Gabriel

&

Esther

A novel
inspired by a true story

Toni Lisa Brown

INTRODUCTION

It feels like it took longer than forever to decide if I should write this book. And then I questioned the major themes of the book. Where should I start? How should I structure the work? How much of the entirety of my life is significant to the themes? Those questions erupted in me over twenty-seven years ago. I *know* … completely startling. Twenty-seven years to answer those questions and write the book.

Of course, there were the inevitable life interruptions. My own illnesses. Geographic moves. Deaths. Inertia. Thought-processing time. Rewrites. A nebulous fear about sharing the filthiest of my dirty laundry. But here it is, either bound between two covers or in e-book format. Clearly it is too late to back out now, or to move to Tahiti to avoid confrontations.

Some explanations: This book is inspired by a true story. What has been changed is immaterial. What is true has been detailed in Technicolor. It is graphic. Bold. Explicit. Sad. Even funny. Often poignant. I chose to change every name, including mine, to write it as a fictionalized memoir. To allow it to read like a novel. Many of the events, locales, organizations, and characters are composites.

Here's the format. Sections of my diaries and journals are lifted from the original volumes. The letters to and from my parents are our actual letters. The details of the major events of my life are accurate. God is spelled G-D because Jewish people consider the very name of G-D to be too holy to write in its totality. My real-time narrative will be in a different font when I find that I need to give you additional insight into the story.

This experience of releasing my newborn into a crazed, often cruel, and highly critical world is scary. But I believe this story was conceived "for such a time as this," and I am compelled to release the work into the great and inscrutable domain that is earth. Let the words, commas, paragraphs, and my often-wretched choices fall where they may.

For: Perk and Alex

For: E and G

TABLE OF CONTENTS

THE FIFTIES

It was June of 1955 and the sight of that green-and-white bus I was about to board made me want to feign illness or just die. Truly! It didn't become a reality to me until that big old bus was six feet from my face. I was about to leave my family to go to Indian Trails overnight camp in the Pennsylvania Poconos for eight weeks, and I was not quite eight years old.

I cried a lot that first summer away. I didn't like being gone for two months. I mean, really! I had just finished third grade. The longest I'd been away from home was for a girlfriend sleepover or a weekend with Bubbi and Zazzi (my Dad's parents). It was from this first camp experience I learned the meaning of the words "to cope."

Eventually, I became an intrepid camper and remained one for nine years. I'm going to share some camp letters to my parents as well as their letters to me. I choose camp letters as a jump-start because it was during rest hour, while writing these silly daily postcards, that my life as a writer began.

I didn't know I was a writer until my early forties. "Writer" was far too lofty a term for me to pin on myself.

Mom and I are obsessed with saving words on paper. I'm not kidding. It doesn't matter if the words are on the back of a takeout menu, scribbled on a recipe card, or noted on a piece of paper towel. If the words do it for us, they are saved for life. Most people don't get it. They might save some of their kids' drawings and a letter or two if they're dazzling. Otherwise, most folks think words are expendable. They come. They go, like youth and a small waist.

1955

Dear Mommy and Daddy,

I'm so exsited. We have try outs for Snow Wite after rest hour. I'm also a nervus reck. I really want to be Snow Wite, but I'll probably be Sleepy or Dopy. Mommy, thank you for sending the care pakage. Everybody in my bunk loves the head bands. Guess what color I chose for me. No not red. No not blue. Purples you sillys of course. Now gess what activti I like best. No not basketbal, dancing you sillys of course. And drama next best.

I got 3 postcards yesterday. So I have to go and rite everyone back. You want to know who they are from?

1) BoBo and PaPa Honey (I love your parents Mommy)

2) Bubbi and Zazzi (I love your parents Daddy)

3) Aunt Lauren (I love your twin sister Mommy. She sent me a cootie game)

One more thing, tomorrow nite at the soshul we are going to go as our favrite movee star. I'm going to be Awdry Hepern. Tell my sweet baby sister Ruthie thank you for the bird fether.

Its OK here, but I miss you sooo much. I cry a lot because I miss you so much.

Kiss everybody for me.

Your dawter,

Leah

1956

June 28, 1956

Leah, my daughter,

With you at camp and me at home, we face another letter-writing span of two months. I enjoy these moments with you each day. A time tucked away for you and me as I sit at your desk near dusk of each day.

Your room is too neat. The house is too still. Meals are too quiet and the piano too silent. This year's bus looked luxurious, even air-conditioned! I trust you had a pleasant trip.

I'm sure you know by now you left Mordecai on your bed. There he sat, that sweet-faced monkey, with his new camp beanie perched like a beret, sitting on your pillow instead of safely in your care. I mailed him off today along with your canteen money. Your riding boots are being re-heeled.

Addie gave your room a thorough cleaning, and we're crisping up the curtains, making certain to keep everything spruced for your eventual return.

Do please eat well.

I have a strong feeling you will have a good summer. There is so much extraordinary beauty that surrounds you at camp, and so many excellent provisions made for your enjoyment. Heap one pleasure upon another, my Darling, and enjoy it all with abandon.

I'm dying to hear everything, and I love your postcards, Miss Muffat! Daddy and Ruthie send hugillies and bugillies and I send some of both too.

Always with LOVE, Mommy

*****
4

June 29, 1956

Dear Mommy and Daddy and Ruthie and Addie,

Yesterday we had a soshul and boy it was fun. I danced with Albie almost evry minute. When somebody cut in on us Albie counted to 10 and cut rite back.

What would you say if I was endgajed. Well I am to Albie. After the soshul he gave me an endgajmint ring. Its red plastic and very pretty.

Addie, I no everybody will miss you when you go back to Jamayka next week to see your family. I miss you a lot every day, especially on Thursdays when we have chow mane. P.U.

Aunt Lauren sent me a pretty bathing soot. It has flowers on it, pink, purple and white. The rest is black.

I love you,
Leah Rebecca

*****

(Letter from Aunt Lauren, Mom's twin sister)

July 15, 1956

Hello, my darling niece!

I don't know who longs for you more, me or my twin sister, your Mommy. Maybe it's because I don't have a "Leah" of my very own. But I think it's because I adore you and am not accustomed to having you so far from home. I watch your Mommy missing you. I know how much you treasure your baby sister, so, just imagine how close your Mommy and I are and how much I feel what she feels since we came out of BoBo's body at the same time.

I think about you so much, Leah, and sometimes I pretend we're reading a story together in the big forest green leather chair in your Daddy's library. Then sometimes I hear you say, "But if I sit with Aunt Lauren then Mommy will be alone, and if I sit with Mommy then Aunt Lauren will be alone."

Right this minute I'd love to toss you on the bed and tickle you just so I could hear you

giggle and holler, "Stop it, Aunt Lauren, you're going to make me pee." Oh, how I love your giggle.

Simply cannot wait for the summer to end so I can squeeze you and kiss you silly.

Stay as sweet as you are.

Forever your, Aunt Lauren

*****

(Letter from Dad)

July 23, 1956

To my one and only Leah,

For certain there could have been no two Leah's. Having you is an adventure, indeed, not to be duplicated now or ever. You were slow in coming. In fact, there were years when all hope was abandoned that there would ever be a Leah. But G-D was with us, and one day you made your presence known to Mommy through her eager pains; and to me, through a sleepless night that held sensations of anxiety and anticipated pleasures.

The above is just a reminder to you, Leah, that our love for you was firmly established before your eyes even met these horizons. I fell in love with you before you were born. There was always an image with me of what you would be like, were you to be a girl.

In most ways you have met my expectations. You are a fundamentally well-balanced, mostly independent, sometimes reckless almost-nine-year-old girl. You show an unusual flair for good taste, and you move with the grace of a gazelle.

Summers take you away from me. I hear from other campers' parents that they feel joyful to have a reprieve from their children. I do not share their sentiments. I endorse your departure because I believe that a summer of competitive and creative activities, shared living quarters and mountain air nurture your development. But I do not like the empty space that your being away creates in my life. You are actively missed, Tiny Mite, by your Daddy.

Ruthie and I are about to watch a Phillies game. Mommy has brought club sandwiches and milkshakes into the library, and I expect we will have a good afternoon.

I await Visiting Weekend impatiently. Much love to you,
Daddy

1957

August 2, 1957

My dearest Leah Rebecca,

What an extraordinary experience to see a little bundle of nothing with big brown eyes, grow into a lovely young lady, a bigger bundle of something with the same big brown eyes. You have come so far, and I am so proud.

The next ten will be more wondrous still, because you will transform from a young girl to a young woman. Braces will give way to beaus, ponytails to permanents, and girlhood growing pains into the serious business of college and career.

Then the most important event in any young woman's life, LOVE! Different from any kind of love you will have known before. All these wonders await you, my Beauty.

It is my dream to be able to guide and teach you to use your mind and heart in a manner which brings happiness to those you touch, and therefore, to yourself. Life for you will surely be good, Leah, because you will be an enlightened and intelligent woman who expects from it no more than she gives.

My love for you cannot be measured.

Your, Mommy

*****

(Letter from Dad)

July 29, 1957

My daughter Leah,

This is being written close to the eve of your eleventh Birthday. As I ponder your age, I suddenly become aware of my own. I am forty-seven, and the best evidence I have to show for my life is fathering Tiny Mite and that bundle we call Ruthie. I have said this to you repeatedly. You are a package of many virtues and some shortcomings. The balance is very much in your favor; those little peculiarities that are yours can certainly be corrected as time goes on. Just a little earnest effort on your part and they will surely vanish.

You're certainly the sum of all good qualities which have been passed on to you. There is maturity for your eleven years, as well as deep recognition of what we expect of you. You have showed a marked ability to make decisions in a way that can only spring from good judgment.

Mommy and I are full of pride at your accomplishments, your show of talent, and your behavior among people. In so many ways I see Mommy in you, and because I love Mommy so much, it goes without saying that I love you.

I look forward to the day when you'll grow into adulthood. And I say to myself with certainty that you'll be a constant source of happiness to us.

Happy Birthday, Tiny Mite.
Much love, Your Daddy

*****

1958

I am now sitting with every camper at Indian Trails around a hot campfire. This is my 4th summer here, and 2 days before camp ends, we come to this spot and sit in a big circle. We sing songs and tell stories and burn marshmallows and then get to write a letter to ourselves. These letters are buried in a steel box and opened at the first campfire next year.

They usually only give us 15 minutes to write, so this year I got smart and have been writing during rest hour for the last 3 days. I love it when next summer everyone gets to see what they wrote.

So, I guess I'll just stare at the stars while the other kids write. I'm also burying copies of Mommy and Daddy's birthday letters for my 11th birthday. I let my counsilors read them, and they can't believe how great they are either.

So, here's my campfire letter for the summer of 1958:
We meet again. Me and me. I'll start at the beginning.

I really and truly didn't want to come to camp this year. You see, I have had kind of an inferior complex this year. Don't tell anyone, but I am jelus of an awful lot of my girlfriends. I think most of them are cuter and smarter than I am and it just hurts sometimes. I know I worry my parents to death. I was a real pain in the you-know-what this year. I'm going to try so hard to make up for everything. I'm going to get all A's in school. I'm going to even practice piano on Sundays, and I'm going to be on pointe by December. I really want to be the daughter that my parents want and think I am.

We went on a fantabulous trip this year. As Mr. Lewis the owner would say, "to the spashus, colosal, Luray Caverns. They were everything he said and I loved it.

And then of course West Side Story. I was a Jet dancer and also helped with the seenery. I REALLY like Dave Schwartz, the boy who played Tony. Boy can he dance!

I ate too much peanut butter and gained 3 pounds. My leotard looks stupid. I hate it. The thing I like most about camp this year is that Ruthie is here too. Daddy wrote that Kennedy beat Stevenson at the Convention. He was disappointed. I'm not. Kennedy's cuter.

About that inferior complex. I really pray it's all over soon. Hopefully before I go home the day after tomorrow. Because I know my parents are going to want me to go to the country club and that's really worrying me. I just can't go over to face those girls. I just don't fit. Mommy tries to understand, but it's just that she wants me to be part of the crowd. I wish I knew what to do. I guess just let things come as they come.

I have just turned 11 years old and Mommy says, "Perhaps your depth and sensitivity will bring you pain." I think she's right. But I haven't found the switch to turn my feelings to happy. I think I need to practice more.

*****

These letters from my parents were the most treasured and confounding words I ever received. I have shown them to countless people over the course of my life. I wanted to understand the disconnection. I wanted to know why the letters made me happy <u>and</u> sad. I didn't really get the full

drift on these epistles until much later in life, after years of counseling, pondering, interpreting, and analyzing. The letters are priceless jewels, no doubt. On the basis of these letters, if my parents were not Jewish, they might have been nominated for canonization or sainthood.

But life with my parents was far from rapturous. Thus, the perceived disconnection. Although the letters flow with encouragement and well wishes for a beautiful life, at home my world was devoid of praise, recognition, or seeming pleasure in anything about me. I was tirelessly criticized, demeaned, underestimated, and undermined.

But oh yes, the letters are fab-o. They came as inevitably as sunrise on my Birthday every year of my life. Of course, I still have all of them, as well as all my letters to each of them, which they ultimately returned to me. But in all truth, I was a scared little bird who was biting her fingernails at age five (I know this from photos of me at that age). It's all easily understood now with the advantage of decades lived, deep introspection, and having watched the interactions among other Jewish kids and their parents.

Recently, I watched *Inside the Actor's Studio* as James Lipton interviewed the cast of *Mad Men* and its writer/creator, Matthew Weiner (a Jewish guy). James asked Matthew, "What was it like growing up in the intellectual power arena of having one parent a psychiatrist and the other an attorney?" Matthew said, "High pressure and humiliation."

I got that, and I'd bet a lot of other Jewish kids got that too. Maybe not all kids were berated in order to push them toward high-level achievement. But Ruthie and I knew what was expected, and we did all we could to meet our parents' academic and social demands because, despite everything, we knew our parents cherished us, and we cherished them.

*****

THE SIXTIES

Dearest Deborah, my very own first diary,

I love you; I really do. I will call you Deborah because it's my favorite girl's name. Mom and Dad gave you to me for Hanukkah. As you can see, you are baby-blue leather.

You will be my best friend for the rest of forever. Really, you're my G-D-friend because you will listen to whatever I want to tell you, just like G-D does, and you will understand. I know you will. I will hide nothing from you and will tell you the whole truth, because why lie to G-D? He knows everything about everything anyway.

Anne Frank was a Jewish girl, like me. She kept a diary. I have read it three times and cried many times. When I'm old, will I re-read my diaries and cry? Will I ever be old? I'm afraid of the bombs.

But I will not think of that now. I will be Scarlett O'Hara and think of sad things tomorrow.

We will have a full and fun life together, I promise. Don't ever forget that I love you.

Leah Rebecca

*****

15

Anne Frank is the reason I persevered as a writer. She is my heroine. Her voice is so fresh and lucid. Her thoughts like living things. Her plight so hideous. Her end so small and degrading. But it is this young songbird in the midst of tyranny and torture whose voice will not be stilled. I love that. I love that she won … that hers is the voice and hers are the words that linger.

*****

January 3, 1960

Dearest Deborah,

It takes me a while to settle into school after the long holiday break. You, of course, were the best Hanukkah gift I could have hoped for. The only problem with you is that there is only one page allotted for each date. Some days, I am certain, I will want to write more, and I will do so in a loose-leaf notebook. Today will probably be such a day because I want to write about the night you were given to me.

It was the very first night of Hanukkah. Our home was festive with decorations. We lit the menorah, sang Hanukkah songs, and read the story of how the Jews in Judea defeated the Syrian tyrant Antiochus IV after three years of struggle. Judas Maccabeus was their leader, and he led the people to rededicate the temple to G-D.

The Jews found only a tiny bit of oil to light their holy lamps. But somehow, the oil lasted for eight days, just like our celebration. A miracle from G-D. Then Mom and Dad and Ruthie and I played dreydl (Ruthie won 23 cents) and then we ate Mom's scrumpshus latkes.

*****

It may sound, from my depiction of ancient Hebrew history, that I actually learned something in Hebrew school. I didn't. To me, Hebrew school was like piano and dance lessons. Just something I had to do. No questions asked. No dissent offered. I attended Hebrew school for many years. I learned to read and write Hebrew, long since forgotten, but I didn't learn conversational Hebrew, about which I've been miffed for years. That would have been fun and useful. Being bilingual in America ... way cool!

But I didn't come away from all those Hebrew school years knowing much of anything about my faith, my Torah, my ethnicity, or my culture. Hebrew school might as well have been chemistry or math.

My Judaic education really came in the form of two Hollywood films: *Ben Hur* and *The Ten Commandments*. All I knew about Judaism, I learned from Charlton Heston. Back to my Dear Deborah.

*****

January 5, 1960

So Deb,

I want to tell you about a family tradition. This really happened two weeks ago, but I didn't have *you* two weeks ago. So here we go. Every year since I was little, my family has watched the TV one-act opera *Amahl and the Night Visitors*[1] by Gian Carlo Menotti during the holiday season. We started watching this show years ago because my cousin Eli sang the lead role of Amahl back then.

---

1 "Amahl and the Night Visitors," *IMDb*, http://www.imdb.com/title/tt0175438/.

17

We continued to watch it every Hanukkah\Christmas season and made it a family tradition because it is a most gorgeous piece of music and a most touching piece of drama. It is the story of three kings and their quest to follow a star and a child. The child's name is Jesus.

Amahl is a poor crippled boy who lives with his mother somewhere in Palestine on the way to Bethlehem. The three kings seek food and rest on their way to bring gifts to Jesus, and they find themselves at Amahl's home. They are invited in. When the kings are resting, Amahl's mother tries to steal some of their gold so she can feed Amahl.

The king's page awakens and starts hitting Amahl's mother until Amahl wakes up and hits the page with his crutch. The kings awaken too, and they are really mad. One of the kings tells the mother, "Oh, woman, you may keep the gold. The child we seek does not need our gold. On love alone he will build his kingdom."

Amahl's mom throws herself on her knees and cries, "For such a king I have waited all my life, and if I weren't so poor, I would send a gift of my own to such a child."

Then Amahl pleads, "Oh, mother, let me send him my crutch. Who knows, he may need one, and this I made myself." Amahl begins to walk; step by step he moves toward the kings, the crutch held out before him. One at a time the kings put their hands on Amahl while singing, "Oh! Blessed child, may I touch you?"

And so, as Amahl pipes the tune on his flute that he played at the beginning of the opera, his Mother stands in the doorway of their hut waving one final good-bye to her son and the kings as they disappear over the hill. Mom and I cry as flakes of snow and the curtain slowly fall.

Year after year I am moved so very much by this story. I hate that Amahl's Mom doesn't go with them. How can either of them bear the separation? And I am chilled clear through by the miracle of Amahl's healing. Just because a baby boy is born in a town called Bethlehem, another young boy receives the use of his legs. How can it be? I wonder and wonder and wonder.

I know that Gian Carlo Menotti made up the story and wrote the music. But I also know a lot of people believe that Jesus *did* cure people and might even have cured a boy like Amahl. I just wonder so much.

Anyway, right after the program, all the lights in our house went dark. It was a snow-white-blizzard night, so the electric power died and made the neighborhood black like ink. Dad managed to find four candleholders and some Sabbath candles. He sat one on the Steinway, one in the library, one in the kitchen, and Ruthie and I were allowed to travel with one.

We traveled up the stairway and straight to the arched window with the floral chintz seat in my all-pastel blue and white bedroom. We were silent while we watched a candle's flame reflect flickers on the windowpanes.

Each of us brought one present to my love-niche-nest. Ruthie went first. Her present was a black leather flute case with her hot-pink initials carved into it. Every year Mom and Ruthie and I pick a color and buy each other little things in that color all year long. We had already decided in December that hot pink would be our color for 1960.

My turn. I knew what the gift was because I asked for it and asked that it be my first night present. I just didn't know what color it would be or what it would look like. Ruthie became extremely impatient with me because I was opening the present too slowly, as though the ceremony was a highly religious experience. Well, to me it sort of was.

You, Deborah, are the gift!!! My new first diary. You are my very forever best friend. Mom knew exactly what I would want you to look like. The loose-leaf I will choose to go with you will also be baby blue. Isn't this exciting! Nobody in the whole world will ever know where I keep the key to unlock inner me. Sleep well, Deborah-Love.

From: Leah-Love

January 10, 1960

Dearest Deborah Diary,

You simply will not believe what happened fifteen minutes ago. While I was writing in you, Dad grabbed my pen out of my hand and called you '*stinkin*'! I don't get it. All my homework is finished, my hair is washed and set in rollers. My clothes are laid out for tomorrow. So now I write by the light of my electric blanket control. HHMMFF on him.

Tomorrow is our first Jr. Varsity game. I'm petrified! I don't know all the cheers, the skirt has a spot on it, the sleeves are too long, the vest arm holes gap, and I feel like a clod in saddle shoes. Ah well, the bra and panties are a perfect fit.

Wish me luck! XOXOXOXO

January 18, 1960

Dearest Deborah,

I heard real interesting news today. Seems that Robbie G. told Patty J. that Jimmy B. was the first boy in our class to "get hot" with a girl! I got really excited about this news. I don't exactly know why, especially since I wasn't the girl. Oh, and one more thing, JIMMY B. ALSO HAD MASTERBATION! CAN YOU STAND IT?

Piano lesson tomorrow. I've practiced my fingers off this week. I have the Debussy piece down pat, but Bach is a catastrophe. Catching a compliment from Miss Binz is like catching a moonbeam. In other words, no holding my breath. Got an A on the history test and an A+ on the *Exodus* book report. Don't even ask about the math quiz, it was a disaster.

1961

Dearest Deborah,

Today, John Fitzgerald Kennedy, that forty-three-year-old dreamboat, was inaugurated as our thirty-fifth president. Being Friday, we were allowed to come home early to watch the ceremony. It was glorious. His speech made me so proud to be an American. I hope I can help our country in some way when I'm his age. Jackie looked stunning, as ever. She is so lucky to be his wife. I can't wait until I love a man. I just know I'll be good at it.

February 12, 1961

Dearest Deborah,

I cried for two hours straight today. Mom and I had another fight this morning. I got so disgusted that I felt like running away. Mom thinks we're up against "an adolescent hormonal struggle." She swears she's giving up on trying to convert me into a decent human being. I don't blame her.

February 13, 1961

Sometimes I just hate Dad. He pulled his "Leah Lecture" thing today. The normal hour to hour and a half of me sitting in the huge, dark green leather chair with his desk swivel chair pulled up so close to me that I'm trapped. He tells me what a bad person I am and asks how I could hurt Mom so much and why did I not get all A's this report card period. He's fed up with my moodiness and my not talking at the dinner table and on and on and blah blah blah.

I can't even speak when he goes at me like that. He demands an explanation, and I just stare and sit in silence. This makes him madder than anything. But what can I say? Am I going to win a point with the president of the debate club at The University of Pennsylvania? I've tried talking and it just gets worse. So now I'm silent and he thinks I'm belijerent. It's not that. It's terror. He never yells, but he's so scary.

I hate that leather chair and I used to love it. Now it feels like a cage for a disobedient dog. And I can't budge until the guard moves his swivel back about two feet.

I need to have some fun. Maybe Rachael's free this weekend.

February 16, 1961

Deb, Rachael and I went to Philly on the train together today. I'm ashamed of myself. Do you know what we did? We went to see *The World of Suzie Wong*. We're not telling a sole. It was absolutely fantabulous. I adored it and could see it again tomorrow.

We read *Lady Chatterley's Lover* out loud for hours. G-D! Can it really be like that? Can it? We also bleached our hair in one spot. Looks cute. My spot turned red and Rachael's turned blonde.

P.S. Oh my G-D! Rachael just told me that Billie T. told her he thinks I have the second cutest tooshie in the whole school! He thinks Gloria Capanelli has the cutest.

March 1, 1961

Hi Doll-Baby,

Guess where I am! At the Essex House on Central Park West. I had to audition today for the new summer camp, Belvoir Terrace, a fine arts center in the Massachusetts Berkshires. Mom and I stayed overnight and we're having a fantabulous time.

I think I did O.K. at the audition. There were so many beautiful girls. There were tryouts for dance, drama, music, and art. I tried out for modern dance, Martha Graham's style. Four girls tried out at a time. We did barre work, had to learn a two-minute routine, and then had to interpret a piece of music by Dave Brubeck … ALONE! Most of the girls look like they've been dancing since diapers. I think I hope I made it.

Listen to this, Deborah. Tonight, Mom and I went to see the Broadway show *All the Way Home*. It was great, marvelous, stupendous, colosal. I cried four times. After the show we stood outside the stage door entrance and waited, and finally Colleen Doowhurst came out. Mom told her, "You are elokwent and magical on a stage. It was a privilege to see your performance."

I loooooove New York at night. We took a taxi to Carnegie Deli and bought three-inch-thick Rueben sandwiches and ate them in our bed while watching TV. It's 1:00 A.M. and Mom's sleeping. I'm watching New Yorkers fifteen floors below me as they drive, bike, carriage ride, and walk the streets of this FANTABLUOUS town!

Goodnight, Sweet Princess.

March 7, 1961

Deborah, today Mom and Dad have been married seventeen years. They seemed gay tonight. Dad even left the plant early, and they looked ravishing as they floated down the staircase to join their friends for dinner and dancing at the club. Will I be as delectable as Mom when I've been married seventeen years? Will my husband be as distinguished as Dad?

Dad gave Mom a diamond watch. Mom gave Dad a leatherbound collection of each of Shakespeare's plays. I gave them a crystal bud vase, and Ruthie drew them a picture of our house and picked wildflowers from the next-door neighbor's field. All in all a glorious day for the Kline family.

Not exactly a duplicate of their wedding day when they were married on a Wednesday in 1944. Mom was on her lunch-hour from work at Red Cross in Wilkes Barre, and Dad drove up from Chester for the anything-but-glamorous ceremony. Dad drove back to Chester afterward and Mom went back to work.

P.S. I passed the audition and will be going to Belvoir Terrace this summer. I think I guess that's good.

August 2, 1961

I am fourteen years old today. I don't feel older than yesterday. Maybe more tired, since we danced for three and a half hours this morning, had a scene rehearsal for *The Glass Menagerie*, and this afternoon had two more hours of dance.

I love all the presents my bunkmates gave me, especially the red cinch belt from Fran and the poodle pin from Laura Lappin.

I walked to the ledge at dusk to have some time alone. Over-looking the Massachusetts Berkshires I feel so close to G-D. I thought and thought and thought until I nearly gave myself a headache. I want so much to be a great person, Deborah. But I feel so insecure all the time. I can act like I'm confidant and poized, but who wants to act all the time. I think everyone is smarter and prettier and more talented than I am. I know I could be a better daughter and a better student. I think I'm a really good big sister and even a good friend, but OH PLEASE G-D, help me during this next year to like myself better and be more machure.

I got my Birthday letters from Mom and Dad today. Our annual ritual is the most important event of all. Masterpieces, that's what these Birthday letters are. I will keep them always.

*****

25

(Letter from Mom)

August 2, 1961

My dearest Leah Rebecca,

Last year as you were entering your teens and turning into a young woman, I thought no scale could cup my joy. But this August, in your second teen year, you have endowed me with still more reason to rejoice. Arriving so excellently and with such grace upon the quivering expectancy of being fourteen, you have braved the girl\woman hiatus with perception and insight, knowing its pain and salvaging its good.

Because I was so like you at your age, Leah, afflicted with exaggeration of my defects and diminution of my assets, I ride right along the heights with you when you soar. And when the depths grab you, there too am I ardently trying to extricate us both.

One day when "to thine own self be true" become meaningful words and you flee the handcuffs of self-torment; one day when you come to accept yourself and fulfill your potential; one day when the wealth of you pours forth, there will be boundless felicity for those who know and love you. The prologue speaks of this when you dance. You reveal a rare sensitivity that instantly touches those who watch. And when you write of your response to beauty, to people and to your environment, I know this is a person whose conscious mind goes well beyond the superficial.

So, you are blessed, my dear daughter. In your own unique way, you could help make this a better world. We are grateful, Dad and I, for having you to love, Leah, and I pray that we be able to share all the flowerings of your growth. You have my heart.

Your, Mom

*****

(Letter from Dad)

August 2, 1961

Good evening my daughter,

At this very moment there is complete quiet and peace surrounding me as I sit alone at my desk with just a single companion, namely, an enchanting symphonic melody pouring from the FM. Such an atmosphere will be conducive to penning a few stray words.

So, here we are at the crossroads of another Birthday. But it is not just another year, because at your age, every year is immensely significant. You are in this period of your life when so much of you is in a state of flux. The body is taking on shape and feminine charm. The spirit shifts convulsively from high mountain points to deep lonely valleys. The mind is shifting, groping, and searching for information that will lead to mature decisions.

These next few years, Leah, will not be easy. But they need not be blighted. I have seen your capacity to have spirited fun, and I've also seen you tackle serious problems seriously. With this dual capacity you should be able to take on these next uncertain years with confidence.

As I look upon you with some measure of objectivity, I feel certain you will make mistakes, but not serious ones. You will grope, but not sink. You will cry, but not wail. You will laugh but not become hysterical; and above all, you will walk through these next years and not run.

Am I overly confident? I want to believe that I am not. And I want to be around to guide when necessary, and the rest of the time sit back and glory in the treasures we have in you and Ruthie. Eugene Ormandy has just finished his symphony. I too am finished.

I do love you.
Have an exciting Birthday!
Your Dad

*****

We never doubted we were loved. It was just part of our culture to be doggedly pushed toward excellence while being thoroughly loved. A form of tough love? A need to assure that if we were rebuffed by the world, which was almost inevitable, we would be able to stand on our own because we were prepared to fend for ourselves? We consciously or subliminally knew, as kids whose families had endured the Holocaust, that we must have professions that didn't depend on our being acceptable to the world's employers.

I was raised in the pressure-cooker of the Northeast sector of America by liberal, Eastern European immigrants who acquired their own high levels of education, had an economically comfortable life, and expected no more from their kids than they did from themselves.

In addition to high academic achievement, we had many obligations. Hebrew school twice weekly. Saturday Sabbath services. I studied ballet, jazz, contemporary dance, and piano. I was a cheerleader and wrote for the school literary magazine. I was a yearbook editor and honor roll student. I read mountains of books each year, was tutored in math from junior high through high school, and as a teen, I volunteered to work with Downs' Syndrome kids. As for TV, I could watch *The Fugitive, Dick Clark's Bandstand, Father Knows Best, Lassie, Leave It to Beaver, Bonanza, Happy Days,* and anything my parents deemed cultural or educational.

So why wouldn't I believe my parents when they admonished me and told me I was less than I could be ... never good enough and an unexpected disappointment? They were bright, educated leaders in our community and were almost always charming, sophisticated, eloquent, and sensible. I thought they were pretty fabulous people and accepted their assessment of me as valid. Here's an example of Dad's extreme demands.

*****

November 12, 1961

Dad is mean. Dad is crazy. Dad is the meanest man in the world. You will not BELIEVE what he did! You know that eighth-grade geography project we have a whole semester to complete and is due in three weeks? The one where we have to write a book about a made-up trip we've taken with our family and fill this book with family photos and magazine pictures of the country we're crossing and include budgets and wardrobe photos and at least seventy-five pages of writing.

Well, Rachael and I were at Sarah's last night working on a Hebrew school project. When I got home, I thought I'd work on the geography project before bed. When I pulled it from its special place where it wouldn't get crinkled or moved, I found every page of my forty-five pages of writing torn to shreds. On top of the shreds was a note from the meanest man in the world: *"You can do better. So do better."* I can't stop crying. I wish I could hit him really hard. DO BETTER! If I could do better, I would have done better. WHAT'S WRONG WITH HIM?

*****

I just about hated Dad for months. I had to write until 1:00 or 2:00 A.M. for weeks to catch up and meet the deadline. But here's the thing: My project, called "The Itinerant Klines from Chadds Ford to Yellowstone," was hailed as the best in all the eighth-grade classes, received an A++, and was ferried from school to school throughout the district. I didn't hate him quite as much after that. His method was merciless, but his critique was spot-on. Ours was a tempestuous relationship, and he scared me a lot. But the love between us was rock solid. It just was ... we both knew it.

*****

1962

Deb, you know how I've been dying to work with Downs' syndrome kids. Mom and Dad have known this for over a year. They also realize no one is going to trust a fourteen-year-old with the education of kids who have Downs. Well, Dad must have called some people he knows on the board because tonight he said, "Leah, if you're really sure about wanting to volunteer to work with Downs' Syndrome kids, I've arranged for you to be able to do that at Elwyn."

*****

Elwyn is a nationally recognized residential facility for severely impaired kids and adults. Years later, when in my thirties, I worked at Elwyn and specialized in therapy with kids diagnosed with autism.

*****

"Dad, that's fab-o! No, I wasn't kidding. I *really* want to work with those kids. Tell me more."

"Well, I've arranged for you to work there after school two days a week for two hours each day. I want you to do this, but I will also be expecting the same grades and participation in your other endeavors. Do you really think you can handle all of this?"

"I won't know until I try. But I really, really want to try!"

*****

I volunteered at Elwyn for three years.

*****

April 16, 1962

Dearest Deborah-Friend,

We had the most wonderful Seder we've ever had tonight. I sang the Four Questions, of course. Everyone was so quiet when I finished that I thought I had messed up. But I hadn't. Mom pulled me to her and when I kissed her tear-wet cheek, I knew I had done well. Everyone wanted one of my kisses and there were lots of tear-wet cheeks. I felt so proud to sing the words I have been singing most every Passover since I was eight years old, and I was really glad that everyone cried.

Mom's matzah balls were fluffier than ever and Bubbi's gefilte fish was scrumpshus. The table looked like Queen Elizabeth was arriving any second for our Seder. I just adore the china, crystal, silver, and linen that turn our dining room into a feast room for parties and holidays.

But the very most fun part of all is the singing before our sherbet parfaits and macaroons. Daddy and Uncle Lex and Uncle Mitch sing so emotionally. Sweat pours from them, so they undo their ties and belt out "Dai Dai Ainoo" and "Let My People Go." Even the kids are allowed to drink icky sweet Mogen David wine while we sing the songs of our people.

During discussion time we heard Dad tell us the story of his own family's flight from Russia. Zazzi (**Hebrew for Grandpa**) owned a huge tobacco plantation. But they were living during scary times in Russia, and often the whole family had to lie under the beds to escape traveling bullets, and pillows were smooshed up against the windows and around the beds to catch the shots and shrapnel.

Dad says he can remember every detail of the panic he felt. These things called tribunals were set up across the street from their house. The hearings were phony and the fate of everybody was death. Dad saw people being shot and hung. Zazzi says it reminded him of the French Revolution. (**It's a fair assumption that a lot of Dad's behaviors and thought processes were birthed from this living-nightmare existence.**)

One day, the Bolsheviks banged on the door, came in uninvited, treated poor Zazzi very harshly, and told them to be out and gone within six hours. Everything that belonged to Dad and his family now belonged to the Bolsheviks. So, everyone in the family who could, stuffed their clothes with jewelry and silver flatware and gold pieces Zazzi had hidden in his sock drawer.

They put on as many layers of clothes as they could and started walking. And walking. Destination: Cherbourg, France, where they would board one of the ships headed for the Land of Milk and Honey.

Stories flowed from Dad about the kindness of the peasants they met along their impossibly long journey. These people provided humble sleeping space and whatever food they could. Without the generosity of these simple people, their trek from Russia to France may not have been possible.

Dad was in charge, because at ten years old he spoke six languages **(even though English was not one of them).** And being the oldest male in a Jewish family of four children, he was accustomed to taking the lead. When they got to Cherbourg, they were put in a refugee camp for people going abroad. Ten days later they boarded the ship that was to glide them to this new world and new life.

They couldn't have known what it was going to be like on the ship. People smooshed so tightly together that when they had to go to sleep, they just went to sleep. The pressure of the people around them would keep them standing up. Plus, all they had to eat for the slow, week long sail was canned sardines. They were packed like sardines and ate sardines, and everyone spent the first two days vomiting. LOVELY!

Their ship pulled into Ellis Island at 4:30 A.M. on July 22, 1922. Hundreds of people stood still and quiet in the dark before the sun came up, as the America they dreamed of now filled their horizon. Lady Liberty, Daddy said, made him both cry AND cheer!

But oh Deborah-girl, check out what happened next. As the ship crawled across the Atlantic, Bubbi noticed that little Sasha's hair was falling out. And it kept falling out until that fateful day when they arrived in American waters and all of three-year-old Sasha's beautiful walnut-brown curls were gone, I mean as in BALD! Bubbi (**Hebrew for Grandma**) covered her daughter's head with a babushka, but that didn't help at all.

The customs guy took tiny, traumatized Sasha and put her in quarantine away from the only people she knew in the whole world. Bubbi and Zazzi refused to leave, so the family was put in a holding area for two weeks!

I thought immigration officers at Ellis Island had changed Bubbi and Zazzi's names. But Daddy said that was not true. Lots of immigrants were afraid of men in uniforms because of their experiences in their homeland. So, lots of immigrants decided to change their names before they even boarded the ships going to Ellis Island. To have a recognizable Jewish name was not a great thing, since Jews were not really respected anywhere. So Rivkah and Nacham Klotzenfeld became Riva and Noah Kline, my Bubbi and Zazzi, before they even reached American shores.

34

Now for the next not fun event: After all the horror, and separation from Sasha, the Customs people sent the brand-new Kline family back to France on the next ship going east. They didn't believe that Sasha's hair had fallen out because she was traumatized. They argued that she may have a contagious disease.

I guess the following will not surprise you. After two weeks in France, they boarded another ship and headed straight back to these North American shores. This time, they had Uncle Joe, Bubbi's brother, meet them at Ellis Island to vouch for them. He had fought in World War I and was acceptable as their representative. Thank you very much, you immigration meanies.

So Bubbi's brother, Uncle Joe, took the family in his brand-new Stutz automobile to Delancey Street on the Lower East Side. This was a part of New York City where ghettos of people from all over the world lived. It was crowded and smelly and noisy, but it was a good start for life in America.

The Klines were set up in two rooms at the back of Uncle Joe's brownstone. Soon, Zazzi got a horse and buggy and started peddling clothes, pots, pans, and chickens. Daddy, of course, helped Zazzi with everything.

Now Daddy, being Daddy, says he looked at the move as a great adventure. Zazzi was brokenhearted to leave his parents, brothers, and homeland. Bubbi was thrilled to see her brother and start life fresh in this land of ease and opportunity.

Daddy was put in first grade. The kids made fun of him, called him "Jew Boy," and beat him up whenever they could catch him. Daddy didn't get it. Why did all these kids who were Italian, Polish, and Irish chase him and call him bad names? Why was a Russian Jew any worse than a Polish Catholic? Oh yeah, and because Daddy was short, he hung around with Dave Long, a big guy who became his bodyguard.

Being brilliant, Daddy got through eight school years in four, and by the time he reached junior high and high school, he was elected president of every organization he ran for.

After five years of peddling, Zazzi started up a small department store. Then he bought some real estate and a new house for the Klines not far from Uncle Joe. But in 1929, the stock market crashed, the Depression descended, and again my Dad and his family were poor. Not for long though! Zazzi is a tough man to keep down and so he started all over again.

When the Depression was in full swing, Zazzi moved his little family to a waterfront town on the outskirts of Philadelphia. He opened a small storefront shop and peddled more pots, pans, chickens, and anything else he could find or buy. Daddy drove the horse-drawn buggy and sold all this stuff too. He said he loved it.

Eventually Dad got a scholarship to Cornell, another one for an MBA from Wharton, and immersed himself in the wonders of wonderful America. He was really lucky to be accepted at these schools because they had quotas back then on how many Jewish people they would allow to attend each year. That year, Daddy was one of five Jews who the University of Pennsylvania actually found acceptable. As for me, I think they were damned lucky to get him at all. After his Masters degree, Dad taught in a high school for several years until I was born. **(He taught American History and English. This, from a Russian Jewish immigrant who a few years prior, didn't know English or anything about American history? What a guy!)**

Eventually, Dad just knew he would need more than a teacher's salary for his family, so he went into men's clothing. Eventually, he investigated textiles and manufacturing, and now, he has one of the biggest plants for men's suits and sportswear on the East Coast.

I, then, am half first-generation American, and darned proud of it! There you have it, Deborah. The Kline family's history. Sturdy little pioneers, aren't we?

October 23, 1962

Dearest Deborah,

We went on a class trip to the United Nations today. It was the most totally scary day of my life. I think the world slides close to war. There is a horrible mess going on with Cuba. It has something to do with something called A Bay of Pigs. I'm embarrassed to ask anyone if it really has anything to do with pigs. (That's because I don't think it probably does.)

I spent a lot of time in the peaceful United Nations meditation room. In the silence I prayed and wrote a poem:

Today the world lies divided.
Brought up in fear of war and death,
I want to live. You want to live.
We all do.
The split grows deeper and wider.
I try to live in hope, but in hope of what?
I would gladly close my eyes to the world.
But I cannot.
I dare not.
They remain open, and I am afraid,
Because I have not yet lived.
But who dares argue with power-crazed men?
Will anyone come to save us?
Lost in an atomic jungle,
There is no one to trust, and no one trusts us.

How could G-D let us live in so much fear?
Just as sure as there are bombs,
We will die.
I cry.
I plead.
Let us live to breathe again

*****

1963

Dearest Deborah,

Thank G-D it's a weekend. I can crawl into bed and escape the world. I know you will hardly believe what I'm about to say, Deb, but I will say it because if I don't tell someone I will burst into a thousand pieces of human flesh. And if I can't tell you, whom can I tell? Without you to talk to, I would be the loneliest person in our galaxy.

I am fifteen years old and all I want is to die. I can't stop crying. I don't even know why I'm crying. I can't think. All I do is feel and what I feel is dangerously hideous. Mom and Dad are so worried. I wish I could hide in a cave. Will it end? When? And why, why, why, have I lost everything I am and been replaced by a person I don't know and totally loathe?

December 12, 1963

Deborah,

I see a psychiatrist three times weekly and they are the only times I step outside. He doesn't help. I think I'm too far behind in schoolwork to catch up. Haven't practiced piano in three weeks. Haven't been to my modern, ballet, or jazz classes. Haven't been to Hebrew school. Haven't been to cheerleading rehearsals, gone to the games, or given a damn, for that matter. My world has stopped because I can't function in it. I don't get it. And now, I don't even care.

My head and eyes hurt so much from crying that I keep wishing I could take my head off and put it in the freezer. Or maybe drill a hole in my brain and stand over the toilet and let the poison drain out.

I'm sick. Sicker than I ever was when I had double pneumonia and measles at the same time in fourth grade. Now I'm in tenth grade and all I keep dreaming of is the peace and silence of death.

What if this doesn't go away? What if this horrible, detestable, miserable, disgusting, disgraceful, and pathetic person who has taken over my life ... *NEVER GOES AWAY?* Lousy joke, and that's the worst part of all. It's not a joke and there's no other person inside me. This is probably the real me, and the other me might be a phony. I'm not nice or kind. I'm a driveling, sniveling, cry-baby do-nothing waste-case.

I think Hanukkah begins in a few days. Haven't bought anybody any gifts. I wish I could be sent away so nobody would have to look at me. Mom, Dad, and Ruthie try to treat me like I'm normal. Now there's the joke!

*****

Here's how clinical depression works in most people who have the disorder. It's episodic. You can feel its approach, but nothing can be done to quell its descent. It falls around you, enveloping you in a charcoal cloud like those that appear before summer thunder. It can take a year or more before the depression is behind you and life is back to "normal."

You are never completely free though, because you know this hideous despair will return. It always does.

*****

1964

September 30, 1964

Dearest Deborah,

I am a high school senior. I thought I was supposed to feel like a big shot. I still feel like a little shot. Not smart. Not pretty. At least not as smart as Betsy or Sharon or Andrea. And not as pretty as Tracy or Lou-Lou or Suzanne. The thought of applying to colleges makes me woozy. I know I'll never get into one of the Seven Sisters schools and maybe not even into one of the Ivy Leagues. Why do I even care? I don't know why I care … I just know I do. Probably because I know even though they don't speak of it, that's what Mom and Dad expect of me.

I miss the summer. I really loved teaching dance to all those darling munchkins at Camp Akiba. And I liked being a counselor too. I loved tucking those nine-year olds into bed at night. I loved it when they jumped on me in the morning and fought over who would comb my hair. I loved listening to all their little concerns and worries, knowing I could say something that would comfort their hearts. I'll be a great Mom, Deb, don't you think?

Tryouts next week for the senior play: *The Diary of Anne Frank.*

There aren't a whole lot of things I've ever wanted in my life as much as I want the role of Anne. I want it so much I'm terrified to try out for it, because if I don't get it, I'll be the most miserable senior at Concord Senior High.

I don't want to play Miep and I don't want to play Margot and I certainly don't want to play Anne's mother. It's Anne, or no one. But that's not how it works. Mr. Tory and Miss Singer cast everyone. They're the co-directors; I had Singer for tenth-grade English

41

and Tory for eleventh grade English. If I try out for Anne and they think I'd make a swell Margot, then Margot it is.

But I know I was *born* to play Anne. We feel like blood sisters to me. I know her. I understand her. We think alike. If she went to my school, I just know we'd be best friends.

Please G-D, let Mr. Tory and Miss Singer see this is my role.

October 3, 1964

I GOT THE LEAD! I GOT THE LEAD! I GOT THE LEAD! I WILL BE ANNE FRANK! OH, THANK YOU! THANK YOU! THANK YOU! THANK YOU!

October 7, 1964

Dearest Deborah,

Today we blocked Act 1. Everyone was "on book" … so although I knew my lines cold, I pretended to refer to my script to dispel being viewed as a hotshot. It felt right. I just knew how Mr. Tory would block the scenes before he told us where to stand. I had created the people-pictures last night before sleep. It's going to be a FANTABULOUS play!

October 15, 1964

Dear Deb,

All of us associated with this production are so stirred by its content, message, strength, and by its ability to draw us into the brave lives of these foreign families in an Amsterdam hideout. Most of us are honor roll kids, so although we rehearse from 7:00 until 10:00 p.m. five days a week, academic requirements and social commitments aren't suffering. We're driven to make this the most memorable play that has ever graced our high school stage.

November 6, 1964

Deborah-girl,

Two more weeks of rehearsal left. We're fine-tuning our costumes and the set is nearly complete.

I like the white dress best, the one I wear when in Pieter's room and we share our first kiss. Bob is fun to kiss. He makes a sweet Pieter with his brown curls and fawn-gray eyes. I wonder every time we rehearse that scene how his girlfriend, Grace, feels about his kissing me.

Do she and Bob discuss it? How does *he* feel? Does he like kissing me? Or does he really pretend I'm Grace?

I hope if he's pretending, at least he's pretending he's kissing Anne!

November 20, 1964

It's opening night. I'm a wreck. I'm scared my memory has been erased and I won't remember my lines. I'm scared I won't punch the "nightmare" scene right. Mr. Tory scolded me the other night saying my "screams resemble those of an adolescent pig having its throat slit." How attractive.

The audience is sold-out. News has spread that the show is a winner. I think Mom and Dad are almost as nervous as I am. It's two hours before curtain. Mary is doing my hair and makeup and I want it all to be perfect. I'll talk to you later.

LATER! Oh Deborah, Deborah, Deborah, it was magical! I could *feel* the audience's approval. It's so much easier with an audience. I tried little improvisational tricks with them I didn't think to try before they were there. Twice, mid-scene, there was spontaneous applause as I produced an emotion that touched hearts.

How I wish this had been Broadway, and my stage family was not high school seniors, but professional actors. Because tonight … that's what I was.

As I spoke my last line, "In spite of everything I still believe that people are really good at heart," the lights began to fade. Thunderous applause. A standing ovation! "Bravo! Bravo!" they shouted. I bit my lip to fight back tears.

In all my seventeen years, Deborah, tonight was my finest moment.

1965

I graduated from high school with honors and accolades and have just experienced a most extraordinary summer. I've been working in Dad's plant five days a week. His gorgeous new line of men's clothing is coming out in September and he's deadline crazy. I'm the official errand girl and unofficial everything-else girl. I love him, but he drives me crazy. Such a nut for perfection. OY!

I will be leaving for Northwestern University on September first. I'm secretly terrified of going so far from home. I feel about it the way I felt about going to overnight camp when I was almost eight years old. Like, it's too soon. Like, I'm not ready. Like, how can I live so far away from my Mom?

Deborah, you know Devon's been my buddy for years, since seventh grade. Well, recently I've begun to feel I want him to be more than a buddy. It's the strangest feeling, since for all these years I've told him absolutely everything about every boy I've had crushes on and kissed and made out with. And now I find *he's* the one I want to be kissing!

When we get off the phone at night, I have to fight with myself not to call him back. And when we meet twice weekly for my tennis lesson, I have a hard time leaving him. He's such a fabulous teacher. My forehand is stronger than ever, and my backhand is coming along great. I could just faint when he stands behind me and holds his hand over mine on the racket and we "follow through."

We're so honest and real together. I trust him. He's so smart, so handsome, so kind and just so dreamy.

August 18, 1965

Dearest Deborah,

Devon and I are in love. I've let him touch me. I can't get him off my mind. I spend all day just waiting to hear his voice. Now we talk from 1:00 A.M. until 4:00 A.M. every night. Thank G-D Dad got me my own line. And thank G-D my bedroom is on the second floor. Dad would pull the phone out of the wall if he knew I was spending early A.M. hours talking instead of sleeping.

I am eighteen years old, and I have never had intercourse. Now, I'm ready for intercourse and he's the one I've been waiting for. I want him. I really want him.

Rachael, my cutie-pie cousin and I went shopping for the white nightgown I will wear. Everything must be perfect. Aunt Mae and Uncle Mitch are going out of town this weekend so Rachael said we can use their house for "LOVE."

August 22, 1965

Oh Deborah,

I am so glad Devon was the first man I ever let enter my body. I will remember every detail of our love's perfection for the rest of forever. He carried me upstairs to Rachael's bedroom just like Rhett Butler carried Scarlet O'Hara. CAN YOU STAND IT? I have written a poem for him that I will share with you first:

> Two prone forms on pastel peach sheets.
> Shadows from lack of light.
> Her long chestnut hair strewn on a pillow. Part of it on
> his chest.
> She watches his chest, his belly, his legs.
> She feels his heat in her hands, his strength abundant
> upon her.

He touches her … the softness,
the smoothness, the velvety sensations, the
shifting shadows, the secret places.
And it is this that they want to have, to share, to give
life to, to be born from, to live in, to love in,
to hold forever.
In her tiny form runs the blood
and soul and life of her.
Having just this … is having all of her.
Passion mounts …
Passion subsides …
Sleep.

*****

(Letter from Mom)

September 6, 1965

My daughter Leah,

All the way home from Northwestern and all the minutes since I have seen nothing but a pair of red shoes and a wee blue freshman beanie skipping with haste across a very wet campus into a new world. You didn't look back after we said "good-bye." So much the better because Dad and Ruthie and I were clinging to each other with expressions which would have divulged our hearts. So, there you are and here we are. Everything has changed for you. Nothing has changed for me, nothing, but everything. Your being away has made all the difference.

I keep thinking you'll pop in the door and greet me with that ridiculous "Charles" thing you call me. Or that you will straggle into the kitchen with your hair askew and at an un-G-D-ly hour devour a cold hoagie for breakfast. I see you whirling into the bath

47

for a sneak spray of cologne or mouth pretty to insure your feminine charms against defect.

We knew this time in our lives would come. I started thinking about it in your junior year. So, my precious, I was prepared but ill prepared for life without Leah. Still, I am glad that you are where you are.

Did you get your trunk yet? I mailed a few more items today, an extra pair of ballet shoes, four pillowcases, and some Noxzema. I still haven't found black gloves small enough in three stores. I'm going to try a children's department next.

Dad and Ruthie were very impressed with Northwestern. Ruthie thinks she too might apply in three years. I just wish it weren't so far away from Chadds Ford, Pa.

I hope you and Amy become good friends and learn how to live together with respect and fondness. She certainly seems like a first-rate girl and, I hope, the perfect roommate for you. I know the only time you've shared a room was during your summer camp summers and that your proclivity for solitude and silence makes sharing a challenge. But you can do it, of course. You can do anything you set your mind to.

So, set your mind on this, my daughter: Learn to like living inside your *own* skin. Study hard. Play hard. Call us every Sunday. And know that your family at home is rooting for you!

HIP HIP HURRAY!

I Love You, Mom

*****

This all sounds pretty good, right? WRONG! The part about only calling on Sundays was like tortuous punishment.

48

It was like abandonment. It was like … what if I have a pressing issue on Tuesday? Do I really have to wait until Sunday to call? I may not have had to wait, but I absolutely believed I did because those were the guidelines Dad set up. And I never ever wanted to cross my Dad. When I think of today's cell phones, I just sigh in utter bewilderment.

*****

September 27, 1965

Deborah, I'm not doing real great here at Northwestern. The best thing so far is Amy. She's just the most wonderful person and comforting roommate. But everything else is practically dreadful.

I'm carrying sixteen credits and ain't nothin' easy. Western Civ. is voluminous. Math is terrifying. Bio (*pre-med bio, no less*) is incomprehensible. Psychology is interesting. English is surprisingly challenging. Phys Ed. is Phys Ed., demanding and jock-ish and I've got it at 8:00 A.M. Swimming, in the gym, which is a half-mile away from my dorm, and it's FREEZING here already!

I study my ass off. Everyone does. I average about five hours sleep a night. My skin's all broken out and I've lost six pounds. To tell the truth, I'm not happy here. I'm trying to be, G-D knows, but I'm just not.

I haven't had a date since I've been here. I miss Devon but we're not really going steady.

We're just in love. Thank G-D he'll be visiting in two weeks. He's coming up for homecoming weekend. I've made reservations at a darling old boarding house on the outskirts of town.

October 15, 1965

Homecoming was a blast! It was beyond glorious to see Devon. I know there will be other loves and lovers in my life, but I also know there will never be another Devon: combination athlete and dancer, panther and teddy bear. I feel like a princess and a porcelain doll with him. And sometimes I feel like a hungry tiger or an evocative enchantress. I know I shall love him always, although we shall never wed.

And when the world hears from him, because he will be a famous jazz sax man someday, I will sit in his audience and blow him sweet kisses.

I'm afraid to actually write these words, but sometimes I think I feel those same feelings I felt in tenth grade when I was so down-and-out I couldn't study, practice piano, talk, eat, or venture away from my bed at Mom and Dad's. And remember, Deborah, a psychiatrist had to shoot Ritalin directly into a vein to even get my mouth to utter a sound.

*****

(Letter from Mom)

October 26, 1965

Leah, my Leah,

Needless to say, you have been in my tender loving thoughts since always, but especially since leaving you yesterday. In the plane my book lay unopened. You occupied me.

Leah, should you wish, you could be all the things you yearn to be. Should you work at it, you could not only be accepted, but popular. Should you relax, you could be a better student. Should you become more sensible, you could be more attractive, because your skin is an outer manifestation of your body abuse.

Your hair suffers from lack of concern. Your little frame is screaming for nourishment. Your filmy eyes beg for rest. Your self-abuse is both alarming and repellant. You're taking a beautiful, healthy body and turning it into an unlovely, neglected shell.

College isn't supposed to be a torture chamber. Give it your sincere effort and then let it go, Leah. Leave time and room to concentrate on health and appearance and balanced attitudes. Level out, my daughter, and seek the beauty that surrounds you.

Look toward your future. It can be a happy one if you allow today to be used well and not be pushed away in fear. You have so much going for you, and yet you never acknowledge the good in you; you only exaggerate the so-called "bad."

It is downright appalling to see what could be a bright and eager eighteen-year-old lousing up her days with an over-emphasis on a single person, a single college grade, a single-minded negativism.

There is an immediate need for self-inventory and an equal need to laugh at yourself and realize the world will not end with Northwestern, for you or anyone there. It's merely a steppingstone to something else, and the stones are exactly what you make them.

I didn't mind flying to Chicago to check in on you. I've missed you and have wanted to "talk our talk" over hot cocoa and see for myself how you were doing. Don't feel that you "made" me come; I wanted to.

Dad is most concerned about you, as is Ruthie. I do believe by Thanksgiving you will be feeling better and looking better and thinking more happily about the world that surrounds you. Meanwhile, stop crossing the days off the calendar with relief; it's an unforgivable waste. I love you, but I'm "mad" at you.

I know you'd want to know your Aunt Lauren isn't doing too well. Her depressions are more frequent and severe than ever, and the recent surgery to remove that grapefruit-sized tumor from her belly has left her drained and anxious. I love her madly; she is my twin, but how I do wish she were sound and whole.

As she heals physically, I see her dread mounting over what she should do next. She panics when faced with a decision. Even the tiniest decisions seem to throw her. I am convinced we must move her from Miami Beach to Pennsylvania, where she is surrounded by the continuous devotion of family. Her plight, it's pitiful. There seems to be no solution to the agonizing facets of her life. I am caught up in the fires of it with her.

Dad is an angel. Even when he's curt or uncommunicative, I can't judge him harshly. He has been so good to Lauren, so unstintingly good.

Well, Miss Muffat, I must leave you now. Addie wants me to make the dressing for our Caesar salad. She's just finishing up some ironing. What would we do without our beloved Addie?

Keep your chin up and know that I love you through "Thick and High," as our little Ruthie would say.

Always your, Mom

*****

November 12, 1965

Deb, Deb, Deb. I'm a mess. I've been seeing the school psychologist and I can tell that he thinks I'm a mess too. I'm rattled and nervous and then I'm depressed and sullen. I hide in the library for hours and dash to the cafeteria just before it closes so that I can eat alone. I'm embarrassed for anyone to see me.

My period is late. My grades stink. My skin is pimply and raw from sub-zero days. As stated, I'm a mess.

December 12, 1965

Now my period is real late. The psychologist is making me take a rabbit test.

December 14, 1965

OH G-D! I'm pregnant. My eyes are so swollen from crying I can barely see this paper. I walked around campus in fourteen-gusty-degree weather for three hours after Dr. Land gave me the news. He said he's going to call Mom and Dad. They'll kill me. They didn't know Devon and I are sleeping together. And why should they? I don't know any girl who confides her sex-capades to her parents.

I could just die. In fact, I wish I would before Mom and Dad get here. What will they do? I'll probably have to drop out of school. I've ruined my own life. I hate every single thing about myself. How can this be? We used condoms and foam! Why, Why? Why?

December 18, 1965

They brought me home. The arrangements were accomplished within six hours. Trunk packed. Dean of Liberal Arts consulted. Good-byes waved. Exams to be forwarded to a college near home so I can be proctored. The eternal ride home was driven in silence.

Mom's gynecologist came to our house to examine me. He said from the feel of my uterus, another rabbit test was indicated; I wasn't swollen inside. The second rabbit didn't die. I still wish I had. So, we've gone through all this and I wasn't even pregnant. The first test had yielded a false positive. Can you stand it?

Mom and Dad don't say much.

I say less.

I am verbally paralyzed.

I only come out of my room for dinner, which I never eat.

I smoke a pack a day and blow them out the bathroom window.

I drink pots of coffee and bite my nails; they're bloody and ugly, as am I.

GRRRR!

They have forbidden me to ever see Devon again. Fat chance. I've been able to sneak two calls. They're so disappointed and hurt and angry. They don't act mean. But I know they could throttle me.

I would have had an abortion, that's for sure. No discussion about that! It was a given. I probably would have had it right in my own bed since abortions are illegal. I can't even think about that. Any more than I can think about what it would be like to mother a baby while I'm still a baby myself. Any more than I can think about adoption. In fact, I can't think about much of anything. I'm just a feeling machine. And all I feel is self-loathing, shame, anger, and a sense of failure as deep as the earth's core. On days like this I need to write a poem:

> Say it ... Say it!
> Hold it in one more moment and you'll shriek.
> And the shriek will be heard globally.
> Tell them.
> Tell them venom is poison.
> Tell them too much love breeds a special sort of hate.
> Tell them emotion requires release.
> Passion requires outlet.
> Love demands freedom.
> Tell them, and then speak no more.

It begins very softly like the life of a feather and then it
grows like a cancer until it all but devours.
It starts very low as the birth of a wave
and then it reaches like a weed until it nearly strangles.
It banishes and buries beauty.
It destroys.
It molests.
It terminates.
It's a mile away and coming closer,
closer,
nearer,
surer.
Soon …. Very soon now …. Just one more kiss before …
THERE IS NOTHING!

*****

Christmas 1965

Darling Devon,

They don't understand. And I don't understand why they don't
understand. They were young once too. They were in love.

How can I stop loving you and the luxury of truth and sincerity
we've shared? How can I abandon the most perfect and complete
love I might ever know?

We unfolded for each other, didn't we, Baby? So vulnerable
for only each other that we stripped away all social conventions
for each other. Through you I have known passion and you have
taught me love. Sweet Devon, I thank you.

We've had fun, haven't we, my Love? Cleansing each other's
souls and blowing fresh sweet thoughts through each other's
minds. I have loved making you laugh with my female self.

So often have I grieved the inevitable "death" of us, while knowing the exquisite touch of lovers that can only give themselves, not forever promises, just whispers of impossible dreams.

We've been so resilient in the face of such adversity. And I do so fear being thrown back into life's death-dance ring without you. Love like ours is as fragile as Tinkerbell dust or sweet angel breath moving skyward toward the sun.

I do not carry your baby. I am relieved and grateful. We are too young. A marriage between us would complicate too many lives. But oh, how beautiful would be the beige baby that my white and your chocolate brown skin would produce.

My first love … my talented, passionate, intelligent Devon.

Thank you for loving me.

Stay at Julliard and excel.

I miss you. I miss you. I miss you.

Don't worry. We will see each other again. I won't always be a minor.

Merry Merry and Happy Happy.

Fly high on angels' wings, my Black Beauty, and know you will always be loved by your, Leah Rebecca

*****

1966

Deborah, I miss me. I have all but gone away again and been replaced by the phantom of depression I loathe. How dare you invade my life, my spirit, and the physical body-house in which I live! How dare you steal my thoughts! What right have you to overtake my brain? How can I kill you without actually killing me?

I try to remember being four or romping on the playground as a second-grader. I have to dig so far down and go so far back to remember a time when I thought living was a cool deal. This sure ain't livin'. This is using all my energy to not pursue death, to not believe the only relief for me is inside a pine box.

I miss Devon. I even miss being a student, a freshman, a girl with dreams and fantasies that included travel and adventure, music, magic, and marriage.

H.E.L.L.O. Leah, are you in there?

April 3, 1966

I see a psychiatrist three times weekly. Into a deep blue vein, he shoots me up with Ritalin so I can speak. Every part of me goes numb when I enter his space, so this drug must be pumped into me just to open my cement-boxed thoughts and feelings. I surge into some fifth-gear momentum as the hot drug courses through my blood in sixty seconds. Then I talk faster than a speeding bullet and leap tall buildings in a single bound. But as the session ebbs into completion, so does the drug, and again I retreat into some dark abyss in my mind.

I'm supposed to be filling out applications and mountain-high piles of entrance forms for The University of Pennsylvania. Since both Mom and Dad are alumni, I probably have a fair chance of getting in for fall term '66. Who cares?

July 4, 1966

Summer school stinks. But when you mess up as badly as I did at Northwestern, you have to pay some dues. U of P. ... oh golly gee. Can hardly believe you've accepted me.

Haven't seen or talked to Devon in many months. Haven't much wanted to talk to anyone. But the ugly devil in my mind seems to have nearly disintegrated. I'm still sad, but not paralyzed. I can enjoy moonlight and neighborhood kids in our pool. I can study and think about time spread out in its illusive way, creating a burgeoning and beckoning life for me.

I had to let Devon go. Leave him to forge his way in his own world. Leave him to his art, his friends, his race and culture. Leave him to a life uncomplicated by Leah. I've read that a first love lives inside someone forever. I believe if I reach rocking-chair vintage, Devon will still reside inside of me.

September 15, 1966

My roommate is *great*! Wendy Shapiro. She's from northern New Jersey. When we're not studying our brains out, we light candles, burn incense, and listen to Tim Buckley. I really love being back in Philly.

Check this out: Yesterday I was walking down Walnut Street taking in the pleasures of mega-metropolis Philadelphia living, when I found myself in faraway fantasies as I peered through Becker Travel Agency's window at the posters that invited me to London, Madrid, and Milan.

When I emerged from fantasy, I saw him in the window leaning against a floor-to-ceiling gothic pillar near the St. Thomas poster. One of those seductive leans … angled, arms folded across his chest, one Italian loafer crossing the other. When he knew I'd seen him, he came to the door, pushed it open, and said, "So, where do you think you want to go?"

"Everywhere," I said. "And someday I shall."

We went out for coffee, Samuel Becker and I. He's fascinating, of course. Sophisticated, world traveled, and great looking. He's also cocky, presumptive, and twenty-eight years older than I am. In addition, and this is a HUGE addition … he goes to our synagogue. Dad and he are peripheral friends.

September 23, 1966

I've seen Samuel a few times. He's funny and romantic and makes me feel like twenty-five. I could really like this man. I better not. I mean, I REALLY better not.

October 2, 1966

I was embarrassed but secretly thrilled when Samuel marched himself into my dorm, had the woman at the desk ring my room, and I strolled into the lobby to find him decked out and carrying a dozen yellow roses. I think the guy truly digs me! Can you stand it? I am more than the apple of his eye. He says, "You're the diamond in my sky."

October 15, 1966

I wish it hadn't been fabulous. I wish he were all talk and couldn't deliver. I wish he didn't make me feel like a fully realized woman. I wish he were a jerk. I always loved the thought of high adventure. I just thought it would happen on the high seas. Oh G-D, when I think about Samuel and my parents simultaneously, I nearly throw up.

I can hear them now: "What's the matter with you, Leah? First there was a black boy, now there's a middle-aged man … a business associate of Dad's who goes to our synagogue! Do you find young Jewish men repellant, or are you just some kind of psycho rebellious hippie?"

October 23, 1966

Though Samuel and I talk every day, see each other for dinner a couple nights a week, and sleep together on weekends, he writes me daily:

"My precious, tiny Leah,

When I met you at my travel agency in Philly, I had no intention of becoming involved with you. A flirtation, I thought, and nothing more. But so soon I am committed and willing, eager and smitten. Though the future is uncertain, it's too late now. I'm sunk. What delight, what ecstasy, how thrilling, how frightening."

"… JOY is what I feel when you tell me you are gaining something good from me. I grow and soar too. Your eagerness is my catalyst. The ingredients are simply man and woman. The obstacles, plentiful. But I wish for a miracle to turn time around somehow, even out our lives, erase disparities, change standards, create something to give hope. I will never stop hoping."

"… I will look for daisies always, love them forever. Daisies are taken for granted. They need a champion: how about you and me. Let's look for converts. Take them off roses and orchids. Complexity versus simplicity. Your thoughts, Leah, envelop me.

I adore your mind and I implore you to keep writing. You may find you'd prefer a major in creative writing rather than in some form of teaching. You don't want marriage as a career. You've got to do something with your intelligent life that really counts. Leave your insignia on the world, Leah. You can become a wife, mother, anytime you want. LIVE FIRST! Discover the world and your place in it. I'd bet a gold mine on you.

Learn from my mistakes, from my adventures, dreams, failures, frustrations, just learn. Your brain, lovely young woman, is both your weapon and your enemy. Be careful. Go slowly. Keep a reign on your emotions.

I know I shall yearn until I see you again. Into this man's life has come one golden woman; now all the others are just shades of gray. Daisies are alive for both of us.

Love you very much, too much. Samuel"

November 17, 1966

OH NO

OH NO

OH NO

OH NO

OH NO!

My period's late. I could choke on fear if I let myself.

Please, G-D, NO BABY! PLEASE!

November 19, 1966

The rabbit died. Samuel and I cried for hours last night. Nothing comforts me. Not his arms. Not his words. Not the bing-cherry ice cream he brought me nor the stuffed bear. I'm not the stuffed-bear type. But how could he know that? He doesn't know me. I don't even know me. Because I sure didn't know that at nineteen, I'd be involved with a man my Dad's age, while my priority is two term papers that are due.

My mind spins. My heart breaks. I now know the meaning of the word *terror*. I can't have this baby. It's not even an option. And abortion is illegal.

November 20, 1966

All I want is Mom's arms. I can't have them. Or I want to awaken and shout, "Thank you, G-D, that it was only a dream." We used contraceptive jelly, a condom, AND foam. And still his sperm found its way to my egg. I hate it. I hate him. I hate me. I hate that I'm still a teenager, he's two years from fifty, and I have to worry myself into near collapse trying to figure out how to rid my body of a growing life.

I pull myself out of bed each morning and vomit into a dormitory toilet. Wendy coaxes me into clothes and guides me to the cafeteria downstairs. The smell of sausage makes my stomach turn.

I summon every shred of physical and emotional strength to get to my 8:00 A.M. class. I sit front row center through the day to encourage myself to listen, take notes, and synthesize the material.

We had to pith a frog in biology today. The formaldehyde made me gag, and I ran to the ladies' room and cried a bucket-full of sea-salty tears.

Wendy is supportive. She's the only one I've told. But she's nineteen too and can only handhold me through this. She can't make it go away. Samuel says he'll handle everything and I'm not to worry. Sure, he may as well have told me not to be brunette or short or Jewish.

November 26, 1966

I report the following saga not knowing whether it comes under the heading of *Horror*, *Science Fiction*, or *Exaggerated Drama*.

Two days ago, Samuel told me he had the whole thing arranged. An abortion, that is. I slipped into a combined state of crippling fear with an overlay of numbness.

I can't even stay with him at night, except on weekends, because of dorm curfew rules. Is this absurd or what? I'm old enough to produce a baby and kill it; my high school friends who aren't in college are old enough to be drafted and kill other kids because of international political nonsense and the global money-hustle. But I'm not old enough to stay overnight in the arms of the man who just arranged my abortion.

Here's what happened. We drove to Camden, New Jersey. We were to meet a man in a tan Ford station wagon, and he was to take me to the abortionist's office. Samuel was not permitted to come with me. We left him at the Maple Diner.

I got into the man's car. He turned the corner, pulled onto a side street, blindfolded me and put me on the floor of the backseat. My heart was pounding. I wondered if I were being kidnapped.

We drove for what seemed like three days but was probably fifteen minutes. Un-blindfolded, he forcibly escorted me into a storefront building. It looked like a tailor's shop, but it wasn't. Inside it was dim, cold, stale, and seemed like a stage setting for a play about something sordid.

Carelessly placed were two torn-up, rusty yellow vinyl chairs and a wooden table. Three "girlie" posters. An overflowing trash can with beer bottles, an empty Jack Daniels, and a Johnnie Walker Black. Two mangy cats slept on a pile of rags. I thought I'd pass out.

Enter the abortionist, from a back room. "So, I guess you's the one who's knocked up."

I nodded.

"Get back there, get undressed, and lie on the table," he ordered.

I obeyed. I wasn't even completely undressed before he marched his greasy haired, beer-bellied, unshaven, T-shirted self into the back room. "I can get through this," I commanded myself.

I laid down on a wooden table covered with a filthy sheet that had faded pink and yellow flowers printed on it. It looked like it had seen a few bloody abortions. A bare bulb swung from the ceiling. He put on those yellow gloves women wear when they're about to use Ajax or Clorox. And then he did a pelvic. I don't know which emotion nearly overcame me. Fear? Disgust? Rage? Humiliation? I felt myself about to vomit so I kept swallowing and clenching my teeth.

He said, "Yeah, you's about seven weeks pregnant. Be back here tomorrow at 10:00 P.M. with $750.00."

"Yes," I said, "Okay."

The driver placed me on the back-seat floor and re-blindfolded me. He dropped me at the Maple Diner and told me I'd see him tomorrow at 9:30 P.M., same place.

I must have looked ashen because Samuel's face stiffened when he saw me. In the diner, I had tea and toast and described the experience. He cried. I couldn't cry. Some of me must believe I deserved such treatment. Abortion is a filthy business. So how could I expect or deserve pleasant surroundings or a clean and sympathetic doctor? I was prepared to return the next day and accept my fate.

"No," Samuel said, "you will not be returning tomorrow. And how can you forgive me for putting you through such an ordeal? I should never have let him take you without me."

I hadn't even considered blaming Samuel. He had done his best. This is all new to him too. He dropped me at my dorm, and I watched until his Lincoln turned left on green.

November 30, 1966

New plan of action. Tomorrow we are leaving on a 7:00 A.M. flight to Atlanta, Georgia. Samuel has a cousin there who knows a legitimate gynecologist who is performing illegal abortions in his office. If all goes well, we should be able to catch a 9:00 P.M. flight home tomorrow night so I can make dorm curfew. G-D help us. This is the worst nightmare of my life.

December 8, 1966

It has taken me a week to even contemplate writing about the hardest day of my nineteen years. I only force myself to record it with the hope that spilling it onto the page will release me from some of the anguish.

The flight was short, and I sat in silence. Samuel pretended to read, but he never turned a page. His cousin was nice. He has lived in the South long enough to have picked up a slower pace than we Northerners, and even a bit of a drawl. His home was comfortable, and he did his very best to make me feel at ease. Yeah, sure. The appointment was scheduled for 1:00 P.M.

One o'clock came and went. So did 2:00 and 3:00 and 4:00 and 5:00 and 6:00. Nobody was telling me much of anything, although I heard muffled phone calls emanating from the kitchen.

Samuel said we may have to stay overnight. The prospect of having to deal with the dorm mother and get parental permission to stay overnight, seemed more frightening than the impending procedure. Usually, she calls parents to check on such a request. I asked

Samuel why the delay. He said the doctor had some emergency surgeries that pushed his schedule off. I sat glued to a chair.

I couldn't read, watch TV, listen to music, or even lie down. I was in suspended animation.

The call came at 7:00 P.M. A close friend of the family took me to the doctor's office. His name is Ted and that was all I was told. We parked a block away. There were no lights lit on the doctor's building, nor in it.

Dr. Marshall answered the back-door entrance. We went quietly to an examining room. He gave me a gown and told me they'd be back in a few minutes. I was freezing and trembling. I wasn't teary. I had resolve.

Dr. Marshall said Ted could stay with me if I wanted him to. I did. And then the doctor said he would tell me what to expect as he was doing the procedure. He said it would be quite painful, but he was sure I'd be able to handle it. I nodded. I was shaking so violently he found a blanket to cover me. It was gray plaid. The procedure didn't take terribly long, and it *was* extremely painful. And all of this, by the way, accomplished with two flashlights.

Dr. Marshall said I had done well and should rest for about fifteen minutes.

After I'd dressed, Dr. Marshall came in with some instructions. I asked if I could fly back to Philadelphia in an hour. He said he wouldn't recommend it, but he thought it would be O.K. if I took it real slow and easy.

We picked Samuel up and Ted drove us to the airport. Once in our seats, Samuel needed to know every detail. They spilled from me without emotion and then I said I wanted to be quiet. We also sat in silence on the drive from the airport to the dorm. When I got to my room, Wendy's arms greeted me. Dear, precious, wonderful, caring Wendy. She made us hot chocolate. We listened to Tim

Buckley while I sobbed through the whole nonfiction-nightmare
story.

Oh, Leah Rebecca Kline, how did you ever allow this to happen
to yourself?

December 18, 1966

It's Christmas break. I have just read the last few entries from
last year's journal. What a mess! I was home from Northwestern.
Leveled from the humiliation of having "almost" been pregnant.
Achingly sad for my parents. Tri-weekly visits to a shrink who shot
me up with Ritalin because I couldn't even speak. Missing Devon
and wishing I'd never been born.

What hideous irony has brought me to a worse position exactly
one year later? I meet Samuel Becker; I play like a grown-up ...
AND THEN I GET REALLY AND TRULY PREGNANT!

Now I live, but just barely, with the fact that twenty-one days
ago I was in Georgia having my baby vacuumed from my womb.

Today, while snow blankets our corner of the world, I sit in
my own room, safely ensconced in my window niche, finished
with finals and those four monumental papers, alone and quiet for
the first time in three weeks. And I feel lousy. No, even *dreadful*
doesn't describe how I feel. It's like the doctor got the "fetus,"
which is clearly a euphemism for my baby, but left something
worse in its place. My entire internal cavity feels rotten, spoiled,
smelly, fermented, moldy, decayed, putrid, and rancid ... as though
he slipped a dead fish inside me where a baby once lived.

I can smile, laugh and "act" normal. But something so restrictive
and sad has penetrated my being that I don't know if I will laugh
and *not* be acting ever again.

I don't blame Samuel. If someone chooses to play with
sex, someone gambles with pregnancy; it is not an illogical

consequence. After all, he didn't handcuff me to the four posts of his bed.

I have nightmares about the abortion. I relive the refrigerator chill of the instruments of dilation and the pull of the vacuum, which surely must feel like labor. No sedative, no numbing med, no nothing but the searing realization of how much I deserved to feel this mind-bending pain. The noise of the vacuum alone could have undone me, if I had let it.

I remember preparing for it like the preparing I imagine is required of those about to face a firing squad or the electric chair. Somehow you steel yourself for it because of its utter inevitability. Afterward, it's like walking around in an afterlife. You know you're still alive, but everything is different.

Why have I gone through this without my parents' help? Because I could, that's why. Because I did not want to scar them, grieve them, or have them look at me with disappointment, disgust, and despair. I've seen enough of those looks to last through forever.

We, the family, have lots of lovely things planned for the holidays. Tomorrow night we're going to Gelotti's annual Christmas bash. They will have a ten-foot-tall tree abundantly decorated with their decades-old family history. We will drink hot toddies, and I will help the kids bake the last few batches of gingerbread men. Then we'll enchant the neighborhood with carols sung in delicate harmonies. And no, Mom and Dad don't worry that I'll fall in love with Jesus just because I sing Christmas Carols every year. (Some Jewish people actually ask me that!)

Since Samuel and I are a secret, I will not see him during this break and will bring in the New Year with some old high school friends.

'Tis the season and all that, but I don't feel too seasonal.

*****

68

1967

I've been back at school for exactly six hours and already I'm
a wreck. My schedule is a horror! Interpretation of Literature II,
Introduction to Social Problems, Comparative Religions, French
III, Introduction to Educational Media, Voice and Articulation,
and of course, on these frigid winter mornings, I pulled hideously
miserable Phys. Ed., SWIMMING … AGAIN, at 8:00 A.M. in the
building farthest from my dorm. Naturally.

The best part of this is Wendy as a roommate and best friend.
I'm making us a cup of coffee. We're going to construct a study
schedule, and then we're off to Sal's for cheesesteaks and hoagies.

My mailbox bulged with letters from Samuel. He wrote to me
every day of Christmas break. G-D, how the man does love me.
And I do take such pleasure in his words.

*****

(Letter from Samuel)

"Leah, my Beauty,

How can I express my gratitude for such a Hanukah surprise?
The shock was so great, at first, I thought I had entered someone
else's home until I remembered you have a key. Through forty-eight years, two marriages, world travel, and fathering, I have
never felt as loved and important as I did today.

The handmade cards, Leah. Each one a faceted jewel of origi-
nality, artistry, conception, and taste. I will treasure them always.

The charcoal cardigan. The kid-leather gloves. Of course, I love
the scarf best of all. When did you have time to knit that, my Lovely?

You could teach women how to love, Leah. You have brought me into a dimension of Utopia, Nirvana, and the Elysian Fields. If I were to die this moment, all the music in your name would still be mine …"

November 15, 1967

It is late Sunday night. What an extraordinary weekend this had been. Samuel is in Colorado on business; Mom and Dad are in New York seeing some shows and whooping it up; Ruthie is skiing at Killington.

I thought it would be a perfect weekend to come home and enjoy the house alone, work on the dyslexia term paper, and start studying for the psych exam. I had just gotten the fire roaring and the hot chocolate hot when I heard a key in the front door.

"Damn," I muttered, almost too loudly. But when Aunt Lauren rounded the corner with Loretta Young style and an Auntie-Mame smile, I was actually pleased. When she is well, she is dazzling!

We talked and talked late into the night and early day. I was so honored that she considers me, at age twenty, old enough to hear about her life. It has been a most daring and outrageous life and she might have thought I would have judged or misunderstood. I didn't, of course. I knew lots of the stuff already. And besides, I can identify with massive melodrama.

It felt safe to ask her about her depressions. As she spoke, I felt my heart tighten. Her symptoms are my symptoms, her fears, my fears. The most engaging fear being that the doctors may never find a solution to her episodic periods of despair. After all, what haven't they tried? Shock treatments haven't worked long-term. The antidepressants don't work at all. Thorazine leaves her feeling and acting lobotomized. Her stints in mental hospitals have left her demoralized but not healed. She lives in dread of recurrence, so even if she is well for one year or two, she knows the despair will return because it always does.

She is twenty-eight years older than I am. I've had several crippling bouts of depression and some periods of savage sadness. Why should I assume I won't have more? It scares me senseless, because when your brain is sick, you're sick everywhere. When you don't have your brain-organ to help you fight illness, you're sunk. You have no defenses, resources, or initiative to research your malady or fight for your life.

I gathered the chutzpa to ask her why she had married her mother's brother, her blood-uncle, when she was nineteen years old. Her answer was so simple. "Because we were madly in love," she stated as though she were talking about why she uses Tide as a detergent.

"Since my Mother was the oldest of thirteen and Jason was the youngest, there wasn't that great an age disparity between us," she continued. "Only twelve years. It was hurtful to me that it was so hurtful to my parents, but not so hurtful that I would decide not to elope. He was the most dashing, romantic, funny, and provocative man I've ever known.

I'm nearly fifty years old now. I've been married twice since Jason and have had a string of sophisticated and intelligent lovers. But no man has come close to Jason in dimension or substance. He was the love of my life, Leah. I have no regrets about our marriage, other than that he died a year into it."

"You knew it was a brain tumor, right?"

I nodded.

Later that night as we examined family photo albums, I looked at the pictures of her and Jason more carefully. Their family resemblance was more apparent, as well as the fiery intensity of their youth and their tenacious resolve to withstand all resistance.

Mom told me about her own position throughout the scandal. BoBo and PaPa Honey forbade her to see Aunt Lauren and Jason. They were livid and humiliated, and poor Mom bore the brunt of their dismay. Mom *did* see her twin, of course. But she had to sneak visits like a thief. Much as I understood Aunt Lauren's lust and determination to be with Jason, I found myself resenting that my Mom had to withstand so much of the heat for Aunt Lauren's unusual choices all through their mutual lives. Never have two identical twins been less identical.

Aunt Lauren has battled depressions, a three-year stint with tuberculosis in a sanitarium, a laminectomy, a stomach tumor, the death of her life-love, two divorces, the failure of three businesses, several relocations, one miscarriage, one hysterectomy, and a long list of other disappointments and setbacks. Although she is now a pastel version of her once brilliant and glamorous self, when Aunt Lauren used to enter a room, she'd make the chandelier look dull.

My Mom, conversely, has always carried herself with a dignified and delicate demeanor that very closely resembles the elegance of royalty. If Aunt Lauren is Loretta Young and Auntie Mame, then Nina Kline is Grace Kelly and Audrey Hepburn.

Back to Aunt Lauren and me. I asked her why she had slipped her key into our door. Hadn't she known Mom and Dad were away for the weekend? Yes, she had known. But she had felt so lonely in her own apartment she thought it would help to be among Mom's things. That made me fight back tears.

She is such a volatile and emotional woman. She reminds me of me, and that feels both wonderful and terrifying.

I almost confided in her about Samuel and the abortion of one year ago two weeks from today. But I couldn't, somehow. It didn't feel fair to encumber her with that secret.

We talked about her childlessness and the emptiness that has created for her. I can't even imagine a childless life, and don't want to. *I will have children someday.*

I will have a daughter whom I take to the Nutcracker ballet every December, just as my Mom and I have done. And afterward we will eat lunch in the ever so opulent Crystal Room of Wanamaker's Department Store on Chestnut Street in Philly, just as my Mom and I have done. And when my daughter is small, we will go to the doll department in Wanamaker's and buy some outfits for her Ginny doll, just as my Mom and I have done. And when she is older, we will go to the junior department and buy a lovely holiday outfit, just as my Mom and I have done.

I will have a son. I will teach him to honor women and never exploit them. I will shoot hoops with him and take him to Phillies' games. We will ride horses together, take weekend trips to the country, buy antiques, sip cider, and commune about the glories of nature.

I WILL HAVE CHILDREN!

Dear G-D, please help Aunt Lauren in her struggle to be whole. She drains my Mom and strains my Dad, and I know she is humiliated by her depressions and pallor of insidious illness. Please allow 1968 to be her year to flourish and shine.

*****

(Letter from Aunt Lauren)

November 17, 1967

Dearest Leah,

I will treasure this past weekend as a highly polished diamond and store it in my memory right next to some other few favorites.

You are a beauty, Leah. You are so significantly wise and knowing for only having experienced life for twenty years. How did you get to be so smart?

Something you said troubles me and I want to speak of it. I do not want you to identify with my illnesses and flamboyance. You are not, as you said, "a miniature version" of your aunt. I see your Mother radiating from you. So many of her qualities have roots in your emergence. Both of you are good, strong, mature, fair-minded, reasonable, understanding, and so, so kind. I am grateful she is your Mother.

It is true without this family I would never have made it this far. All of you inspire me to reach for wellness. When I was so sick last year and had to stay at your Mom and Dad's home, and you had just returned from Northwestern, I came to really appreciate what you are made of. Your warmth, empathy, and gentleness touched me so much. Your tiny hands holding and compressing my ribs while I coughed delighted me because of how deeply you care. You will never ever know how much I adore you.

Listen to me, Leah. Depression will not overtake you. You are strong and you can fight. Don't give up and don't give in. And don't ever let me hear you say the word *suicide* again. EVER! Do you hear me? You just keep right on going to those doctors and therapists. If they want to try a new drug on you, let them. If they want to shoot you with Ritalin because you are unable to speak, let them. I know you don't like it. Who would? But you can handle it. You simply must. Mental illness does not have to be your legacy. You may not win every battle, but you will win the war. I know it. I just know it!

Great good fortune brought us together this past weekend. Thank you for sharing yourself so generously when you had papers to write and exams to study for.

Be good to yourself. Be careful. Be all that you are, and all will be well. I adore every centimeter of you.

Aunt Lauren

*****

1968

(Letter from Mom)

August 2, 1968

Leah Rebecca is twenty-one years old today, so vulnerable and firm, a study in paradoxes. She is a chameleon at once young and mature, indifferent and thoughtful, rash and premeditative, a bundle of complexes, exultant and sad.

She is only fifty-nine inches, but not to be looked down upon. Her hands belong to a child, elementary, as if they had not fulfilled their promise to grow. Her feet are shapely and nicely rounded. But it is her eyes and voice which reveal the most about her. Both are mellow and rich brown velvet with expression. Instruments she uses with consummate skill, spilling ice and fire over her world.

She moves with grace, like a woman should, not the self-conscious gait of a model, but with a genuinely exquisite softness. What a feminine creature, Leah.

Volatile loves and misjudgments have flung her into bogs of quicksand from which she seemingly emerges unscathed. But the quality of her behavior grows more constant now, and the spectrum of her responses steadier.

A humor sharp and cynical and inward-directed saves her from a sometimes too-acute appraisal of herself. The practical and the romantic merge. The bitter and the sweet become one. Leah grows to be a lovely and excellent woman.

Your Mother

*****

(Letter from Dad)

August 1, 1968

My very dearest Leah,

It is our special ritual that I sit down to pen some thoughts your way during the early moments of August. The second of August is a most significant day for your Mom and me. Unique and memorable because, being the oldest, you foisted upon us a new sense of responsibility and a completely new source of pleasure.

Until the day you were born, Mom and I had only each other to both give and take from. Although this is normal during the first years of marriage, it was a largely selfish existence with the giving limited between two people.

I've always believed that love, in its broadest sense, is the fundamental cornerstone for human relationships. I believe the more one is able to give, the greater must inevitably be his pleasure. Just think, if love were the prevailing force in the world, how little use there would be for war or strife.

So you see, my Darling, your arrival unshackled us from a circumscribed love to a wider concept of sharing. We welcomed you with open hearts and you became the center of our existence. We lost the past limits of our emotions and embraced the flowering of a widening swell of love.

This then, is what you have given us. You have opened completely new and untapped sources of joy and surely some pain, but one does not usually exist without the other. It seems to be the faculty of parents to allow the cheerful remembrances of their children to linger and permit the distasteful to fade away.

How immeasurably rewarding it has been to have you come into our lives! Where there might have been loneliness, you give life much joy. Where there could have been emptiness, you give rich meaning; and where selfishness might have been our way of life, you lead us into the rich fields of giving.

Your great contribution is simply that you are our Leah Rebecca, ALWAYS!

All my love to you, Dad

*****

1969

Deborah … Samuel and I had the most delicious New Year's last night. We went to the Bellevue Stratford Hotel in Philly, danced to a big-band sound, devoured blood rare fillets with a mushroom and wine sauce, drank a bottle of Dom, and made love in an elegantly appointed room until 4:00 A.M. He takes such pleasure in spoiling me. Frankly, and thank G-D he really does know this, I'd have been just as happy at his house with a pizza.

And that's where we are right now. In his gigantic bed, reading *The New York Times* and *The Philadelphia Inquirer*, and a pizza is on its way. I'm so happy here. The only part that hurts is that we must be clandestine about our love.

In six months, I will graduate from The University of Pennsylvania with a Bachelor of Arts in speech path and a minor in Special Ed. Then I'll go on for my Masters. Nothing substantive can be done with a mere Bachelors. So, although I am sick to bloody death of school and exams and papers and pressure and competition and students and rah-rah-junk that has never appealed to me, I will persevere for another two years and learn the meaty stuff, so I can really help the kids who need help.

I've decided to focus my Masters on Autism. My professors have encouraged me to do so. I seem to have an uncanny ability to reach the unreachable. Maybe because I'm as oddly altered as they are.

January 15, 1969

And just when everything seemed so lovely, everything is now totally unlovely. I feel as though I've been clubbed and beaten silly. Two nights ago, Samuel and I were eating our favorite Italian

delights at Antonio's. It was amateur night, and every aspiring oper-
atic star and groupie was given a chance to perform. It always tickles
me to see humanity doing its thing, unencumbered, unfettered,
blushing, sweating, and swigging Chianti to make it all possible.

Soft, feather-light snow was falling when we emerged. Philly
was silenced from the white fairy dust that blanketed streets and
muffled car sounds, foot sounds, and people sounds. We too stood
in silence and then kissed, rocked, and watched the white powder
sprinkle our hair and coats. We stuck out our tongues to catch its
purity and freshness. And then the world stopped.

Mom and Dad and Mr. and Mrs. Rosen had pulled into Antonio's parking lot and were walking toward us en masse. "Oh, no!"
I gasped.

"What's wrong, honey?" Samuel asked.

"It's Mom and Dad and the Rosen's, Samuel. What should I do?"

"I'm not sure," he said. "Let's see what they do."

Well, here's what they did. Dad dead-eyed Samuel.

Mom said, "Hi, Leah. Hi, Samuel. Anything great on the menu
we should know about?"

"Not really," I murmured.

Nobody shook hands.

Dad said, "Call us later."

I tried to worm out of it on the phone later that night. I was
totally graceless, and they accused me of lying. They told me to
come home next weekend and we'd discuss it. Now that sure
sounds like a cracker-barrel full of fun. Samuel feels rotten, but not
nearly as rotten as I feel. *His* parents aren't going to lay into him.
They're dead. *His* parents aren't going to pull him out of school.
He graduated a hundred years ago. *He* isn't going to have to look
into the faces of two people he loves and see total disappointment
and disgust.

My family has known Samuel since I was a kid. He was the proprietor of a store not far from Dad's plant before he opened his travel agency in Philly. He occasionally attends our synagogue; sometimes he and his kids show up for High Holy Day services. He's been divorced for decades.

Samuel doesn't quite grasp the enormity of the consequences that are about to befall us.

January 18, 1969

Well, despite being twenty-one, Mom and Dad have forbidden me to ever see Samuel again. And the only reason I can stay in the dorm and don't have to commute an hour and a half each way is because they don't want to cripple my study time.

Now Samuel is beginning to get it. Of course, neither of us has any intention of never seeing each other again. It's just going to make it a damned-site harder and a lot less festive.

I could scream. Instead, I cry. I guess I should write a poem.

A few years ago, when I was about seventeen, I found a piece of paper on my seat in a train-car as I sped toward New York. The words seared me. I remember getting home that night and trying to catch the essence of those words in my journal. Here's my version, from that journal, of the feelings those words carved into me. They are so apt right this very second:

> And there are men and women. And we seek each
> other.
> And it is right that we should.
> For there is no beauty that can touch that of man
> woman eyes meeting.
> The wonder. The testing. The journey into each other.
> The revelations.

The quest to find those missing parts of ourselves.
We will go to all lengths to merge:
To sheets. To grass. To floor.
We will go anywhere to feed together and share the
lightning chill that explodes behind my eyes and in his
groin.
We will try anything to ascend, as one, to the sun
draped hillside of beauty and giving.
Ah … to know and be known.
To touch another human being touching me and to
know myself.
On rare occasions this wonder transcends itself.
Then I stand naked as a child between worlds, ages,
stages of life, sex and all else.
I stand between what I am and what I may become.
Between self-love and self-sacrifice.
Between my desire to have and that to give.
And then there is that wish … to grind myself indelibly
into him.
And the wish is all consuming.
Frantic. Frenetic. Passionate.
It is beyond the raw beauty of our naked bodies spread
face to sighing face.

March 5, 1969

I think what I experienced yesterday can safely be labeled
"psychotic rage." Today I am "raged-out" and have slipped into
scathing pain.

Samuel was supposed to call me the day before yesterday. He
didn't call then. And he didn't call all day yesterday. I couldn't
study or think. I paced. I mumbled. I was on the verge of getting

really weird, so at 7:00 P.M. Wendy suggested we take a bus to Samuel's house and see what we could find.

The house was dark, and his car wasn't in the garage. I let us in. Nothing looked odd, but nothing looked right. I felt a headache marching my way and went to the bathroom for some Excedrin. First sign of trouble, his toiletry kit was gone. I ran down to the cellar. Two of his suitcases were gone.

Panic descended. Or was it more like dread?

My Dick Tracy mode kicked in.

Wendy followed me around like a sheep dog.

She didn't say much. How could she?

I had the air waves covered with tyranny and hysteria.

Within minutes I found the incriminating evidence: a letter in his charcoal, cashmere overcoat.

"Dearest Samuel, The French Quarter will always be 'our little corner of the world.' Now, I love Creole and Jazz as much as I love you. Thank you for a most glamorous weekend, Darling. I'll await your phone call next week. You're absolutely divine! All my love, Cindy."

"DIVINE?" I raged. "DIVINE?"

No, not divine. A cad, maybe. A chump. A jerk. A bastard. A cheat. A lowlife. But, not divine. Never again, DIVINE!

It was hours before Wendy cooled and calmed me sufficiently to get me on a bus and back to the dorm. I didn't even pretend I could sleep. I sat in the TV room and watched programs, with no volume, until colored vertical lines filled the screen. When the National Anthem came on, I walked the corridors. And when the girls started waking for their 8:00 A.M. classes, I went to the cafeteria for coffee.

That was yesterday, which has bled into today. Now it's 10:00 P.M. and he still hasn't called. Off with Cindy somewhere, I guess. Cindy who? Cindy what? Her letter was postmarked from Denver.

He goes to Colorado all the time. Which time did he meet her? How old is she? What does she look like?

G-D, I hurt. I hurt so deeply I didn't even know I had a deep this deep. We're through. It's finished. Did he ever love me? He's bored with me; that must be it. I'm too young for him. What was life like before Samuel? I forget. I wish I could pull a Scarlett O'Hara and think of sad things tomorrow. But this pain will not be stilled.

May 26, 1969

In two days, I receive my Bachelor of Arts. I will be graduating magna cum laude with departmental honors for my work with autistic kids. Mom and Dad are throwing a splash for me tomorrow night with about fifty of their friends and mine. It's a pool thing. I want it casual. Nellie is catering and Spence is bartending, and the Caruso Brothers will be blowing their horns and banging those ebony and ivory keys. I'm excited.

I haven't seen Samuel for eleven weeks and nine days. Some minutes I wish he had died in a car crash. Then all I would have is the pain of loss. This way I have the pain of loss plus the hurt and anger from having been cheated on.

"I love you, Leah, I'll always love you." I wish I hadn't believed him when he first said those words. And I wish I had slapped him when he said them the night I confronted him about Cindy. I wonder if I'll ever really trust a man again. I mean *really* trust.

Cindy is only five years younger than he is. I'm sure she's more interesting and obviously more experienced than nearly twenty-two-year-old me. But why couldn't he have just told me he was interested in dating women more nearly his age?

Why did he just go off and have a seven-month affair and not tell me anything at all? I don't get it. I'm not sure he does. Unless, of course, it can just all be explained away through selfishness, ego, and greed. He wanted it all. And he wanted it all his way.

Oh well. I have much to be grateful for. My undergraduate education is complete. I'm going to Europe for the summer. I will be attending George Washington University upon my return. And … dat-da-da dat-da-da … (sung musically) … my depressions have been tolerable.

So, for all the blessings in my life, thank you. I know I am a privileged young woman and with privilege comes responsibility. I will use my education to help those who suffer. And I will forever try to be happier and more emotionally healthy.

June 15, 1969

Mom leaves tomorrow for Miami Beach. Her precious Dad, my PaPa Honey, is failing. Eighty-one suddenly seems young to me because PaPa Honey seems far too young to die. He has lived eleven years without BoBo. I've always thought death means black vacuum, void, nothingness. Now I find myself hoping I'm wrong, so BoBo can greet PaPa Honey when he dies.

Aunt Lauren is a mess. I'm really worried about her. There's no sparkle left in her at all. She looks like green paste and gray dust. What is to become of her, G-D? What is there left for her to try?

June 18, 1969

Aunt Lauren is dead.
She killed herself last night.
Mom is flying back from Florida but hasn't been told why.
Dad just told her he needs her to come home immediately.
He's picking her up at 5:00 P.M.

June 19, 1969

It's like an enveloping cloak protects me from feeling too much at once. I burst forth with great sobs and heaving convulsive cries, and then it goes away. Like labor … there is a respite between contractions.

Dad took Mom to the Sheraton on the way home from the airport. When I asked him why he chose to tell her there, he said he didn't know.

Mom cries and then she looks numb, as though she's wearing a mask. She walks ever so slowly and sleeps little. She sips brandy and has eaten half a bagel. An enveloping cloak protects her too. I don't think it has registered, set in, been chronicled, documented, and absorbed.

It's a surprise and it's not a surprise. What else could Aunt Lauren have done? Nothing and no one has helped. She was a vacant soul in a badgered shell. This last depression was just too much for her. One defeat too many. She looked haunted clear through. And so embarrassed. So ashamed. So pained to be a burden.

I understand her choice. I just wish she hadn't made it, or I wish someone could have helped her. I don't like that I'll never see her again. I don't like that Mom must bear this grief and loss. I don't like that we can't even tell PaPa Honey about Aunt Lauren because he too is days or even moments from death.

We will place Aunt Lauren next to BoBo tomorrow. I dare not write any more just now. I don't want to stir up all there is to be stirred within me.

July 5, 1969

Mom sits next to me at our pool. Ruthie is scrubbing the tiles; she's been at it for hours. A mindless and consistent task seems to soothe her. She has cleaned every kitchen shelf and the pantry, hall closet, and even the garage and shed.

Mom is less numbed out and in more conspicuous pain. It is not guilt, which I've read other relatives of suicide victims feel. She couldn't have given more nor done more. It is LOSS, LOSS, LOSS. Her identical twin, her soul sister, her best friend, her literal other half … gone from this earth.

Two funerals in as many weeks. We never did have to tell PaPa Honey. He passed eight days after we put Aunt Lauren to rest.

Today, Mom, Dad, Ruthie, and I are going to the cemetery. We're each putting our favorite flowers on their graves. Mom will bring lilies and Dad crimson roses. Ruthie will bring pansies and I shall place my dainty daisies on the ground where they rest. Are they resting? Is that what happens? I think about G-D more than ever now.

Five days from today Mom will usher in a Birthday … her fifti-eth … alone for the first time since she and Aunt Lauren burst into this world. How will she come to "celebrate" this milestone year? She won't. She's devoid of celebration.

July 28, 1969

I didn't go to Europe. No heart for it. We whimper and limp through the summer. Aunt Mitzy gave Mom a puppy, a miniature schnauzer. We call her Bridgette; she sleeps with me.

Mom and I are planning to go to Pasadena in a couple of weeks. She has cousins and an uncle there who want to hug and love her through this pain. As a surprise for everyone, I've already packed a suitcase full of family photos and scrapbooks. Mom will think the bag is filled with shoes, scarves, and hair supplies.

How irresistibly adorable the Rosen twin girls were in their matching childhood clothes. Mom is demur. Aunt Lauren more daring. Even in the rolls of film I've shot of them over the past few years, their differences overshadow their similarities.

Is there anything more grievous than the grief of loss? G-D, wherever Aunt Lauren, PaPa Honey, and BoBo are, please watch over them and keep them safe.

*****

(Letter from Wendy)

August 30, 1969

Dearest Lee Lee,

I miss you more than I thought I would. After sharing a room with you for three years, I find myself bored silly with my present roommate, my half-sister, Elizabeth. She's a noisy, loud-mouthed twelve-year-old, and she makes me long for the sweet, dulcet tones of your mellifluous voice.

How's your Mom doing, Leah? Last time we spoke she was in and out of touch with her pain and even with herself. I think about you and your family a lot. All of you were so kind to me during our years at Penn. I will treasure always the memory of those Thanksgiving dinners and "fantabulous" Seders.

Your Dad is so emotive and professorial when he speaks of his native Russia and the Bolshevik takeover that forced his family's exodus. You never failed to move me with your rich tone as you chanted and nearly wailed the Four Questions in your impeccable Hebrew.

Your Mom is truly first-lady material in her graciousness and talent at creating food-art and flower-art and setting a tone of both reverence and majesty. And Ruthie, well, Ruthie is winsome and warm and makes guests feel like family. Does it sound like I'm enchanted with the Klines? I am. You guys are great!

In that my Dad is Jewish and my Mom thoroughly Catholic, I never knew much about these traditions until I met your family. Now, I celebrate them too. Thank you for giving me back my heritage.

I went to Woodstock. I guess you've read all about it. I wish you'd been there because you'd have loved it, Lee-Lee. It was colossally wonderful. Our favorite sounds went on for three rainy days and nights, and I gloried in the driving, drowning cacophony of it all.

I remember a nervous official stepping in front of a mike as the festival opened. Four hundred thousand kids, a vast sea of the faithful, stood before him as he reminded us, "If we're going to make it, we'd better remember that the guy next to us is our brother."

A sense of mystical communion seemed to bathe us. I only hope that through our rain-drenched gathering we have ignited in our doubting elders a hint that the hippie ideal of peaceful co-existence can prevail, and a recognition that just possibly, we, the youth, can move the human race ahead a step with our anthems of peace and love.

So, Little Lee, where were you on July 20th when across the air waves a voice from the command module Apollo 11 affirmed: "Houston, Tranquility Base, here. The Eagle has landed."?

Can you *stand* it?

All those photographic images of a bleak and eerie moonscape have heightened my passion for the natural beauty of our own planet. Suddenly, the cosmos seems quite small. We have extended our human presence to another world, and I wonder who visits us.

All of our discussions about God and the meaning of life float back to me now. Oh, I do miss your lightning-fast mind and the fluid way you have of turning a thought.

I leave for New York the day after tomorrow. All the grants and loans came through, so I start Columbia Law with a clean slate and a clear mind. Wish me luck, Leah. And I wish you the very best at George Washington. Promise you will write. Maybe we can see each other over Thanksgiving break. I hope so. I still play my Tim Buckley albums.

I love you, little non-blood sister. Your best friend, Wendy

THE SEVENTIES

Deborah-girl …

I love my DuPont Circle second-floor walk-up apartment. At this, the beginning of my second year of graduate school at George Washington University, I am happy to report that I am raring to go.

I like the course work. I like the Profs. I adore the city. Two more semesters and I will be equipped to really help children with special needs. I haven't decided whether I want a children's hospital, rehab setting, or clinic.

Wendy's coming to visit next weekend from New York. Both of us are eager to get out of the rush and rhythm of the big-city hustle. We're cruising down to Skyline Drive to catch some mountain air.

This is the longest stretch of time I've been without a boyfriend since ninth grade. Just a bunch of ho-hum dates, most Saturday nights either spent with Ivan and Petra, my two best friends at school, or spent completely alone. But I don't really care. Samuel Becker was enough to cure me. I wonder about him a lot, but not enough to find him.

May 13, 1970

Mom and Dad and Ruthie are staying at a hotel on Embassy Row. I graduate tomorrow. They're excited. I'm relieved and exhausted. It has been grueling. I need a break. I'm taking a break. I'm off to Europe for an open-ended stay and will be using the money BoBo and PaPa Honey left me. Mom and Dad are all for it. They applaud and appreciate the six years I have slaved to earn a Masters. A suma cum laude Masters, at that! I'm grateful for these years of study. *And I pray this trip be safe and enlightening.*

June 5, 1971

Kennedy Airport. Waiting. Waiting. Fatigue. Exhilaration. I'm going to Europe … can you stand it? A 4:00 A.M. take off. The giant wings of a mechanical bird are right outside my window. I'm so high I feel like I could fly without the "bird"!

Max Stein sits next to me. He's from San Diego. A UCLA med school grad. He just finished his residency in internal medicine. He's so handsome I could faint. Instead, I think I'll talk to him.

June 7, 1971

MAX! MAX! MAX! I'm practically in "love"! We have not left each other for even an eye-blink of time. It's as though we were assigned to sit next to each other. Amsterdam! Glorious, extraordinary, tulip-infested, fragrant Amsterdam! Is this really happening?

June 9, 1971

Yesterday was the most romantic and erotic day of my life. I will be twenty-four years old in less than two months, and if I were to perish tomorrow, I could not say life had not offered me the best of itself.

And so it began. Thin, gentle rain fell on us as we walked to the Modern Museum to breathe in the genius of Rembrandt, van Ruisdael, Vermeer, Van Gogh, and Mondrian. We met two guys named

Haans and Volt and drank peach tea at their favorite café. They talked haltingly in English. We talked through gestures, smiles, and a Dutch-English book of words and phrases.

I left Max with our two new friends and went to our hotel of antiquated charm to await him. To prepare. I filled our room with flower-stand bouquets, a bottle of delicate French champagne, sweet rolls, pale-yellow butter, and the most succulent pears in all of Amsterdam.

I chose to wear a violet and cream-white cotton sun dress. The sinking neckline revealed my cream-white skin and large violet buttons held the dress together all the way down to my pale pink sandals. I was ready.

Far down the hall I heard the iron gate of the elevator close. The footsteps fell silent and I opened the door before he had a chance to use his key. His arms were full. Red tulips. Two gold boxes with brilliant royal-blue bows. Inside them, a breath-defying red-and-turquoise silk scarf and fresh hot pastry.

It was instant. His arms were quickly filled with me. The cork bounced off the ceiling and we sipped and shared and cross-locked our arms the way it's done for special toasts.

We cooed at each other. We ran our fingers over the clothes that concealed our rising passion. G-D, how I love the way he wears his clothes: A baby-blue silk collarless shirt. Beige cotton pants with the faintest blue silk threads interrupting the solid cloth. He is irresistible.

"I love you in baby blue," I said.

"I love you in rainbow," he said.

Soft jazz sounds penetrated our room, arriving through the air from a small club across the street. It was all perfectly perfect. And we knew we were on the threshold of creating a moment to be treasured for each of our eternities.

Piece by piece we fed each other a ripe yellow pear. His mouth took pieces from mine. He smelled like June air and his very own unique scent. I breathed him into me. My spirit accepted him sense by sense. His sinewy proportions caressed my eyes. His skin warmed my fingers. His laugh kissed my soul.

Button by button. Then each sandal. He even took the earrings out of my ears with a surgeon's precision. I felt like the provocative being I have so often struggled to suppress. He handled my body as a sculptor handles clay, all the while looking into the liquid brown warmth of my enveloping eyes as I peered into the azure blue of his.

Slowly, I unbuttoned, unzipped, and unlaced everything of his that separated our bodies. His long equine beauty was now stretched on the mound of goose down bedding and my hands feather-touched his outline.

Two sea-salty tears escaped my effort to hold them back. His essence created a harmony in me that was uncharted. I found myself loving him, if only for those moments. We got silly to break the spell.

A warm, fragrant bath evaporated the muscle tension of our ardency, as we both secretly chose to make the day linger and last. The bath oil caused the water to bead on our skin. We sat and watched the beads roll down the gentle curves of our outer selves.

He wrapped me in a generous terry towel and carried me to mint green sheets. The palm of his artistic hand lifted the back of my head and his fingers laced through the Hershey-brown silk of my hair. He turned my head with authority and blew his champagne breath into my ear.

He whispered the murmurings of his heart … raw, vulnerable, uninhibited emotion. We were matched touch for touch, both of us expecting and receiving the full, heady measure of sensual intimacy.

Each minute seemed interminable and yet ended too soon. Time built, hovered. We were riveted on each other's faces.

Soon our lazy bodies, now replete, were still and eager for sleep. But we lay in the aromas, feelings, and sensations that could never be severed, knowing it was barely dusk and the whole night lay before us as an open-ended possibility. Amsterdam. Sweet Amsterdam. I shall never be the same.

Perhaps I shall marry this man.

June 13, 1971

I accompanied Max to the airport. He was off to Leningrad, Odessa, and Moscow. When his plane was past sight, I took a trolley and got off at the stop marked Westermarkt. I walked down a tree-enhanced street and saw a crowd gathering ahead at a house numbered 263.

It was not an atypical house for a Holland canal street: narrow, multiple-storied, large windows bringing summer sun through. The house was Anne Frank's during her two years of hiding in Nazi-overcome Amsterdam. Old feelings ignited upon entry. I once again was Anne, thirteen and afraid, but hopeful and filled with budding, acute awareness. I walked up the stairway to that door above the warehouse, entered, and felt the door close on the life Anne had walked away from.

Do I dare describe the myriad emotions that swept me along from room to anguished room? Oh, Anne, how I do understand you. You are my champion.

I stayed for hours, caught up in passages I remembered from playing the role. So sacred a spot for me. There were others around.

I saw no faces, heard no voices. I was transported to far away and long ago. What a profound privilege to view my friend's last home.

How I wish Max had been with me. He needs to see this hallowed spot. I need to tell him how important it was to me to play her. I need to recite my lines to him. I need to hold him and rock and sway and try to push back the tide of emotion that Anne and all such Anne's evoke in me. How treacherous is the history of the human condition.

Yet, how poetic is the depth and style of a young Jewish girl who unwittingly had the wisdom of sages. She flew high, soared with stars and comets, and inside the context of her tiny, shrunken world, she transcended the unparalleled evil of her time.

I will leave Amsterdam tomorrow. It is a sad city to me now without my intriguing Max.

Please keep him safe and thank You for permitting us to meet and for allowing me to experience such harmonious and priceless "love."

*****

I traveled in Europe for over a year. Not much of it is pertinent to this story, except for one compelling surprise and a provocative stay in Israel.

*****

(Letter from Mom)

July 18, 1971

My darling daughter,

Your letters and cards come as gifts, delightful surprises, filled with thoughtful, soulful responses to all you are seeing, meeting, doing, and being.

It has been a unique experience for me too, Leah, to live through your adventure. Your letters spring from a heart so filled with wonder, warmth, interest, intensity, and the acute sensitivity of one twenty-four-year-old electric-bright mind.

And so it is that time of year when *Happy Birthday* is circled around August second on my calendar. You are away again on your Birthday and so feelings and wishes must by necessity be confined to paper.

It is safe to say that should I wish you the eager open joy of *now* to continue through your life, the exultant awareness of the sacredness of individuals, the consummate desire to understand and appreciate cultures that make one people different from another and yet, the same, the continuous growth in mind and spirit of an already flowering woman, I would be offering you more endless summers of richness and fulfillment. AND I DO!

When you are ready, come home to all of us who love you. You are cherished and missed, and, and, and. But it will wait.

Birthday wishes for all the precious things in life, my daughter. Your Mother

*****

December 25, 1971

Deborah … Christmas in Paris. Why not? I choose to spend the day alone, although I really never feel alone when I'm writing. In fact, maybe that's when I feel least alone. I am glad to have this pot of tea, loaf of bread and plate of apricot jam. I am glad to have biting cold Paris outside my window and this divine new worsted-wool army-green and ballet-pink plaid scarf encircling my neck.

I am *not* glad about how very lonely I have become during these many months of travel. I could go home, of course, but that would be giving up and giving in. There is more to see and more to be and I shall not give into a feeling.

It's not that I don't meet people. I do. Constantly. And our interactions are not superficial. Lots of kids from all over the world travel alone in Europe and I enjoy each encounter. It's so loose here. Kids invite me to their parents' homes or their own homes for dinner and a place to sleep. Parties erupt from casual talk. It's just extraordinary. But the deepness, trust, and richness that exist between lifelong friends and newfound friends is as distant as the North Star is from Paris.

I miss Max. I've only gotten one letter from him since his return to the States. But I cherish the memory of his surprise visit in Zurich.

I shall relive it now. I was sitting at the bar in my hotel. It was storming. The kind of fierce, dominant thunder and lightning that only arrive in late summer. I thought I felt warm, soft wet lips on the back of my neck and it frightened me. *Who would dare,* my mind questioned. I turned angrily and his eyes caught me and his arms held me.

"Surprise!" We went promptly to my room and loved each other for hours. The next day, an excursion to Mount Pilatus, elevation, nine thousand feet. If part of G-D is experiencing a mysterious, mystical, and untouched part of man, then I found and experienced that part of myself that day. Clouds below us, some above us, others embracing our bodies.

I reached out and let the soft, cool dampness of white cotton-candy clouds pass through my fingers. We both had marked physical reactions to the elevation and change of altitude. Our hearts raced, but our thoughts and movements were slow. I could only whisper, and really did not wish to speak at all.

There is no medium that can capture the experience of being so close to G-D's art ... the strength, power, and peace of natural things. I find this realization a comfort. Nothing man creates can attempt to harness that which G-D designs.

Wars and destruction, illness and anguish ... all seemed more preposterous than usual that day. I wished to kiss the world, and I wondered how anyone could hate or fear if he or she had reached the apex of some similar summit. That day, I felt I was truly re-born.

We spent two days among the Swiss. Paddle-boated on Lake Zurich with the sun beating against our nearly naked skin. Fondue for dinner and long walks through the affluent streets of unimaginable beauty. The Swiss are not the friendliest of people, but they are polite. I don't think it has anything to do with snobbishness. They're just close knit, self-contained, and don't depend that heavily on tourist dollars. I approve of the Swiss. They are sturdy and refined.

I didn't like taking Max to the airport in Zurich any more than I had in Amsterdam. He was going directly to San Diego to connect with his family. Then he was going to apply for a job in medicine "somewhere on the East Coast."

I think he fell in love with me for a minute. Ya know ... Europe in the summer? We were ripe. I could fall hopelessly in love with this man. Ah, baloney! Who am I kidding? I *have* fallen hopelessly in love with him. But he was not interested in talking about "the future." He gave me his parents' phone number and told me to "give a call" when I'm finished discovering myself and the continent.

I shall leave France tomorrow and snake my way over and down to Israel.

*****
99

1972

When my plane landed in Tel Aviv, I found a bus station. I wanted to walk the streets of Jerusalem.

Old Jerusalem is a serene city, as old as time and dirt. Its streets breathe primordial tradition and solidity, in spite of missiles, devastation, an over-abundance of cemeteries, and remnants of war all about. There is a conquering stoicism about this place and these people. How massive the courage required to bear so much anguish from the ravages of time and circumstance, and still laugh, dance, party and love. Indeed, these are mighty warriors with intense emotions.

The Wailing Wall on a fair spring Sabbath night where I prayed and cried, as millions before me have done. I embedded a written prayer into a small space between two massive stones. Reverence and solemnity bathed this ancient ruin. Since there was a Sabbath calm that night, I basked in it and walked the streets of this city, my city, my home.

Before arriving in Israel, I was holding in thought the possibility that I would not love Israel, and if that were so, I planned to hitch to Haifa and board a ship to Athens. I would be greeted by Nicholas Alexandrides, a guy I met in London when he was attending the London School of Economics. We became friends and he invited me to his home in Athens any time at all. We've been corresponding.

But there is something inexplicable that is drawing me into the very soul of Israel. I feel a stirring in my spirit I have never felt before.

The air has its own distinct quality. These people are my people. This is my country; its earth is mine.

Within this group, I sense pride, defiance, and an ingrained willingness to die for this tiny strip of real estate. Israel imitates nothing else. It is captivating. Mysterious. Electric. It is the spiritual capital for three major religions.

Everything seems heightened for these people, as if today may be their last because it might be. War is part of the fabric of their lives and their interior worldview.

These people are W.I.L.D! Not sedate and soft spoken. They are forever arguing among themselves, but they are fiercely united and interdependent. They are stallions and gladiators in a war-weary society but remain ferociously intent. They are voracious and vigorous after exiles, wanderings, deportation, massacres, and genocide.

I've been here for so short a time, and yet cannot ever imagine leaving.

April 15, 1972

I'm on fire. I can barely sleep. I feel an urgency to not miss a pebble, stretch of sand, vista, lecture, ruin, monument, night club. My body is drained, but my mind and spirit beg for more.

I've had to think about who we are and how we got here. So here it is: We are a teensy-weensy nation on the eastern shore of the turquoise-blue Mediterranean Sea. Independence proclaimed in a house in Tel Aviv in 1948, in the name of thousands of people who declared themselves free at last. Free, that is, while millions of militants were crossing these borders, swearing to exterminate us once and for all.

It was after World War II that Jews started to migrate back to their origins. No one else wanted us, and indeed it was this pressure that ignited our courage to return "home."

I feel a mixture of dramatic emotions. I have not settled in yet, so I must give myself a minute. I'll figure this out.

May 4, 1972

The men are friendlier than the women. What's new? I have allowed Baruch to become a friend. He's a guide with boundless energy and unfaltering enthusiasm for all that is Israel. He took me to the Weitzman Museum of Science today. Fantastically impressive. One just knows important things happen here … progress, learning, experimentation, and results.

The evening was cool and lovely, and we shared it. A motorcycle ride. A sweet, ripe, red, drippy watermelon. An apartment that glowed warm feelings. Israeli musical sounds. A couple of dozen candles. Kinishes and red wine … feeling safe and happy.

May 7, 1972

I explore on my own a lot. Yesterday … Mt. Zion and King David's Tomb. A Moslem Mosque and an Arab market, called a *souk*. Arab markets are set up *by* Arabs and *for* Arabs. The tourist has never been and will never be anything more than an oddity in the daily workings of exchange.

I wonder a lot about the conflict between these two people, Jews and Arabs. O.K., so we represent two cultures and two religions and two ideologies. But why is it that we can't get along? Americans find a way to blend dozens of cultures reasonably harmoniously.

Arabs and Jews are kinfolks, for Pete's sake. We share the same father, Abraham. Doesn't that make us not just stepbrothers, but actual half-blood brothers? Yes, it does. So, O.K., you guys, squabble if you must. But machine guns, bombs, dead kids, and limbless bodies? What a ludicrous, costly, agonizing atrocity.

Oddly, by dusk, a different mood emerges. Star-bright nights bring music and dance which change both the tempo and focus of sun-drenched desert days. I get it. We're Jews. We will not forget to party!

I often dance the night away at Jerusalem's Khan Club. How good it is to release the dancer in me that craves release. Mony, a professional dancer, often sweeps me onto the floor after he and his troupe perform for the tourists. We dance the Samba, Cha-Cha, Meringue, and Tango. It's nearly effortless to follow a professional lead. We're encircled and applauded, and I feel powerful, exotic, and drunk on the energy and competence of my body to do everything I ask of it.

Israel, how grateful I am that you were born.

June 12, 1972

I have a second favorite spot in Israel, and it is Bethlehem. I looked forward to making this journey to the city of Jesus' birth, though I don't know why. We bussed through Hebron. It is a yesterday world, and my response was strong. I wished to be invisible and not part of an American group on an air-conditioned bus, flaunting expensive cameras that snapped ... without thought ... poverty, destitution, hovels, beggars, a man with a wooden leg.

We arrived at the Church of the Nativity. It instantly felt like the zenith of sacrilege that the place of Jesus' birth is a commercial tourist attraction with souvenir shops, soda stands, and little boys hawking Kodak film. I'm not a Christian, but come on, how loathsome for the people who are. I am a solitary soul though, so I found a way to walk into my own secret self and approach this site with the humility and awe that slowly rose in me.

Jesus, "King of the Jews," they wrote on a plaque, nailed to the two trees that formed the cross that held his crucified body. People in America tell me, "You Jews killed our Lord!" Is that true? Why would we do that? How could I have killed him? I didn't even know him. Who was that guy, and why do people love him sooo much?

I will never ever forget Bethlehem. It is permanently inscribed.

June 15, 1972

Jericho: And the walls came tumblin' down. Arab women are weighed down with loads on their heads. Donkeys are urged on by men or little boys. It is a biblical landscape with the sweet aroma of a blossoming oasis. It is lush with the promise of fertility.

But juxtaposed to these thriving blooms, rest abandoned refugee camps. Jericho exudes an unexpected stillness, with heat and ubiquitous dirt and soil spreading hot dust into windless air. I sense a type of unhurried, heart-stopping, tentative calm.

Here, in Israel, a daily visceral experience for me, is being part of a majority population.

Here, I am not part of a minority who stands as a universal scapegoat. Here, I stand firm and proud in my homeland. Truly, a unique sensation in my life experience.

*****

(Letter from Mom)

July 4, 1972

Leah my daughter,

It is a warm and lovely day in Chadds Ford, Pa. Being a holiday, we are leaving shortly for the club with the Kauffmans and Blooms.

You have been gone one year and one month today. Had I not been getting such favorable reports from you and from the Bloomberg's when you met them in Rome, I would have to come see for myself that you are flourishing.

We are so happy your response to Israel is what we hoped it would be. The more you know about your heritage and traditions, the more you'll identify with our people. Much can be said for thousands of years that brought Israel to its refusal to die, now or ever. The same can be said for the torture and deaths; they were not for naught. The Jews have as much right to a homeland as the Italians or Danes. That you learned this lesson, has allowed missing you to be worth it.

All goes well here. Ruthie has a new guy. His name is Jonathan Goldman and she's wild about him. It's delightful to see your sister so happy. Dad is better. Please believe the stomach tumor was benign and he has been back at work for weeks. Now he wants a respite in the Poconos before the crew at the plant starts their summer vacations.

I heard from Wendy. She misses you, as do we all. The Bloomberg's said you look too thin. Don't starve yourself, Leah, and please rest. The heat over there can be truly deadly.

I hope you plan to come home soon. I do tire of this a bit now.

I love you with unrestrained emotion, Mom

*****

(My Letter to Wendy)

September 26, 1972

Dearest Wendy, oh Wendy, or should I say Wendala ...

Thanks for writing so regularly. Your words arrive like Hershey kisses for a chocoholic deprived for far too long. I miss you dreadfully. This on-the-road suitcase life can get old and stale. It's exciting, but it's demanding, rough, lonely, and sometimes even scary.

You want ALL the news, you say? Okay. I will write until my fingers nearly fall off. I'm infatuated clear through with this wondrous country about the size of New Jersey. It has everything, Wendy. History to die for! I had a non-duplicable rush while standing at the top of Masada. I allowed myself to feel what the martyrs must have felt as they decided to kill themselves rather than be captured.

And the site of the Last Supper ... well, I just wept like a child. Jesus stuff makes me cry. Don't know why. Always has.

At Galilee it seems as though every blade of grass, every stone, every puff of dust remains permeated with Jesus' memory. I intuit that most people who visit here must sense him and be moved.

The geography is nuts. Obscenely gorgeous turquoise blue water. Gracious mountains majesty. Endless and ominous deserts. Cosmopolitan cities.

Want a tiny history clip? During the 1800s, in the hope of establishing a nation, Jewish immigrants drained swamps, irrigated deserts, sank wells, and planted forests. Farm settlements erupted and useless land became fertile. It's lush, Wendy-girl. It's Paradise and the Elysian Fields. It's Never-Never Land and the Garden of Eden.

The best food I've ever eaten in my whole life is right here! It's sumptuous, artfully prepared and fresh as air in April.

I'M CRAZY NUTS ABOUT THIS PLACE!

Israel feels like worn-in sneaks, favorite jeans, corn and tomatoes on a summer eve. It feels like the best version of "home" one could fantasize into existence. Wendy, the whole Jewish population interacts as *one* family. What I've longed for since I was old enough to long for anything, I have found here: the country almost exists as though it were a singular family/community.

This lifestyle births a population of people who care about total strangers because we share a bloodline, race, culture, and religion. I even wear a Mezuzah now. Can you stand it?

One little itsy-bitsy problem. I think I've overdone it with the amphetamines. I'm down to ninety-three pounds. Now don't shriek. My realistic goal was one hundred, so I'm not cadaverous. Will any girl I know ever stop obsessing about her weight? I'm such a pain in my own ass.

I'm also deep-dark tan and my hair is waist length. It's super casual here, so, like everyone else, I wear short-shorts and for once, am not humiliated by my thighs. What a sensation!

Going to bed now. Will continue tomorrow.

September 27, 1972

Hey Wend … I'm back.

I know you want to hear ALL the dirt, so here's a really low-down, sad, and grimy story for you. Flash back with me. Picture this … the road starts to descend and from around a bend the Dead Sea appears. It lies there, three thousand feet below in a heavy haze, lifeless and parched; mountains encircle the sea.

The story begins … I am floating effortlessly because of the density of salt in the Dead Sea. It feels like a board is holding me up. Two young men swim close. Mind you, we have been

107

conditioned and warned to be suspicious of aggressive Arab men. So when they banter with me, and I can't tell if their "English accents" are Hebrew or Arabic, I snub them. One of them says, "Is this any way to treat Israeli soldiers?" Embarrassed, I soften and listen and speak.

We play in the Dead Sea, then they escort me back to my hotel. They go to the bar for a beer. I go to my room for a shower. Their names are Shmuel and Raffi.

The three of us get very chummy over the next several weeks. Not sexual. Just chummy. One or both of them has to leave now and again to defend a border; otherwise, we are always together.

Shmuel is a Yemenite … swarthy, muscular, ruggedly handsome. He is kind, dominant, and cautious. He has assurance, defiance and command. He is one of twelve children. His youngest brother was killed in the Six Day War.

No, we're not lovers. Why, you may ask. Instinct, my friend, instinct. You travel this long, you hone some delicate antennae. Raffi is sweet, funny, boyish, and hangs around Shmuel because he feels protected. I feel protected by Shmuel too.

So many adventures. A scooter ride with Shmuel all the way to Tel Aviv, the New York of Israel. We wind up bowling and then spend hours at an outside café that floods to capacity as people watch people and people meet people and people flirt with people.

We spend lots of nights at the Israeli Soldiers' House at the army base. In some ways it feels like a frat house … young men and women, dancing to *The Beatles* and *Blood, Sweat & Tears*. The air is filled with body aromas, energy, and youthful zeal. But it's also stark, austere, and war oriented.

One night while sharing a Kiddush and substantial food, we get word that a twenty-two-year-old Israeli soldier accidentally ran over and killed a five-year-old Arab child. We leave to pick up the truck he'd been driving and find the soldier in a paddy wagon, trembling, the parents in a police car, sobbing.

So much happens all the time. It's close to overwhelming.

An example of a communication hassle: Shmuel said, "Tonight you, me go home of friends marry."

I assume we're going to visit some married friends of his. But NOOOOOOOOO, we walk in on a Yemenite wedding! Wild joy and chaos, casual clothing, an Israeli band, songs sung in harmonic Hebrew, so much love. Oh G-D … what beauty!

Sometimes Shmuel seems haunted. He cries a cry that emanates from numberless centuries of pain. He rambles on about the war in '67 and the brother and friends he lost. He wouldn't dance at the wedding because, "My brother dead. I love him. No can dance." No dancing. No movies. No laughter. His eyes belong to an aged man … murky, troubled, sinister, and sad.

He told me after the war he was hospitalized for two months, in shock. His senses deadened. He wouldn't eat. Couldn't sleep. A specialist from New York stayed with him a third month attempting to coax him back. Slowly he revived, but much of him remains lost. It was bravado I first sensed in him, not the command of unbridled confidence.

Uneasiness ignites in me the night he says, "You are new moon to me. Peace in me when I'm with you. You be my life." I don't want to be his LIFE. OH G-D, HELL NO! Just a buddy. The responsibility of his pain begins to strangle me.

That very night he got word he must leave for Jericho. Two of his friends were killed the night before, doing the same work he does. I flipped. I freaked. I sobbed. I took my Mezuzah off and put it on his chain. Something of mine to embrace him. Something of G-D to protect him.

Fast forward to the next day. I was forlorn and decided to meet some American friends at the King David Hotel. I stopped at the Shalom Restaurant to say hi to Moshe. He's the owner and a friend. Shmuel and I eat there often. Moshe told me Shmuel had been there the night before with an American girl. No, couldn't be, I assured Moshe. Last night he was on his way to Jericho to protect this country from enemy threats.

Moshe shook his head. "No, Leah. It was Shmuel."

My mind spun like a drunken top. What's the deal? Is Shmuel reducible to a liar, a fraud, a con? Is he one of twelve children? Did he have a brother who died in the Six Day War? Was he nearly comatose for two months? I remember wishing I'd been born a piece of impenetrable granite or a spinning star in a sparkling sky.

I returned to the hotel and there was a note on my bed. Shmuel called. His sister Eva poured kerosene over her body last night and ignited herself. He was at the hospital all day with her until she died. Eva, a human torch! True? False? My brain was shot through with Novocain. I barely believed the day even happened … too surreal to be real.

I wanted to be home, Wendy. I wanted Mom. I wanted you and the people who love me, people I trust.

The next day I call the number of Shmuel's aunt in Haifa. He gave me the number for use in emergencies. I identified myself as Shmuel's American friend. His "aunt" screamed, "What kind of friend are you? I'm his wife!"

Oh Wendy, it took days to figure it out. But here's what I figure. Shmuel is an artist of deception. He set the stage, played with my vulnerability, encouraged me to depend on him, believe in him, and truly care about him. A game. And he knew he'd won when I put my Mezuzah around his neck. Then he was on to his next victim, the American girl at Moshe's restaurant.

Here's the wind-up. A few nights later I went to the Soldiers' House to see if Raffi could explain any of this. As I'm about to be buzzed through the gate, I heard Shmuel call my name. I turned but didn't see him. Then from his concealed perch on a tree limb, he jumped in front of me with his machine gun held in firing position.

"You know truth. Now you must die," he said with the look of a crazed animal sprawled across his face.

I froze. At that split second, an Israeli soldier came up behind him, took him down by the throat, and handcuffed him before I even had time to gasp.

My mind spun off into limbo-land. I was struck hollow.

Somehow, I got to this kibbutz. I don't remember how. Escorted by angels, perhaps? Oh, my G-D, Wendy. Oh, my G-D.

How could I not have known? I was eventually told that the Israeli army was watching him, waiting for him to do something truly psychopathic so they could prosecute or institutionalize him.

I'm so glad they got what they wanted, at my peril and potential demise.

So here I am holed up in a kibbutz called Hanita near the Lebanese border. While here, my mind slowly clears, and I have a response to this haven. I think, ah, how lovely. A kibbutz is so satisfying, sensible, safe, and sane. Healthy children. Shared interests, duties, and responsibilities. Shared money. Common ideals. A whole community raising everyone's kids. The love-in of a lifetime.

But last night in bed, writing in my journal, after a long day of folding filthy burlap banana bags, I hear what could only be interpreted as a barrage of machine gun fire. I rush to find Yona, a new friend.

Arab terrorists have crossed the border and been met by waiting Israeli guards. Nine men lie dead some one hundred yards from my cabin.

Oh, Wendy, I'm so tired.

Yona has chosen to take me under his warm wing and cajole me back to health. He is dear and gentle, yet strong and deliberate. A man's man. A woman's dream.

When we were picking bananas today, I asked him, "Yona, how much do you love Israel?"

He responded, "Leah, how much do you love your Mother?"

Yona is a musician, singer, composer, and bass player. He has his own band and is genuinely gifted. I could imagine a lifetime with him. But Sabra (Israeli-born) males of fighting age are not given visas often or easily. The military does not want to lose even one of their available men for service. But, oh Wendy, he moves me. He's electric and silk in the same moment. He has the intensity of a high fever and the mellowness of a balladeer.

I know he likes me too. And I know he knows we could fall hopelessly in love. But why should we? The probability of us materializing into permanent love is nigh to nil. Yet the unfettered joy he brings me is worth the inevitability of loss. I will want to forget him, but likely never will.

He is so unlike Max, Max the medical man with ambition and a plan. Yona glides through his time and space with the lyricism of an ascending musical scale. I miss Max. But I long for Yona. Oh, and did I fail to mention, Yona is drop-dead gorgeous! Almost painfully gorgeous. He catches me staring at him. I can't help it.

Beauty is my drug. Yup, beauty. It could be the lined face of a Mexican elder, an iris, a cottage in the woods, an Oriental rug, a Herman Miller chair, the arch in an athlete's foot, a pinkish-gray boulder, a Parisian scarf, baby teeth, sculpted metal. I'm hopeless for beauty and so grateful to be. Sadness or depression could never hinder my response to beauty; it is thoroughly ingrained in my DNA.

Wendy, I think I'm afraid to come home because I don't know if I can get a job and I don't know if I'll be of any real value to autistic kids and living here is like living in a novel. I'm part of it. I'm engrossed. I don't want to finish it because I'll never again live another story this extraordinary. You know what I mean?

I'm glad you're in love. She sounds lovely. A poet and a potter, no less. Thank G-D you'll be an attorney in a year. All determined artists need a benefactor. Please tell her I am most anxious to meet her. Much joy to you, beloved friend, Leah

*****

(Letter from Wendy)

October 7, 1972

Leah, Now Hear This:

As your former college roommate and loyal friend, I'm taking a stand. Listen to me. Get a plane ticket, get your ass on the plane, and come home this very minute. I mean it, Leah. Enough is enough. You write a great letter, but frankly, I wasn't all that amused. You're exhausted, and you've badgered your body with amphetamines. Your judgment stinks, and you've been gone too long. You need a job in the real world. You'll be a fine therapist. You have excellent training and you're a natural with kids.

If you don't want to live with your parents, you can live with Kate and me until you find work. I will pick you up at Kennedy Airport. Wire me and tell me when to be there. I expect to hear from you within forty-eight hours of your receiving this letter, which should be in nine days. In other words, wire me around October 16th.

Do it, Leah, Wendy

*****

November 5, 1972

I dutifully did as Wendy suggested, and left Israel within two weeks. It wasn't pretty, leaving all the glorious people I'd met, especially Yona. Leaving him was viscerally painful. But of course, I believe I will go back to Israel or Yona will move here, and ain't it blissful to dream.

I can't see staying at Mom and Dad's for more than a few more weeks. I have outgrown their milieu. They adore me. I adore them. But at twenty-five years old, I'm too independent and have a bushel filled with my own living habits that aren't all that congruent with theirs.

No sense looking for a job here. I don't want to live and work near where I grew up. And Wendy and Kate are sincere about their invitation for me to live with them until I find a job. So, I'm going to New York City.

P.S. I really like Ruthie's boyfriend, Jonathan. He's a good man and they're good together.

November 21, 1972

Deborah … I miss Israel so much. I miss Yona. What a joy he was. Such a love boat. His affection and attentiveness brought me back from some outer-worldly numbness. I allowed him to take care of me, though I had little to offer him. He writes and I write, and we speak of what-if's and what-might-have-been's. But I doubt I shall experience his laughter or see him dancing naked on the beach, in the moonlight, ever again.

Mom and Dad look older. I hate that. Their hair is more densely gray, and they move with less speed and determination. Their relief at my arrival wounded me. It made me know I should have come home sooner. Ruthie was aloof for a few days, mad at me for having worried Mom and Dad and engaged myself for so long in my own selfish odyssey.

*****

My sister Ruthie keeps journals too. Not as prodigiously as I do, but she keeps a sparse record of her earth life. Yesterday, Ruthie's journal was lying open to a page that began with my name and so ... I read the entry. Okay, shoot me ... I was beyond curious. Allow me to quote her. She is riotously funny to me (and yes, I did ask if I could quote her here):

*****

(Ruthie's own journal entry)

I learn things about Leah as I read her journals. **(I told Ruthie she could read anything of mine she cared to while I was away. I did hide some written things I want no one to ever read. But with her, I pretty much allow my life to be an open book. Pretty much.)** Well, Leah sure got one thing right. I WAS mad at her for traveling more than a year. Jealous too, maybe, but mostly I was ticked off she left us, poof, just like that, gone.

She missed my college graduation. She missed my first euphoric months with Jonathan, my honey of a husband. I didn't have her counsel about which MBA program to choose. I had to watch our parents agonize about her safety.

Leah, the free-spirited hippie artist was in odyssey-ville and I was left holding the proverbial bag. She would have been a great friend but as a sister she is just too, too ... too everything: unpredictable, reclusive, odd, savvy but with the trust of a naive

115

wide-eyed three-year-old, silly but dead-serious, reckless, impetuous, wise like some sage sitting in a hooded robe.

Oh, who knows? The woman was, is, and no doubt always will be, just uncompromisingly odd, at least to me. Her friends think she's fab-o and merely exotic.

Let me put it this way: When I was in ninth grade and she was a senior, we had to wait for the school bus together while she carried a kid's Cinderella lunch box and wore winter leggings! LEGGINGS! Like really little kids wear as part of their snow gear. She humiliated me.

I'm a CPA with my own firm. My husband commutes to NYC three days a week to work on Wall Street. We belong to a country club, vacation several times a year, and have subscription box seats to the cultural and sports events in the City of Brotherly Love.

Leah sits under trees and writes poems.

Oh, and I love the memory of this one: Leah was a cheerleader. She didn't particularly want to be a cheerleader; she was recruited. She's really short and they needed a shorty to balance the configuration of the group. You know, tallest gal in the middle, sloping down to short on each end.

Well, Leah, in her flippy-dippy little way, one day, got up and started doing literal cartwheels on the field because she heard cheering and assumed we'd just completed a touchdown. WRONG-O! HELLOOOOOOO! It was the opposing team's goal. OUT THERE! The chick was truly out there. Maybe she was day-dreaming, or humming a Broadway show tune. She could have been dancing an imaginary duet with Gene Kelly.

*****

Now that's truly funny, don't you think? Really, I'm not the slightest bit insulted. How could I be? Ruthie nailed me.

*****

November 30, 1972

I'm staying with Wendy and Kate. They have a teensy one-bedroom at 71st and West End in New York. I sleep on the couch. These days do not remotely resemble the dorm days of 1966 through 1969. In fact, I don't feel I can stay here much longer. I'm glad they're songbirds singing a love duet, but I want my own space! They're a little too militant for me. New York seems to have given them license to protest too much and too loudly. I find myself needing to defend the entire male gender.

O.K. It's a man's world and both have been hurt by that. Who hasn't been, including men? Women's pay must be equal to men's pay … obviously! But I can't seem to muster enthusiasm to have "women" as my card-carrying cause. Jews are persecuted too. Blacks are often treated as less-than. The disabled can't physically get into some of my favorite restaurants. War legally permits young boys to kill other young boys. It all stinks. Why single men out as the enemy? Human nature is the enemy.

I've been pounding the pavements looking for a gig. So far, no bites. It's hard to even secure an interview … as in, I've only had two in four weeks. And I've sent out fifty-eight resumes!

The day after tomorrow I have an interview at a medical clinic in Harlem. It's located at 125th and Lenox Avenue. That's about as Harlem as it gets.

December 5, 1972, 11:50 P.M.

OH G-D! OH G-D! OH G-D! Deborah, you will not believe what happened to me on this spooky December day. CHECK IT OUT!

I puffed my way up eighty-three steps to the medical clinic, which was just yards from the subway stop … thank G-D. I was directed to take a seat and told the director would be with me momentarily. Momentarily took fifty-six minutes. His name is Richard Rothman. Full bearded and shoulder-length hair. Intellectual. Princeton undergrad. Penn Med School. A Long-Islander. Very sweet.

"We're definitely looking for a special ed. person," he said, and then he went on, "I'm going to ask our associate director to sit in on this interview, if you don't mind."

"No," I assured him, "I don't mind."

I heard the door open behind me and footsteps approached. Richard said, "Leah Kline, I'd like you to meet Max Stein, our associate director."

My mouth invisibly plummeted to my knees. I extended my hand.

Max took mine into both of his and said, "Leah, how good to see you. Richard, Leah and I met each other in Europe in the summer of '71. You're lookin' great, Leah. How've you been?"

"Great," I said in a barely audible tone.

"Well," Max said, "So, you're in the market for a job. Is Harlem your heartthrob or is the market just tight?"

"Yes, the market's tight and Harlem is still an unknown."

So, I figured it was one of two things: He saw my application and resume and so I wasn't a surprise to him, or worse, I *was* a surprise, but not a big enough one to send his adrenalin rushing into overdrive.

They escorted me all over the office and introduced me to everyone. It felt okay. The people were friendly and clearly dedicated to helping those who really need help. The employees were composed mostly of Jews, some Puerto Ricans, and a few black men of all ages. Some doctors who have made poverty-medicine their career. A few upstart docs who think they might want to, and some who are probably there to get a pulse on how to run a clinic. A mega-smart group of people.

Richard said the job was mine if I wanted it. "There aren't that many people with a Masters applying for this gig," he said, "so if you think you can handle the high-volume caseload, long hours, a $7,500.00-a-year salary, and great Chinese food at the place around the corner, you're in."

I asked Richard if I could have forty-eight hours to decide.

"Sure," he said. "I'm positive we won't have a rush of applicants in the next two days."

I wanted to talk to Wendy … BAD! But she's impossible to reach on her public defending gig. And Kate … well, Kate was probably feeding pigeons in the park.

I wasn't home twenty minutes when the phone rang.

"Leah, it's Max."

"Hi," is all I decided to say.

"In answer to the questions I'm sure you've posed to yourself: yes, I had seen your resume, and no, I hadn't said anything to Richard. I didn't think what happened between us almost a year and a half ago was any of his business."

"Uh-huh," I said, still unsure of what to say.

"Are you living alone?"

"No, I live with Wendy and her girlfriend, Kate. Remember me telling you about my roommate, Wendy, from college?"

"Yes," Max said. "I do. How long have you been back?"

119

"About six weeks ... three at my parents' home and three here with Wendy and Kate."

"So, have you been profoundly altered on some primitive and indefinable level by your odyssey?"

My, how sarcastic, I thought. Was this defense or something else being vaguely disguised? Hell, I wasn't sure he hadn't married in the past year and a half, so I decided to ask.

"Now it's my turn to ask some questions, Max. Are you married? Engaged? In love? If so, why are you calling? If not, why are you calling?"

"The answers are no, no, no, no and to ask if you'd like to have dinner at this great Cuban place on Broadway not far from where you're staying."

I immediately felt a calming rush of joy and said, "Yeah, I'd like that." We decided to meet at 6:00 P.M.

For the interview today, I looked business appropriate in my navy gabardine calf-length straight skirt, white blouse, and waist-length single-buttoned matching jacket. I wore my hair in a chignon. But tonight, I will exude a siren, because even in his dungarees and flannel shirt today, Max looked like a model for men's casual wear.

New York's air disguised itself and seemed crispy clear as I walked the eight blocks to the Cuban restaurant of his choice. I was wearing a red matte-jersey dress that skimmed my ankles ... the one that reveals a hint of cleavage, cinches my waist, and has a built-in flamingo look below the knee that makes me look like a sumptuous mermaid. I let my hair fall into its full nearly waist length and tied the long red-and-turquoise scarf into my hair ... the scarf Max had bought for me in Amsterdam. I let it trail over my shoulder. In my ears I wore my silver hoop earrings that are nearly the size of my fist, and on my feet, black granny tie-up boots with dagger sharp toes.

He was waiting at the bar with a full pitcher of sangria; in it floated huge pieces of fruit. I was so nervous, I wished to ingest its full effect and be just this side of tipsy. Instead, with uncommon reserve, I sat next to him without touching or even grazing him.

"Smashing as ever, Leah. You have as many looks as a chameleon."

"My Mom says that about me too."

"You still have the scarf!"

I nodded.

"Richard showed me your resume a week ago. He said he thought it looked interesting and wanted my opinion about whether we should interview you. Seeing your name at the top of the page nearly toppled me. So, I told him, 'Sure, we should interview her. How many suma grads do we have applying for this job?' It's wild, isn't it, Leah? I never thought I'd see you again. What do you think? Coincidence or divine plan?"

"Feels utterly divine to me. Almost like I've been rocketed to heaven. How did you wind up in Harlem? Is there really no woman in your life?"

"I wound up in New York because I really want to experience New York. I wound up in Harlem because I really want to make a difference. There was a woman in my life until about six months ago. We were engaged. Her name is Susan Bannister, an ophthalmologist. A debutante type from Vermont. Taller than I am and as blonde as a Norwegian ice queen. Ultimately, that was the problem. She was cool as a mountain stream, and I guess I like my women hot and exotic."

I fought with my hands not to grab his hair and press my mouth against his words. (Patience, Leah, patience. It's always best if one waits.) "Well, do you like New York?" I said in an all-out effort to avoid talk of anything hot or exotic.

"I love it and I hate it. It's glorious and disgusting. It makes me want to dive in or run like a fugitive with dogs on his heels."

"I can relate," I said.

"Let's get a table, peel some spicy shrimp, and get blotto."

We talked for two hours about everything. My year abroad and how I've barely begun to assimilate the immensity and diversity of it all. I told him about the loneliness of travel, the exhaustion. I told him I never stopped thinking about him and found myself looking for him in throngs and crowds, on trains and in market squares. I didn't tell him about Yona.

He told me of Leningrad, Moscow, and Odessa. He told me how his surprise visit to Zurich sealed his feelings for me and he tried for months to pretend I never even happened. Just a summer fling. That's how he boxed me into a compartment in his brain.

He met Susan Bannister at a medical convention in New York shortly after he arrived, and she wanted him. He let her have him. But she ended it when she realized she need not settle for a man who wasn't completely there for her. How grateful I am she is a confident woman who knows her needs and acknowledges her rights.

Finally, he extended his hand and ran his fingers through my hair, taking the red-and-turquoise scarf with him. He draped it around his neck. I took both of his hands and kissed both of his palms. We left, turned the corner on 75th Street, leaned into each other against a building, and kissed the kiss I've longed for since our last kiss at the airport in Zurich on the hottest summer day I'd ever known.

Then we walked back to Wendy and Kate's in silence. We hugged and swayed for a minute, then he was gone. I know he'll call tomorrow.

Christmas Eve, December 24, 1972

I am dangerously happy.

It's the night before Christmas and all through our house, not a creature is stirring, not even our uninvited kitchen guests … a critter family of roaches. Seems to me all New Yorkers have roaches, shrinks, and dogs.

Max will be back in a couple of hours. He's off doing last-minute this-and-that's. I lie in his bed, which has become our bed, in the bedroom that was his and now is ours.

The Hudson River winds its murky brown way past this window on Riverside Drive. We have so little space, but it is space enough since we're in love and never want to be more than two feet apart anyway.

What a volcanic year for me. This job is demanding of everything I've ever learned, been, or felt. These children have special needs educationally, emotionally, socially, financially, and spiritually. They are burdened with cares far too weighty for their little frames. Their learning deficits are almost the least of their pressures. So, squeezed in with teaching, I give them whatever it is I think they most need. Hugs and laughter, a heart-to-heart about their mother's drugs or their father's absence. Sometimes I help with their homework.

Charlene, who is 13, and Natasha, who is 11, both get a special "S" from me each week. "S" is code for "Surprise!" They're both about my size, so I usually bring them items from my closet that I can live without. Many of the kids I want to wrap in ribbons and take home.

Working with Max is pure pleasure. We goose each other in the hall and catch kisses in his office between patients. He works at a fevered pitch and seems to thrive on being needed, which he is … profoundly.

Carmen has become our friend. She is Richard and Max's secretary. A Puerto Rican beauty who is tall as a tree and raven-haired. She throws her head back when she breaks into laughter, and the length and abundance of her thick black waves look like a blanket rippling in the wind.

She's a salty, zesty woman of thirty-five with two kids and an ex who left her and fled, she thinks, to South America to avoid child support. I rarely leave the office without her or our security guard, because on the streets, no one messes with her or the gun-packin' guard. Me, they mess with.

We have Carmen and her kids over for dinner a lot. She's teaching Max how to make Puerto Rican specialties.

I spent a portion of today luxuriating in *LIFE*'s "The Year in Pictures." Most of this year I spent in countries other than my own and paid less attention than usual to the news, so here's a summary of the year I missed.

- Bombardments on Hanoi and Haiphong were heavier than ever this month. Kissinger's declaration in October that "peace is at hand" turned into hollow phonetics, similar to the "I love you" so often whispered or shouted at orgasmic release and believed only by fools.
- Nixon visited China in a flamboyant display of international diplomacy. Didn't hurt him much last month when he crucified McGovern at the polls either.
- We had death at the Olympic Games when Arab terrorists invaded the Israeli team's quarters. Two died there. Nine more shot at the airport. Five terrorists and one policeman, all dead. At the time, I was in Tel Aviv at Baruch's home watching TV with his friends and a grieving world as even Olympic majesty and unity transformed into tyranny and carnage.

- Israelis\Arabs. Arabs\Israelis. Hate seems so easy among these people who physically look alike because we're truly blood relatives. I just don't get it; not really. When the Olympians' broadcast came through, the people I was with at Baruch's home went numb or walked out. One older woman became hysterical, but only she, because for Israelis, terrorism is a life reality. I wept unabashedly.
- Liza captured glory in Cabaret.
- Liz turned forty.
- Alistair Cooke, Mark Spitz, Tom Eagleton, and the Cookie Monster were emblematic of the year.
- Fischer beat Spassky in world-class chess.
- In May, Wallace was gunned down, paralyzed forever.
- Clifford Irving nearly perpetrated a grand fraud with the literary scandal of the decade. But Howard Hughes, the unrelenting recluse, exposed Irving and off to jail he went.

In my own life:

- I had the exalted pleasure of seeing Judith Jamison, from Alvin Ailey's company, perform the dance solo Cry, and I did, copiously. I have rarely seen anything so moving in movement before and may never again. A tree-tall African Queen in yards of supple, white fabric. Fully stunning!
- It was a year of tumult and change, for me, and for the whirling sphere we call our home.
- I believe in my secret heart Max and I will marry next year.

For all my blessings, for my family's health, for Max, I do thank you, G-D.

*****

1973

January 7, 1973

BIG NEWS! GREAT NEWS! NOW HEAR THIS!

Last night being Saturday, we decided to opt for our one splurge dinner of the month. French was the mutual decision. We dressed beautifully and took a cab to *Deux Cheminées* on the East Side.

Spoiled and coddled from the moment the doorman greeted us with a *bon vivant,* "*Bonjour. Comment t'allés vous?*" we were seated where we requested, a nearly secluded corner from which to view all, without being viewed.

A need for grand and exquisite romance is implanted into my genetic code, and Max is ample-enough expert to keep me sated. With his edges of irony, thin veil of mystery, and saturation with the melancholy of Rimbaud, he is perfectly cast as my fantasy lover. He chooses fascinating nuances to tantalize my primary erogenous zone … my brain.

He ordered in French, of course. And soon, tuxedoed men with an airborne touch delivered delicacies at a serene pace. *Escargot ma façon* and *velouté crabe marguerite* … snails with garlic and basil served in a puff pastry and this divine cream-based soup laced with Scotch whiskey. To die for!

It continued this way for hours. We finished up with *Normandarin-Mercier Cognac*, raspberry parfait, and white chocolate sorbet. OY VAY!

We bought Sunday's *New York Times* on the way home. When we arrived at our door, Max said, "Baby doll, mind if I shower first?"

"No, of course not, Max." I wanted to flip through the magazine section and breeze through the mail anyway. In keeping with my reflexive habit, I went to the freezer for the pint of chocolate ice

126

cream and my only piece of sterling silver flatware … a long handled, ornately carved teaspoon.

I nestled into our sofa, flipped to the cover story, and popped the lid on the pint. There, perched bright and shiny, staring at me like a flashlight, was a big round diamond surrounded by a whole bunch of gold!

It's not easy to laugh and cry at the same time, but I've perfected the art over the years. Max appeared, dressed only in his black bikini, wet hair dripping all over his shoulders, arms outstretched. He knelt beside me.

"Will you be my wife, playmate, best friend, and graceful goddess for the rest of our lives?"

"You bet I will!"

He pulled me to the floor, and we rolled all over it like two kids who only recently discovered the fun of touch tumbling.

Making love didn't feel the same. I was no longer just someone's girlfriend. Here today, tomorrow gone. I was Max Stein's fiancée. Our passion was headier and verbal expressions safer, deeper. Touching his body was like touching my body. His skin was mine. I embraced his vulnerability. I memorized the joy on his face and can still taste the salt from his tears as he whispered, "Leah, Leah, Leah, Leah, Leah …"

At midnight we called both sets of parents. Mom was jubilant and I could feel her wedding gear crank into place. Dad was genuinely pleased. Finally, at age twenty-six, his daughter has found happiness with a man her own age, Caucasian, American, Jewish, educated, and a genuine sweetie-pie.

Max's parents were generously supportive. They offered help in any and all ways.

Mazel-tovs were exchanged in delighted joy and suppressed relief.

It's frightening to be this happy because I've lived too long to suspect it can last.

April 11, 1973

New York, New York. It's a hell of a town. So few places where the place itself gives pleasure. I didn't ever, before New York, realize the impact of environment. If I'd grown up in the tenements of Harlem, I'd be mean. I'd be ugly.

The smells! My most sensitive sense abused all day. Irritation mounts subconsciously until I pass a flower stall or smell some yummy cooking, then the memory of caressed senses soothes my sanguine heart.

I wish I could describe myself as other than depressed. I'm engaged, for Pete's sake! (Who is "Pete" anyway?) Something dark umber and ominous encircles me. My world is grey-edged. Some days I'm unable to immerse myself in work; at the clinic today I was bored, sad, sullen, and unfulfilled.

My mind, the great enemy of my spirit. I wish a mind could be exchanged like a blouse that doesn't fit. I would purchase a mind that conceives the world as wide and gracious. It would be sunny too, and easy paced. There would be utopian days, and breezes kissed with soft, smooth petals caressing me at night. And the people … the people would be warm and simple, give-and-take type folks, everyone a potential friend or gentle lover. We'd be a blended group whose synergy is heavenly.

May 18, 1973

Max slips away from me. He hasn't wanted to touch me for weeks. Now we consider seeing a sex therapist. He contends I'm "over-sexed" and he feels pressured to "perform." How did this happen? I thought sex was one of our best things! Maybe he's really turned off because I'm sad and plodding, and he's just using this performance thing as a red herring.

My shrink has me on two new antidepressants. How many drugs have been tried on me since I was fifteen years old? Seven? Twelve, maybe? Is there a drug manufactured that can help someone like me?

Perhaps I should write in code. I anguish someone might read my journals and have access to the very core of me.

Secret of secrets, silence alone, isolation and desolation. Waves of despair wash over me, threatening a drowning.

Max and I are so perfect on paper. We are:

- The same age
- The same nationality
- Of the same cultural and religious heritage
- Have about the same number of years of education
- Have similar sensitivities, similar taste in clothes, friends, furnishings, and films
- Share almost identical values
- Love the theater, museums, and long rides to absolutely nowhere
- Love Alfred Hitchcock and Perry Mason
- Love Chivas Regal and lox and bagels
- Love cats and kids

But do we love with the love required for a marriage?

Living with each other has uncovered more than I wish it had uncovered. Does depression cloud my vision, or is my inner eye painfully acute? This persistent doubt disquiets me, making peace foreign and nerves brittle. Deception is a poison. But the truth is too frightful to fully admit.

Am I hoping for the hopeless? I know we will not work if he hides himself from me or denies us the electricity of our bodies sharing each other. He thinks he makes up for all the lack by being kind and good. His goodness makes me less good.

- He tries, I mope.
- He cares, I defy.
- He listens, I grumble.
- He bears, I cry.

Prove me wrong, TIME ... PLEASE PROVE ME WRONG!
Something at the root of me nags, "Don't marry. Don't marry."
I should heed my head and not my heart. But I won't.

So, what is there left to say, really? Perhaps there is only this left to say: Leah Rebecca Kline, pull up from the center of your being and beat this mental misery of melancholy. Don't wallow, woman. Try, please try to secure a less morose approach to life. It is so devoid of nobility or honor, and serves no one, least of all yourself.

Love this man, Leah, as he does his best to love you. And pray G-D grants both of you His blessings and His peace.

* * * * *

1974

It is the night before Max and I marry. I have a strong suspicion
what I'm feeling is not what I'm supposed to be feeling. That
is, unless it's kosher to be feeling doubt, fear, and OH MY G-D,
WHAT AM I DOING? I mean really, Leah, how many women do
you know who would marry a guy they're already in sex counseling with?

I do deeply love this man. He is razor-sharp smart, entertaining,
mysterious, witty, adventurous, sensuous, and I believe he loves
me. But we have issues that may be insurmountable:

- I relate from my gut; he relates from his cerebrum.
- I emote; he ponders.
- I need his affection and attention; he is now emotionally and
  sexually unavailable.

But I *cannot* and *do not* and *will never* forget our first torrid
summer days in Amsterdam.

There is an emotive and provocative man inside the barricade
Max has constructed around himself.

Do I dare believe I am woman enough to break through steel?
G-D help us. We will need it.

In an hour I will become Mrs. Max Stein, wife of Dr. Max Stein.
My heart has migrated to my throat.

I sit in my arched window niche for the last time as a single
woman. Through the glass I see the white tent, the circular
tables with green-and-white-checkered cloths and fanciful floral

centerpieces. Strings of twinkle lights adorn trees and tent posts. Baskets of flowers hang suspended from oaks and maples. We have created a chuppa from a white lace tablecloth and hung it from four weeping willows that surely were planted for this very purpose.

I see Mom consulting with the caterer. She is lovely today in a soft pink hand-crocheted knit that skims her matching silk pumps and hugs her proportioned body. I guess I won't see Dad until the ceremony.

If I must say so myself, and it seems as though I must, I have never looked prettier. I'm so glad I decided to have this unspeakably gorgeous dress made rather than try to feel all virginal bride-sy in a white gown. This suits me. Free-flowing, full-length floral chiffon with a deep scoop neck and deep scoop back and a wide sash to pinch my waist. I am wearing heeled sandals that I hand-painted with flowers. My hair is piled high with the tiniest of tiny white flowers woven through. I shall carry white lilies. Long. Graceful. Feminine.

Max and I shall walk through my parents' garden of ancient trees, along a freshly laid path of tiny white pebbles, to the shade of the chuppa. We did not want any bridesmaids or groomsmen. So, Max and I will be joined from the first step of our walk that begins our life as husband and wife.

We are conducting the whole service. The rabbi will bestow a blessing near the end and lead the wine tasting and glass smashing. The cantor will sing whatever it is that cantors sing on this occasion. And both Max's father and mine will welcome us into their respective families. Otherwise, it's our show. Let us remember our memorized vows, G-D, and kindly protect and guide us all the days of our lives.

*****

In retrospect, there was something about our wedding day that I didn't think about until maybe ten years ago: I did not have a good time at our wedding. I pretended to, but I knew I should be feeling a fascinating mix of feelings that I just wasn't feeling. And here's the capper: guess where Max and I slept on our wedding night?

He was slightly looped and slept in my single bed in the room I grew up in … and I slept on the floor next to the single bed. The sad part is, I didn't give it a thought. I didn't even think to question our sleeping accommodations on the most important night of our lives. There's a term for this kind of non-thought and numb behavior. It's called …

NO SELF-ESTEEM.

NO SELF-WORTH.

I didn't think I deserved better.

But once we married, a type of love I'd never known grew branches and floral lovelies. I knew I was in it for keeps and, somehow, we would work through our issues and be all the stronger for it. I breathed Max into my center and embraced him as my husband.

*****

1975

January 1, 1975

Max, my darling Max,

To my husband of four months and twelve days, I say HAPPY, HAPPY NEW YEAR!

I love you so much, too much, too emotionally. Do such words sound hollow pouring from such a tortured soul as I? Ah, but there's the rub, Max. Mental anguish does not prevent the sun-bright emotions of passion and love.

I dream glory dreams for us, my Love. And so I do swear to you, I shall search for and find the solution to wrestle the demonic tiger inside of me until he is dead.

If love is defined through sensation, I tell you with all truth, I sense you running through my blood.

Your patience in the company of my unbridled despair embarrasses me. What have I done to deserve you? My heart is yours, this New Year's Day and always.

Your, Leah Rebecca

*****

(Letter from Max)

February 14, 1975

HAPPY VALENTINE'S DAY TO MY WIFE, LEAH REBECCA.

Last Friday night a gentle snow fell hour upon hour on our twirling world. Crystal flakes brought me translucent peace, permeated me, and made me feel clear and cleansed.

134

With delight I have experienced the bright glow from an autumn sun before she hid herself behind the far horizon.

I have been dampened by the most thunderous storms and frightened by the electrical death that sparked around me.

I have known you, and you have brought me to a loving appreciation for all things in a new and spiritually complete way. You, Leah, bring wonder and delight into my world.

You will be healthy and strong, my Lady. We will see to it. I can wait because I've experienced you healthy and strong, and I know you are worth the wait.

I love you, Leah Rebecca. I shall always love you.

Ineffably, Max

April 15, 1975

The last few weeks have been W.I.L.D.! I often lost large blocks of time. Max would start analyzing a movie we'd seen, and I wouldn't remember having seen it. I had crying jags that lasted hours. They'd start as a whimper and crescendo into hysterical wails. I would even head-bang, lip-bite, and face-scratch myself as a distraction from the deepness of the mental and emotional torture. I'd sweat and stink. My skin broke out. I couldn't sleep.

The self-hate was so intense I couldn't look in a mirror or check out my reflection in store windows. One tiny aspect of me I call intuition watched the rest of me in stoical silence, calm and patient, accepting and nonjudgmental. I clung to that tiny aspect of myself because that was the only sane aspect left of me.

Actually "working" while at work was a sorry joke. It took everything I had to just appear somewhat normal. And then, about a week ago, I think it was about a week ago, I crashed in my office. My heart wouldn't stop racing, or my head pounding, or my ears ringing. I felt a volcano of sick lava about to burst from me, and I buzzed Max's office. I don't remember the rest, but here's what Max described about the week to come.

He rushed in to find me on the floor, eyes rolled back, saliva dripping down my face, my body in convulsive heaves. An ambulance was summoned, and I was taken to Columbia-Presbyterian Hospital. The seizure abated in the emergency room and then the tests began. Grueling and gruesome.

Since the hospital was full, they had to put me and three other women in an enclosed sunporch. It was damp. It was noisy. New York is no place to be sick.

The group of doctors who probed and stuck me thought it was a reaction to the antidepressants. Swell. I wonder how many other depressives can claim the drug they take to fix themselves revolts on them and hurls them into a psychotic break and epilepsy.

I stayed in the hospital for five days while they tried to determine the cause of this medical mess. They were stumped; that was clear. So, they put me on two different antidepressants and created a schedule to slowly wean me off the ones I was on. Oh, what fun!

Back to home-sweet-sort-of-sweet-home. Max and I were both terrified to leave me here while he went to work, and so I went to work with him and pretended to work.

I feel overwhelmed. Work exhausts me. A sexless relationship with my husband unnerves me. Our sex counseling drains me. My own therapy confounds me because of the volume of levels we must sift through. Max's therapy threatens me because I'm afraid he'll discover he married a hopelessly crazy woman who is all wrong for him. If Max leaves, I will be indelibly wounded. I will not blame him. I will simply wish to cease breathing. Ceasing to breath, my default stance.

I'm so lonely in New York. Wendy and Kate are so involved with their jobs and each other they have little time for me. Max and I have too little time to spend enjoying New York, and we don't have a lot of throwaway cash. We bank my salary and live on his, and the limited space in our apartment now feels limiting.

Max stays focused on what is now titled "The Trip" (This is why we bank my salary.) He has atlases and travel books all over the living room, remaining inalterably convinced that by June, 1976, we will have enough money to travel the world for a year. High adventure for my high-flying hubby. I don't know that I want to travel the world for a year.

He dreams of foreign intrigue. I dream of silent peace, so tantalizing.

October 18, 1975

Oh Deborah,

This is a very sad saga.

The day was jammed. I had stacks of paperwork to wade through and four reports to write. Unexpectedly, Madeline entered my office and seemed edgy; I was in no mood for her secretarial complaints.

She seemed on the brink of tears though, so I told her to take a seat and spill it.

"Leah, I have something to tell you. I've wanted to tell you for a long time, but I just couldn't. You know I care about you and have been worried about your health. That's one of the main reasons I haven't told you. Well, everybody else in this clinic, except you, knows what I'm about to tell you, and that just doesn't seem right to me anymore. So, here goes: Max and Carmen have been having an affair for over a year."

Too surprised to cry. Too numb to feel. Empty.

She asked me never to tell Max. I looked at her as though she had two green heads.

"O.K. Never mind," she said. "I'll tell him I told you."

"You do that," I said.

A few minutes later he walked into my office. "Do you want to talk?"

I told him I had nothing to say but would listen.

"I'm sorry, Leah. It's been over for a few weeks. I'm so sorry." He slumped into a chair.

Some of the numbness wore off, and I felt a burn in my stomach hot enough to sizzle steaks. "Is that all you have to say, Max? Surely there's more. Like, *where* have you been doing her? How did it start and when? How could you have permitted us to have her and her kids over for dinner so often? Cheap, sick thrill for ya, Max?

"So, what was the turn-on? Her long legs? Her anorexic frame? You can have sex with Miss Puerto Rican slut-queen, but can't make love to your own wife? For over a *year*? Really? Did this start when we were engaged? What is *wrong* with you, Max? Never a clue. I never had a clue. You never left a clue. What a cunning, deceitful, masterful liar you are. You're in the wrong profession, darlin'. Maybe you should switch to law or P.R. or used car sales."

He took my coat from the hanger and said, "Come on, Leah. Let's get out of here and get a drink."

We subway-ed down to 72nd and Broadway. In a dark corner of a dark bar, I heard harsh, hard, piercing words. The only words I can imagine wanting to hear less would have been, "Your Mother is dead," or "Your Father is dead," or "Your Sister is dead." As it is, only I am dead.

The words: They made a baby. Carmen carried his baby. Or so she convinced him. In my unimportant opinion, it could have been any number of men's baby. She had an abortion. An illegal one for which he flew her and himself to a Caribbean Island. He paid. Or should I say, *we* paid.

They had each other in *our* bed. And sometimes in her bed. Whenever I was out of town or when he knew I'd be gone for hours.

I will never trust him again. I will never believe in him again.

So many things make more sense now. Like, now I understand why he helped Carmen find a car, went to her cousin's funeral, and wrote a letter to her brother's parole officer. And I thought all those gestures were so kind and thoughtful. I'm a schnook. Noodnick. Space-cadet.

I ping-pong between hurt and rage. It's been nine hours since a nuclear blast fried my world. I think I'm coping rather well.

Back to the details. I must write or I will shriek until my vocal cords plead for mercy. Degradation. Humiliation. Right now, I could rip the skin off Carmen's body. Why *should* he have tried to make our relationship work? He had a part-time woman and sex whenever he wanted it.

I have used so much restraint not to sleep with other men.

For what?

I guess I know … "for what." Because marriage meant monogamy to me. And I knew adultery wouldn't be worth it because I have too often felt the emptiness of loveless, commitment-less sex.

Damn him. Damn him for this pain!

I asked him if his shrink knows. Yes, the doctor knows. Max said the doctor doesn't see it as a major issue. Max's affair is only symptomatic of a larger problem. Max and I don't have a sexual problem; we have a relationship problem. Well, thank you, Dr. Freud. And screw you, Dr. Freud.

There was only one thing to do when we got home. Get stoned. He wanted to make love. Can you stand it?

It didn't work. I had sharp visual images of him on top of Carmen and could feel her in bed with us. He was loving, but I was shut down. He was remorseful and that helped a little. Very little.

Rushes of disbelief and revulsion.

They made a baby? They made a baby in our bed?

He sobbed in my arms. Now he sleeps.

The perverse part of me wishes to get dressed, go to a bar, flirt with a guy, go back to his place, and sex myself blind for a week.

I'm grateful it's Friday and I won't have to look at Carmen's sneaky puss until Monday.

October 21, 1975

The weekend was revealing. Late Saturday afternoon, neither of us out of our pajamas, he opened up. A monologue spilled from him. Essentially, he said, "I exist on two levels: intellectual adult and frightened child. I fear abandonment. I need copious amounts of approval and overt love. I need to be constantly reassured I'm okay.

"Five years ago, I was profoundly depressed for two months. I vowed it would never happen again. To assure this, I stopped allowing myself to feel. When I fell in love with you in Amsterdam, I both feared and rejoiced that a relationship with you would force me to deal with my issues and I would emerge from emotional hiding. You are so brazenly emotional; I thought it would rub off on me. In your demand that I confront myself, I have grown to loathe what I see. I hate my insecurity being the motivation for my being so 'nice.'

"When I kiss you, I feel my barricades crumbling and it terrifies me. When I kiss Carmen, it's just lust. I'm afraid of wonderful sex with you because I'm afraid of commitment. Commitment means dependency, loss of control. An absence of sex controls the depth of our relationship. It's what I use to ensure the upper hand. Your passion, your range, your insight, your raw emotion renders me defenseless."

He must have said, "I'm so sorry," ten zillion times during the weekend.

"I'm so sorry too, Max," I said almost as often. Despite everything and probably because of everything … I love him more than ever. I feel responsible for so much of his unhappiness.

October 23, 1975

Monday morning. Carmen didn't show at work today. Can't say I blame her. Can't say I missed her. Can say I wish she'd quit work, or a truck would run her over before tomorrow morning.

*****

(My letter to Max)

October 28, 1975

Oh Max …

Sorry about last night. I guess I had been a good sport for as long as I could be. The hurt morphed into rage. I'm glad my ballet slipper missed you as it hurled through space.

Is there anything more powerful and painful than love? Have you any idea how completely I am yours? How much of myself I have committed to you? Sometimes I feel close to bursting from the comprehensiveness of my involvement with you. Long ago I let go and allowed myself to be inextricably entwined with you.

I am not myself alone anymore. I am you and me together. Letting go was based on unyielding trust. What should I do now, Max? I'm not much good at gauging emotional output the way you do. I know nothing of restraint or caution or percentages. I invest all.

The wounded part of me and the part responsible for self-protection warns me against you now. I'm afraid of your unlimited power to severely hurt me. I'm afraid of your capacity for deceit. I don't want these fears to interfere with my love for you. I want to believe in you. In fact, I must.

My love is not conditional, Max. It is stable and constant. But my belief in you, trust in you, respect for you *are* conditional. These things are earned. They are not gifts.

Our life together can be the stuff of which dreams are made. It is what I want most from the years I'm allotted. To love you. To love you. And I do. And I will. Just help me.

Leah

*****

1976

Max and I limp along as days pass into seasons. The thought of Carmen, their affair, and their baby still make me feel as though a sacrificial sword has run me through.

I just got back from a two-hour session with my shrink, the ever-penetrating Dr. Ellen James. The onion skin layers of my psyche are being exposed. It doesn't frighten me. I want to defeat depression and its horror show.

Dr. James seems to think most of my issues were born from a childhood that was just "too safe, too protected, too loving." She says, "Clearly, nothing has been as safe and satisfying since you left your parents' home as a college freshman. You were gratified too consistently."

What? Is she nuts? Has she been listening?

I'm terrified of my father. The demands on me have always been outrageous. I'm undermined no matter what I do or how well I do it. What's so safe and satisfying about that?

When I lived at home before college, nothing ever got talked through. Every issue was quickly locked in safety deposit boxes or pushed under Oriental rugs. Anger was not permissible in any form. Mom and Dad's marriage has always been difficult, and it affected Ruthie and me daily. Dad is almost always distant and demanding, and Mom's life with him is sad, which is so painful for me to watch. We never go on family trips. We never did or do much of anything together except go to the club.

And since age sixteen, I've been Mom and Dad's marriage mediator. Yet, what I suggest to them is never attempted by either

143

of them. And still, I'm bombarded with phone calls from her berating him and phone calls from him berating her.

"Safe and satisfying"? Hardly, Dr. Ellen James. HARDLY!

*****

I reiterate, we all knew Dad loved us, and he knew we loved him. But there was little doubt that my being in his presence would create contention, tinged with cayenne. He greeted our dog with more affection and tenderness than he and I ever shared. It shattered me and I was jealous of the silly dog.

One of Dad's psychiatrists once told Mom and me, "Sol is as emotionally closed as a cement box." Years later another of his psychiatrists told me, "If you, Leah, were to win both the Pulitzer and the Nobel Peace Prize on the same day, you should not expect an 'atta girl' from your Dad."

*****

Hearing those words really was the embryonic beginning of giving up my silent quest for approval. It would not be forthcoming.

*****

February 15, 1976

Oh Deb … our stay in New York will soon end and we will begin the year-long trip Max has been planning for over two years. I think I'm self-deceived and foolish to believe I can do this.

Like, I'm conning myself, and Max will end up cheated by my dishonesty.

February 22, 1976

I explained something to myself today. These journals allow me the mind space to contemplate my past and present. Sometimes a kind of synthesis evolves, or an epiphany occurs. This was a day like that.

Most people outgrow an idealized perspective of their parents fairly early in life, if they ever had one at all. I took an inordinate amount of time to see my Mom realistically.

I saw in her a fragile beauty … a delicate woman with grace and charm, creativity and talent, sensitivity and wisdom. And those assessments are accurate. But Mom never saw those attributes in herself. Her own childhood had not birthed self-confidence or self-esteem.

In Mom's distorted view, even though she and Aunt Lauren were identical twins, she was the plain and inelegant duckling. Aunt Lauren was the exotic beauty, the homecoming queen, the lady with panache that drove men wild. Mom constantly covered for Aunt Lauren. She did Lauren's homework and wrote her papers, allowing Miss Popularity the excitement of a life gone wild. Mom was meek and shy, still is, but she compensates with a regal bearing and a spirit held high.

As a kid, the huge part of me I called intuition knew Mom didn't see herself as the self she projected. And I reasoned she was lying when she said, "Oh Leah, you're so adorable." Nina Joy Kline, that lovely creature at her prime, a perfect size eight, graceful and gracious, was just trying to make her homely daughter feel better. That's how I saw it.

Because if she didn't think her natural beauty and charm were anything special, how was I to believe as an adolescent … with pimples, fat thighs, bitten nails, and glasses … that I was anything special … much less adorable?

O.K. So I have a loaded question for you, Hidden Subconscious: *If my childhood was so full of love and security, as Dr. James suggests, why am I guilt-ridden, angry, emotionally dependent, self-conscious, a compulsive eater, regularly despondent, and terri-fied of abandonment? I will await your response.*

February 27, 1976

A series of several months, a string of dirty days until … New York is not our home!

I know New York is a phenomenon. If this were ten years from now, I'd probably never leave.

We have all the camping gear bought and paid for. The itinerary is shaping up. It will not be a worldwide trip, as the prince hoped. It will be a driving trip to include as many states as is logical and possible, huge sections of Canada, most of Mexico, and as far into Central and South America as we dare drive.

I'm so scared. How shall I explain this? Let me count the ways: We are both at critical points in our therapy. Dr. James has voiced her concern about my delicate psyche and the unpredictability of travel. Max and I are still trying to recuperate from the aftermath of the Carmen-the-Slut-and-Max-the-Cad Sexcapade. He hasn't touched my body for I forget how long. There will be no one to talk to and laugh with and share secrets with, except him. I will miss Wendy and my Mom and all the other people in my world who help me remember I'm an O.K. person.

What will so much free time feel like? I like silence and solitude but have always known I require the discipline of projects and

146

structure. Without these two confines, I fear I might break down and crack up and become truly unglued. (*Dr. James assures me that beneath this despair is a woman with ego strength, a strong sense of reality, and a developed sense of identity. That all sounds great. So how come I feel soooooo bad?*)

April 21, 1976

Today I had another lightbulb-thought of self-explanation. Here it is: A posture of guilt protects my world. It's a catch-all stance. When I don't feel up to dealing with a problem, I cop a guilty plea, something like, "I know I'm impossible." "I don't see how you could love me." "I'm so sick and repulsive." Who could berate or abandon someone so pitiful and defenseless? Works every time. What a lowlife am I … a formidable actress with purpose and an agenda. Just pathetic.

Another revelation: Why, I asked myself, do I spend all my energy hating Carmen? It wasn't just she who betrayed me. It must be safer to hate Carmen. If I hated Max with even a sixteenth of the intensity I direct toward her, Max and I would be unable to co-exist. No how. No way.

June 19, 1976

And so, it happened. Today is day two of our projected year-long odyssey. Leaving New York was a breeze. Packing up our furnishings and storing them was a cinch. But leaving Mom and Dad and Ruthie was awful, worse than I anticipated. Max and I drove to our first stop, D.C., in near silence.

I prepared for this trip as though I were helping someone else organize, systematize, list-create, and list-complete. I didn't really want to believe I would be going with Max, caught up as I am

in someone else's fantasy. He is like an expectant child eager
to attack this time of travel and explore himself, cultivate new
interests, study the cultures we'll be exposed to. I deal with more
basic issues, like … separation anxiety, fear of limited adaptability,
disappointing Max, disappointing myself, roughing it, coping with
complete freedom. I don't feel up to this challenge.

July 19, 1976

We've been gone for one month today. I must admit I love
documenting these days with accumulating words and photos. It's
not that they have all been easy days, and some days are not even
close to fun. It's hard to never know where we'll be sleeping or
even in what town. Playing it loose is daring and often leads to
drama or at least irritability. But I wouldn't have missed this for
nuttin'. Everything I thought would be hard for me, has been. But
I have no choice except to soldier on and so I do; this breathes new
respect into me.

Yesterday we had an ever-so-charming breakfast at a diner in
Biloxi, Mississippi. While eating eggs and white toast, sitting on
red vinyl stools at a royal blue Formica counter, we started a chat
with the toothless guy next to us. He wore a green baseball cap
advertising local chewing tobacco. His hands had black grease in
the nail beds that likely had been there for decades. A truly hard-
working man.

He asked us where we're from, having already told us that,
"Y'all's Yankees, I kin tell that. So, where's y'all from?"

I said, "Philadelphia," and Max said "San Diego," but we told
him we'd both been living and working in New York for several
years.

"Y'all ever seen any Jews?" he asked.

Instinctively we knew not to say, "Well, sure we have. We *are* Jews." I nodded at Max to handle this one.

"Why do you ask?" my honey asked.

"Well, I's hear tell them Jews have horns growin' out their heads, and I's jus' wonerin' if you ever seen any a them horns."

"No, can't say that I have," Max said while sipping his java. "Can't say that I have." We finished our chow and our second cup, shook hands with our dining companion, and got the hell out of a place too far south for Jewish folks. *Horns*? How do people come up with these things?

September 21, 1976 – September 23, 1976

Entering Mexico

Now variation from our norm is *really* about to kick in. Ready. Get set. Here we go! We're prepared! We're cool! All our official papers and documents are in order. All pot paraphernalia is gone … left on a college campus in Brownsville, Texas. All car seats and carpets have been vacuumed and re-vacuumed from every crevice of our car's interior to rid the vehicle of potential telltale signs of weed or seeds. We go all through Mexico with no problems.

(There are tons of South of the Border stories, but this is not a travelogue. I'm sharing highlights.)

Finally, we're at the border of Guatemala. Customs. Immigration. Registration. Visas. Money exchange. Hours of tedium and boredom and the bureaucratic hustle. It's a hundred and twenty-two degrees in the shade. And pouring … naturally.

The first three checkpoints after Customs are no problem. We pull up to the fourth checkpoint and estimate we're about fifteen miles into this Central American country.

Greetings are exchanged. They check our papers. We naively expect … "O.K., we're outta here." NOPE, not even close! A platoon of men appears out of tissue-thin air. They look mean, really mean. They sport machine guns. Strips of black leather holding real gold bullets crisscross their chests. It's clear they have dispensed with decorum.

One soldier opens Max's door and then another soldier opens mine. They stick their rifle butts under our arms and pull each of us out of the car. They motion us to stand back. One of them kneels near the driver's seat and another kneels next to my seat. They start a search.

The soldier near me holds up a pair of pinched tweezers indicating that he has found something on the floor of the car. He glances back at me, looking meaner by the millisecond. I shrug my shoulders. They continue the search.

Three soldiers are now scouring the car, for what … pot seeds? I guess. Maybe. They each have tweezers and tiny white paper bags.

I begin to fume, and an ounce of indignation erupts from me. Max has moved to my side of the car and is now squeezing my hand into fractured splinters. He leans toward my ear and whispers with total command, "Be still and keep quiet. Now listen to me. We're in deep shit. There's no one in the world who can help us now. No political clout or family money can buy us out of this one. I'll do the talking."

My lips remain still but in my body I scream, "OH NO! OHHHH NO!"

(Now it's tomorrow, and I still haven't come off the adrenalin rush.)

They handcuff us. We stand in silence as they take apart our lives. Onto the red-dirt earth they pile all of our stuff from the trunk and the car's interior.

Some funny part of my brain gets tickled, and I find myself remembering Max asking while we were packing, "Leah, do you think we ought to pack the lawn mower?" I giggled. But Max knows we need everything we brought. Warm and cool clothes. Camping gear. Books. Tapes. Water jugs. Toiletries. Camera equipment. Maps. Binoculars. Blah. Blah. Blah. Strange how the brain reacts to terror and the memories that surface.

They escort us into the Customs building. The officer in charge pulls out a large ledger. He says in Spanish, "I need your passports." He and Max go back to the car to retrieve them.

I thought he would simply write down the important information from our passports and hand them back. But NOOOOOO! He writes down some stuff and then puts the single most important documents in our world into *his* desk drawer. My knees weaken.

I count the number of banditos. There are thirteen of them. One, a guy maybe two inches taller than I am, comes up behind me and puts his knee just under my buttocks and starts a slow vertical climb. I slam my eyes shut, determined not to whimper. Max spots this action and he whimpers for me.

Officer Sleazebag then moves in adagio around my body and stops when our eyes are a breath apart. He removes a knife from his belt, picks his teeth with it, and then places the knife at my throat and slips its point under my gold chain. He pulls sharply and catches the airborne chain with his free hand. He dead-eyes me, kisses it, then slips the chain Max gave me for my twenty-fifth Birthday into his breast pocket as he winks at me.

I want Mom and Dad and Ruthie.

I see our camping gear head up the road in the arms of some teenage boys (the sons of the banditos?) All of the men help themselves to the objects of our physical lives. It means nothing. Stories float by in visual form inside my forehead. Stories of the thousands of American kids rotting in foreign jails around the globe. Hell, I watch *60 Minutes*! I've seen the stills and footage of the pitiable kids from our generation in tattered remnants and long dirty hair, bare-foot and numb, skinny and sick.

No consulate or embassy has any clout. That is fact! I feel that fact in my solar plexus with the force of a torpedo.

The officer in charge lays the contents of the white bags on his desk. I count eleven dried-up seeds. He says in Spanish, "You have a big problem. This is marijuana."

Max had three years of college Spanish; I had two years. So far, I am following this guy. My Max says, "No, señor. Tenemos nada. Estos no son marijuana. ¡En el auto hay nada!"

The señor is not impressed. He continues in Spanish, "In Guatemala, seeds are considered to be the same as marijuana. You have brought these seeds into our country to plant them and later harvest them and export them for big money."

"Señor," Max pleads in Spanish, "my wife and I have saved our money for several years in order to be able to visit your country. We have no pot with us and no intention of planting those dried-up seeds. The car wasn't even ours originally."

(And it truly wasn't. It was Max's uncle's Oldsmobile; he'd passed away shortly before this trip and the car went to Max.)

My honey continues, "Maybe the former owner smoked pot."

I had no trouble understanding the officer's next sentence: "You are going to jail." Most of the officers now sport sly grins. They revel in the terror they create in us. The officer in charge says he'll have to call his superior.

Max does not let up. "You know these things are nothing, señor. You've searched the car and you know we have nothing. I am a doctor. I'm not about to jeopardize my career and our lives for eleven seeds. We are on an extended holiday."

In a weak, breathy voice I've never heard slide from me, I say, "Señor, por favor. Solamente un viaje, un vacacione. Queremos visita a Guatemala. Nada mas. Por favor, señor. ¡Por favor!"

He does not flinch. He escorts us into another office and says that Interpol will have to be informed. I've never even heard of Interpol, but I see thoughts express themselves on my husband's face.

We are forcibly escorted into two separate cells on opposite sides of the building. My throat is drier than hay. I begin to pray, a prayer that starts very low and skyrockets out my brain. Please don't allow us to live out our lives and rot away in cells in Guatemala. What an unspeakable punishment. Spare us, G-D.

Hours melt by. If Max stands in the far-right corner of his cell and I stand in the far left of mine, we can see a portion of each other's faces. So that is where we stand for hour after hideous hour.

Periodically, through a tiny slit of a window, I see other cars stop for their routine Customs' check and then move ahead on their journey. I wonder why we have been singled out with such maliciousness.

I know there were no seeds left in that car. We had made it all the way through the countless checkpoints in Mexico, and *they* had trained dogs sniffing foreigners' belongings and vehicles. But go argue with militaristic, barbaric little men draped in artillery.

Max makes his move. He asks if he can speak with me. They comply. Nose to nose we whisper our fright, and he explains his plan. He says the officer's reference to Interpol, an international crime network, seemed a bit like grandstanding. Eleven seeds do not a high-powered international crime-case make. So, Max is ready to offer a bribe and asks what I think.

Here's what I think: "Be honest, Max. Tell them if offering them money will be held against us, then we're not offering them money. But if money is what they want … they've got it." That's a difficult enough concept to put across in your own language without being self-incriminating. My husband is facing the most rigorous challenge of his twenty-nine years.

Max motions for the head-honcho officer and then states his case. The officer just stares back at Max. One last hurdle. We have already exchanged a lot of our travelers' checks into Guatemalan currency. We are savvy enough to know they want red-hot American dollars. Not American Express checks or their own currency. Max shoves his hand into his Wranglers and pulls out $50. Mr. Head-Honcho-Bandit grabs it, sports a grin that can span two coasts, and opens my cell door. Once he releases the metal cuffs from our wrists, he gives us our passports, walks us to our car, shakes our hands, and says, "Tell no one of this."

We drive off slowly. Fifty bucks! A lousy $50 turned their world into paradise. This is so sad.

In silence we drive to Penajachel, a village on the hem of Lake Atitlan. A red, white, and blue awning catches our homesick eyes, and Max walks in to inquire about accommodations.

Directly from heaven we are sent Jena and Richard Blake. They own the hotel with the patriotic awning and hail from our nation's capital. We spill out our story by candle glow, late into last night's diamond-lit sky.

Richard said, "You guys are lucky. Kids from many foreign countries rot, as we speak, in the jails of this country for having seeds in their car carpets. It's also fact that border cops plant seeds in car carpets and conduct ruthless shakedowns. This is a funny country. It's politically corrupt, but the people, mostly peasants, are shy, happy, gentle, friendly, and kind. We love it here. That's why we spend six months a year running this hotel."

When not running the hotel, Richard does his attorney thing in D.C. and Jena gives piano lessons and tutors high school and college kids in Spanish. The four of us fall instantly in love.

I remember talking softly, explaining, and describing, "They went through my purse and our film canisters. They pushed coat hangers down the window spaces in the car doors. Max was incredible. Incredible. He had all the legal ramifications to consider. He was understated. He was unflappable."

I cry all night, between sips of liquor and bites of lamb. I continue to ramble, "I've been mugged and I've been held at gunpoint, and neither of those violent experiences can compare with this. Because violence is fast, but fear that crescendos hour upon hour is paralyzing."

As I rock like a schizophrenic child, I say, "Isn't it ironic? We're not heavy pot users. We've never sold drugs. We haven't so much as toked since leaving Texas. We've seen scores of kids wrecked, stoned, high, and wiped-out on pot and opium, and we are targeted to be terrorized."

As I write this account that I feel the fear and anger ebb. Good thing, since there's no point in trying to persuade Max, we must leave this country this very second. He has made it abundantly clear he hasn't driven five thousand miles to Guatemala to turn around and hightail it back to the States.

So, Leah, I tell myself, let it go. Think about something else. Write about something else. Eat food. Chill out. Take a nap. You'll be seeing all there is to see, so flow with it.

September 28, 1976

Let me describe this spot in visual paradise. Penajachel lies at the base of a circle of volcanic mountains. They are bathed in mist.

155

It is other-worldly and still here. Bird calls and church bells are the solitary sounds that break up an otherwise pervasive calm.

The lake is mystical, magical, moody. It is obvious we are in another sector of the world. Even the air is different. I feel as though I have walked into a painting.

Tiny men stand in tiny boats and use big oars to glide across the horizon. Women and children sit along the muddy curbs and weave threads of color into fabrics of incomparable beauty. These are the fabrics that become clothes. The village looks like it's dressed up for a festival honoring the artistry of costume through a rainbow of embroidered cloth.

Men wear pants that end just after their knees, and their heads are shaded with darling little straw Panamanian hats. The babies are priceless. Dark round faces and shiny, straight, spiky black hair.

Men are stooped from the loads of grain they carry on their backs as they ascend steep inclines. Children beg. Although it keeps pouring … piles of rain and hills of puddles … the natives do not own raincoats. They tie sheets of clear plastic around their necks and smaller pieces over their heads, and hardly anyone wears shoes.

Tonight we're having dinner at a Chinese restaurant with Jena and Richard. I feel better now.

September 30, 1976

Oh, these are some wild-ass times!

Back to the Chinese restaurant from a few days ago. It's one of the only restaurants in Penajachel, so when Jena and I are not up to cooking in her mega-modest kitchen, we dine Chinese. It's a crummy little joint with wooden tables and benches on what the owner has the audacity to call "the veranda." This means the floor is mud with plywood planks laid over it and the walls are plastic sheets that howl with the wind. The Four Seasons, it ain't.

There are no menus. You eat whatever they're cooking that night. That night, they serve steak, eggs, and coffee for $.75. Two flies crawl out of my eggs. They are too tired to fly away, and I must coax them off my plate. They land on the mud-covered dog who lies at my feet.

Jena and Richard's hotel is comprised of a circular series of little thatched huts. The center of this circle is a splendid tropical garden. Stalks of red, yellow, and purple flowers tower over me. Palms sway and bamboo grows, and the earth is blanketed with delicate wild flowers. Jena and Richard live in the largest of these huts, so at night we usually convene at their house and play Gin or Scrabble and share the stories of our lives.

They are golden people. Everything about them shrieks health. Their bodies are shades darker than ours and are strong and sinewy from physical work. They are in their mid-thirties and consider adopting children. Adopting children. I ache for children of my own. It feels as though "Mommy hormones" constantly snake through me.

For reasons unknown, I often have nightmares about a kid dying in war or a kid being dragged by a car. It's always awful, and it takes hours to shake the nightmare of too-vivid visuals. And sometimes I seethe with envy when I look at women with baby carriages or mothers demurely breastfeeding their tiny treasures. My response seems so exaggerated. What's wrong with me? I still have plenty of time to have children.

Only You, G-D … know how I long for a child to raise into self-assurance, strength and the full capacity of his or her potential. But you also know I am an unstable and emotionally damaged woman. How could I raise a child when I'm barely able to raise myself? I'm defective. I'm seriously flawed. I have nothing of merit to offer a child. Will I ever be well? Will I ever be the stellar Mom I long to be? I pray I will be, but I really don't think I will be.

Jena, Richard, Max and me: Sometimes the four of us lie in their bed under their Austrian goose down comforter because it's the only place in the country to feel warm or dry. Their little fireplace takes some of the raw dankness out of the air, but not much.

We will be friends always. We've entered each other's bio-rhythms, and a forever friendship is inevitable.

I'm sure you won't find this hard to believe, oh Deborah-pal-of-mine, but our journey to Chichicastenango, Guatemala, was another melodrama.

Permit me to set the stage. My stomach is rotten, but Max has his heart set on visiting ChiChi. So up, up, and away we go, over hill and dale. Rotten turns to rotten-er, and by the time we get to the village, I need a bathroom *bad*.

We hire a kid, Guillermo, who locates a bathroom. This bathroom is located down a perilous row of ancient stone stairs in the basement of a chicken warehouse. Dead chickens with slit throats hang on multiple lines and stacks of them litter the floor.

Damn, I've been in nicer outhouses. Even mouth-breathing cannot prevent the years of stench from penetrating my nostrils. Toilet paper? Nah. Just a stack of newspapers piled on the floor. Now my ass sports yesterday's Spanish headlines. As I'm exiting, the owner screams at me, "Señorita, tres centavos." I keep walking, longing to, but refraining from, flipping him the bird.

We walk to the church … El Dominican Santo Tomes Iglesia … where Indian men (*tribal representatives*) burn aromatic incense to honor their ancestral pagan deities. Inside the church, men and women throw offerings of rose petals and pine needles onto the stone floor. They pray before the crucifix and altars. They burn incense from sod beds. The beams and ceiling are blackened from the candle soot of centuries.

It is a unique combination of religious customs: worship of pre-Hispanic pagan gods and Catholic practices introduced by the Conquistadores.

There's a crowd. Hundreds of Mayan-Quiche Indians. Busloads of tourists. An assortment of American hippies and artists. The customary hordes of children, pigs, chickens, turkeys, donkeys, and a couple of cows. What sights. What smells. I'm getting sicker by the second.

I dry heave and sweat cascades from me. I'm dizzy and the world spins. Max leaves me with Guillermo because he's off to find help! The fact that Max is a doctor is not of much value right then. I remember thinking if all else fails, we could always call on the witch doctor we'd seen on the church steps who was decoratively clothed, coiffed, and had the demeanor of the truly unhinged.

Max returns. Couldn't find a doctor. Guillermo says in Spanish he knows where there's a "doctor." THANK G-D. They each grab one of my arms, and we walk about a quarter mile. Through the haze of my own liquid sight, I do, in fact, see the decoratively clothed and coiffed witch doctor walking toward us as we approach. Max and I look at each other and start walking in the opposite direction as we drag Guillermo along with us.

On our way to the car, an Indian man gestures in a vague resemblance to sign language that there is a hospital he can lead us to. I don't remember much of this, but Max later described it graphically.

My honey places me in the car, which is approximately one foot wider than the streets themselves. He then drives this monstrous Oldsmobile down the street while the Indian runs ahead to show the way. An entire community is disrupted. Herds of people must pick up their goods, wares, chickens, fabrics, pots, pans, and children to make room for the Gringos with the way-too-wide Olds.

At long last we reach the hospital, but alas, it's closed for lunch. No joke. The place is padlocked and the sign reads *Siesta Tiempo*. I pass out.

So, we make our way up and out of ChiChi and somehow arrive at the lake. Max says he's grateful I was out cold because I would have shrieked at the mountain passes. The grade was so steep he couldn't see the road ahead of him; the car was pitched at an angle that allowed him to only see the car's hood. We're talking a vertical climb.

October 3, 1976

We never did see much of ChiChi and Max missed his anticipated day of shopping. My delirium passed within twenty-four hours.

Last night was great fun. The four of us were sauntering the streets when we heard some jive music and singing. The doors were open, so we walked into an Assembly of G-D revival meeting. Hallelujah!

Once again, more Jesus people who stamp, holler, shout, and sing the praises of this dude called Jesus? Is it a spell? I'm tellin' ya', it's WEIRD! Tomorrow we're off to Santiago on the far side of the lake.

October 8, 1976

By dawn we catch the mail boat that traverses Lake Atitlan twice daily and glides visitors to an anachronistic village. Through the mist emerges a vision of colorfully clothed women washing vibrant clothes on the huge boulders at the water's edge. They work so hard to pound out the dirt and mud of their daily lives.

Girl children descend like birds of prey. Hustlers. They begin this occupation as soon as they can walk. Their little straw baskets brim with trinkets, beads, ceramic birds, talons on key chains, and fertility charms.

"Me Delores. Buy from me. Five for twenty-five cent. Buy from me." They are relentless. They tug at our clothes. They push their goods into our hands.

It saddens me. Not the poverty. It is all they know. It is us whom I resent … the tourists with cameras who stop and stare and take what we want from these people. Were these Central Americans happier before the concept of *turistas* ever entered their world?

Max and I buy from every kid who begs. And each time I snap a photo, I pay them for their portraits. We buy yards of woven cloth whose beauty is pure enchantment; their intuition for color and composition is inspired.

We decide to spend the night at the only "hotel" in the village. Our room opens onto a courtyard of luscious foliage. The manager proudly boasts that after 6:00 P.M. we will have running water and it may even be warm. There are three military cots in the room, two tin candlesticks, a clay water pitcher and a swinging light bulb with an inverted paper shade. It is very damp and cold …. what a surprise!

The hotel's proprietor, Miguel Sanchez, directs us to a restaurant for dinner. We arrive at the restaurant and are warmly welcomed by a man and woman. They move their five kids, three high-chairs, and mangy dog, then motion us to sit down.

We ask for a menu. No menu.

She says, "*Quiero pollo?*"

Sure, we nod, chicken sounds great. A half hour later the *señora* brings each of us a half-raw chicken leg, a slice of not-yet-ripened tomato and a parboiled potato. We pick at it and eat a little.

Max asks for *la quenta (the bill)*. Everyone looks at each other hesitantly; it appears they don't know what to charge. They huddle and start the bidding for our two meals at $.50 and increase the price by nickels among themselves.

At $2.10, Max tells them to, "*alto*" (*stop*). We give them $5.00, and everyone hugs, smiles, and says *gracias* lots and lots. We leave. Very strange. But I have become almost comfortable with strange. Travel continually expands my perception of my outer limits.

November 23, 1976

We leave this paradise tomorrow. Although we had planned to drive all the way to Panama, even Captain Courageous is anxious to hear "The Star-Spangled Banner." It is now time to make the three-thousand-mile trip back through Mexico. I shall not even begin to describe the dread that fact ignites in me.

Final Thoughts: Despite our inauspicious entry into this land, I have grown to admire these people and appreciate their country. Truly, this is an Eden that is sumptuous, bountiful, and scenic. It projects an air of pageantry. It is softly exotic and steeped in the images of ancient civilizations.

I shall miss Jena and Richard. I wish we could sweep them up along with our baggage and carry them with us for the next several months of our adventure. But I know our lives are permanently meshed, so I also know soon again we will hug, laugh, spin tales, and play Scrabble.

December 10, 1976

I got a letter from Ruthie today. Picked it up at Western Union when we drove across the border into Texas.

*****

(Ruthie's letter to Leah)

December 1, 1976

Leah, Hi Sis.

I've got a question for you. So, you really did mean it when you said you guys are going to travel for a year? Damn, Leah, why can't you ever do anything the way everyone else does? What would have been wrong with a nice ten-day cruise or a week in Milan and Rome?

You may be interested to know that Mom and Dad practically worry themselves sick about the two of you. They weren't great while you were in the States, but now that you wander through Third World countries, their worry is more worrisome. I know you're not about to jump on a plane and forego you plans, but jeez, Leah, a whole year?

Anyway, I'm in love with this guy named Jonathan. He's utterly fab. You'll adore him. I'm actually "happier" than I've ever been. This one may *be* the one. I'm practically euphoric. Will write again soon. Love you despite the fact that you are you.

XOXOXOX, Ruthie

P.S. O.K., I suppose I should qualify my remarks by saying I could never do what you are doing. I wouldn't have wanted to or dared to. Never knowing what city you'll be sleeping in or if you'll even find a motel. A fifteen-dollar-a-day budget. Staying in flea-bag joints with bare swinging light bulbs, water bugs, towels the size of washcloths, and locks that don't lock?

And Max had the flu in the middle of a town with limited plumbing? Nice. How go the plans re: Max quitting smoking, you reading a book a week and learning the alto recorder, his desire to learn and eventually teach hypnosis, and your ever-present obsession with losing weight? If it sounds like I'm annoyed with you, it could be that, or it could be jealousy. You're very brave and I'm sort of proud of you. More XOXOXOX.

*****

We pulled into Mom and Dad's driveway two weeks short of a year of travel. I'm going to pull final observations from my last journal entries:

Almost every day I see things I've never seen before, giving me a forever panoramic view of forty-three out of fifty states, Canada, Mexico, and some of Central America. We've seen remote ghost towns, metropolitan cities, forests, deserts, hot springs, volcanic mountains, tangled wilderness, dunes, beaches, craggy cliffs, rocky caverns, waterfalls, snowfields, fishing streams, farmland, alpine meadows, ice caves, lava flows, wildflowers, and wild animals. We even slept in a sea lion cave for a night. Not on purpose. The elevator that brought us to sea level .... broke!

We've been to stock car races, horse races, dog races, armadillo races, drag races, motorboat races, rodeos, lumber mills, universities, museums, county fairs, craft fairs, movies, theaters, arboretums, and easily sixty percent of all the state and national parks in this grand land. And let me not forget the celebrations honoring chewing tobacco, Lone Star beer, and hefty steer.

Ruthie made it a point during one of my phone calls home to spend some of the call in wails of laughter picturing me camping ... in August ... in the Everglades. We camped a lot. I loathed it.

*****

1977

Deborah, I feel I should go to a hospital to recover from this year-long odyssey. "Weary" doesn't hint at capturing the fatigue that has invaded my being. My brain is fried … easily hot enough to panfry flounder and so crowded with a year of accumulated stimuli that I feel as though I need to be debriefed or deprogrammed or just dee-ed.

It is not that I'm ungrateful for the most thrill-a-minute year of my life; I'm just punchy, emotional, overly everything-ed. Now hear this! If I don't eat in a restaurant until the Arctic thaws, I won't moan, I promise. If I don't sleep in a motel until Santa forgets Christmas, I won't gripe, I swear it.

We're at Mom and Dad's. They marvel at us and look at us with newfound respect. I suppose we did embark on and complete something rather spectacular. Being immersed in it, living it, didn't afford us the opportunity to focus on its outrageousness. Only in retrospect does something of this scope penetrate the hollows. And retrospect has not yet had time to even consider awakening.

We've been in touch with Jena and Richard. They're pleading with us to stay with them until one of us finds a job. Max longs to find a practice to join that's near my family. I don't know that I want to live this close to everything and everyone I've known since birth.

What I do know is something happened between Max and me on this trip. Something born from too much time alone together, something that acquainted us too deeply with each other's unrequited love. Does he not ache for my touch as I ache for his? Could he really have shut down so completely as to no longer need the heady rush and intoxication of passion?

How foolish was I to think he could not possibly resist me forever? Max is lion strong, and he can do whatever he wants to do. Vanity and confidence in my sexual prowess boomeranged, and I have the knot in my heart and the ache in my soul to prove it.

It makes me feel like an ugly, dried-up old witch that my husband cannot even run his fingers through my silken hair much less examine my nakedness or tantalize my mind with whispered words. My prime ebbs away with my youth, thirty years old only months from now.

I fight depression away like a bear protecting her cub. Do not *dare* take over my life again, you cruel and hideous disease of my mind. Do not *dare* steal my sanity and rob me of all but breath. That's what's most cruel about you, you insidious, hideous mind-crusher. You take *everything*, with the notable exception of a capacity to breathe, which any veteran of depression would gladly give up. You leave us to rot in our own decay, but you insist that if we die, it must be by our own hand. Truly, if there is a devil, you … depression … are his premiere agent.

June 20, 1977

It's Friday night and we've just spent a languid evening around the graceful curves of an oval pool in the valley behind Jena and Richard's house. I hadn't realized how much I've missed Washington, D.C. During my Masters program, my eyes were stuffed in textbooks, so only through osmosis did I breathe in the city. But I have always thought I could live here.

I respond to this gracious home that is casually decorated with care and imagination. I see things around this space that Jena and

I found in the crevices and secret places of Guatemala. I like her style, probably because it echoes shades and reflections of my own.

Max and I have the third floor, a lovely room with sharp angles and sloping lines. A tight hot-pink rosebud awaited us in our bathroom, where a porcelain tub is perched on four brass feet.

Fantasy stuff. But here, it's for real.

I don't want a job in speech pathology or special ed. I don't want to have pimples. I don't want to be a slave to my paltry emotional development. And I don't want Max. I want rest and freedom. Will they ever be mine?

It's all hopelessly stupid. Life predicaments. Juggling acts. Displaced emotion. Safety valves, but no safety. Remorse. Heaviness.

I stop writing a lot and stare at the wall across the room. I'm laden with insignificance and meaningless detail.

*****

(Note from Jena)

August 2, 1977

Leah, will you be upstairs in your retreat in time for me to wish you a Happy Birthday? I'm giving you a Mont Blanc pen to remind you that you must keep writing.

My wish for you is that someday you know the joy of love given and love freely received. If not with Max, then with someone else, someday. You could make a guy feel like a king, and you have a right to be treated as his queen. Jena

*****

Okay, Leah Rebecca, listen to Jena. Read a book and take a bath. Pull yourself back into the relentless current and pray you don't drown yourself on purpose.

September 17, 1977

Serious clinical depression has broken through the steel door where I attempted to stand guard. But depression has no respect for guards. Depression would laugh in the sadistic face of a Gestapo guard or Hitler himself, for that matter.

If I could take half of my emotion and flush it into the world's sewer system, I would. No hesitation. I'd just do it. Because this degree of emotion is an albatross of incomparable weight. I'm forever about to burst from excess.

Part of Max as a life choice was my belief he would soothe me with his easy style and patient pace. He doesn't soothe me. More and more, the reasons why I chose Max as life-mate dim into extinction.

All the self-soothing tricks I've used over the decades on my aching psyche aren't working anymore. I can't hide from myself as effectively. I can't pretend. I'm wounded and I know it. Max can't help me, and he knows it.

September 18, 1977

I've stopped dancing. I'm white-faced and red-eyed from crying. Why do I lie awake unable to sleep? Why is my face pushed into a pillow to muffle my screams? I don't even know where to look for me.

Overwhelming! Totally devastating! I ask of G-D, "Will I mend?" "In time," he says, so quietly I almost miss it.

September 24, 1977

Max left early today. Annapolis? Virginia Beach? New York? Pennsylvania? I don't know. He didn't say. He's freaky these days. He envies me. He hates my successes in friendships, most recently with Jena and Richard.

Even when I'm well, I can't be who he wants me to be: Less verbally alluring. Less easy with people. More reticent and withdrawn. I'm afraid to be myself with Max because he doesn't seem to like the Leah that I like best. He's afraid of that woman. I'm too much, too emotional, just too. He's afraid. He has his own issues from a difficult past.

It isn't that I don't know my weaknesses. I know the ways in which I hurt him … through my own insecurities, emotionalism, abandonment issues, depressions, and the insanity that surrounds depression. Of course, I know.

But one thing is certain. He's most at ease with me when I'm weak and vulnerable. Oh, he's attracted to my strengths, no doubt about it. He often tells me he admires my courage, resolve, and ability to get things done swiftly and efficiently. Mostly, he says, he's captivated by my capacity for love, my mind, my sensuality. (*Yeah, right. The sensuality that seemingly repels him.*)

I can't win. When I'm sick and depressed, he's put-off by me. When I'm strong and determined, he's uneasy with me. This relentless rotation has worn me down as flat as unleavened bread, and I've stopped trying so hard. He resents my retreat.

Jena's mad about not getting a chance to vocalize her opinions. And about his controlling the group through his silence, and by his not fessing up about how he started to feel when he started to feel it.

I don't want to leave here, but I know Max does. Chances are excellent that we will. Right now, I smell so pretty from a bath. I'm wrapped in beige cotton and lace. I'm feeling renewed sexuality. Five hours out of his sad and dampening company and I begin to stir, to feel the first rush of me, my favorite me.

It was sheer stupidity to ignore what I knew before we married. Why did I neglect basic me ... the lover, the eternal and hopeless lover of beauty, grace, sexuality, sensuality, relating from my gut, talk that lasts for hours?

I'm a fool.

I'm afraid.

I'm kitten weak.

Strength is a memory.

I don't allow myself the beauty of relating through my senses anymore.

I've slammed the door on animal me.

I'm tired of writing.

I'm tired of everything.

September 30, 1977

Depressive symptoms are now in full blast. The smallest tasks seem monumental: balancing the checkbook, looking up a phone number, filling in a job app, even washing my hair or walking downstairs for a cup of tea. I'm waaaay too familiar with the inca-pacitation that accompanies this "thing." This "thing" that feels like a curse from a powerful brainwashing, mind-twisting expert. This master sends the person who usually inhabits my body far, far away and replaces her with a slimy, worthless, pathetic drain of a schnook. Nobody likes her. I despise her.

October 29, 1977

A minor miracle! I felt well enough to venture out today. Not far, but it is a baby step toward something that feels "normal." On this most gorgeous leaf-dazzling afternoon, I took a moment of reprieve to breathe in autumn's air. I spent time under an umbrella of a tree, embraced by the sun and surrounded by crinkled brown leaves, a thermos of hot tea beside me and my neat, truly neat new burgundy penny loafers.

I've reverted to the safest decade I can remember, the 1950s: Bobby Rydell, Paul Anka, Tab Hunter, the Mouseketeers, Dick Clark's Bandstand, bunny hops, poodle skirts, circle pins, and ice cream sodas. That was the decade when my worst problem in all the world was, "Will he? I don't know. But I hope, I hope, I hope Chucky Hammerick invites me to the Friday Night Dance!" Ah, for the simplicity of the fifties.

I know Max is within a shake of getting that job in Philly, and I will likely be able to find a position at one of the rehab centers or children's hospitals in the city. But my minds screams, "Noooo! I don't want to go. Don't go. Don't go."

November 7, 1977

We leave tomorrow. Max got the job he wanted with a group of internists who are in a suburb on the periphery of Philly. He starts in three weeks.

Everything is cloaked in mud and dust. I can't think. We'll be staying with Mom and Dad until we find a place. Nothing more to say. Nothing to say. Nothing.

December 12, 1977

We found a place in Narberth, a suburb of Philly, a sweet little rental in a nice little neighborhood … two floors, two bedrooms, one bath, and a yard with honeysuckle and azalea bushes that will be glorious in spring.

This week has been pure madness. It's the week we move into our house rental, and we're accumulating all the stuff we stored before "The Trip."

Since leaving Jena and Richard's, Max and I haven't spoken about anything, except things of minimal importance. He smells depression all over me, and I know it's nauseating to look at, much less be married to.

We deposited our most vital documents in the fireproof area at Dad's plant. After all our furniture and stuff was unloaded into our rental home, we went to Dad's plant for the vital docs. It was 10:00 P.M. We were both beat, but Max was anxious and full of nervous energy from having weathered his first week of work. I wanted to accommodate him.

It started to pour after both of our cars were loaded. He said he'd drive ahead of me and I should keep up. I always try to keep up because I'm not good on back roads and if I lost him, I'd be lost. So naturally, I lost him on a stereotypical rural Pennsylvania road … it rocks, it rolls, it curves, it meanders.

The windshield wipers in this 1965 relic of a Volvo needed changing, so the windows fogged like a steam bath, and I felt aggravated by Max's obsession with old Volvos and seethed that he didn't keep his eye on me in his rearview mirror.

I became more aggravated when the accelerator stuck to the floor and my careful fifty-mile-per-hour speed crept to seventy-five miles per hour. I approached a steep hill and roller-coaster rode it at ninety. The red needle disappeared off the gauge after one hundred miles per hour.

Oh, and the brakes quit at the same time the accelerator stuck, and the steering mechanism failed too. I felt a rush of sweat encase me, and I experienced the pre-death adage. I really did see episodic flashes of my life and I formed the thought, "This is how I'm going to die."

I went up an embankment, and the car rolled back down turning itself over and over, three, maybe four times. It skidded across the road on its roof and came to a halt … an indescribable sensation. But no panic and no tears. I just crawled out the driver's side where the window used to be. The car was barely recognizable as a vehicle. I briefly thought I might be dead.

But I could stand and move all my parts, and I spoke aloud to see if I had a voice. I watched our vital documents kite-fly with wind gusts and rise into the rainy night. This upset me enormously. Eventually, a trucker came by and called an ambulance on his CB.

I was taken to a hospital. Max arrived. I was petrified he was going to be furious about his beloved Volvo and our lost records. He wasn't. He looked whiter than Casper. I endured hours of x-rays because they thought I might have sustained some nasty cervical damage and possibly would be permanently paralyzed in about eight hours. But at 7:00 A.M. they let us go. And all I had to show for this near-fatal mishap was a three-inch rip in my jeans, a brush-burned knee, some bruises, and a sore neck.

A recurring thought now lives in me since the accident of over two weeks ago. It was not an "accident" that I survived. There really is such a thing as an appointed time to pass out of this life. I wouldn't tell anyone but you this, Deborah, but I keep hearing these lines going around in my head like a record needle stuck in a groove: *"You have work to do. Hang in. Hang on. You have My work to do."*

How I do wish you were truly real and could answer me back, Deborah. Because I would ask, "What do you think of that? Am I really and truly loony-bin material, or is someone trying to tell me something? I don't think G-D communicates with us like that. Does He? She? It? All?"

Anyway, what kind of work can a sniveling, driveling waste-case handle? But somehow, life is just ever so slightly more precious to me now because there is no logical reason I escaped death or serious injury from that Volvo wreck. I knew it had nothing to do with luck. There was supernatural involvement. A guardian angel? A protective shield? G-D Himself taking time out from His busy schedule to assure my safety? I dunno. But I am devoutly convinced Lady Luck had nuttin' to do with it.

If you're listening, G-D, I say, most humbly, "Thank you." And if it is You who planted the broken-record message about my future, then I plead … fix me! Because I can barely make toast, much less handle Your work or anyone else's.

I know You know all of this. Yup, I'm sure of it.

*****

About two months later this depressive period began to wane. A veteran depressive intuits these things. Dark clouds lighten, thinking is actually possible, physical movement is a beat faster. A spirit of hope slowly returns.

It was best we did leave Jena and Richard's. Max was right. We needed to move on with what was left of our marriage and see if there was any hope for revival. Plus, I

really needed to study for the boards for a renewal license to practice speech pathology in Pennsylvania.

I was ready for something new in my life; I needed something new in my life. I could not have known what this "new" thing would be. If I had known, I would have moved to Siberia.

*****

1978

I've met a man named Robert England. He is an adventurer, a Robert-son Caruso, a daredevil barely contained. He is a total experience, a non-duplicable Superman. He looks like a British aristocrat and rugged outdoorsman squished together … only Robert is more refined.

He is blond, tall, rugged, patrician. He teaches at The University of Pennsylvania, consults, lectures internationally on aerodynamics, restores Mercedes, designs furniture, loves his wife.

I can't seem to make myself walk away, even though I know I'm a temporary explosion in his life. I make him feel emotional, loving, and passionate. I make him feel like a total man and not just like a producing machine.

March 3, 1978

Robert begins to complicate my life as well as add to it. It's no longer easy to separate from him. It stings, and the only place the sting can lead to is *pain*.

I told Robert today if Max and I were to leave each other, I wouldn't be able to see him anymore. I couldn't bear him leaving me to go back to his other life. I couldn't bear one-hour meetings and lunchtime love. He agreed.

He also said he'd step back anytime to avoid hurting me. He said the only way he can deal with his own guilt is to know he has promised me nothing. He said if it ended, he'd throw himself more ferociously into his work. He'd be pissed. He'd be hurt. He'd get over it.

He spoke of the image I initially tried to portray of myself of being independent, strong, free. Now, he sees the holes in that portrait, although he sees me as far more sensitive and dimensional than he had assumed. Hell, he ain't seen nothin'. Not: hyper-un-worthiness, hyper-emotionalism, hyper-love-needs. Not me: depressed, withdrawn, angry, sullen, directionless, lazy.

Now, when Max is distant and withdrawn, or when he punishes me with silence, I do not feel guilty about my Mr. Wonderful. Because this brilliant, blonde Adonis has put a burn back into my thinking and revitalized my energy and drive for creation.

I love him. Oh G-D, I'm really starting to love him.

March 10, 1978

I stink at having an affair.

If only Robert were an ordinary guy. A guy I just dig seeing once a week. A guy I dig for sex but not for making love. A guy I like to talk to but am not mesmerized by. A guy who likes me but doesn't know me so thoroughly. A guy I could distance myself from and not miss, crave, yearn for and even love. Oh no!

Robert would leave me if he knew all this. He's already begun to control me in the only way he can … by spending less time with me. He can't make me love him less.

Marriage and sex counseling with Max has become unbearable. My own shrink knows about Robert, but our joint shrink doesn't. What a joke! And my own Dr. Stuart suggests I should mentally and emotionally compartmentalize my life. Realize I can't get it all from Max, and if I stop seeing Robert, or confess to Max, it would be "sealing my own doom." I'd end up bitter, frustrated, and enraged. My relationship with Max would deteriorate.

So, the doctor suggests, "Take what you need from Robert. Then walk away from him, back to your husband, your job, and your responsibilities." I will likely take his advice, although it is the shoddiest, sleaziest, and altogether most ruthless and immoral piece of advice I've ever been given.

I'm just selfishly terrified of going back to my life as a nun.

March 22, 1978

Robert rented a furnished hide-a-nest for us … a love nest. It's wonderful … a space in Philly overlooking the Delaware River. A top-floor apartment with angles, arches, points, and projections. Recessed lighting and a stone fireplace. A dining niche with a Sheraton dining set. An old oak roll-top desk with marquetry inlay, tiny vertical slots for filing, and little wood-dot pulls used as drawer handles.

In the bath there's a peach tub with aqua trim; the outer tub is covered in mosaic cut tiles.

Wall art is created from the broken shreds, shards, and slivers of seashells. Best of all, I love the bleached oak ceiling fan suspended from the highest arch in the highest peak in the prettiest bedroom. He hung it there for me, knowing I would love to see it as I lay on my back on a white eyelet quilt as his swimmer's body undulates with mine. This place gives me breath. It gives me fire.

(I was genetically predisposed to design. When I was twelve and Mom was in her early forties, we took an aptitude test for design. She scored in the 99th percentile and I was in the 98th. Aptitude is aptitude no matter one's age. So, why do I have a Masters in speech path and special ed., when even as an adolescent it was obvious I belonged in the arts? Answer: No

guidance. No self-awareness. And the ever-present parental dictate that I major in something that would earn me a living.

A lot of my friends ask me to help design their homes, and it is always my pleasure, especially since the work is play for me. But I digress.)

Dr. Robert England, I'm so comfortable with him. Even my self-conscious parts don't seem unsightly. He sees so deeply into me; I can't get stuck on one body part while he's seeing straight through to my center.

When I sit on his lap, I feel petite but gigantic, because I know for brief moments, I have from him as much love as he has ever felt or shared. I give him all that I am because he not only can handle it, he adores it!

We met when I was hunting through the stacks at University of Pennsylvania's library, researching the latest goods on autism. He was writing a paper on aerodynamics that he's presenting in Brussels in the spring. We chatted, and after our fourth planned meeting at the library, we went out for a drink. I felt myself falling into him. He laughed when I was funny. He parried when I made a point he found weak. He appreciated my passion for sick kids and couldn't understand why I repel Max. That's because he's never lived with the mentally insane and cannot imagine that the person he finds so enchanting could be the anguished depressive I describe.

The first time he took my mouth into his I weakened to the point of nausea. Could barely breathe. Had to push him away. Had to cry. Had to leave. The next time I devoured him like a panther who had gone without food for a month. But it was only me, a woman in her twenties who had gone without sex for almost four years.

*****

(Letter from Wendy)

March 24, 1978

Hi-Ho Leah,

Greetings from your vagabond friend, Captain Wendy Shapiro, just home from a three-week sail in the Greek Isles.

So sorry we didn't connect when you got back from your year-long trip. Before our sail, I had been in Albany working on some radical legislation for feminist and gay rights that you might find excessive.

It has always interested me that you are so protective of a gender that's responsible for most of the world's ills and your own misery. I guess I may never really "get" you.

I've read the fifteen-page letter that awaited Kate and me when we entered our pad that was house-sat by a kid from NYU who all but trashed the place.

I will try to respond to some assertions you made in your letter. You and Max have never made any sense to me. He has the emotional range of a tadpole and you're an emotional hurricane. He's an intellect and you're a smart, savvy, sexy, hopeless romantic. He's sexually repressed and you're a hot tamale.

But does his revulsion surprise me? *Hell no.* You are unbearable when you're depressed. Really just about too much for anyone to handle, and your pain is dreadful to look at for anyone who genuinely cares about you. Anyway, what can you really offer him, Leah? Max never knows when a depression will descend. You arouse his mind and spirit, and then you disappear indefinitely into the ugly zone. I don't understand why he doesn't just cut his losses and run.

And by the way, Leah, did you truly not know how hard it was for me to live in that dorm room with you for three years? Did you not know the effect you had on me, or were you just a heartless tease? I never really could find a bottom-line answer for that one.

And now we have this U. of P. professor in aerodynamics. Having a really busy little life, aren't we, Cupcake? I hope he doesn't twist your heart into a pretzel, but he will and you'll let him.

So, I give you fair warning, be careful out there, Leah Rebecca. It's a jungle.

Love, Wendy

March 30, 1978

Deborah ... *Do you believe her?*

Real nice response, Wendy. Real nice.

I could throttle her. Damn her. I didn't know she "wanted me" when we shared a dorm room. I really didn't know. Was I zoned out or what? How could I not have known? But why should I have known? I never caught her mooning over me or staring. She never touched me suggestively. We played like sisters. We shared like best friends. And besides, she had a girlfriend!

I'll give it a rest until I cool down, and then Ms. Shapiro, Esquire, will be hearing from me. Oh, Wendy, please don't do this. Don't ruin a twelve-year friendship. Don't abandon me. Give me another chance.

May 14, 1978

I don't feel so hot. Really, G-D, this is not funny. A gray funnel-cloud moves toward me knowing I'm the target.

May 15, 1978

I haven't written for six weeks. Now I have a story worth reporting.

There he was, Robert England, at the Atlantic City bus station, all adorableness and happy to see me. Tight at first, scared I wouldn't be on the bus.

We drove to Brigantine. I felt round, sensuous … not like a chubette, as I had all week. We walked to the beach. The most gorgeous hour of the long-short night. On a sheet. In the dusk. Fully clothed. Rocking and cooing and telling each other how much, "I love you."

Robert is exquisite in the great outdoors. His unabashedly blond maleness complements dune shapes and rock formations, and his skin is so like the color of sand. I adore his face. Simply and totally adore his face. G-D, I was happy.

We drove his van to a secluded strip of beach where he held me, took me, loved me. I always melt from the way he watches my face. And in my mind, whenever I like, which is often, I can pull up from memory his face in strained ecstasy, as he never takes his eyes from mine.

We drove to a pier and walked out over the ocean. White caps in the dark, with the roar and the sea-salt smells, the black vastness, the rage, the power.

The hours became gentler as we unwound. The boundaries, always there when we first meet … broke. We went to a club to listen to jazz and shared a pastrami on rye, onion rings, and a pitcher of root beer. I talked about my job and "my" kids. He talked about his job and "his" kids. His: the future scientists of the world. Mine: the future residents of institutions.

(*I haven't written much about my new position at Children's Hospital of Philadelphia. I'm nearing the beginning of my third month in the speech path department, working with autistic kids. I like it but can see where this could be a burn-out endeavor.*)

In the jazz club, I told Robert about Tracey, one of my kids at the hospital. She's being moved to a residential facility for severely impaired autistic kids. After next Friday, I will likely never see her again. She has never spoken, but consistently allows me to hold her on my lap as we sway and I hum show tunes to her. We have obtained eye contact maybe five times, but I know she loves and trusts me and will miss me, or miss something, and not even know it *is* me.

We crawled back into his van and made more love-saturated love. He called his wife. I did not call my husband. We started the drive back to Pennsylvania at 1:00 A.M., stopping in joints along the way. We watched disco dancers in scanty little unbecoming clothes, pool hustlers hustling, and beer drinkers guzzling. We dropped coins in jukeboxes and did the twist and the jitterbug, and when the slow tunes played, he held me to himself like a sailor about to deploy for a year.

We drove a bit more and then stopped to sleep. It came easily, wrapped in his warm body and smelly sleeping bag.

Up again. More driving. He dropped me at my car. I hated to leave him, to go back to my life of empty air and seething silence.

May 16, 1978

Want to hear a real joke? Today I was laid off, with twenty-six other employees, from The Children's Hospital of Philadelphia (CHOP) ... ya know, the place where I'm chair of the speech pathology department. My boss saw to it, as I knew she would. Guilt grabbed her though, and she arranged for me to interview for the position of director of public relations at a private psychiatric hospital on the Main Line outside of Philly.

A *psychiatric* hospital? Now that's rich. But the chief administrator, an Israeli, liked the way I handled myself and I got the job. Still, I'm a pathetic PR director. I can write, but I can't sling crap and that's the chief job requirement of a public relations gal. The bigger joke is I'm crazier than two-thirds of the patients … maybe even three-quarters. I'm thirty and as lost as a swaddled baby left in a wooded glen.

May 17, 1978

It's Sunday. A day to breathe. Phone off the hook lest the outside world rob me of the solitude I need to glue myself back together enough to go to work tomorrow.

This sweet little rental house in this perfectly peaceful, graceful little neighborhood is my only salve. I stay in bed as much as I can. Horizontal is good. It demands so little. Now I will force myself to think of lovely things. Ready! Get set! Go!

Leaves of autumn. Streams of spring. Perfume of clover. Bark of oaks. Wind breezes lifting hot orange-red leaves off park benches and swirling them around like dancing fairies. Mother-of-pearl glaze on rocks submerged under the surface of a slow-riding creek.

Are there answers to these mysteries? If there are, I can't crack concrete and see into their illusive meaning. No, I stand as a reticent girl\woman, wondering why it is my friends, family, and colleagues lead safe and meaningful lives, while mine is one of quietly torturous despair. My fear is that my despair will become so visible that I'll be sent away permanently to dwell with the truly deranged.

May 19, 1978

I'm so confused. My thoughts are slow. My speech is slow. I'm withdrawn. I have no energy. Music unnerves me. I want my Mom but no one else. I sleep fitfully. Even food doesn't draw me with its tantalizingly compulsive lure.

Rachael and Sarah have moved back to Philly from Chicago, and I'm glad my cousins are here and plan to stay, but I can't reach out to them. I feel like a giant embarrassment ... a drain, a drag, a dark and ugly canker sore that sucks in air she doesn't deserve to breathe and takes up space she doesn't deserve to claim.

And then there's that literal cloud that descends and colors my world a dingy, smoggy, stale, pasty color of coffin gray. It's the worst. It lets me know the depression is in full swing, and only when it starts to fade by slow-motion degrees do I suspect I may make it through yet another round of crippling mental illness. *Mental illness.* Such a polite term for something as dehumanizing and disfiguring as leprosy.

You hear all this, right, G-D? Sure, You do.

May 28, 1978

Mind mechanisms. Mind machinations. Mind nightmares while wide awake. And the age-old recurring nightmare always just a subconscious dream away. The screaming children, vultures, and wolves all emanate inside my cranium as I run wild through a forest maze.

My mind is so very sick. I'm alive and aware, but just barely. The psycho brain is now in full control.

June 4, 1978

I don't know what to do. I can't generate a thought that inspires joy or comfort. I don't want it to be a weekend, and I don't want it not to be. I don't want it to rain, but the sun doesn't soothe me. Some depressions are so dense I cannot see through their sea swamp. This is one of those.

I want to find my gone-from-my-life husband and hold his face an inch from mine and ask, "Max, do *you* remember when I was fun? When I laughed with childish ease and talked of grown-up things? When my smile wasn't forced and I moved with unaffected grace? Remember? When I wore my clothes with flair and walked the confidant walk of a woman in charge? Remember when I spoke of the limitless possibilities between you and me? Remember? I hardly do." I feel loathsome and ugly.

Animal ... Primeval ... Before what we knew ... Base ... Sacrificial ... Poison ... Black tunnels ... Convolutions and cerebral misfiring between synapses.

I want to be dead more than I want to be well, because dead means I won't have to face this again.

I ask you, G-D, what is there left to try after internists, psychiatrists, psychologists, endocrinologists, nutritionists, holistic physicians, medications, vitamins, jogging, diuretics, hair analysis, and fasting? Now I know exactly what I need: *The End.* I wish all life functions to cease.

Dr. Sandburg wants to put me in an institution; he is an aspirin when morphine is required. I don't want to be a prisoner behind caged doors. I can't give myself away. I can't do that to my parents. I can't lose this job. But ... I can't function. I can't stop the hideous flood of sick, molten anguish that seeps from my skin and tear ducts and any orifice it can find. My air is filled with personal stench. I can't stop wanting to stop it all ... all that is me, this ludicrous, undersized, volcanic eruption that is me.

G-D of the Universe, do you know I think of myself as a "mistake"? **Maybe some of us are sacrifices ... examples to healthy people of how to waste a life.** Anyone who looks at me would beg for my advice on how to avoid becoming like me.

How I do wish this were sloppy melodrama … merely a poorly written script I could walk away from. It's all so sad. I pull Mom and Dad toward me out of need and push them away because of a gnawing sense of self-disgust that rejects their care. I don't deserve love.

June 9, 1978

Here's another true story for your entertainment, journal of my secret life. It has a comic tone, but it wasn't all that funny. Really, it wasn't. I got so sick, scared, and panicked at Berwyn's Psychiatric Hospital yesterday that I pulled and pushed everything out of my credenza, crawled in, slid the door closed, and started screaming.

I don't know how long it took for them to locate me. From the scorched sensation on my vocal cords today, I'd guess it took a while. They let the Director, Mr. Head-Honcho-Israeli, slide the door open and confront me. He pulled me out of the credenza, cradled me for a minute, and then lifted me into my desk chair. He offered me two options: He would either drive me to my parents' home or admit me to the psychiatric hospital where I have the job title of PR director. I let him drive me to my parents' home.

Mom and Dad convinced Dr. Sandburg to allow me to stay with them rather than go you-know-where (the institution). He's going to double my meds over the next two weeks and said I must seriously consider a round of shock treatments.

I guess I'm having a breakdown.

June 13, 1978

FREAKED … BROKEN … CRAZED …
Nothing makes the pain stop. I try to sleep the day away but can't. I try to hide in television noise, but my eyes won't focus.

Mom and Dad allowed me to bring my feline boys to their home. G-D bless these people. So, Oscar, Bentley, and I stay in the guest suite on the third floor. My bed has four walnut spiral posts, and from the circular window in the deepest eave, I can see the first signs of summer flora and the crest of the hill that falls into the pool. This is the only stimulus I can handle because I want as few reminders as possible that the world keeps revolving, and people are having fun.

My spirit is so depleted, and a type of fear I've never known has grabbed me hard. When Mom comes up, I cling to her like a terrorized child, and when she leaves to market or conduct some business, Addie must come up and stay with me. I lay my head against her chocolate pudding skin while she strokes my hair and hums the tunes from her native Jamaica, which she has been humming since I was three years old. I wish I could anesthetize my brain ... coma deep.

June 16, 1978

I have always felt if I did not write about the pain, and therefore expunge some of it from me, the accumulation would take up so much space that one day I would explode ... firecracker loud and sparkly.

So here are today's outer-scribblings from inner-space: It hurts like knives driving into flesh. It hurts like war and injustice and bigotry. How I long to be "normal."

To have: Internal harmony. A sense of balance. An ability to handle life on its own terms.

To have: Friendship. Love. A relationship. A child. Work I enjoy. Travel. Art. Dance.

To have: Music. A garden. Some land. Fresh flowers. A window near the kitchen sink.

To be: Free. Unshackled. An amoeba. A lily pond. A piece of snow.

June 20, 1978

Times I've cried today: Eight

Meals eaten: None

Phone calls: I can't even mouth "Hello."

I nearly drowned in a tidal wave of tears today. The fear and paralyzing sadness now seem to emanate from a different inner spot. In this lovely third-floor bedroom suite, I feel permanently and indelibly alone. Though the phone keeps ringing, people who love me calling to say so and offering help; it doesn't help.

If only there was movement, even subtle movement, so that with time spread out in its illusive way, I might say, "I'm moving and it's good. I'm not hiding. I'm still afraid, but less so."

If only I could say, "I so dearly adore life. It is challenging and evocative, and I am up to the challenge because each of my days is charged with my own unique spirit."

Instead …

I hurt people I love because of depression. I pull people into my death-dance spiral unintentionally. I want so much to add to people's lives, to bring them joy and a finer sense of themselves. I want to make them laugh. I want to help them see the beauty in themselves. I want to give physical pleasure. I want to be the Leah that I am in between depressions … enigmatic, entertaining, and often brimming over with life.

When depression descends, Leah Rebecca transforms from:

Petite, Sharp, and Foxy

into

Short, Dim, and Frumpy.

I want to experience timelessness and feel my existence as it stands separate from, while united with, all else. I want to be so sensitized that I feel my organs in their relative positions in my body and hear my blood sliding through channels and inner spaces. I want to feel the power, potency, and wonder of my brain … its capabilities and eccentricities, its neurological integrity, and its developed sense of sensitivity. I want to know I am everything, and at the same time, I am a molecule in eternity, a blink, a speck of lint, a flash of light, and even less. I want. I want. I want to be normal.

July 15, 1978

It's now two months since I wrote a journal entry. Max and I grow micro-meters closer to each other these days. It's easier to be patient with him now that I am no longer celibate.

He has wanted a cat, so yesterday he brought home a six-month-old chocolate point Siamese whom we've named Oscar. Today, he brought home a two-year-old seal point Siamese from the SPCA. They were about to put this feline to sleep because he's deadly ill. But my husband, the pet world's savior, arrived in the nick of time. I wanted to call him Meyer, but Max slammed the door on that. He will not have his "sons" mocked in an Oscar-&-Meyer hotdog way. We've named him Bentley.

Max begins to consider a private practice. He needs one. He deserves one. I'm all for it.

July 23, 1978

Let me paint a plan: I will take all of my abundant, rich, honest emotion and put it into a small, ancient, beautifully hand-painted box. I will put the box on a conspicuous shelf and will not touch it until I am well. I will now elevate myself out of my emotions, into the world of my cerebral strength.

Would that I could! Dear G-d, I wish that I could!

July 28, 1978

We've done some weekend traveling and have attempted all the sexual intimacy exercises our therapist has recommended. Like, now we can touch each other's face and shoulders for five minutes. No longer. No less. That's the exercise.

Wasn't there a time when Max and I were hot together? Fun to be with? Downright provocative? I remember when I thought we looked like siblings and I imagined we'd have a home bustling with children, neighbors, and friends. We would influence senators and rally activists and have lives that made a difference.

At our self-written garden wedding, among ancient oaks and weeping willows, although I was besotted with doubts ... when we declared our love with eloquence and emotion, I wanted so badly to believe in us.

I see Robert less. Some of me misses him. Some of me wishes we'd never met.

August 1, 1978

Tomorrow I will be thirty-one years old. We're having dinner with Mom, Dad, Ruthie, and Jonathan. Perhaps because I *am* turning thirty-one, I've been thinking about children a lot. How can I even contemplate a childless life? But will our marriage last? And do I want to chance subjecting a child to a splintered life? And how can we make a baby when we don't even make love? And how can

I expect to care for a child, when much of my interior life is spent trying to stamp out thoughts of suicide?

So often, I feel so crazy. Quite literally, only G-D knows what keeps me from breaking into human fragments, like Humpty Dumpty. But I wouldn't even need to fall off a wall; I'd only need to let go and swallow the whole bottle of antidepressants that don't work anyway.

August 2, 1978

It's me, thirty-one years old on my Birthday, and floundering like a dying fish on the banks of some decaying stream.

I search for my "Jerusalem," for that fantasized spot within me that is "home." I make myself old with anxiety. I frazzle the very organs that keep me alive with so much self-imposed torment. I'm ashamed of who I am.

You know what I would love? To fill these pages with thoughts unconnected to me. To write of the world and its complexities. To offer thoughts and impressions of people and how they work. To see beyond me and use my fertile mind to create strings of words that are useful to other people. Is it an unfulfilled purpose? Or simply the naive wish of a girl exposed to far too many fairy tales?

But ... I choose to believe, G-D, You do not wish this to be my life, and somehow, someway, someday, You will bring me to health, stability, and purpose. You've created everything; You know everything, so I know You can fix me. I believe You *must* want to see me dance in a meadow, sing into the wind, and give love as I so yearn to do. I must believe You will do this for me. Help me to believe it, G-D, and I shall.

September 6, 1978

How I wish Max and I meshed like the lace in doilies. I do so love his tenderness and intensity, his intellect and subtlety, his humor and style, his daring and drive. If only we had met ten years from now. If only there were no if-onlys. G-D help us. I force myself to try to imagine life without him. It's impossible.

September 15, 1978

MY PERIOD'S LATE!
A WEEK LATE!
OH NO, G-D. NO. NOT POSSIBLY. NO.

October 8, 1978

I cannot imagine ever having to write three sadder words: I am pregnant. I found out two days ago. AMAZING! I think I can't slip any lower in my life and then I surprise myself and do. I'm scared. I'm devastated. I can't even pull up the words to shape the feelings, so I will only describe the details.

I called an abortion clinic. They will perform abortions fifty-six days after the first day of a last period, not sooner. So, they recommended a different procedure. Menstrual extraction, which is not fool-proof and very painful. Unfortunately, there are times when the procedure has to be repeated. I freaked out.

I called my gynecologist. She said to call St. Vincent's Hospital. They informed me I will need written consent from my husband. Yeah sure, that'll work.

I called my therapist. He said he'd check around discretely to see if it can be done in New York without consent. My panic escalates.

I couldn't reach Robert. Tears, a flood. So much revulsion and fear. Finally, I located a women's center that will not require spousal consent but will require the fifty-six day wait.

O.K. G-D, I give up. How am I going to live with Max for the next two months while pregnant with another man's child, hide morning sickness, lethargy, fear … and go t work and act perfectly normal? I guess the fact that I'm never perfectly normal will be of some value here.

When I finally reached Robert, he was Robert-like … cool, interested, offered to pay, and offered to go with me. Sure, he can pay. No, he cannot go with me. I have no desire to see him. He's not terribly inconvenienced by this, is he? Our baby doesn't grow inside of him. Business as usual for him and his wife.

I cannot believe my life. Why aren't I about to attend my own funeral instead of my baby's? Why was I even born? My whole experience of forever has been so desperate and sad. I wish I were a drunk so I could numb myself out. Obliterate my liver. Get this whole damned lifetime over with.

I can barely look at Max. Some minutes I love him, fear losing him, and know I don't deserve him. The next minute I could strangle him for never touching, enveloping, desiring, or even confiding in me. I feel I was silently pushed into this affair. I am not ninety-five years old with a withered libido. Damn it! I am a woman, a woman, a woman!

October 11, 1978

Time is long and treacherous. I procrastinate about writing because I don't want to have to decipher, decode, and deliberate. Feelings happen. Writing would require I relive the feelings all over again.

The abortion is scheduled for October twenty-eighth, a Friday, so I will have the weekend to recuperate. The wait is eternal. I despise this growing thing inside of me. I dare not love it.

October 17, 1978

Wow, sure has been an interesting couple of weeks:

- I find out I'm pregnant.
- Max's cathartic revelation. (*The outcome of which includes the epiphany that he married me for neurotic reasons and may not want to live with me anymore. He laid that one on me last night, a conclusion reached with his psychiatrist.*)
- My boss's declaration that I'm in the wrong field and her strong suggestion I resign.

"You're a liberal-poet-artist-free-spirit. What are you doing in a children's hospital? You're just too unconventional. If the state knew some of the things you do with these autistic kids, we'd probably lose our license."

She is being **ludicrous!** I'm inventive, loving, and affectionate. What' so flippin' perverse about that?

Yo, G-D, you have got to be kidding!

October 26, 1978

The abortion is two days away. In a sense, I'm less anxious the nearer it gets. I've made it through eight weeks, and soon it will all be over. I cannot crack. I cannot break. I must handle this.

I saw Robert yesterday. He gave me $140 of the $160 abortion fee. I didn't even ask why. He was very tender, romantic even. I observed it but did not experience it. I have slipped into chilled numbness.

Things I remember he said: "I wish we didn't have to kill it. It would've been such a cool kid. I'm worried about how you'll respond emotionally and if there'll be any medical complications. Now, Leah, don't spend this money on anything else." Insensitive bastard.

I'm not really scared of the pain. I've learned how to ride pain, transcend it. Physical pain is a calm breeze compared to mental lunacy.

November 5, 1978

The torrential flood of emotion now escapes through crevices of unprotected territory. I can't stop crying. This is the first time I've let myself respond since that terrifying Friday, the twenty-eighth.

I didn't suspect there would be an aftermath, other than relief. But instead, I feel betrayed by my diaphragm, his condom, and this painful IUD. I hate everything I know or have ever known: my husband, my lover, my family, my values, my religion, my ninth-grade algebra teacher, my job, and my field.

I feel ruined, filthy, old, used up, ugly, unsavory, unwholesome, and worthless, worthless, worthless.

G-D, what is it that You want from me? I must be a mistake. I feel like the only reason I was born is to experience torture and shame. I feel people pitying me. The circles under my eyes are so dark and deep, children could use them for hide and seek.

I'm so alone. Robert hasn't called. In fact, he hasn't called once since the day he found out about the baby. Not once. I guess he figures $140 about covers his responsibility.

The weekend after the abortion was so strange. I walked around in an envelope of fog. Max and I went to Harrison Park on Saturday. We sat on a blanket overlooking a bluff ... ate brie and drank a superior Chablis.

I experienced the oddest sensation that day. I felt as though we were on a date, and I wanted so badly for him to like me. Once I blushed. Twice I giggled. I wonder if he noticed.

- I wait like Damocles for the sword to fall.
- Will he fall in love with me or won't he?
- Will he stay with me or won't he?
- Will he decide I'm good for him or will he decide I'm not?
- What a trap. What a prison.
- I loathe rationalizing his kindness for love.
- I loathe feeling apologetic about my very existence.
- I loathe not being desired.
- I loathe myself for staying and allowing him to decide my fate.

How could this have happened to me? The little love-goddess begging to be loved. All my dreams … so far away. All my plans … a memory.

Dropping back to Friday and the abortion: I was out of the house by 6:00 A.M. Wendy came down from New York to be with me and we met at the clinic. Thank You for her, G-D. Thank you that we made-up after her last castigating letter.

Long wait in line to register. Long waits all day. Standing room only. A cross-section of people. Teens through early forties.

I remember … a teenager with braces and both her parents looking worn and worried. Half the women had their men with them. A few women had no one at all. There were very few minority women.

Wendy lost money in the candy machine and approached the woman at the desk. She had long oily bleached hair with long black roots, gold front teeth, dagger-long-chipped red nails, and her name tag read *Delores*.

She said to Wendy while smacking her gum, "Well, your money isn't *our* problem, is it, Deary? There's a 7-Eleven around the corner."

After a two-hour wait, I asked Delores how long she thought it would be. "I don't know," she said. "The doctor's been detained." I thanked her while inside I shouted, "Why the hell don't you announce that fact to all these overwrought women? Why? Why are you so insensitive and devoid of compassion?"

Many women who arrived after me were taken before me. (*I found out later they were back for their three-week check-up.*) We had to fill out an overly detailed questionnaire. I felt the answers were none of their business and left them blank.

A little after noon, Jane called me into her office. She was an attractive woman in her mid-twenties with shoulder-length ginger-colored hair. She wore a tailored khaki suit; she was competent and marginally pleasant. She took the money and asked if I had any questions. I said, "No, but I have a few suggestions: Announce if a doctor has been detained. Explain why some women are taken before others who have been waiting longer. Give a hand-out on what to expect in terms of the wait, the process, the steps. Get a new receptionist."

More waiting. A blood test. More waiting. A group meeting consisting of me, five other terrified mothers, and Jane. Finally, an explanation of the procedure, step by hideous step. We were told to anticipate pain during dilation of the cervix and while the vacuum was pulling. No anesthesia. Lastly, a detailed discussion about birth control.

I guess a chastity belt would be my best bet since contraceptive jelly, foam, a diaphragm, condoms, and the Pill ... have only helped me to become pregnant twice.

More waiting. I'm first on the list of the second group. When I heard my name called, I catapulted to steel inside. My mind snapped shut.

I was taken to a small room to change into a paper gown. Blood pressure checked along with pulse and weight. I went to an examining room where the doctor would measure the size of my uterus to estimate how many weeks into this pregnancy I was. A 'nurse' helped with the stirrups. Another woman entered the room. When she approached my body, I blurted out, "Are you the doctor?" (*Geez, and I thought the receptionist was seedy!*)

She was a teeny-tiny woman with a bloody operating room gown, oily frazzled hair, silver-capped front teeth, adolescent acne, and truly dead, beady eyes. And these are the people and hygienic operating procedures associated with *legal* abortions? This is just ALL wrong.

The only words we exchanged were in response to my two questions. "Yes," she was the doctor. "Seven or eight," in response to, "How many weeks pregnant am I?"

More waiting in an adjacent room. The girls and women in my group started to filter in. What a pathetic, sad-looking, paper-gowned group we truly were.

Finally, at 3:10 P.M., I was called. On the way down the hall, I said to the 'nurse,' "I'm scared senseless." She made no reply.

On the table. Legs in stirrups. Enter the doctor. She never said one word to me. And why should she? What could she say, really?

"I'm so sorry we're about to kill your kid"?

"Relax, this won't hurt a bit"?

"Beautiful day, isn't it"?

The pain started. I tried to remember to breathe deeply. The pain worsened. I flashed to Max and Robert and stared at the fluorescent light overhead. The torturous sound of the vacuum on and off … five, maybe six times. It was achingly reminiscent of December 1, 1966. Once, the 'nurse' came over, squeezed my hand, and said "You're doing great. Only a few more minutes." More searing pain. Deep breathing didn't help. Nothing helped. Then it was over.

I saw the vacuum bottle. A lot of blood and a clot that held my baby. I wondered why they hadn't attempted to hide it from my view.

I was wheel-chaired into the recovery room. Seven beds. One was mine. Severe cramping. Light-headed and nauseated. I was determined not to freak, vomit, or complain. In an hour I was up and dressed. Wendy and I went out for coffee. We didn't talk much. I couldn't cry. I just wanted to go home and get in bed.

The phone was ringing when I walked in the door. Ruthie. She was in tears because of a last-night argument with Jonathan. I played Big Sissy as genuinely as I could until I heard a racket blaring from the living room.

I met up with Bentley, who was running around in circles. Oscar and the seventeen-pound stray tomcat who hangs around our garage were into some vicious combat in my living room! The sound of two cats duking it out sounds like a brutal jungle war. The screen was mangled. Three plants were splattered on the kitchen tile. Clumps of hair were flying.

I got a broom and started swinging. Eventually the tomcat left the same way he entered. (*He had jumped from the ground to a ledge, to another ledge, then right through the kitchen screen.*)

Oscar's face instantly swelled to the size of a baseball. The whole thing felt like a conspiracy.

Although I was exhausted, traumatized, drained, and crampy, Oscar and I left for the vet.

I wasn't home ten minutes when Max walked in. No time to think. No time to mourn. No time to process. I couldn't look into his eyes. When I *had* to look at him, I stared directly at his nose.

I took a shower. We ate tuna fish sandwiches. I blindfolded my brain and got into bed. After I heard the rhythmic breathing of his sleep, I went to the den, smoked a half pack of Parliaments, and stared at the sliver of a moon. Oscar had to stay overnight at the vets.

*****

I now know legal abortions aren't a whole lot different from illegal ones. They are no less horrific and no less scarring. Legal just means women don't have to use coat hangers to abort, and that's a really good thing. But to hope for a squeaky clean, nicely orchestrated abortion, is nonsense. It's all seedy, grimy, and filthy. And once you've seen a teen in your own college dorm, bleed-out in a corridor from a coat-hanger abortion, the Roe vs. Wade conflict takes on new meaning.

I don't believe anyone really likes the idea of killing tiny babies. Women just want to choose and not be dictated to. The blatant truth is that if women want that tiny life extracted from their body, they will find a way, even if it means sterility, bleeding-out or living in perpetual denial, shame and loss.

Morality cannot be dictated or legislated. I am so torn by Roe vs. Wade. Legalized killing is nuts, and so are millions of damaged women who cannot cope with the aftermath of their abortion choice. But are dead or emotionally shredded women who at any cost will extract life from their womb any less horrific?

I'm beginning to wonder if the issues of my adult life didn't have their genesis in that first abortion. I didn't have a food issue before then. I didn't have horrific nightmares about children before then. I didn't have much self-esteem, but it wasn't as absent as it ultimately became. I wasn't as anxiety laden, nor as restless and ungrounded.

One thing I know for certain ... crippling neurochemical depression was an ongoing drama, but it was not created by outrageous behavior. Two dead babies, conceived by men who were not my husband, was self-created drama, causing agonizing loss, basement-level self-worth, no true core values, and an identity that reinforced what I believed was my Dad's opinion of me.

*****

November 23, 1978

It is twenty-six days since the abortion. I saw Robert at our love-nest yesterday for the first time since that black abortion Friday. He explained his position. The baby ordeal was painful for him because of two factors: (1) His inability to change or control the situation, and (2) his uncertainty of my ability to handle the situation. He was scared, really scared ... that something might happen to me medically or emotionally, or that Max might find out, or worse, his wife.

He said he always felt I silently blamed him and the only reason I didn't verbally blast him was because of how well he handled the situation.

"Bull crap, Robert," I assured him. "At no point did I blame you. I blame myself for participating in this affair, for irresponsibility, and for my hedonism. Furthermore, what do you mean how well you handled the situation? You handled nothing. Absolutely nothing!"

I will not be seeing Robert again. I knew that from the moment I found out about our baby. It has all become too gruesome and macabre.

I wrote him a letter a few days ago. He read it in our love nest and handed it back to me, as he had all previous letters I had written to him. We wept together in the same bed in which we had created life. And then we devoured each other with desperation and abandon. As I left, I felt his eyes pierce my back and his sorrow pierce my heart. Robert England will linger in memory.

*****

November 20, 1978

Dearest Robert,

How many times have I written to you and watched your face as you read my words, my heart, my mind?

I have shared all of me with you. You breathed life back into me, Rob. I was so wilted and dry when we met. You became my oasis of renewal.

Your face and body are exquisite, and I treasure them, but it is your mind I have most loved. It is so agile, quick, and inventive. It is so incisive, deft, and compelling.

So often have you forced me into words when I was more comfortable with elegant silence. When I wished to speak through leopard-like movements over your body and silent love songs expressed through my touch.

I have always had a thin veil of mystery about me, even with my closest friends. I have been denied that with you, since you demand I be exposed, raw, x-rayed. But I am grateful, because it is an honor to be known so completely and loved anyway. Though you said it seldom, I felt your love. As much as you could allow yourself to love me, you did indeed love me.

Sometimes I have felt so young with you, almost like your little girl. Sometimes I have felt like your mother, your sister, your confidant, your buddy. I have so enjoyed all of the "you's" loving all of the "me's." You have challenged me to stretch and see beyond my conception of myself and I thank you.

I'd like you to know why I never asked you the myriad questions I could have asked about your wife. The more anonymous she remained, the less guilty I remained and the less threatened. I'm sure even through description I would have found her formidable in ways in which I am not, and I didn't need encouragement to be jealous or insecure.

I have memorized you. With so little effort I can smell you and intuit the curve of your shoulder. I can feel your weight engulfing me but never smothering me. Taste the inside of your mouth. Feel every part of me coming alive as your hand feather-glides over me.

I remember how it feels to awaken all the precious parts of you. And I remember the rush I always felt when I first saw you. How you have made me sparkle with delight, Robert.

Ours was the very best baby I could have hoped to bring to life. The combination of our genetics would likely have created a supremely unique child. A sensation that transcends explanation tells me that our baby was a boy. And that is how I shall remember him. That I have killed him, is the saddest sadness I have ever known.

I have loved you, Robert. You have moved me. I would have devoured you with love if you had let me. It would have been sickening. You'd have hated it.

Missing someone is such a singularly personal experience. Everyone I've ever missed, I've missed differently. I cannot define how I will miss you; I only know that it will likely last a lifetime.

I am glad today is as grey as yesterday was blue. There is no sunshine in my world this day, as I bury that which was "us."

G-D keep you safe. Leah Rebecca

*****

New Year's Eve—December 31, 1978

Deborah, it is the eve of a fresh new year, and I am alone with the beating of my heart. I pulled out one of my old journals this afternoon. It pushed me to pull all the letters, including the battered leather suitcases filled with all the camp letters I saved from Mom and Dad and even my own letters to them that they gifted back to me. I even dug out all the letters I've ever received from anyone and all the photocopies of letters I've written. How inspired of me to save and copy my written history. It doesn't allow me to imagine, distort, or deny my past because here it all is, in hand-written clarity, with the honesty of immediacy keeping it real.

New Year's Eve makes me nostalgic. I ran my fingers over the row of diaries and journals I've written since the early 60's. Unconsciously, I stopped at the beige one with the pink pansies on the cover. I hadn't remembered what year it represented just from the cloth cover, but once I opened it, a flood of memories from 1966 cascaded back. The year of my first abortion.

Now I sit in the bed I share with Max, with this year's journal, a cup of tea, and the winter sun about to set, ready to reflect on that day in 1966 that will not go away.

I never recorded why Dr. Marshall had been hours and hours late the day of that first abortion in Georgia. He had been in jail

205

all day. Early that morning he was arrested for performing illegal abortions. He was released on bail just a half hour before he suctioned my baby from my womb.

G-D only knows how Samuel and I flew back to Philly that night and how I made it to my 8:00 A.M. class the next morning. Wendy was my G-D-sent guardian angel. What would I have done without her?

I believe now that my relationship with Samuel would have wilted more quickly had it not been for the abortion. We'd known each other for so short a time when we were faced with a crisis pregnancy. Unlike for Robert and me, the abortion did not splinter Samuel and me. Instead, it deepened our emotional bond, and we became interdependent.

Samuel helped me with my studies, quizzed me before major exams, and sat beside me for hours in the library while I researched and wrote. I know now I helped him by simply loving him. I doubt that at age forty-eight, he'd ever known such innocent and complete adoration.

On Saturday nights we would dine and dance at stylish clubs and eateries. People would stare. We didn't care. We were a May-December duet of lyrical love, and we stayed protected in our own tiny world.

I remember so clearly that electric fear that shot through me when Mom and Dad caught Samuel and me embracing in the parking lot of the restaurant they were about to enter with the Rosen's. Things were never again the same between Samuel and me. The strain was too great for both of us, and the disclosure of our secret life punched a hole in its magic.

He told me right before we split up that he'd gone to Mom and Dad's a week after they had caught us outside the restaurant. He told them he would end it between us and begged for their forgiveness. Cindy was already a part of his life, and our conclusion was imminent anyway. When I found the letter from her in his overcoat, I knew what it meant even before I read it. It was all that I needed to fall into a hell-pit and my trust in men turned jaded and my naiveté waned in scope.

Samuel had felt like a boyfriend to me in spite of our twenty-eight-year age gap. But so clearly now do I see he was cast in the role of male parent. He took care of me. He protected me. He treasured me.

He saw in me great potential and vast heart, and he reveled in it. And because he was genuinely in love with me, I never suspected he was my substitute Daddy, the one I never had. I had a father, but I never had a Daddy before Samuel. Such a complex mix was I … grown up in social finesse and a pubescent emotionally.

It's hard to feel very New Year's Eve celebratory after reading about the 1966 abortion and still trying to recuperate from the one just eight weeks ago. I'm still Leah, but I'm not the Leah I remember. Something inside me died in addition to my babies.

Max doesn't suspect a thing. He's not really paying attention. Now I know why he was able to pull off his secret life with Carmen. Lying is an art form.

We're going out to dinner with two couples from his office. They will be absorbed in doctor chatter; I will listen and pretend to care. New Year's Eve. Truly, so what?

G-D, are you there? I want help. I want out. Can't You arrange for a car accident that "works" this time? I can't kill myself. I can't do that to my family. But I can no longer endure this agonizing life that only incorporates misery after misery. Please make my life go away, G-D. NOW, I'M BEGGING.

*****

207

1979

(My letter to Max)

Okay, Max,

You say you want to know what I want. Maybe you'll be sorry you asked. But here it is:

I want what I apparently can't have. I want you. Short of that, I'm not sure.

I know this, I feel defeated and dried up. I feel my patience stretched to its limit. I feel pain that words cannot capture. I feel angry and mean and jealous.

My heart has a constant migraine, and nobody will kiss it and make it go away. What I want seems so simple. A man who loves and wants me. A man who enjoys the range of my capacity to give and receive love. A man who adores me unabashedly, with vulnerability and honesty.

That's what I want from a relationship with my man. Open, fully realized love. Are you that man?

I know when I'm well, I'm a whole lot of woman, sometimes more than some men know what to do with. But, I need to be embraced for who and what I am. I shouldn't have to shrink myself or water down who I am to be loved.

I will not pussyfoot around with you anymore, Max. I will not pretend this is satisfactory. If you want me, fight for me. Show me. Tell me. Do something.

I love you. The thought of leaving *you* makes me as ill as the thought of making love to me, makes *you*! But I must be given a reason to stay. Some hope. Some visible sign that you're trying, or even that you want to try.

I think to myself, *"What's Max going to think as he looks back on these years when he's old? Will he feel regret? Will he see how sad it was to create obstacles to living and loving? Will he be sorry to have lost his Leah?"*

Stop punishing us, Max. Drive the wedge in much further and we will splinter. Three hours a week consisting of *our* marriage counseling, *your* therapy, and *my* therapy is not enough. We need to talk every day.

You rationalize and justify our lack of progress, I sometimes think, by being in so much pain yourself and pretending we can't work on us until your pain stops. Max, the pain won't stop *until* we work on us. You look for ways to exonerate yourself. We've both done cruel things to each other, said cruel things to each other. But that's marriage, not a death or divorce sentence.

I know you love me, Max. I know you don't want to lose me. It's so ironic. The last thing either of us wants is exactly what we're pushing ourselves toward.

I feel all grown up. I'm not hysterical, only deeply sad. I'm not even scared, at least not today. I will be able to function on my own. I will date. I will know love. But all I want is you. I already have what I want. Take an honest look, Max. Don't throw us away unless you're sure that's what you want.

Cry. Scream. Tell me. Make me understand. Give me a morsel, a handle.

I just want to love you, Max.

Leah Rebecca

*****

(Letter from Max)

January 30, 1979

Dear Leah,

I have an hour break between patients, and I need to respond to your letter. No, I need to respond to you.

You don't have the market cornered on pain, Leah. Neither "you" nor "us" are my only problems. I think I've finally unraveled enough of my stuff to be able to enumerate the issues.

I have a lot of unanswered fundamental questions. Like, here I am, thirty-one years old and who am I? What do I want? Where am I going? Why aren't I happy at work? What would I rather be doing? Is our relationship based solely on neurotic needs?

We've never had the best of each other, you know. I feel as though I hold you back and I feel as though you hold me back. I know I don't allow you to be your full self, but maybe I can't handle your full self.

Maybe we're just not each other's type, and maybe we just don't intrinsically turn each other on. Never mind, even I know that's not true.

I've been trying to fit into *your* life because I don't have one of my own. Maybe if we never married, we could have been good friends, maybe even good lovers.

Since I don't know what my needs are, I can't fulfill them myself and can't expect you to help me fulfill them.

This is the very worst period of my life, Leah. I cry every day and pace at work, and it requires all the strength I can gather to just keep going.

It was kind of you to let me "rape" you last night. I was harsh, impersonal, and I'm sorry. I couldn't look at you; I know and I'm sorry. You're a courageous little lady, Leah. There's so much I admire and respect about you. You provide me with a sense of wonder and a fresh take on almost everything. The way you love people captivates me because it is so apt and subtle; you fluently consider who a person is and what he or she needs. You tune in because you care.

But I don't know if I can live with you much longer. You want things from me I feel disqualified to offer. It's not that your demands are outrageous. I guess what you cite in your letter are things all women want. I wonder how many women get them.

It's time to tell you something I feel certain you need to know. You need to know what happened between Jena and me. We had a close and special relationship. She made me feel important, attractive, smart, and capable. She was very adept at pointing out your limitations and weaknesses and made me see how they contribute to our issues. I could have fallen in love with her. That's why I was so insistent we leave. I didn't think we needed her to break us apart. We seem to be able to handle that without her assistance.

She's not a safe person, Leah, and we were both too vulnerable to escape her shrewd and calculating nature. We were pawns in her world. The whole arrangement was too hazardous, especially with our marriage in troubled water.

I know you are exhausted from trying to extract information from me. I know you are weary from supplying me with options and having me multiple-choice pick the ones that apply. Sometimes I allow you to do so just so I can bask in the amount of thought I know you extend in attempting to understand me.

All of the alternatives you suggest for my not wanting to converse with you are dead-ringer right.

1. I don't really give a damn what you're thinking now because I'm totally preoccupied with me.
2. I don't want your opinions or observations influencing my thinking.

3. I don't want to have to consider another set of emotions
   because I don't want to know how much I'm hurting you.

A part of me fears I will never again meet anyone who knows
or loves me so thoroughly. We can try to ride this period out, Leah,
but I'm not feeling very hopeful about us. It is possible that too
much bad blood has spilled.

Let's go to Luigi's tonight. I'm wanting pasta and veal marsala.
Love, Max

*****

January 31, 1979

Deborah!

Jena did what?

Max and Jena … *Whaaaaaaaaaaaat*?

No wonder she hasn't answered any of my calls. And no wonder
when I call and Richard picks-up, he invariably says she isn't
home. She's home. She's just afraid Max has told me this stuff
and I'm calling to give her a piece of my mind. Well, I sure *would*
like to ask her what the hell she was doing to our minds and our
marriage. And I thought *I* was the only sick one in the house. My
illness is red-hot visible; her malady is a silent killer.

I'm medically sick; she's just low. And sick really is a pony of a
different color compared to crafty maneuvering.

I'm aghast. I'm numb. I don't know whether I'm more stupid
than naive or more naive than stupid.

Let's not quibble. I'm both.

March 3, 1979

Deborah,

Too long since I've written. Too sick. I'm so sick of being too sick. Max left on February twelfth. Marriage counseling transformed into divorce counseling after he found the last letter I wrote to Robert.

I kept all the letters I wrote to Robert in a suitcase hidden inside another suitcase in the bottom of my closet. One day I had a splintering headache and I asked Max to retrieve a Tylenol with codeine from my navy purse. That was the pill I had chosen not to take the day of the abortion. Along with the Tylenol, he brought back a face drenched in anguish and my final letter to Robert. It had not made it from my navy purse back into its secret hiding place.

And that was it, really. We lived together a few more weeks until he found another apartment. I knew his pain intimately because it echoed mine over Carmen. What a grotesque piece of human irony … his affair and my affair both resulting in pregnancies and abortions. Hideous business, these immoral extramarital liaisons and the byproducts of lust that get flushed down sewer systems. I repulse myself.

One thousand visual images of Max swim inside me and never let me rest. When I sleep, he's there. Awake, he's there. When working. While watching TV. All of his postures and the nuances of his speech.

I see him drying his hair and sitting in the Windsor rocker reading a medical mag. I see the lines on either side of his sun-lit face as he laughs, and I hear that hearty sound as it erupts from him. I see him in his candy-striped nightshirt. In his tall black cowboy boots. In his forest green plaid flannel shirt. In his tux. In his beige wool jacket with the brown wool turtleneck.

I can almost feel the black coarseness of his hair and those to-die-for hands that doctors have, and the way those hands, fingers spread, comb through his hair while in concentration he seeks to make a point.

I smell his after-shave face when it's near me saying good-bye. I see him in scuba gear and skydiving gear. I see all the shapes of his body parts that sometimes I want to touch more than I want to breathe. I see him confident. I see him scared.

I'm only pretending to live. I miss him so much. I miss me so much. This is not living. This is merely surviving and waiting for the end.

March 9, 1979

Attending to living things helps a little. Feeding the fichus, fern, and cats ease me into life's current more surely than dusting. I've tried it all. Things that cannot be rushed or hurried, machine made, or mass produced … these are the things I cherish so dearly now.

Mom's matzah balls.

A poem written to me by Wendy's partner, Kate.

Aunt Lauren's knitted sweater I've had since tenth grade.

Re-runs of *The Mary Tyler Moore Show*.

April 1, 1979

I left Mom and Dad's yesterday and moved back to my little Narberth home. I'm so glad I didn't have to raise or parent me. And I love my parents enough to wish they didn't have to parent me either.

Sarah and Rachael helped me move back in. I'm far from well, but I'm well enough to stay alone, fry an egg, feed the cats, and change my sheets.

I love these two women, my cousins. We were strolled in baby carriages side by side over three decades ago. Their mothers … my aunts. Their siblings … my cousins. Their husbands … my friends. And they have been part of my rescue team since returning from their temporary jobs in Chicago.

But sometimes, oh sometimes, I do truly loathe them for the normalcy of their daily lives and the way they take being able to work and create and love and make babies so for granted. As though it were owed to them. As though they may have done something to deserve brains that function "normally".

We ordered a pizza and listened to Mathis, Belafonte, and The Pointer Sisters. They danced and drank a rich burgundy while I nursed an herbal iced tea. G-D forbid I should mix fermented grapes with toxic doses of antidepressants. So sorry, G-D. I don't mean to appear ungrateful for finally being well enough to return home. I am grateful! Honestly! Hallelujah glory and amen!

April 6, 1979

My savings account runs out in a few weeks, and I've been frantically seeking employment. Yesterday I failed a typing test; even Kelly Girls won't have me. I walked out in tears.

I've considered babysitting for working parents, but I'm not sure I trust myself enough yet. What if a crying jag descends and the stress of screaming kids unglues me?

For one totally crazed moment I considered bartending, until an administrator at the Bartending School told me I was too short to reach the overhead glass racks.

I have the persistent thought there simply are not enough pills in all the pharmacies on the whole East Coast to fix me. A horrifying thought.

April 9, 1979

Max opened his own office. I heard that months ago. And that is all I've heard because for over a year he has refused all contact with me. He hates me. I wish I hated him. But yesterday, he called me, summoning me to his new office without allowing for an answer as to why.

I was agonizingly adrenalized when I walked in. I followed his receptionist's directive to take a seat among his waiting patients. I'm no doubt sicker than anyone in that waiting room has ever dared imagine being.

Thirty minutes later I was escorted into his inner sanctum. It's nice. Real nice. Seems that my idealistic-do-gooder-let's-help-the-poor-and-underprivileged husband, has turned a corner.

We're talking maxed-out bourgeois surroundings and accouterments. Why was I surprised? I did not rise when he entered. Too afraid I would fall. He did not touch me but moved behind his carved mahogany desk and sat in his throne-like cowhide tan leather swivel. He was so smooth, so cool, so like the Max I remembered from Amsterdam.

"You look tired, Leah. Are you okay?" he asked.

"I'm fine, Max. Why am I here?"

"I've filed for divorce."

(*My face fractured. I'm sure of it.*)

I lied and said, "Oh, I understand. But what's the hurry? Are you getting married?"

"Yes, I am, Leah."

I stood, turned around, and walked out. I thank G-D that Max did not follow me. Today I feel like the earth broke and forgot to fall on me.

I want to die. I want to die. I want to die. I want to die. I want to die. I want to die. I want to die. I want to die. I want to die. I want to die. I want to die. I want to die. I want to die.

More than a chapter has ended; a whole set of encyclopedias has ended. And I know I was rejected by him because I reek of illness and was too heavy a burden even for friendship.

May 16, 1979

Dear Deborah,

It has been such a strange day. Nearing midnight and I'm drained, but I must write. Rachael and I went to Sarah's today. Our midweek ritual of meeting for an early dinner at one of our homes. It was over spinach quiche and fresh baked croissants they broke their "news" to me.

"Leah," Rachael said, "we know you're not ready for full-time employment yet. You're still reeling from the fall-out from your most recent depression, Max's news, being unemployed, and living with your parents. But we believe with all our hearts you must have a little something to do every day. Since you love to write, wouldn't it make good sense to learn to type? Then you could type your diary entries instead of handwriting them, and you might even be able to find a little non-stressful part-time work."

It didn't sound entirely crazy to me. I thought I should try, since Rachael and Sarah were so intent.

They handed me the Yellow Pages and insisted I flip to the business section and pick the Yellow-Page school of my choice. This seemed excessively daunting. I tried to defer but they insisted the choice be mine. So, I let my fingers do the walking and I stopped dead at … The Sleeper Business School.

Ya know, Deb, the name just sounded so non-threatening and easy paced, I thought maybe this school would not be a pressure-cooker. "Sleeper," sounded good, so I dialed the number.

"Sleeper Business School. This is Janet Sleeper. How may I help you?" (*Oh. Sleeper. The proprietor's name.*)

"Hello. My name is Leah Kline and I'd like to learn how to type."

"I have an opening at 9:00 A.M. tomorrow morning if you'd like to come in then, Ms. Kline."

"That'll be fine. I'll see you then," I said.

From halfway across the room, Mrs. Sleeper approached me with genuine warmth and an extended hand. When we were about four feet apart, her hands flew up to her face. She gasped and said, "Oh my goodness, you're the one!"

"Well, yeah, I am," I confirmed. "I'm Leah Kline and we have a 9:00 A.M. appointment."

"Never mind, dear. Just never you mind. You come right into my office, and we'll have a cup of tea. Do you like strawberry tea?"

"Yeah, sure. That'd be nice."

Clearly this woman knew in a slice-of-a-second the last thing I needed was to learn how to type. Months of suicidal despair had me looking like an over-shocked mouse in a wire cage.

She seemed nervous. She pulled out some books on nutrition and vitamin supplementation. I wondered what this had to do with typing. She dead-eyed me and said, "Leah, you are not here by accident, but by providential design. I'll tell you how I know this some other time."

I was about to say, "Wait! Whoa! Tell me now!" but there was no time. She started firing questions at me and wanted to know everything about me since my beginning.

I started with nursery school and told her about *The School in Rose Valley*. AGAIN, she threw her hands up to her face. Get this! Mrs. Sleeper was the principal of that school and taught there from 1949 through 1959. I attended from 1950 through 1953. When she checked her *Rose Valley* files of "some favorite students" that she had kept all these years, sure enough, there was the data on little Leah Kline.

Wow, now *I* threw my hands up to my face. Strains of the theme song from *The Twilight Zone* marched through my cerebrum.

Good golly! Now I'm paying attention! This just got too weird for words. We bonded quickly and discovered similarities and synchronicities in our backgrounds. She was divorced, had suffered severe depressions, been suicidal, and survived a near-deadly car crash.

"I want to tell you, Leah, about how I escaped the ravages of mental illness and became a fully productive, joyful woman. It was God, Leah. God healed me. I know He can do the same for you. More importantly, He wants to. He longs to."

She mentioned Jesus; I mentioned I'm Jewish. This did not faze her. She went on and on about Jesus, so I listened. She was interesting and I was desperate.

"From my heart, I ask You, G-D, is this my course too? You know I'm looking for You.

"I'm trying to be still and hear You."

I said "yes" when she asked if I would go with her to a community chapel in Newtown Square this coming Sunday. After all, what did I have to lose?

Sunday, May 20, 1979

Deborah, today I became a child of the Lord, though I really have no idea what that means. Mrs. Sleeper took me to a church meeting today. It was held in a modest little hall. There were only about twenty of us. It was announced that a Messianic Jewish Rabbi would be delivering the sermon today. So, what's a Messianic Jewish Rabbi? I wondered.

I don't remember a thing the man said, but I do know when he asked if there was anyone present who wished to accept Jesus into his or her heart as their personal Lord and Savior, I felt as though an invisible puppeteer prompted my arm to rise. I didn't fight it. I simply stood.

The Rabbi came up to me and the congregants surrounded me. I repeated the phrases required of me and that was that. Suddenly, I was one of the flock and was showered with love and hugs and kisses. It was bewildering. Overwhelming.

I still don't know what happened or that anything did. But I choose with my heart to believe that I have been touched by the Spirit of G-D, that He loves and accepts me, and that I will hear Him as I listen for His guidance.

Jesus (that feels so weird to write), I have a thought-question and I don't know if it's normal or if I should be embarrassed by even posing it to You. But here goes. I don't know what to tell my parents. I fear they will feel I've rejected my heritage and all they stand for. But I don't feel that way. I don't feel as though I've "converted" or given up anything. I don't feel any less Jewish than I felt yesterday. In fact, I don't feel much at all.

*****

Get a load of this. I actually decided I would give G-D five days to heal me. Chutzpah to the max! My rationale was, since He made a gazillion galaxies, certainly He could heal me in

five days. By day five, not good! Certainly, not healed. In that I was not fixed, healed, or even a smidge better, I reclaimed my Jewish stance that a man cannot be G-D. Or if He is G-D or G-D's Son, He isn't G-D or G-D's Son for Jewish people.

*****

May 25, 1979

Deborah, I know I've said, "You won't believe this," more times than there are stars, but I think I've maxed out on the truly outrageous, phantasmagorical, and definitely supernatural. Here's the deal. I've been miserable since last Sunday. I've prayed the depression would lift because of the bold step I took of accepting Jesus last Sunday in a public setting. If anything, the penetrating despair has deepened.

I've gone through the motions of being a living person, but I've only known I'm still alive because everything hurts so much. The ninety-plus pills at the back of my panty drawer is now very, very, very hard to resist.

Throughout today I talked to Mom and Ruthie and Wendy. There was so little ability in me to create a voice with levity or interest, I terminated each call quickly.

By 8:00 P.M. I knew I had to escape the pills and drive anywhere forward motion would take me. I drove to Wilmington, Delaware, and back. I drove to Philly and back. I was tired, but I was so afraid to go home and more afraid to impose my sickening self on anyone who loves me.

By 11:00 P.M. I was driving on Route 322 to utterly nowhere. It was a dark night; the sky was an ink-black vastness. No one on the road but me.

I sobbed. I dry heaved. I pleaded with G-D for mercy. "Fix me or kill me, G-D." My eyes moved upward to glimpse a light that appeared in this moonless night. Nah, can't be.

No moon, so where was the light coming from? Okay, get ready, Deborah. The light was coming from a luminescent cross … a distinct, sharply defined, brighter-than-bright, but not harsh or blinding … C.R.O.S.S.

Out loud I said repeatedly, "G-D? It's G-D. Oh my G-D, it's G-D! G-D is visiting me?" Adrenalin shot through me. My shirt was drenched in sweat. I held my breath, dropped my speed, and pulled over to the shoulder of the road.

It just hung there. The cross just held its position in stoical regard. This was uniquely for me, Leah Rebecca Kline. This was a visible sign to assure me that my acceptance of Jesus into my heart last Sunday was not silly or stupid.

"Okay, G-D. I won't kill myself. I promise. I won't kill myself. WOW! Thank You, G-D. Thank you for loving me. Thank you for hearing me. REALLY? You really are real? Is there really a G-D who pays attention to everything? And this Jesus, this Jew, this Nazarene guy born in a manger and said to be your son, does that mean he's really real too?"

A thought penetrated me, one that didn't seem to originate in my own cerebral process. It was more like a message being transmitted to me: *All the answers you seek are available to you through faith. Just believe. Just believe. Just believe.*

Okay, G-D. I'll believe. I'll believe in You.

G-D gave me time to synthesize the appearance, for it was not until I accepted the supernatural miracle of this visible sign and made the promise I would never take my own life, that the cross lessened in heavenly brilliance by slow-motion degree … until it vanished.

I awaited normalized breathing. I tried to think but I couldn't. That was a first.

My mind was uncluttered of poisonous thoughts and complex logic. I just felt peace. I guess that's what a "normal" mind would call what I felt.

I had to tell Mrs. Sleeper when I got home. It was so late, but I decided to wake her. She cried, or was it more like laughter through tears?

"Mrs. Sleeper," I then asked, "why did you gasp, 'You're the one!' when you saw me when we first met nine days ago?"

"Leah, you may not understand this," she said, "but I will answer because you've asked. I embraced the Lord in my life when I was exactly your age, thirty-two, almost twenty-five years ago. As I studied Scripture and allied myself with other Believers, I came to realize we Gentiles only have this Jewish Messiah because of everything that was promised to and fulfilled by the Jewish people.

"Never forget that Jesus was born a Jew and crucified as a Jew and that Christian beliefs have Judaism as their cornerstone. When true freedom reigns on this earth, it will be the Shema *("Hear, O Israel, the Lord is our G-D, the Lord is One")* that is sung by all the world's people.

"We have everything we have, most dearly eternal life, granted through belief in this Jewish Messiah, because of the Jews, and what they have suffered and what, someday, all of them will come to embrace, just as you have.

"You see, Leah, when all of this became clear to me, I started praying for God to send a Jewish person into my life so I could help guide this person 'home' to his or her Messiah. It became a desire that became a yearning that became an ache. Two days before you called my school, I had a dream that assured me my prayer would soon be answered. And when I saw those sad brown eyes in your sweet sad face, the Holy Spirit whispered to me, 'She's the one!' You are an answer to prayer, Leah. You were hand selected and chosen by God to be sent to me.

"Everything in your life has led up to this, and everything in your future will be affected by this. Don't be afraid. God will heal you of depression, and you will have work to do that will fulfill the very purpose God designed for your life.

"I'm here for you, Leah. Now you must go to bed. You have been through a war and you have won. Enjoy the sleep you have earned. Call me tomorrow, precious."

I must do as she commands. Go to bed. I can't write anything more, not even a comma.

*****

It quickly became evident that my joyous assertion that I had accepted Jesus as Lord, and even been sent a cross in a night sky, was not a popular declaration. The general consensus was, "Oh no, now she's hallucinating and seeing things in the sky! It may be time for us to seriously consider institutionalization for her."

I quickly and frequently said with assurance and certainty, "Yeah, I was just seeing weird things from the effects of the antidepressants. Don't mind me."

It was years before I ever spoke of that cross in the sky again.

*****

June 5, 1979

I live with the knowledge that I have embraced Jesus, but I don't know what to do with that choice. Since most of my world is comprised of Jewish people, and I *know* I dare not even mention the "J" word around them, I feel lost.

Mrs. Sleeper is out of the country for a few months. I don't think I'd feel comfortable just strolling into a church. How do I find out about Jesus? What books should I buy? Are there people who counsel people like me? And how many "me's" are there? You know what I mean, Deborah? How many Jewish people have taken Jesus into their hearts?

August 15, 1979

The High Holy Days approach. I will attend with Mom, Dad, Ruthie, and Jonathan. None of them wish to speak at all about my having embraced the Lord. I can tell that Ruthie and Jonathan feel confused and compromised by my choice. Family gatherings are now uncomfortable for me as I sense them pushing me into the background, like a dunce in a corner with a pointed hat. As though what I've done is contagious. As though I'm a person in bad need of a crutch and a cause. How little they know me.

I have no idea why they, or anyone else, would give a damn if I believe in genies in bottles, Tooth Fairies, or the Seven Dwarfs. I am no different than I ever was in my behavior or demeanor. I have not turned into a religious zealot who pickets in front of synagogues or evangelizes anyone! I honestly don't know enough about this Judeo-Christian subject to be truly informative, so, I say nothing.

Oh, but I will! Just wait! I most certainly will! Jesus was not a flippant choice.

It's all a tad sickening to me, frankly. I've never understood why Jews have such an active antipathy for Jesus. He was born and died a Jew. What did He ever do to us that demands our scorn? Sure, religious wars have been fought. Jews have been killed, and maniacal Hitler quite nearly exterminated us. But was any of that Jesus' fault? Human nature and its resulting behaviors are the motivations behind every atrocity.

I heard recently that we live in what is called, in Judeo-Christian speak, "a fallen world." As in the fall from grace after the mess in the Garden of Eden. My mind is only wrapped around a thimble-full of information now, but you can bet my base of information will leap exponentially as weeks and months pass. I will have answers for these naysayers. After all, they weren't the ones who saw that cross in a night sky. So yes, eventually, I most definitely will have answers!

Most people have never battled mental illness and so have no idea what that cross in the sky means to me and how fully I believe the promises G-D whispered to me on that spring night in May of this year.

The fact that I've never been overly impressed or swayed by other people's opinions of my opinions is of great help to me now.

September 18, 1979

Tomorrow ... Rosh Hashanah, New Year's Day. How will I feel in our synagogue when the congregants know of my embracing the promised Hebrew Messiah? I expect I may be escorted out like a dangerous ideologist. It is abundantly clear now that the synagogue of my youth is no longer my home.

October 23, 1979

I've now read just enough library books to know there are Jews like me sprinkled around the globe. I am not the first, nor will I be the last, to embrace Jesus as the Messiah. Would I even be sitting here today if I had not? I think not.

When I was young and naive, I once held my breath until I fainted, thinking it would be a clean and easy way to die. How disappointed I was to discover that upon passing out, one starts to breathe reflexively. The truth in my change of heart is knowing that without Jesus, those pills would have been swallowed and I would simply have taken my place among the mentally ill and desperate people in my family who have already taken their own lives.

December 31, 1979—New Year's Eve

I am becoming accustomed to New Year's Eves spent alone. Anything anyone does repeatedly becomes less shocking, more tolerable and part of one's "normal." Somehow, we learn to protect our psyches and adapt, like a cat with three legs, or a man with one eye.

*****

THE EIGHTIES

It took almost eight months for me to tell Wendy about embracing Jesus as Lord of my life.

*****

(Letter from Wendy)

January 12, 1980

Leah, you did **WHAT?** What is it with you, woman? Is there no end to the absurdity of your life and your choices? This is really too much. What in the hell does, "I've accepted Jesus in my heart" mean?

I can well understand your parents' response. Haven't they been through enough with you? Now you take it upon yourself to undermine their entire ancestral history!

I choose to write instead of call because I wish totally to avoid anything confrontational with you, but I have some things to say. You're not going to like any of them, but this letter is overdue.

Of late, our conversations are empty and awkward. I can't tell you what I think you want to hear, and I know from experience you don't want to hear what I have to say. Since I never want to say what I'm thinking, I end up making idle chatter. The quality, caring, uplifting, sharing of insights, and all the great stuff our conversations used to be made up of, are gone. What is left is heavy, flat, boring, and depressing.

Your characterization of my attitude toward men as "hostile," was very wounding. And by the way, some have likened my attitude to "heightened awareness." What if all these years I had equated your depressions to "craziness?" Wouldn't you have felt that to be a blow to your jaw? I have been consistently supportive of your varied and multiple issues for thirteen years now through letters, phone calls, visits, sharing information, turning you on to the latest studies about brain enzyme dysfunction, the Brain-Bio Center at Princeton, recommending cleanses and handholding you through two abortions.

You, on the other hand, stand on the sidelines waiting for me to process my childhood molestation issues, and I'm talking about your immediate and firsthand lack of response or support. Which I actually knew couldn't and wouldn't be forthcoming.

I know I just recently told you about my father molesting me, and I understand that you're in the early aftermath of another mental collapse, but come on, Leah. Have a heart. Sing me a lullaby or write me an essay. *Do something*!

Being molested has blown a lot of things apart for us and revealed some major irreconcilable differences between us. These differences touch on class and privilege and the ensuing protection that provides for some people, especially you.

I feel like your distance from feminist community, dialogue, theory, literature, etc. leaves me at a disadvantage in your understanding of the dynamics here. Specifically, I am referring to the upper-middle-class fear of dealing with conflict and anger versus working-class women trying to deal with upper-middle-class privilege vis-à-vis protection. Do you even have a clue what I'm talking about?

Bottom line: You just don't want to deal with my feelings. I guess the violence and sexual abuse was just too sticky and touches too much on things you don't want to look at. So, here's the point: Heterosexual women, because of their dependence on men and male approval, do not want to look at their "male" capacity for abuse (of every kind) toward women, whether acted upon or not, and what those manifestations or ramifications are in their own lives.

And here's where the issue of leading a protected life comes in. You were bred to be protected by men in whatever form that takes, which of course, quite logically, defines the parameters of your insight into them.

I was bred from the larger and, shall we say, "lower" class and culture and therein lies the difference. From as early an age as I can remember, I was tuned into the power differences between males and females and what that power difference signified. This inequity revolted me. I knew I would never be interested in "boys," because I wasn't interested in this "master class" having power over me. I also found boys intrinsically boring and predictable; basically, a lower form of life, akin, say perhaps, to an earthworm.

I was interested in more highly developed mammals, *girls*! They have, still do and always will engage my total interest. My feminist consciousness was there from the get-go; something you, in your dreamy princess realm, have deigned to designate as "hostility."

Since we don't speak a common language, writing to you of my feelings and perceptions feels like trying to explain to an Eskimo what spaghetti tastes like in comparison to pizza.

But I will miss you, Leah. I did so enjoy your zest for life that surfaces between illnesses, your artistic sensibilities, your struggle to defy insurmountable health issues, your tenacious will, and your gracious and easy way with people. But what we have touched on here is a nerve. We could continue to pussyfoot around, have a knock-down drag-out, or endure a grueling demise. But I'm finally able to admit it can never be the way it was in a U. of PA. dorm because we can never be who we were back then.

And I might as well add what I've known for years. You only *think* you're a raging heterosexual. You're not. You're just pretending in order to avoid an alternative that isn't easy or acceptable to many people. Most women are gay; they just don't have the guts to look it squarely in the eye and say, "Yeah, I dig women."

You may feel I've deserted you, and, if you do, know the feeling is mutual. I'm not trying to cause you pain; I'm only trying to end my own.

I hope this Jesus thing works for you, Leah. But I think you're grabbing at straws here.

Really, I do. Wendy

January 28, 1980

Deborah, stand aside. I need to speak with my Lord. So, Jesus, I have a question. Is Wendy's response one I can expect from all whom I tell of my newfound dedication to You? Is this indicative of the Scriptures that state, in paraphrase, "You will be persecuted for My name's sake. You will be persecuted for righteousness' sake? If you're not being persecuted, you're not living the truth or walking the walk."

It is just over a year since I embraced You as Lord of my life, and really, Jesus, I don't know if I'm up to this. I still feel weak, tired, scared, and mentally ravaged. I cope with loss, grievous loss, and painful abandonment: my husband, my lover, my babies, Wendy, and my job. I have lost a kinship with the field I am trained for, and all markings of a sense of selfhood. Will there ever be gain?

Now I know why they say the pen is mightier than the sword. I wish Wendy had just run me through with a warrior's blade rather than annihilate the fabric of my being with words.

She's right about my having been an inadequate friend. But she's sopping-wet wrong with regard to the reasons. I'm not afraid of discussing her feelings or her problems from the molestation she suffered. G-D, literally *only* G-D knows, I am not afraid! Words, talking, writing, dissecting issues, working through tough times with words … these are my passion and talent!

It's just for the past sixteen years I've focused nearly all my energy on trying not to kill myself. There's "great friend" material inside of me; it just fades into absence when I'm in the throes of mental illness. I mourn. I grieve. I cry. I scream.

I guess I should pray for her. It must be an incomparable burden to consider half the world's population the intellectual and moral equivalent of earthworms. Poor Wendy. Poor me. Lord, was that You? I think I just "heard" You. Did You whisper to me, "Rooooooooooooll with it, Leah. Be an ocean wave." I'll try, Lord.

August 2, 1980

My 33rd Birthday, it was one year ago today I said to You, "If You haven't fixed me before the bells toll on my next Birthday, I don't think I'll be here to usher it in." But here I sit, and I'm not fixed. We both know the reason I'm still here is because a year ago I promised You I would never take my own life. And then, of course, there is the persistent knowing that if I kill myself, I might as well just shoot my parents too.

I'm not liking this at all, Jesus, and I wonder when You'll make good on Your promise that I'll be well and have specific work You've planned just for me. This is interminable, Jesus. Come on. Help me. I'll hang in, of course, but *please* … ENOUGH ALREADY. Anyway, thanks for listening to Your pitiful but sincere devotee. Over and out.

October 3, 1980

Snuggled up in my bed in my cottage. A mug of hot cider perched on my nightstand. Through my window I see the fire-tinged leaves of fall spill from the oak if a puff of invisible wind passes by. I'm so grateful. I'm not yet employed but have started up my private practice with my kids from before this latest sojourn into mental madness. I have missed them so much.

I didn't have the steam or interest to summarize a past journal on my Birthday in August, but I can tackle it today. With my hand hiding my eyes so I wouldn't know what diary year I chose, the 1969 journal caught my fingers. Here goes!

Wow! I just skimmed the whole year of my scribblings. What a year! What a decade! Amidst the tumult and change that characterized the sixties, I attended junior high, high school, and college: from 1960 through 1969. How could I have avoided becoming a by-product of that era's thinking?

Oh my, such high drama, comedy, achievement, and anguish as I lived that whole decade maxed out on themes and trends ... as did nearly everyone else I knew and loved. High school and college friends made all the likely choices. Some joined the Peace Corps. Others, in search of a dream of embracing honesty and simplicity, abandoned city life to settle communally. A few left for Canada to conscientiously object to a war we could not condone. Two of my high school friends came back from Asia in pine boxes draped in American flags.

- We had Chicago rioting.
- Watts burning and college students being shot by the National Guard.
- We had The Beatles ... those Liverpool wizards who pulled it all together for us with their parodies of the vapid materialism of our time.

• We had spy planes, a German Wall, and missiles in Cuba.

My fashion was my signature; it made my mother sick. I tired of Lord and Taylor's and started to shop in thrift stores and Goodwill. I found boutiques where fanciful used clothing hung from hat stands or from wooden pegs projecting from walls. There were worn wooden fruit boxes spilling over with shirts and sweaters. Some stores offered tattered divans that invited patrons to linger over cocoa and cookies.

I developed a deftness akin to stage sorcery in creating moods with scarves, hats, strips of lace, embroidered hankies, crinolines, and military surplus. Like a seasoned rag picker, I dressed in scraps from any period and every society. Some days I probably looked like a pre-Raphaelite angel, and on others more like a member of a guerrilla fraternity.

Dad built a bomb shelter near our cluster of weeping willows. More than halfway through the process, he quit. He conjectured, "What if Leah was in Philly when the bomb hit? And what if Ruthie was visiting her best friend six miles from home and Mom was in New York? If the four of us can't be together, what's the point? And if relatives, friends, and neighbors pleaded for admittance, how could I refuse?"

Eventually, we named the shelter "Solomon's Folly" and decorated it with posters, day-glow paint, some funky furniture, and insisted Ruthie practice her drums in there.

Somewhere along my way, I came to understand that in the record of history, the times of greatest change and progress are never tranquil. Although America in the sixties was frantic, troubled, turbulent, and angry, I believed the travail would yield a better world. I believed it with the vigor of youth and the blindness of passion.

We lost PaPa Honey and Aunt Lauren in 1969. I lost Samuel and our baby.

I never wrote the details of Aunt Lauren's suicide in April. For the longest time I couldn't even say the word *suicide*. I called it her "accident."

Dad found her. He had expected her at his plant that day, to help him with some inventory. When she was two hours late and there was no answer at her apartment, he went in search. The manager let him in. There she was. Ghost grey. No pulse. An empty prescription bottle lay beside her on the bed. She was wearing the peach satin negligee we had given her for Hanukkah. There was a note.

They pumped her stomach at the hospital, but it was too late. She had not been seeking attention. She meant to die.

Mom did not choose to share Aunt Lauren's note with me until two years ago. Of course, I made a copy.

*****

(Aunt Lauren's suicide note)

April 16, 1969

Dearest Nina,

You will grow to forgive me. I had no other choice. I ran out of hope and fight. You were breaking under the strain of my illness, and your little family had put up with enough. You did everything you could and more. Remain blameless, my lovely twin sister.

Everything I have is yours. My will is in the drawer with our mother's silver. The pain of depression is incomprehensible to those who have never known it. I am grateful you have never known it.

Thank you, Nina Joy Kline, for your relentless care and for nearly fifty years of being my best friend.

I love you with all my heart and with my last breath. God willing, we will see each other again.

Your beloved twin, Lauren

*****

I would guess that in my personal recorded history, 1969 will stand as a time of great heartbreak and imposing life change.

*****

December 13, 1980

John Lennon was murdered five days ago. A globe of people mourns. He was a tornado of creative genius, a breath-giving legend, a blazing idealist whose vision I relished. He was a voice in a void, a poet for here, for now, for always. John's literal voice was stilled on the night of December eighth, when a maniac shot him at near point-blank range.

But we, the youth, know that the Beatles ushered in something garden-fresh and enduring. These four lads will all be gone from this earth with the passage of time, but they will never "die."

I stopped mourning for John when I found something far closer to home to mourn. Yesterday it was confirmed that Mom has breast cancer. If someone had asked me three days ago, or a month or a year ago, "What's the worst thing that could happen to you?" I'd have said, "Anything happening to my Mom. She's the central person in my life. She's my stability, sanity, voice of reason, and the person who loves me most in all the world."

Now, I'm in a stagnant time warp. My Mom, my soul sister … her life is in jeopardy.

What to do? Hold on. Take this second, then take the next. Be strong for her. Be near her. Distract her. (After Aunt Lauren's death, my relationship with Mom slowly evolved in scope, depth and intimacy.)

How will she handle disfigurement, and for how long will it matter? Who will make her feel feminine and lovely? Who? I can't, and I don't think Dad knows how to anymore. He acts like a shattered little boy. Scared to death. I bleed for him. I need him, but he holds me at football-field length. What can I do for him? I don't even know what being "a good daughter" means to him. All I know for sure, is that in his eyes, I'm not one.

Ruthie and Jonathan hold each other all the time. Have they any idea how blessed they are to have each other? How *could* they know? They've had each other since before they even knew who they were alone, much less together.

I have never felt this isolated. Barely stabilized from over two decades of depression, and I face the loss of my Mother. I'm so mad. I'm so scared. Why have You allowed this, G-D? I want to know why. Why my Mom? Why her?

Fear is what's most gripping. It just can't have spread through-out her body. Please let her live. Please. What can I give? How can I make a trade? I don't suppose You bargain, Jesus, but would You consider a sacrifice? I would give anything for her safety. What could I give that would equal You sparing her life? Amahl had a crutch. What have I? Hear me. Help me. I can barely draw breath.

Leah, snap to! Get a grip. Remain single focused. Stay strong. She has asked you to.

You must.

*****

238

1981

Mom had a lumpectomy. In a few weeks she will start five days a week of radiation, and after that, chemotherapy. She is so brave and daily puts on soldier's armor, but it is merely a veneer. She does not fool me. We hold hands a lot and take slow walks in the neighborhood.

A friend of Mom and Dad's told them to take me to a doctor who is the prez of a psychiatric hospital in Delaware. A doctor named Mel Myerson … so off we go and tra-la-la. He said it's not my fault. He said to think of depression as I would high blood pressure, diabetes, or heart disease. Not my fault. He said he can "fix" me if I give him a chance and allow him to use an experimental drug on me. The dosage he wants to quickly build to is considered illegal by FDA standards. If they knew of his mega-dose philosophy, they'd shout, "Crazy man!" and suspend his license.

I've heard it all before, Dr. Myerson. This is not new news to me. Lots of doctors told me I'm sick and not crazy, but none could fix me. O.K., so you're some kind of Ph.D. bio-chem genius with a degree in psychiatry. Am I to be impressed? I'm not. I don't really believe for a second you can fix me. Why should you succeed when countless numbers of your colleagues have failed?

Another doctor. Another drug. I wish his optimism would soak by osmosis straight into my psyche. But to me he just appears to be an egotist, another medical man ever so enthralled with his stature and accomplishments.

239

What have I to lose though, really? I've already all but lost my mind, the most valuable of all human organs, and to disallow him to experiment with my neurochemistry would be to give up and give in, and I guess I have not yet quit. Maybe this is a "G-D promise" finding resolution.

O.K. then, Dr. Myerson, mix your potion and do your cauldron thing. Stir up a concoction. Pump me up with chemicals and see if you can straighten out the debris that is my mind and life. Go for it. Fix me. I dare you.

June 17, 1981

Deborah, it is six months since I met Dr. Myerson, and I now allow myself to believe, almost believe, I will be well. Dr. Myerson truly is a "cutting edge medicine man."

The drug is slowly taking hold of my neurological mess. Depression lifts by centimeters, slowly but certainly as the hot air balloon in *Around the World in Eighty Days*. With quiet determination my thoughts, as the balloon, ascend. There now lives in me less of a desire to die, along with a growing sense that I may indeed have specific work to do and may even be well enough to do it.

Mom is facing a death sentence, and I use all of me to appear even tempered and helpful. We take delight in the smallest of things. If Mom can go to a movie, we cheer. And today, we sat on their porch, had cups of tea and tangerines.

I am by no means steady, surefooted, or strong. But something so deep inside of me I cannot even phrase it, believes that depression will not always shape the course of my life. It may take years of being depression free for me to have absolute confidence in my mental stability ... but I can wait, because now I have hope that it can and will be so.

So, Lord G-D ... bless you for working out all the elaborate details so I would find Dr. Myerson. I dare not tell anyone my burgeoning joy, lest they think me a pathetic dreamer for believing this drug may provide neurological stability.

I have dreams for my I-hope-not-too-distant future. I want the paper I wrote on neurochemical depression published in *Philadelphia Magazine*. I want to be interviewed about depression on the radio-talk show *Ask Why*. I want to apply to the Academy of Interior Architecture and Design in Philly. And in the intervening months before I can work out financial aid, I will continue my private practice with special-needs kids.

Indeed, I have dreams and I have plans, and with G-D's help I know all things are possible. But I must remind myself, "Go slowly, Leah. Don't rush the healing process. Don't go out into the world with guns-a-blazin', thinking you can make a significant contribution by next weekend."

So, it's a pharmaceutical ... a tricyclic anti-depressant. That was not what I conjectured G-D would use as one of His healing tools, since so many drugs have not worked before this one. But as the adage goes, "We make plans. G-D laughs."

September 10, 1981

I started design school today and I'm praying I'm actually whole enough to do this. The syllabus is daunting. I will need much stamina and focus to see this degree through to completion. Friends and family think it is waaaaaaay too soon for me to be taking on a second Masters. I just hope this occupational choice is more suitable to my gifts and interests. Hey G-D ... I know You know this, but just in case, I need You a lot. A LOT!

*****

1982

Do I really give a rip-roaring damn about designing a ski lodge this second semester? No!

Categorically, I do *not,* but I must. Is life ever anything more than a never-ending procession of have-to's? Other people seem to be having fun. I'm so tired.

Mom slogs through chemo and is devastated by the sight and smell of people all around her in death decay. Yesterday she spent vomiting. Today she deals with hives.

I have nightmares about her not making it. Grotesque and ghoulish dreams. I try to hide behind frenetic activity, but my fright and sorrow never abate ... never, not in night sleep or day dreams. Dealing with Mom's cancer, this new degree program, and the remnants of decades of depression make me feel I'm in over my head, bobbing up for air the third time in deep ocean currents.

Deborah, some more real not-good news: I tried speed (*metham-phetamine*) at a fellow designer's home-party two weeks ago. I've bought some. It makes me feel energized, confidant, in charge ... albeit artificially.

I've managed to pack in endless amounts of cancer research and treatment alternatives with this fifth-gear momentum. I've called all over the U.S., Canada, and Europe. Materials pour in; it's unnerving. The alarming statistics. My confusion because of the varied approaches. Who's right?

Dad's deeply depressed, sick himself with fear about Mom. I know his pain intimately. Who of us knows hers? I take relief

where I can find it, like when the breast surgeon decided to perform a lumpectomy and not take half of her upper body away.
There was lymph involvement, but the surgeon's decision was an
expert opinion and so we simply concurred. I can get through this.
We can all get through this.

Mom's little dainty B.K. (Bridgette Kline) lies with her on the
sofa in the library all day. The teeny miniature schnauzer Aunt
Mitzy brought Mom after Aunt Lauren's death is *her* dog, all hers.
If Bridgette were a woman, she'd be Nina Kline; and if Nina Kline
were a dog, she'd be Bridgette. It's uncanny how similar those
two are.

April 15, 1982

Time to fess up. I'm addicted to meth and I've messed up my
nose and last night was the second time in two weeks I cut myself
so badly chopping carrots I had to go to the emergency room again
and get my finger stitched up. My little dainty hand now looks like
it belongs to Joe Frasier.

I'm wired. I'm fried. The feeling of invincibility has been replaced by paranoia, and my sadness is so conspicuous I look like a
little homeless woman sitting at a bus stop with nowhere to go.

I called a rehab center today and talked to the director. After
hearing all the details of this sordid tale, here's what he said: "Ms.
Kline, I recommend strongly you drop out of school for a term and
admit yourself to our center to dry out and clean up. You cannot
do this alone, but you shouldn't have to be here more than three
weeks."

"Afraid not, Dr. Jackson," I retorted. "We'll have to think of
something else, because what you suggest is simply not an option."

Can't you just hear it? "Hi Mom. Hi Dad. Guess what? I'll be
out of touch for a few weeks because I've made a little boo-boo.

I've gotten myself hooked on crank, and I'm admitting myself into drug rehab to get un-hooked. Don't worry about a thing. Talk to you when I'm released!" Yeah. Suuuuure!

Plan B: I will call Dr. Jackson twice daily for pep talks and encouragement. I will go to the center every other day to have my vitals checked. Nice goin', Leah. This is one of your finest moves yet.

May 2, 1982

Been off of meth for two weeks. Don't ask. Probably haven't slept a total of twenty hours in ten days. I can't hold a mug of coffee steady. I can't eat. My mouth is drier than hay. My eyes are drippy. To state my mood as irritable would be like describing Mt. Everest as a hill.

I'm keeping away from the family. They think I have the flu and don't want to expose Mom to a virus with her immune system so compromised. I don't even want to expose Oscar and Bentley to me. I'm glad my feline lovelies have each other. I wish I had a plot of ground dug deep to six feet. *Geez*, I am so tiresome about suicide. Listen Leah, either do it or shut up.

May 26, 1982

Still coming down from meth, shaky and wanting to scream every seven minutes. Although I only used meth for five months, just that amount of time can profoundly tangle someone up.

I'm hating school and realizing how nuts it is to be designing buildings and interiors I care nothing about when I just want to be with Mom. This month's assignment is to create blueprints, finishes, design boards, and a polished presentation of a self-designed three-floor spa from the ground up. Oh, joy! And that's just for one class. One out of five.

I have other priorities. Like: Mom's life, my tremulous health, and the non-fiction knowing that I am alone. "No man is an island." Really? I'm a half-inch dot of unused soil and rock in the expanse of the Pacific. I am an island so small it cannot be spotted. No one even knows I exist.

I'm attempting to be grateful each and every day that she's still alive and I'm not in bed shrieking and wailing. I'm grateful I'm living in my cozy cottage and not with Dad and Mom. I'm grateful I can eat more than a half piece of toast, but mad as hell that the number on the scale belongs to a small hippo.

Someone *finally* told me that I need a Bible to learn about Jesus. No kidding? What a revelation. I ran to my nearest bookstore and bought the NIV (*New International Version*) translation of the Bible. I started in Genesis. *Very* interesting! Truly! I like this book a lot. How can anyone not know that the place to find out about the Messiah is in a Bible? Have I lived a life in the sea with other ill-informed ocean species?

August 31, 1982

Ruthie and Jonathan are pregnant.

September 2, 1982

Ruthie and Jonathan are pregnant.

September 4, 1982

Ruthie and Jonathan are pregnant.

I'm not a person given to jealousy, at least not crippling or handicapping jealousy. I wish I could say what I feel is envy, in the way I've envied birds, dolphins, and the moon over Jamaica Bay.

But this is stale-green jealousy … no disputing it, no muting it, no brain-numbing to make it go away.

I'm thirty-four years old, single, the mother of two dead babies, and my kid sister is pregnant. Hold your ears, Deborah, I'm about to scream loud and long.

September 7, 1982

First day of the beginning of my third semester in design.

O.K. So I've joined the hip-hip-hoorays and ain't-this-fabulous family gaiety. I've started buying presents for our new family member. A collection of *Grimm's Fairy Tales*, a musical mobile of neon stars and half-moons for the crib, mint green crocheted booties, and the tiniest Phillies baseball cap ever designed or worn with pride.

*****

The day Adam was born, I cried and giggled all day. I love this boy as though he were my own. I knew instantly and intuitively that I would always be a fixture in his life. And that's how it has progressed. In some ways, we're so alike it's both spooky and fantastic. We understand each other in indefinable but so totally satisfying ways. We zig and zag in rhythm with each other's waves.

I do have the advantage of not having to parent him, so we share secret stuff and trust each other with unyielding faith. Last summer, when he was fifteen, we traveled to Greece and Morocco together for three weeks. What a blast! He's a fab-o traveling companion! Mom and Adam hold places in my life and heart no one else ever has or likely will.

*****

1983

Deb, can you believe this is the beginning of my last semester? School is truly challenging.

Taking care of Mom when I can and calling her a couple times daily takes sections of my smashed heart and twists them into sailor's knots.

I stay alone most of the time because the school workload is vast, and I barely want to look at people and inadvertently encourage small talk. I'm not clinically depressed, but I'm sad, anxious about school, and scared senseless Mom will leave me here without her.

Last night Sarah and Rachael insisted they take me out for dinner. I didn't want to go out to dinner. I'm still in survival mode, and just barely able to make it through the day. Truly, I was not interested in chatter or Greek food.

Anyway, the girls won and off we went to a neighborhood Greek place in West Chester, PA. Soon their motive for dining Greek was clear.

Rachael said, "Leah, you haven't *really* interacted with people in a long time. School barely counts. You're pulling into your tortoise shell and disappearing. We miss you. The whole world misses everything you have to offer, and they don't even know it. This is your pattern, Lee, and we have a plan to turn it around."

"Oh really?" I said. "Do I get a vote? I'm not sure I'm as ready as you two think I am."

"You're ready," Sarah said. "Here's the plan. We've already called this guy named Peter who works at a nearby regional theater. He's the chairman of the Scenic and Lighting Department.

He said he'd be happy for us to come over, and he'll talk to you about ushering at the theater on weekends."

"Oh, really?" I said.

"Yes, really," Sarah repeated.

They also won this round, and off we went to Peter's place.

Peter lives in an ancient farmhouse mansion along with a five-member rock band. The farm sits on multiple acres; horses with heavy blankets stroll the pastures.

He greeted us, and we followed him to his room, which was delightful in the way an artist's bedroom would be. There was a fire blazing, bass guitars were all about. The wall art was comprised of his own creations. Plaster walls were painted muted green. High ceilings were beamed and stained with soot. Wooden baseboards were seven inches high, and his bedspread was patched in squares, rectangles, and triangles from the costume shop's toss-away bin. Soooo enchanting!

We all sat on the floor, and everyone talked except me. I was feeling shy, inward, wordless, and out of place. Eventually, Rachael left for one of the other bedrooms to nap. Sarah stated she was off to finger the harp she saw in the band room. I *could not* believe these two women left me alone with a stranger. My cheeks flushed and I played with the fringe on my jeans.

Peter talked in soft tones and asked appropriate questions. He discerned my discomfort and so he served to comfort. I did the best I could. I agreed I would try ushering at the theater but said I would be surprised if I could memorize the house seating chart. He assured me everyone would be helpful and he'd keep an eye on me too. Well, okey-dokey then.

As we were leaving, Peter shouted into the winter wind, "Hey, how about I make us dinner on Thursday?"

I kept walking, and Rachael and Sarah turned and said, "Okay. Great!"

"Well, actually, I meant Leah," Peter clarified.

Huh? I turned slowly and said like a sheepish sheep, "You mean me?"

"Yes, I mean you. I'll get your number from Rachael sometime this week. Okay?"

"Okay," I managed to whimper.

April 16, 1983

We've been dating for about eight weeks, and at Peter's invitation, I've semi-moved into the farm mansion, but we stay at my place a lot too. I don't want to love this man so soon. He doesn't love me. That's not hard to discern, and he hasn't said he does. Maybe my feelings take flight because of years of sexual deprivation with a husband who wouldn't touch me. Maybe it's because Peter is completely adorable, and I just can't help it.

He's not the type of man I would imagine could take my heart. He's the type of man I could see as a buddy, a pal. But no, I surprise myself once again and find him irresistible. Six feet of lean muscle with all his shapes and curves those of male statuary.

You think I'm exaggerating? Deborah-girl, I promise you, I am not. Even the arch in his feet and the shape of his toes. The muscle mass in his calves are like those of a swimmer. His shoulders are in complete ratio to the rest of him; they are straight across, no dipping, no sloping. His hair is silken brown and skims his shoulders. His eyes are Mediterranean blue.

I sound like I've described an Adonis ... but he's not that. At first, I thought he looked like a cross between Johnny Appleseed and Ichabod Crane. But you know how these things work. Once you love a man, he looks like someone other than the person you first met. Now his face and all his shapes are, for me, the music of his essence.

I look at him as he crosses a room and feel schoolgirl butterflies. I see him in his bikini briefs and force myself not to touch him. When I hear his Karman Ghia hit the gravel driveway, I force myself to continue my task and not run to the door and devour him before he puts his stuff on the counter. This is appalling.

He told me he now understands how women can feel objectified. In other words, I want him far more than he wants me. I've been in the desert crawling across sand for years and he hasn't. Plus, his work is so demanding and requires so much focus and so many hours … there is little of him left when he gets home. He just wants a meal, very little talk, and some mindless TV.

But I can handle it all, because the time we do spend in merriment is so scrumptious. He cracks me up. He's a born comic. Last night, while at an ATM, with me waiting in the car, he pantomimed robbing the ATM with an imaginary machine gun. He looked furtively around, hunched over as though making himself invisible, and when the machine spit forth the bills, he grabbed them and sprinted to the car like an Olympian. He's the "funnest" man I've ever loved.

July 27, 1983

I got the design degree and will be looking for a job in the fall. Meanwhile, this summer I'll continue private practice with my kids.

Peter and I just finished packing the car for our ten-day sojourn to Cape Cod. I'm psyched.

Camera, film, and telephotos packed along with a fresh new journal. Walking shoes and sailing gear. Scuba masks and fins.

Lotions and potions and reservations at some of the loveliest bed and breakfasts on the Cape. A new adventure to catalogue in our book of adventures.

Journeys with Peter are so easy, like liquid gold. We find ourselves mirrored in each other as we sway into our blend with grace.

September 22, 1983

I secured a position at an interior design firm in Philly. It's a prestigious firm, so they only let me do gopher work until G-D-only-knows-when. I guess it's okay, though, since we're still having to deal with Mom's ordeal while I continue to adjust to a new-ish relationship and fight the ever-present uphill battle of just being me.

December 23, 1983

Getting a teensy bit bored with gopher status at the design firm. Come on, you guys, give me a shot. I think you'll be pleasantly surprised. Really, I do.

December 24, 1983

I'm so excited! Tonight, Peter and I are wrapping our Christmas gifts for each other. Being my first for-real Christmas, I asked Peter, "So what's the deal? A stocking? A gift or two?"

He said, "Sure, a stocking and a significant gift or whatever you feel like doing. Anything we do will be great."

I've spent a lot of December making and collecting gifts for him. I have loved it! We've hand-made cards to send to friends and family.

This Christmas thing is grand and wondrous. Hanukkah is fun too … but because this is new to me, it feels a lot more thrilling, caught up as I am in the whole seasonal madness.

Peter decided instead of an evergreen, we would cut down one of the dead trees behind my rental house in Narberth. We've spray-painted it white and dressed it in silver tinsel and things we've been making for about two months: Photos of each of us in various stages of growth. Strung cranberries. Skinny strips of glittered tissue paper. A tiny nativity he's had since he was five years old. We strung a dreidel and hung it conspicuously along with my little plastic menorah. He made a haloed angel to top the highest branch, which he accidentally placed off center. But it pleased both of our artistic sensibilities, sort of a drunken angel, if you will.

Peter was raised Catholic and now practices nothing that is orga-nized. But he seems like the essence of a spirit-infused man. There is no malice or judgment or anything hard or angry about him. He is soft pink light and clean air and as refreshing as iced tea with mint.

We don't talk about Jesus or religion, but in my heart, I carry that cross in a night sky and know I belong to the Messiah who saved me from certain suicide. I'm looking for a support group of other people who love the Lord that I love.

Back to gifts, decorations, and Christmas cheer. Well, I didn't much like the stocking idea, because there were so many things I wanted to give him. Instead, I filled three pillowcases with gifts and painted stockings on them. When I dragged them in on Christmas morning, Peter howled in disbelief. But we had a blast opening the stuff, and I shot two rolls of film to capture his delight.

My significant gift for him was a Gibson bass guitar (*just like his*) that I had a jeweler create in white and yellow gold to hang on a sterling chain.

His stocking gifts to me were all purple or violet because that's my fave-o color. Each one was something I loved or wanted or needed or didn't need. Peter pays attention! And he bought me a

Nikon camera and a series of photography books! Now I can toss the $35 camera that I've been using for years. So much joy on the best Christmas I might ever know.

*****

1984

Deborah, I wish I were not writing about my life. I wish I were writing about a fictitious life, because what I'm about to report feels as though it *should* be a psycho-drama or horror movie, anything in all the world but my life.

I awoke two days ago and thought my lips felt weird. I went to a mirror to check out what the feeling looked like. It looked like someone had pumped my lips full of helium and they now spread over about half my face. I freaked. Then I looked into my throbbing mouth and saw blisters lining my tongue on either side and on both interior cheeks. I couldn't even think clearly enough to know who to call.

Call Peter? Not a chance. When he's at the theater, no other world exists for him. He has been patient and kind, but there is no doubt he is way past turned-off and tuned-out by the episodic remnants of my depressions, Mom's cancer, and the various other problematic issues that litter my life. How could he have possibly anticipated the complexities of a life with me?

I remembered the oral surgeon my parents know personally. I called, and he said to come in.

He wasn't sure, but he thought it might be herpes. Herpes! I haven't been exposed to herpes. He sent me to a dentist; he wasn't sure what it was either and didn't feel like guessing. By now the pain escalated to twenty-seven on a ten scale and tears stained my face. G-D, listen to me, please. NO WAY! Not one more illness. Not one more infringement on this freakish, out-of-control life. Can't handle it, honest. You want my attention? Fine. What do You want from me?

I can't go to work tomorrow. I look like a circus sideshow act, and there isn't a chance I could be of any value on any level to anyone.

*****

I was about to commence a thirty-month battle with this oral-blistering disorder. And it was this anguished journey that created a spiritual turning point for me and changed the trajectory of my life.

*****

February 13, 1984

Today is our Adam's Birthday. There's a party at 2:00 P.M. Again, I awakened to a mouth full of fire and lips the size of those red wax lips we wore for fun as kids.

My tongue and gums and the inside of my cheeks blazed with fire. Within an hour, I again had a mouthful of red-hot blisters. This is the second month in a row.

I sat in my car a half a block from Adam's party and watched the people with presents enter the house which was covered with banners, bows, and balloons. The clown they had hired parked behind me. She saw me weeping before I saw her coming, and with classic clown aplomb, she tied one of her own balloons to my door handle and blew me a kiss.

I left and drove through the Pennsylvania countryside for hours.

March 6, 1984

It's back … the swollen lips and fire-raging blisters inside my oral cavity. Whom should I call? What specialist might have an inkling what this scorching inferno is? Maybe a dermatologist? How should *I* know? But I'll try.

June 25, 1984

Every month the same story. A bonfire in my mouth that renders me unable to work or play or eat or kiss or talk. I just lie still and moan a lot. The dermatologist had no idea what this is. I've now been swabbed and biopsied. I've taken antibiotics and must hold three ounces of lidocaine in my mouth for hours at a time to numb the burn.

It looks like there's a pattern emerging. I feel my lips tingling, which leads to the lip swelling, and then all the blisters appear. This happens about two to three days before my period. Is it menses that triggers this thing?

Now I've scheduled appointments with an endocrinologist and my gynecologist.

August 12, 1984

I'm so tired of being sick and telling the same story to a parade of doctors who have no idea what this is. I've had to take a sabbatical from work, because what employer is going to put up with an employee who can't function for ten days a month? Are you kidding me, G-D? Have I done something egregious to totally turn You off? Do You despise me?

November 26, 1984

I AM NOT DOING WELL! I feel defeated. I don't know what else to do or where to turn for help.

*****

1985

Two more specialists are trying to figure this out: a PMS specialist and a holistic physician. I think I've consulted with eight doctors now. Or is it ten? And I've had three more tissue cultures, viral cultures, titers, more blood work, more biopsies, hair analysis, and cytological testing to add to the diagnostic potpourri. WWHHHEEEEEEEEEEEEE!

June 18, 1985

Hey, hey, Deborah, it's the medical anomaly, just checking in. I'll add the new diagnostic and therapy tools for this "fire mouth," as I have affectionately come to title the ... disease, virus, condition, plague? I dunno.

New drugs that haven't worked: Zovirax, Dyclone, Tetracycline, Kenalog solution, Prednisone, and Dapsone. I've also taken pharmaceutical tours with an anti-malaria drug and one used for leprosy. Leprosy! Nothing helps, and there are some gruesome side effects not worth using the energy to write about. And as you can see, I don't wish to write about anything else.

August 13, 1985

Finally, the chair of the Department of Dermatology at the University of Pennsylvania Hospital believes this is a viral disorder called *aphthous stomatitis*. Ain't that swell?

The only advantage of having *aphthous* instead of herpes is that *aphthous* is not contagious. But no one believes that. It looks like herpes, only worse, and kissing is the least of my sacrifices. I can't eat or talk either. I'm a mess.

Now I'm researching and reading everything I can find about this virus. I've called the research departments at the University of Chicago, the University of Maryland, John Hopkins, NIH, *Prevention Magazine,* the Health Information Clearing House, the Brain-Bio Center at Princeton, and even Dr. Wray at the Western Infirmary in Glasgow, Scotland. No one is encouraging. They say it's chronic and incurable.

This is another disease that completely disallows me to partic-ipate in a normal life? I am seared, scorched, scalded. Will I ever draw another joyful breath? Talk to me, G-D, I'm broken, scared, out of hope.

September 12, 1985

I went to see my Uncle Harry, a cardiologist, for counsel and support. Here's what he said: "You do indeed have a chronic and incurable disease. Be glad it only takes up ten days of your month, and not thirty. Learn to live with it. Be brave."

I walked out of his office, and something snapped in me. No, I thought; it doesn't take up only ten days. After the outbreak, it takes me several days to find my way back to where I was before it happened. And then days before the next outbreak, I'm anxious while anticipating its arrival. My whole life is ravaged. I can't work and I'm in no mood to play. This won't do. If the medical world can't help me, I must help myself.

September 20, 1985

Deborah, I've put the three-inch-thick file of accumulated medical research away and started a new file called "Spiritual Solutions."

I remembered my psychiatrist had recommended an acupuncturist, so I made an appointment. I also called a minister in Indiana said to have the gift of prophecy. She told me my body was pharmaceutically over-drugged, I would find my answers through seeking G-D, and that I would be relocating in six months. Really? Swell.

This week I finally found and joined a support group for people who also know G-D must be central to their lives. I've been given two books and a few tapes. The info is pretty interesting, but I don't think all these people are "Jesus" people. We study three huge volumes called *A Course in Miracles.*

*****

In total, almost three years passed before the outbreaks dissipated and my body and life began to heal.

The process was slow and demanding, but I was determined. Although I had been blessed with that cross in a night sky, I had not begun a vigorous spiritual quest as a result. There is nothing that rivets one's attention as completely as pain. Now, physical illness rather than mental illness had me paralyzed, and I was compelled to reach for G-D. I embraced the challenge and have not paused from a spiritual quest ever since.

Decades later, I can state I am grateful for that virus, because it helped me to unleash the Holy Spirit's healing power that lay dormant in my being. I was blessed to once again experience that through prayer, affirmations, and unyielding faith and trust, I would fall in love with G-D's mercy all over again.

What else could we desire but the truth about ourselves? Through my healing process, the patterns of my life unraveled. I began to see how I subconsciously believed illness brought me affection and attention. (And it did. I had my parents' undivided attention when I was ill.)

I began to hear the festering words my lips held back. To sense my denial of self. To feel my shame and guilt and fear. To acknowledge my anxiety, my dread, my buried wounds.

Honesty triggers surrender, and there is no defense against surrender. Surrender is at the core of every spiritual experience. As I laid down my barriers and became open to receive, I opened to the power of the Holy Spirit.

But surrender is not passive. Oh no! It is an active expression that requires enormous energy. After all, to demand the ego surrender, requires a warrior's courage. Love can be many things, but surrender is only surrender.

My faith and my Messiah rescued me when I gave up and begged for His guidance and mercy. Because it was not through any works of righteousness or research, but through the suffering He endured on those two trees in the shape of a cross, and the anointed blood He shed on that cross, that I was healed. His mercy bathed me, once again, in His healing touch.

When I decided to walk outside of earthly solutions, and pursued G-D with focus and vigor, G-D helped me to agree to the path He had for me. And with that came the healing. Amazingly, I was granted another medical miracle. I was awed and honored. I remain awed and honored.

*****

October 2, 1985

Jesus, I'm getting mighty tired of being told I am no longer a Jew by the Jews who know I've embraced You. They say I can't be both a Jew and a Christian. Really? Isn't that exactly what You were while on earth, Jesus? You managed beautifully to be both a Jew and a Christian, even though the term *Christian* wasn't coined until centuries past Your resurrection and ascension.

Yo, Jewish folks, G-D made me Jewish. It isn't something man can take away. It isn't that I'm proud of being a Jew any more than I'm proud of having brown hair. In both cases, it was not my fault, request, or achievement. It happened through genetics and G-D's plan for my life.

But I have conjured a tart reaction to people who tell me I am no longer a Jew. I get all excited and throw this gleeful expression on my face, and then with the enthusiasm of a gambler on a winning streak, I exclaim, "Oh boy, oh boy, then I guess that means I'm no longer a Tay-Sachs carrier either. How *fabulous*!" That usually quiets things down.

*****

Tay-Sachs is to the Jewish population what Sickle Cell Anemia is to African Americans. I happen to be a Tay-Sachs carrier, which essentially means if I were to marry a man who was also a carrier and we had a child, that child would show signs of this dreadful disease at three to four months and likely die by age three or four. That is why silence falls after I tell Jewish people I'm a Tay-Sachs carrier and am, therefore, obviously still a Jew, no matter what they believe.

The degree to which Jews have been both conditioned and blinded to even investigate their promised Hebrew

Messiah is something I understand, having been one of those Jews before 1979.

Think about this. Isn't it preposterous to assume a Jew, one sunny Saturday, would awaken and say, "I think I'll accept Jesus Christ as my personal Lord and Savior today"?

And let's just say that later that day, this imaginary person is sitting around his country club, sipping a vodka and tonic, getting psyched for a round of golf. Why in the world would he think he needs a Savior? Why would a member of the Chosen People, who has enough scratch to belong to a country club, think he needs a Savior, when he's already "chosen"?

It's a mess. If I had not tried everything there was to try to rid myself of mental illness ... there isn't much chance I would have turned to Jesus for help. It wouldn't have even occurred to me.

Only something as crippling as a twenty-two-year battle with mental illness and a preoccupation with suicide could have caused me to declare, with a sense of hopefulness and expectancy, that I believed Yeshua Ha Mashiach (Jesus the Christ) to be my personal Lord and Savior and the rightful redeemer of all people.

That, in all truth, is why I'm grateful for the years of neuro-chemical depression. It brought me to my knees and forced me to seek a spiritual solution to what the medical world could not fix. And when one asks, seeks, and knocks, doors and windows fly open, and questions find their answers.

For me, it required mental illness and aphthous stomatitis for G-D to permanently secure my attention and devotion. (I'm not implying that G-D "gave" me those two diseases. I'm suggesting they got my attention, "because all things work together for good for those who love G-D and are called according to His purpose.")

For those who may not know, Jesus was a Jewish boy born into a Jewish culture. Jesus is the English translation of his Hebrew name, which is Yeshua. His Mom, Dad, disciples, and friends all called Him Yeshua, because that was and still is His name. Yeshua Ha Mashiach is the Hebrew translation of "Jesus the Christ" or "Jesus the Anointed One" or "Jesus the Messiah." I just thought I'd explain, in case you weren't aware.

*****

October 18, 1985

Oh, Deb …

Life in Pennsylvania grows increasingly hard. You know the interior design business I started after I left the design firm in Philly? It's a total bust. What in the world made me think I could run a business? I have the talent for the design portion of the biz, but that's just a portion of the biz, and without a command of the business end of the biz, there simply is no biz.

Not surprisingly, I'm in the red because three clients will not pay their bills. One wealthy gal is simply not satisfied with the dye lot of the custom-made fabric on her custom-made sectional and insists she simply ain't payin'. I cannot pay for a $15,000 sofa. She had signed off on the swatch after I told her it might be a few shades lighter or darker, depending on the dye lot.

The other two clients are just tardy, as in four months tardy. They don't *feel* like paying and can read *not a businesswoman* written in red marker across my forehead. I will need to take them to court. Isn't this fun?

Peter and I limp along. He's almost six years younger than I am. I met him when he had just completed his Master of Fine Arts and I was already a divorced woman who had lived in several major American cities and traveled large sections of several continents.

I find him outlandishly adorable, comedic, talented beyond what should be legal, a sensuous lover, and endlessly endearing. But we're in different stages of our lives. He's career obsessed, which is appropriate, and he's still very much tied to his birth family. I factor in, but not that high on his scale of things that are crucially important. It hurts. I'm overly accustomed to not being of transcendent importance to anyone but my parents.

And speaking of my parents, I'm exhausted from attempting to be their marriage counselor. Exhausted and fed up. This role I play in their lives started when I was just a teen. Not fair and not productive. I'm the spilling-well into whom they spill, and it hasn't exactly turned their marriage into euphoric splendor.

These aspects of my life are helping propel me in the direction of a geographic move: Parents. Stagnant relationship with Peter. Failed business venture. Insidious restlessness.

*****

Although Mom and Dad's marriage has difficulties, as most marriages do, these two people genuinely love each other. They aren't a superlative match, but their core values are certain, so they never could subject Ruthie and me to a splintered life. Divorce was not a frequent occurrence among Jewish people before the 1970s.

As mentioned, there was always an undercurrent of unresolved junk in our home, but somehow, we got through.

Love will carry people along a rushing current for a long time before they give in, give up, and sink.

My parents' correspond with each other regularly, as does everyone in my family. We do our most effective communicating on paper. No interruptions. The points made are covered thoroughly. No arguing or getting stuck on one point.

I have the letters my parents wrote to each other over the course of their relationship, more than six decades of captured words that map a courtship and marital journey. Fascinating. Heart-wrenching. Exquisite.

That which was most precious to Mom is that Dad unequivocally knew, wrote about, and verbally acknowledged that Nina Joy Kline was a rare and extraordinary woman, and without her he would not have become the man he became. That acknowledgment carried her through some treacherous times.

*****

November 5, 1985

I toy with the idea of moving to Virginia Beach. Since Mom was born there, a few family members still live there. I've gone to the Beach for years when I've had a week to play or a long holiday break. But I'm scared. I'm not really feeling adventurous. I know I need to create something new for myself and I want to begin with a fresh deck and a new group of people who don't know the mentally ill, oral-blistering, divorced, career-changing weirdo I am viewed as on these familiar byways.

I know who I am and who I am capable of being, but I don't think it's in the cards for the *real* me to emerge in Pennsylvania. Too many strikes. Too many misconceptions. Too little respect.

So how about it, Lord? What do *You* say? I'm not budging an inch until I hear from You.

November 19, 1985

Okay, Lord of my heart, I'm beginning to feel You stirring in me. I'm beginning to sense Your direction for me. You're right. I can try the Beach, and if I hate it, I can move somewhere else or move back here. Nothing is absolute. It's not like moving to a space station. It's just down the coast about two hundred and fifty miles. I can come home often to see Peter, Mom, Dad, Ruthie, and Adam. I'll ponder longer and listen harder, and maybe I'll hear a love song chanted by You.

November 30, 1985

Not surprisingly, Lord, You have helped prompt a plan in a blink of time. Tomorrow the loaded U-Haul will be driven to Virginia Beach by two friends who will haul my stuff, my felines, and me to the coastal town of Virginia Beach, Virginia.

I make this sound easier than it is. This is not easy. This is wrenching. Mom and I could barely stay in each other's company today. Peter and I walk around each other without saying much, although this is not a break-up. This is just the two of us living in two different states and visiting each other as often as possible.

I'm excited and scared. Probably more scared than excited. But once I have resolve, it's a done deal. I've secured a job at a design firm and have sublet a small apartment from a woman who wanted out of her lease.

Oh, Lord, please stay close. Guide and lead. Comfort and counsel. Please help me be all You wish me to be and teach me to know You more completely every hour of the time You lend me on this earth.

*****

In spiritual-word speak, Virginia Beach is considered a vortex in the United States, as is Santa Fe and Sedona and some other hot spots determined by energy fields and other physics concepts I have no understanding of at all. VA Beach is a New Age mecca, partially, I assume, because of the work contributed by Edgar Cayce and his Center for Research and Enlightenment.

I explained earlier I did not vigorously pursue a Bible-based congregation or even know to buy a Bible in the time immediately after embracing Jesus. I was very easily drawn in by the notions and practices of the New Age movement proliferating in Virginia Beach in the mid-1980s.

I was deeply involved in the movement for four years, naively assuming everyone in the New Age loved Jesus as much as I did. Even though I knew little about Him, I couldn't help but love Him. He had healed me of mental illness. He had healed me of aphthous stomatitis. He had given me the courage and direction to move to the Beach, amidst a host of other glorious gifts and guidance.

Because this is not a book focused on the New Age, I will not belabor the subject more than needed; however, some things must be explained in order to make sense of what happened after I disengaged from the New Age movement. Here goes.

*****

December 30, 1985

Deborah, in so little time here in Virginia, I've now experienced a past-life regression and attended two seminars: one on out-of-body experiences and one on channeling. I've participated in a chakra cleansing, and I've read a book on crystals and their healing power. My next-door neighbor, Suze, built a pyramid in my living room in which I sit to chant and meditate. (*I'm so glad my parents don't live around the corner. I know they would think I've completely lost my mind and would just be ever so concerned.*)

I watch as others do automatic writing and hear them channeling otherworldly voices from their vocal cords. I see them ooze with fascination at the power they embrace through crystal healings. I see them buy armfuls of books to digest, and, once again, I can't keep up.

I can't channel. I can't do automatic writing. The crystals sure aren't fixing anything and my past-life regression assures me I was Anne Frank's boyfriend. Right. Uh-huh! I'm paying close attention, Lord. I'm giving it my undivided focus. I'm committed. But I'm a New Age dolt.

It's worse than when I needed a tutor in math nearly every year of junior high and high school. That was humiliating and reinforced my firm belief that I was stupid, but this stuff isn't dependent on intelligence. (***Decades later it was determined that I have a specific learning disability***.) This is just me failing again at something those around me find enlightening. How come? I have my little bedroom shrine. I listen to meditation tapes. I've been to Sedona and chanted under the red clay rock formations of unimaginable beauty. I don't get it. Will I ever belong to anything that feels right for me, G-D?

*****

1986

I've become friends with a woman named Shirley. I met her shortly after I moved to Virginia Beach. We go to these seminars together and have gatherings in her home to enhance our base of New Age information. Shirley has been paying attention to me and is apparently much more interested in my health than in whether I can keep up with New Age practices.

She had a long talk with me last night. I hated every word she said, but I knew in my heart most of her words were true. She cares enough to tell me she watches as I deteriorate into a dim version of my former self. She knows my job at the interior design firm is sapping me of vitality, health, and drive. And my only job there so far has been to organize the chaos in every closet, drawer, and cabinet. She reminds me that at the end of each workday, all I have left is enough energy for a bath, a sandwich, and a bed. That's true. She knows I cannot make it on $8.50 an hour. That's true. I asked her what she had in mind as a solution.

She said, "Cut back. Work part time and ask your Dad for three hundred dollars a month to supplement your joke of a salary."

"Oh no! Not that! Not going there!" We argued into a near screeching match over that one. "Listen, Shirley. Dad put me through several degree programs. He doesn't owe me a nickel. If I'm having a tough time financially, well, tough nookies for me."

Shirley reminded me that everyone else in my family lives affluent lives and do whatever they want, whenever they want.

"Yeah. So?" I said, "That's their good fortune, and I don't happen to share their fortune. That's not their fault."

Shirley countered, "Right, and it's not your fault you're an unconventional, free-thinking, inspired artist who just hasn't come into her own yet. I've been watching you for a while now, and you are not lazy, not derelict in your responsibilities, not a leech, nor do you complain. But you're getting sick, Leah. You'll end up in a hospital if you keep this up.

"So what if you don't have your Dad's constitution or aptitudes. You just are who you are and that's plenty. You've been underestimated and undermined your whole life. Do you really think if your parents saw you right now, they'd be pleased or want you to continue with this path?

"You're not a parent, Leah, and that puts you at a disadvantage. Parents don't want to see their kids sick and struggling. You just don't see yourself as worth three hundred dollars a month. You really, really don't."

"Yup, that's right. They've done enough for me, and the last thing I need is Dad coming down on me for having two Masters degrees and not being able to earn a living."

"What's the crime, Leah? Does that make you a worthless schnook or crook or con? Does that make you so unworthy that you can't ask your Dad for an amount of money that's pocket change to him? I'm telling you, Leah, I'm not going to be able to watch this much longer."

"What does that mean?" I asked.

"It means if you don't ask him within the next month, I'm calling him."

"How dare you! Who the hell do you think you are? Stay the hell out of my business!"

"Wait," she said. "There's more. You tell me your sister and I are the only people you've allowed to read some of your past journals. I believe you, because if anyone who cared about your professional life had read them, they would tell you what I'm about to. Now here this: You're a writer. I don't give a damn what your degrees are in. I'm a speed reader and a prodigious reader. I know good writing when I read it. You need to work part time and write part time and rest when you need to rest. Here, I got this workbook for you and I really think you ought to seriously consider sitting down and doing the exercises it suggests."

"Wow! And you say *I'm* a hopeless romantic and dreamer?" I responded. "I'm not even in the same league as you. A writer! You're nuts. I'm just someone who keeps diaries, journals, and scribbles on the back of napkins."

"Right," Shirley said. "That's what you've been doing. Practicing. Now it's time to get down to work. I know you can write a book, no doubt several books. You've got the cadences and rhythm. There's lyricism in your words. Your thoughts are deep and rich, and they teach without lecturing. You're a natural. If you had taken even one writing course, someone might have told you that. So get up tomorrow, it's a weekend, and just sit down with that book and do some of the recommended exercises. Would you just try, Leah? I'm more or less begging."

*****

I did as Shirley requested and I liked it. The exercises led me to construct essays, stories, quips, and observations. About six years later, I had a book. It was published in 1993.

About two months later I worked up the steam to call Dad about the three hundred dollars. He wasn't overjoyed, but he wasn't mean. He knew I wouldn't waste time lying in bed watching soap operas and eating Godiva chocolates. We didn't even have to discuss that.

*****

1987

Shirley suggested we drive to Louisville to visit her family.
She had a few days off, and I needed a break from writing. I've
known Shirley's family for a while. They're growing toward sec-
ond-family status for me, and I adore Kentucky … the splendor of
the land and the horses that have the grace and power of animated
creatures. There is crispness and flair here, flavor and panache.
The people are kind, and the place has a select feel to it, something
distinct and singular.

At dinner everyone was merry, telling family stories and devour-
ing Southern delicacies.

My northern humor and stories found their way into the night,
and we all went to bed around 2:00 A.M., sated with all that the
evening held.

Here's the 3:00 A.M. part of the story. O.K., I had to pee. The
kitchen drew me with enticement to the freezer. Earlier, four gal-
lons of Breyer's ice cream had sat upon dessert trays. I had taken a
demure amount of chocolate.

But at 3:00 A.M., damn it, I ate the rest of the container of chocolate. It felt great going down! Afterward, mortified and sweating
guilt, I meticulously washed out the container, placed it in a plastic
grocery bag, and put the bag in my suitcase. Leah Rebecca!!!
WHAT???

Somebody help me! I'm in my forties and acting like a dessert
thief. This must remain forever exclusively between you and me,
Deborah!

The next day, Shirley's Dad asked casually at lunch if someone
had eaten the rest of the chocolate ice cream. Everyone said no. I

just focused on my cornbread. I know this man. He wouldn't have cared who ate the rest of the ice cream. He just didn't think he had finished all of it the night before. And if he really wanted more chocolate ice cream, he would have just sent one of his grandkids to get more.

My G-D! Do I need a rehab facility? Am I a future Food Thieves Anonymous participant?

I could just cry.

*****

In March of 1987, Mom was diagnosed with breast cancer in her other breast. It was not a metastasized cancer; it was brand new. Dad, Mom, Ruthie, and I were all in her surgeon's office when we got the news. Dad and I asked myriad questions. Mom and Ruthie stared out the window. The surgeon called her oncologist into his office.

These two doctors love my Mom. They both treated her during her first bout of cancer. She was pampered by these two men like the untitled queen she is. It was wonderful for us to know Mom would not be a faceless number.

Same game plan: a lumpectomy, radiation, chemotherapy. Mom was now sixty-seven years old and didn't have the vitality she had before her first bout of cancer. The stress on her diminutive body had taken its toll. I was frightened for her and for all of us. We were so not ready to lose her.

For over a year we plodded through the morass of the mess that is cancer. She was leveled when it was over. More quiet, less enthused, more reticent.

*****

She must not have totally fulfilled her earth-life purpose, because she became a long-term cancer survivor. Blessings from heaven.

*****

1988

I've been crying pretty steadily for at least three months. It's Peter. No, it's Peter and me. And Mom. And Mom and me. G-D, how I do love these two people.

I knew it was past time to let Peter go, let him fly, let him find his way down his own life path. When I love someone, I love him always. The end of a relationship never means the end of love for me. I know Peter will never entirely leave me, but I knew we were not meant to be.

You know our journey, Deborah. Peter and I weathered this geographic separation and visited each other often on weekends for over a year and a half. But it has worn us out, and something weighty as cement is settling in between us. I know he knows exactly what my spirit and soul tell me. He's far too sensitive not to pick up on the strangeness of this different vibe seeping into conversation and lovemaking.

I can't talk to him about this now because he's in the midst of opening two shows next month. He's stressed, overworked, irritable, and nervous. He, like every artist I've ever known, never thinks we'll be able to pull the magic together one more time. Each blank canvas or page or stage is a new challenge that is daunting, even terrifying. But I know both these shows will exemplify his stunning artistic workmanship in scenic design and lightning. He was born for this work, and someday he'll probably be internationally recognized.

I feel so sick inside, like I'm about to choose an amputation that will hurt so badly I might never again delight in kids or G-D or my own artistic expression.

275

March 10, 1988

Peter and I cried together for hours on the phone last night. He knew this was coming, as I suspected he did. He even wanted to initiate the end himself but just didn't. I'm not sure how I can endure this severe a loss and actually live through it. There's no one to cry with or even talk to, and who would really understand or care? Everyone processes loss differently, and I have no interest in what anyone has to say anyway.

Lord G-D, if I have ever needed You to help me breathe and keep putting one foot in front of the other, this would be the time. I'm devastated. I'm pierced. I don't even want there to be a tomorrow when I awaken and cannot call Peter to wish him a happy day and tell him, "I adore you."

*****

When Mom called a couple of years later to tell me Peter's father died, I immediately called him and asked if he wanted me to drive home to Pennsylvania from Virginia to be at the funeral.

"You would do that for me?" he asked.

"Yeah, Peter, of course I would do that."

I drove home. I knew he had married.

Mom said she absolutely wanted to go with me, not only to support me, but she loved Peter too. When we saw him standing next to his wife in the receiving line, Mom and I looked at each other, reading each other's thoughts: Peter and his wife were G-D-given gifts to each other. They looked right together. She's in the theater industry too, and they design shows together all over the country.

When we finally reached them in the long line, I found her charming, gracious, and completely lovely. I could see why I had to be moved out of the way, literally, to create space for them to meet. It was a reality check I must have needed. The in-person visual was more profound than anything my active imagination could conjure.

It took years for me to stop missing Peter with tears and longing. But once enough time passes, all things change. Tears stop. Treasured memories remain.

*****

November 22, 1988

Deborah, I'm not sure any more about these New Age principles and practices. I'm so confused. There's a restlessness in me more urgent than my normal restlessness. It could be other issues too. There are always issues involved in the business of just living. But now, this internal disquiet about the New Age feels more dimensional in scope than my mere inability to do the "tricks," as I have come to label them.

Now, this discomfort lies deep in my belly as though I've swallowed a rock. There's a fuzziness in my rational, logical ability to think things through. I feel out of place, misguided, out of sync, a round peg in a triangular hole. Considering I've never felt truly at home in any group, maybe I'm just having a strange period and it will gradually fade. Still, I think I should pay attention to these rumblings.

*****

1989

Dear Deborah,

There was a musical I saw on Broadway eons ago called *Stop the World, I Want to Get Off.* Now … that's me! I want out. I want off. The New Age movement is too extreme even for me. Those feelings I was having months ago have crystalized. I now know I've seen enough and participated enough to be certain I'm ready to move on. I want my Jesus back. I want people surrounding me who are rapturous about Jesus. I've tired of hearing my LORD called an ascended Master or a really cool Rabbi or one of many sanctified spiritual Super-Dudes.

There is usually one thing that pushes someone off a cliff or around a bend or into a new home or job. But for me it wasn't one thing; it was more like multiple months of accumulated things.

So yesterday, all by myself, in a gesture of *I'm-not-kidding*, I took every gorgeous crystal I love down to the Atlantic Ocean. I wrapped them in my old Chivas Regal drawstring bag. I waded out into the chill of not-quite-summer ocean temperature and threw those things as far as my "pitcher's arm" would allow. Yup! Gone with the wind and the tide and the wishful thinking they could in some way fix me.

Tossing the rocks and crystals hurt me a lot because I loved those rocks and crystals. Not because they had or didn't have healing power, but because they are G-D's art, my favorite art: Sunrise and moon glow. Ocean currents and ten-thousand-foot mountain summits. Iridescent abalone seashells. Rock crystals of various weight, hues and texture that formulate directly in the

278

earth's crust. These are life's pleasures for me; I'm madly in love with G-D's artistry.

Then last night I got permission to use the club house, so I built a clumsy fire in the fireplace. I burned all four years of my accumulated notes. Yup! Can you stand it! Me! Burn my words! A first! Unheard of! About as out of character for me as anything I've ever done. But I felt a push from G-D to do so and, therefore, the task was not something I could forego.

This morning, I put all four years of my accumulated New Age books in a sheet and dragged them to the Dumpster. I hoisted those heavy books, a few at a time, and threw them into the world of trash and garbage. Now I feel much lighter. I'm going to bed until I feel like getting out of it, and I'm going to think and pray and ponder and see what G-D has to say to me about anything and everything.

This is your cue, G-D! Talk to me, please. Give me answers to the sizzling questions only You know I have.

August 14, 1989

Deborah, one must be very careful about what one asks for. I asked G-D to show and tell me the answers to my heart's questions vis-à-vis the New Age and other more personal things, and along with many answers, He gave me a directive. This directive is high on my Hit Parade of things I would *never* want to do.

Never.

But G-D more than sort of said ... He distinctly said (*in that still small inner voice you know sure as hell isn't you, because you would never say this to yourself*): "Leah, about those two abortions you had in 1966 and 1977 ... well, it's time to deal with them now. It's time to come out of denial and stop thinking of them as though they were merely tooth extractions."

Oh no. Not that. I don't want to think about those abortions. I really, really don't. But I know G-D is not interested in my stomach-churning objections. It isn't as though I felt His anger or even conviction. It was more like knowing your Dad has given you sound advice even though you despise it.

So, what now, Deborah? What does He even mean by "deal with them"?

September 25, 1989

G-D's work is more than "mysterious;" it's curiously congruent. Answers are supplied when needed and not a nanosecond sooner. I call Him my "11:59:59 G-D." He's never late, but he's never even a finger snap early. I have a hunch this is because He wants to build our faith and test our ability to wait for His perfect answer, His perfect timing. But I could be wrong. It's just a hunch.

When I started to investigate how I would or could find help to "deal with" my two abortions, it took only a couple days to locate a crisis pregnancy center not far from my apartment. The office was cozy and unpretentious. I was graciously greeted and handed some brochures to peruse, then I was escorted to an office by one of the counselors. She explained about their post-abortion program of individual and group counseling and how all courses can be retaken if so desired. I asked a boatload of questions that generated more questions; her responses all made sense logically and therapeutically.

In recesses deep in my spirit I knew I'd found the right place. Although I had no desire to do this painstaking, wound-opening work, I felt I had no choice.

September 30, 1989

What have I gotten myself into? Oh, my G-D! This is torturous, and I've only been to my second session at the crisis pregnancy center. There are about twenty-three of us. Two of us are men who are post-abortive. They are "man enough" to face their participation in their partner's choice and acknowledge the baby was theirs too.

We have hours of homework from a workbook specifically designed to take post-abortive people through the gradual steps of repenting, grieving, and healing. Sobs emanate from the room during each session. Some people walk out to collect themselves.

The stories are unique, heart-opening, and heart-searing. There are a few women like me who don't have any living children. There are people with a ton of kids. We each grieve differently for different reasons.

What I love most about this group is the unbridled honesty. No one tries to weasel out of their choice. No one is defensive or cavalier. We are a broken group with nothing to hide; we are transparent in our need for help.

October 5, 1989

Deborah, today was my fourth individual therapy session. Oh, puulleezze! This is a type of self-inflicted torture that just better result in some substantial healing. Suzy, my counselor, showed me a film today depicting what really happened to my kids during the extractions. Will these images ever be released from my psyche? No. Of course not. How could they be?

This film needs to be mandatory viewing for the world, certainly for students and for girls and women considering abortions. Minds that are certain they *think* they want an abortion would inevitably be changed by at least a percentage of females. This is a grotesque form of human destruction that's simply not clear to the girls and women in panic mode, who cannot think clearly and are not truly informed about their choices and the potential consequences.

I know that panic vividly from 1966 and 1977. But during those decades, I did not seek counsel nor was I shown films or talked to about my choices. Abortion is huge business, as I am learning; one of the most lucrative industries in the world.

Why would people doing these abortions or running these clinics want to stop the enormous flow of cash pouring into their coffers? Answer: they wouldn't.

But they are self-deluded if they think they're helping women. They're helping their bank accounts. Maybe some male abortionists are naive because this isn't happening to their bodies. How can they REALLY get it? Well, maybe they can sort of. Maybe not.

This is certain: abortion is a heinous hell-storm that destroys potential little people and often ravages post-abortive mothers. We're the silent walking haunted, suffering a grief that is forbidden and scorned. Trapped in unconscious feelings and aberrant behaviors that we may not have had prior to our abortions. But few of us suspect that the genesis of these issues may have been born because our babies weren't.

November 25, 1989

Deborah. Deborah. Deborah, can someone have the most horrifying day of one's life and come out with a prize that makes up for all of it? Yes! Because that's what happened to me today. I was in individual counseling, and we were getting deeper into the effects these two abortions really had on me.

I was truly in La-Dee-Da Land with regard to how these choices affected me. I had a zillion other things on my plate every year of my life, and why harp on something far in the past when there's nothing one can do about the past?

Here's why it's imperative to deal with the past. There is a Post Abortive Syndrome that has been studied in great and grave detail. One post abortive effect is that harmful, unconscious thoughts and deviant behavior can develop and linger after an abortion. I have many of the symptoms.

Lots of post-abortive women have addictions to food, alcohol, street drugs, sex, gambling, or shopping. Many of us have no ability to trust men and therefore go through a parade of them, unconsciously thinking of them as scorpions, liars, cheats, and self-serving jerks.

Many women have trouble bonding with the children they have later in their lives. Some of us cannot stop mourning the children we aborted. Many of us cannot keep a job. Some of us roam from city to state to country feeling misplaced, angry, restless, unfocused, and so sad, so, so sad. Many post-abortive women and men have basement-level self-esteem. Many women are angry at the fathers of their babies who pushed them to abort, or the parents who drove them to their abortion. Most of us live with a nebulous guilt or feeling of dread we don't understand. Recurring nightmares about children are common.

Some women hate the sight of baby carriages, mothers in the park, or families in general who don't have to deal with this issue, which can easily destroy relationships and family unity.

This is a sinister syndrome that can eat you alive. Denial is lethal. It forces you to live a lie. It turns your thoughts into warped truth. It creates a make-believe world where the truth of your pain is so buried or distorted that it causes you to be an imitation of yourself.

I won't declare this is *everyone's* life who lives with the aftermath of abortion. That would be a generalization too wide in scope. But I will never again back down from saying many women are marked for life by the abortions we so easily dismissed. We go directly back to the lives we lived before the abortion(s) and send all evaluation into distant space. We put evaluation anywhere at all except into conscious thought.

Potential solution: a woman wanting an abortion should have two hours of mandatory counseling with a post abortive woman who is no longer in denial and has herself been counseled. This should occur before an abortion can be approved. I think it is a key to a truly informed choice.

Okay … so here's what happened to me today!

One never really knows why something hits on a particular day or hour. I couldn't have anticipated today with the aid of an auditorium filled with sages, seers and crystal balls. I don't remember what Suzy said about my two abortions that triggered a response that tumbled from me with ferocity and volume. But I know I found myself on the floor of her tiny office in the kind of hysteria one remembers for a lifetime. Mucus poured from my nose and my eyes became swollen slits in an unnaturally crimson face. I muffled my screams into a pillow and humpty-dumptied myself right off the wall into a zillion pieces of stinkin' rotten egg.

What I had chosen during those pregnancies came into a kind of focus that didn't blur or mute any aspect of my choices.

- This was true contrition.
- This was the searing pain of loss.
- This was humiliation before my G-D.
- This was me begging my children to forgive me and allow me to breathe and carry on with a life of meaning.
- This was repentance in textbook Technicolor.

- This was a fractured, humbled, weary woman who was left
  with no place to hide from the consequences of her choices.
  This was me in the lowliest state I'd ever known.

But, my loving G-D, what have I ever done to deserve what
happened next? I was prompted to lift my head from the carpet and
when I did, You gave me a vision that will sustain me for life.

Clear as crystal in sunlight, I saw the backs of my two
kids as they held hands. They were walking through a diaphanous,
fluid scene of pinks, corals, and violets into an unknowable adventure. The little girl was taller, wearing a butter-yellow shirt and a
red skirt that had little red suspenders. She wore white socks and
red Capezio shoes. The boy was in navy blue pants and a white
collared knit shirt with white socks and navy blue Keds.

My heart nearly leapt from its home in my chest. I knew
instantly who they were. And then, my caring G-D, You whispered
into the core of me, "Your oldest child is Esther, and your little boy
is Gabriel."

All crying ceased and I just stared in disbelief and relief. Then,
Lord, You slowly allowed the vision to penetrate every hollow
of my being before You gently dimmed the vision of my son and
daughter into non-existence.

I couldn't talk. I didn't want to. Suzy had no idea what You
had allowed me to see. I nodded at her indicating I had to leave. I
left, came home, started writing, and here I am … whispering of a
vision that will impact everything about my loss, everything about
my knowing they are safe, everything about my assurance we will
be reunited, and everything about my knowing that indeed I am the
mother of two children who frolic in another dimension.

It will take time for all of this to filter in and find a place in me
that is sacred and safe. But G-D, You could not have done anything

to bring peace to my being with more clarity and assurance than what You chose to do today. My babies are alive! My babies are alive!

Esther and Gabriel ... my kids are alive!

*****

June 21, 1989

Esther, my daughter,

I believe you know me, and therefore you know I have written countless letters over my forty-four years. But never to you. Dare I come to you now? Is it ever too late?

Esther, forgive me. I had so little understanding as a girl of nineteen, that what I was doing was denying you life and denying me motherhood. I feel you have forgiven me, and I believe you are grateful I have finally faced the act which claimed your life, because now, we can be truly connected.

I acknowledge and bow in humility to the sacrifice you submitted to. Did you know, prior to your implantation in my womb, that you would never see the earth's blue sky or the brilliant yellow of a daisy's center? Did you know you would not be comforted by your mother's arms or share in the joys and struggles of our mutual lives? What did you know, so long before I knew anything?

Although I have only actively missed you for two years, having lived in denial for over twenty-three, you may know I am an intense woman and so I have packed decades of longing for you into two years of accumulated days.

Sometimes I fear I might die from the pain of the loss of you. Sometimes I fear I will not die, and that's almost worse.

Esther, it is embarrassing to me that I have not tenaciously clung to life, and that the prospect of longevity holds so little appeal to me. Maybe you know that decades of an anguished life, lived through the biochemical debris of my mentally ill brain, allowed me to consider suicide as my best friend. Was it you who prayed for my survival?

If so, as you can see, your prayers have worked.

I know now if G-D creates a life, He has a purpose for that life, so I really had no right to extinguish your life. It was a slap in G-D's face that I anguished over how, as a nineteen-year-old, I would provide for you. If I had *really* known G-D, I would have known He had the answers for both of us.

But I didn't know *that* G-D when I decided to end your life. All I knew was I had term papers due, tests to study for, and a long-range life agenda that did not include a child at nineteen years of age.

I have read touching novels and autobiographical accounts of how women perceive their aborted children. Dare I believe you are really well and happy and we shall laugh someday together and play among the stars?

Yes, I do dare, and I hold to the dream in the hope that it is a promise. How does one apologize for so vast a choice of selfishness? Words are powerful and incisive, but there are no words that could begin to encompass the enormity of my pain in denying us each other.

By denying you an earth life, I denied myself motherhood. All of the beauty, the sorrow, the nurturance and sacrifice, the facets of character that develop through motherhood, have been lost to me. But I learn fast, so perhaps as we move forward, we will be able to have a spiritual life together. A life whereby we cannot touch, see, or hear each other, but a shared life of sensing and intuiting each other.

Come to me in dreams if it pleases you, Esther. I will receive you.

And in spite of the swift end of a shared earth life, I will always be your mother. You will always be my daughter. I am so grateful to G-D that He cares for you now.

December 21, 1989

I had a very no-nonsense thought today. Many soldiers come home from every war with various issues and physical handicaps. One of the worst is post-traumatic stress. My thought is that killing is truly unnatural, even though it has been going on unendingly. So, to not expect our boys and men to come home damaged by seeing and participating in the human atrocity of killing, is to be ill-informed or flat-lined.

Why would a woman who is not in denial about her abortion be any different from a shell-shocked vet? How could we possibly expect she will not suffer from post-traumatic stress?

During war, men kill total strangers.

During abortions, mothers kill their kids.

I could say it nicer and all, but why bother?

Another thought: Too often I have been told that women are not killing babies; they are removing a cluster of cells, a non-viable "thing" that is useless without a womb. A fetus or a not yet fetus, a nebulous blob.

Really? Well, then what is this blob? It's definitely not a radio or rose or river. If left alone, this blob will develop into a fully realized person called a baby. It will not develop into a fully realized radio, rose or river. It's just a teensy, weensy, itsy bitsy baby. Case closed.

*****

THE NINETIES

Deb, I know I've heard the title "Messianic Judaism" before, but it wasn't until a few days ago I learned Virginia Beach actually has a Messianic congregation. This means that Jews … actual real-life blood Jews, who believe Jesus was, is, and always will be the promised Hebrew Messiah, choose to worship in a Jewish context, along with many Gentile Believers who also wish to join in the worship and teachings that reflect the foundation of their faith. This would include the thirty-nine books in the Old Testament\Covenant and twenty-seven books in the New Testament\Covenant.

Messianic Jewish Believers simply believe G-D wouldn't stop telling His truth on the last page of the Old Testament and start lying on the first page of Matthew, in the New Testament. Together, both of these Testaments make up one Bible. To not read part two **(the New Testament)** would be like closing a novel and not reading the last twenty percent of it or walking out on the last twenty percent of a film. You'd be a noodnick and miss the best part, the resolution, the power, and the promises.

The truly neat-o thing is that every prophecy about Jesus in the Old Testament is fulfilled in the New Testament. EVERY SINGLE ONE OF THEM … and that would be hundreds of prophecies.

G-D is just so astonishingly brilliant! And every one of our own life stories is handled by G-D with as much precision and attention to detail. We think we know ourselves? We know a fraction of what G-D knows about us, including our needs before we need them and our thoughts before we think them. I am sooo in love with G-D. And for sure, He's the best friend I'll ever have.

The day I accepted Jesus as my Lord in May of 1979, a Messianic rabbi gave the guest sermon in the little church that day. It was with him that I said the salvation prayer that brought me into the Lord's kingdom. See what I mean about the details? I mean REALLY? A visiting Messianic rabbi for His mentally ill Jewish daughter? What are the chances? It was the first time the Rabbi had been to that little church.

Deb, are you ready for another serendipitous happenstance that brought me to a Messianic congregation in Virginia Beach? Yup, I thought you would be. My toilet broke. I called a plumber. He saw a note I wrote sitting on the kitchen counter that read, *Find Messianic congregation.*

He said, "Ms. Kline, is it you who's looking for the Messianic congregation?"

"Uh-huh," I said.

"Look no further," toilet dude said. "That's my congregation, and if you want, I'll give you directions to get there."

The first Friday night Sabbath I attended this synagogue, I bonded in a flash with the rabbi and his wife because they too are Jewish, from New York, and we had many things in common. Home at last. A community of like-minded people who don't think of me as a clown-freak-with-hay-for-brains because I proclaim Yeshua Ha Mashiach as Lord. Life is lookin' up.

*****

1991

I now spend time at the crisis pregnancy center to help in whatever way I can.

This is the work that gives meaning to the entirety of my life. This is the classic take on G-D turning sour lemons into the sweet elixir of lemonade. I have purpose. I have things to say and things to offer and help that actually helps! These women in crisis pregnancies or in post-abortive regret have been led to this humble building and effective ministry in a sleepy coastal town on the shores of the Atlantic in VA. Thank G-D for this place.

I went to a memorial service yesterday, and it moved me so deeply I wrote about it:

*****

The Cemetery of the Innocents

It is the kind of day poets whisper about and artists endeavor to capture. The sky's shade is translucent lavender blue. Spring's youthful baby-green leaves birth themselves on arched branches. Pine needles soften the earth to feel like a cloud.

We are surrounded by elegant buildings of brick symmetry that speak of majesty, solidity, power, and grace. Hundreds of acres and century-old trees cloak us in a secluded haven.

On the green blanket that covers brown earth, four thousand four hundred small white crosses stand in silent homage ... stand in stoical regard to honor the memory of those we have chosen to deny life.

I am not alone. A male friend has accompanied me. He cares about me enough to share my pain.

The crowd of mourners swells. There is a unique beauty in this gathering. It is the quality of beauty born when two or more are gathered in His name. Every humble little cross represents hundreds of thousands of babies. Every mourner represents throngs of the walking wounded.

We open in prayer and song. It is a muted and reverent sound that flows from us. A gentle woman invites any or all of us to take a rose from the white wicker baby carriage, choose a cross, place our red symbol of nature's perfection at the foot of that cross, and memorialize, sanctify, bless, and mourn the lives who live in another dimension.

My friend holds my hand as we choose our flowers and choose our crosses. I will never, ever, forever and ever, forget the image of a brokenhearted sea of mourners kneeling, praying, wailing, holding, and sharing.

I sensed G-D's pleasure in our acknowledging our capricious choices that ended the lives of those to whom He had given life.

How we do thank You, Father G-D, for Your patience and generosity in caring about our transgression and selfishness. How we do thank You, Jesus, for the relentless ways in which You intercede for us, break us, change us, build us, heal us, love us. How we do thank You, Holy Spirit, for empowering us, guiding us, and being our instantaneous help when we call for Your wisdom and words to pour through us.

In the soft air and pale sky of an April day, we cry out and up to all of you, our precious babies, who died as courageously as any soldier in battle or any martyr slain for G-D.

May the Lord bless and protect each of you. May the Lord's face radiate His joy upon you. May He be gracious to you. Show you His favor. Give you His peace.

We miss you. We love you. Forgive us.

*****

By now, I had been writing my first book for six years. It was a laborious love effort. I was learning about Scripture and about the LORD as I wrote and re-wrote. I would beg people who were seasoned Believers to talk to me and teach me and sometimes I came to these gatherings with a pad filled with questions. How the book came to be published is a doozy of a story, best saved for another time. It took three years after the book was complete to see it in print. It is called AWAKENINGS… A Jewish Woman's Search for Truth.

*****

1993

Deb …

This was another one-of-the-best-days-of-my-life days! This is the day my first book, my precious work of love and labor, came off the presses. Shirley and I went to pick up some cartons at the printers.

I laughed. I cried. I transformed into a Mexican jumping bean. Then I stood silent and gazed. I checked out the binding, the color saturation on the cover, the gold leaf stripes at the top and bottom of the cover.

I felt, in a not-off-the-wall nonsense kind of way, as though I had birthed something. I held all the book's wonders with reverence and awe, knowing that only the Lord could have orchestrated this just the way He did. I wonder what He has planned for its flight into the hands of readers.

August 14, 1993

Every year there's an international Messianic conference in the summer somewhere on the globe. This year it's in Virginia Beach and my rabbi is chairing this weeklong international event. About six weeks ago the rabbi asked if I would like to present one of the essays from my book to the largest crowd of the conference, which gathers on Sabbath, Friday night, before the conference's conclusion on Sunday.

I naturally said, "Oh, yeah," even though inside I was shouting, "Hell, no!" This was a terrifying invitation. Naturally, I had to make it more difficult by declaring I'd lose fifteen pounds before the conference.

I chose to present the essay without any notes. Memorized. Just me and a blackened auditorium holding fifteen hundred people. A follow spot will light me and a lapel mike will broadcast my voice. No visual distractions. Not even a standing mike. Not surprisingly, I have been sick-nauseated with stage fright for days.

I've rehearsed the thing a ridiculous number of times. I probably could recite it backwards ... and still I feel ill. Thin, but ill.

My rabbi has never ever heard me speak publicly, and he has asked me to do this! G-D must have assured him I can do this, because he has no reason to believe I can pull this thing off without embarrassing him or myself.

Mom is flying in to see me present.

August 20, 1993

Mom is trying to act calm to keep me calm. Not working. We're both a mess. I have to get dressed in a few minutes. I'll be wearing all black ... a slinky form-fitting full-length skirt with a respectable slit to just below my knee. The tuxedo jacket with black satin-lapels is belted, and I look lean and about as statuesque as someone four feet eleven inches can look. Well no, let's not be ridiculous. Not statuesque. More like a facsimile of pulled-together. Better than cute. Maybe sophisticated and self-assured. But my insides do not look self-assured. I wish Dad were here.

(*Later, about midnight*) Please indulge me while I shout, "Oh G-D! Oh, Wow! What a rush! Enthralling!" The standing ovation made me cry. Talk about being judged by a jury of your peers! Fifteen hundred Messianic Jews from around the globe screaming their approval and applauding with thunderous enthusiasm. I could see Mom because they brought the house lights up to dim brightness during the ovation. She was crying while throwing kisses from the second row as two women on either side of her held her steady.

It felt *almost* surreal. But I was fully conscious, knowing I was standing center stage as my mind, with ease, glided back to me at age thirty-two: depressed, suicidal, a woman who had run out of hope and rope. And here I am tonight, a dozen years later: A herald. A messenger. A harbinger.

Now I understand what G-D meant on May 25, 1979, when He sent me a cross in a night sky and assured me. He had work for me to do and I was *not* to take my own life.

Thank You, Lord, for giving my life validation, vindication, purpose, scope, and the unbridled joy of moving an audience because of the message You sent through me. Every bit of suffering has been worth the wait.

I bow to Your timing, wisdom, and the gifts You have so generously given to me. Mostly, I praise You for choosing me to choose You! Never will I receive a more priceless gift than You as my Lord, best friend, heart's delight, and fulfiller of dreams.

I LOVE YOU SO MUCH, DADDY-G-D.

*****

May 26, 1993

Mom, Happy Birthday, sweetie-face…

I am so relieved this May, as in all preceding ones, you are with me and I can say, "Happy Birthday. I adore you."

I am in constant awe of the grace G-D extends to this family. The assailants who entered Dad's plant with sawed-off shotguns and shot him twice, could have ended his life. Cancer could have twice eaten you alive. My car accident in 1976 could have claimed my life, and if not the accident, surely suicide might have been my choice. Ruthie might have died from meningitis. Each of us has been spared and continues to breathe air and watch dogwoods bloom.

I listen as you speak of the achievements of your girlfriends. It's not the measure of a life, Mom. The "achievement model" has grabbed many people and even cultures of people. This leaves many people who have not achieved tangible recognition, feeling less than adequate.

But I meet people as I journey my path, and most are not caught up in the achievement model as a measuring rod of success. Like you, it has been hard for me to abandon this zealous model.

I'm still navigating through debris. I still feel guilty if I'm not doing something constructive or productive. But at least now I see the falsity of that perspective. It induces guilt, low self-esteem, an unhealthy comparison to others, and a spirit of over-the-top competition.

Achievement is simply that and nothing more, Mom. It says nothing of one's heart or character or humanity. It doesn't measure how G-D or other people view us. It only measures how we view ourselves.

You are blind in not seeing who you are and what your life has brought others. A Type A personality is not the only legitimate one. The world needs type A's. They are the movers and shakers who get things propelled. But G-D created balance for the whole of the universe. It wouldn't work at all if everyone had a mania to produce and achieve. Who would rock the babies? Who would sit at the sea's edge and watch the currents change?

Some of us were born to create, using the artistic gifts bestowed to us. What holds you back, Mom, could never serve you well. A fear of mediocrity. Inertia. Procrastination.

Your soul longs to create. All the other stuff is just hooey, Lovely Lady. The act of creation is pleasure enough for someone who's creative.

From whom do you think I genetically acquired the ability to write, paint, photograph, design interiors, string beaded jewelry, create floral arrangements, and entertain audiences? Certainly not from Dad.

Dad is the economist, scholar, business genius, orator, organizer, leader, and visionary. That is not who you and I are. Dad is our earthly king and without his gifts, our lives would have been hard in ways they are not. Certainly, each of us has suffered deeply, but we have not known the anguish of poverty or the agony of children we cannot afford to feed.

Everything I love to do and execute well are *exactly* the things you love and execute well. You might start an endeavor, but so soon, you abandon your joy in what you produce. You quit.

You and I want our lives neat and tidy before we indulge in the "superfluous" arts, but guess what, Mom? The errands and trivia will still be there after we've exploited our gifts. The stuff of life will be easier and accomplished faster because we're juiced from what we've created.

I will be merciful but relentless with you because I know you have enough steam if you'd just do it! Go shoot a roll of film of your grandson. Buy some beads and string them.

Just use your plethora of artistic sensibilities and *have fun*! Since you're still breathing, it's not too late.

For your Birthday, in the box with the rainbow ribbons, I have sent watercolors, brushes, a tablet of watercolor paper, and a book on how to just make the leap and start.

I treasure you. I'm proud of you. You are the Mom I would choose if all the Mommies who ever lived were lined up in a row. You are my exalted role model. Your simple presence graces this planet. As you are my champion and cheerleader, I am yours.

G-D bless your every breath, my elegant and delightful Mother.

Forever your, Miss Muffat

P.S. REMINDERS: You have a degree from an Ivy League school. Headed the department of Social Work at our local hospital. Helped Dad in the plant for years. Volunteered to do horticultural work with challenged patients. Worked for Red Cross. Wrote for the synagogue bulletin. Chaired design committees for many formal balls. Had a dried flower business. And, know it or not, you've had a letter writing ministry all your adult life. People tell me they still have letters you wrote to them decades ago. Enjoy who you are, Mom. Everyone else does. Xoxox

*****

1994

Deborah,

I'm on a plane headed for Los Angeles. Lizzie, my Public Relations person, lined up six weeks of speaking engagements for me, all through the many and majestic miles of California. I'm frightened it will all be too much for me. I fear I won't have the stamina. Will I be what people want or expect? Of course, if I bothered to factor G-D into the equation, I might be more confident and less pathetic. Maybe I should give that a whirl.

Speaking gig number one: Completed! It was at the Women's Mission Center in downtown Los Angeles. A group of downtrodden women walked into the small auditorium. I asked the Christian band that was playing before I spoke, to pray with me. Our prayers were saturated with meaning, and we spoke in our individual prayer languages for about ten minutes.

I couldn't take my eyes off a woman who was probably about thirty-five but looked sixty-five. She never glanced up and was holding a dirty, ragged fabric doll clenched tightly to her chest. I knew her issue without being told. She was depressed, probably suicidal. As my testimony unraveled, including the story of how my depressions were healed by the Lord Jesus, she furtively looked up at me, then swiftly back down. The longer I spoke, the more she glanced up. My testimony ebbed to completion.

I asked if anyone wished to be prayed for, and this woman raised her hand. The band members and I approached her, and I slowly coaxed her out of her chair. We prayed a long, vigilant prayer, and after an extensive time, she began to exude strange guttural noises, grimaces, contortions, and then her eyes rolled back. She slumped to the floor, and we slumped with her. All of us knew what was happening. Demons were being released from her. I'd seen this type of demonic purging before. I knew what I was seeing but could hardly believe I was seeing it.

She trembled long and hard, almost like an epileptic. The anguished expressions that crossed her face, drenched in dread and terror, very slowly transformed into a face with a gentle half smile and a look of wonderment. She appeared decades younger within twenty minutes.

She embraced me hard and sobbed in my arms. The employees of the mission took over while we ministered to others, and as "our" woman was exiting the auditorium, she gave her doll to a staff member.

Am I honored? Am I stunned? Am I bewildered that G-D has chosen me for this work? Could G-D have selected a better place for my first speaking gig? I think not.

I sense these next six weeks may prove to be another turning point in my life. The shift on my own personal axis started this very day. I have never been more humbled.

*****

The six weeks were unparalleled in their impact on me and others. I, along with those planning the book tour, was astonished at the doors G-D opened for us. I even spoke at several New Age bookstores. The proprietors knew I was going to be speaking about Jesus and my own foray into the New Age.

I had the advantage of living New Age principles for four years, so nothing I said was tinged with disrespect, judgment, or holier-than-thou nonsense. I was just a woman with a story, and that packed enough of a wallop.

I spoke at Fuller Seminary, a prestigious Christian school of divinity. I spoke at several Barnes and Noble bookstores, Borders bookstores, churches, Messianic synagogues, halfway houses, schools for troubled kids, missions for both men and women, battered women's shelters, and a women's prison.

My favorite gig was at a mega-church in Los Angeles, where on Friday nights they allow people with little money to get a week's worth of groceries if they listen to a gospel message. I was the gospel message this Friday night.

The auditorium was filled with Armenians, Latin Americans, and Russian Jews. There must have been six to seven hundred people, speaking three different languages. Three translators translated consecutively after I said a few sentences. To hear people laughing in rounds, so to speak, as they each heard my words in their own language, was hilarious to me.

Of course, the presentation took three times longer than usual, but it didn't seem to matter. Everyone had a grand time! When three pastors who spoke these languages delivered the altar call at the end of my presentation, over fifty people came forward to receive their Savior. I was up all night with starry-eyed wonder!

*****

1995

March 3, 1995

My dearest Dad,

I've been sitting in my own puddle of tears for an hour. Wondering how to say what I long to say, knowing our style is to write; so, I will write.

Dad, time downhill skis toward the end of our earth lives. It will come as certainly as daily sun rises in the east. So, I dare not risk never having you know how torturous our relationship is to me and the persistent ways it affects my life.

Love has never been the issue between us. Neither of us could possibly love each other more. But oh my G-D, Daddy, we have missed each other in a fog of rubbish and drivel. We could enhance each other's lives, but instead, we exist in a cold war. No nuclear bombs, but always the threat.

For me, the nagging knowing that I am not respected, admired, approved of, or understood by you has trumped the fact of our mutual love. The lack of these longed-for responses from you, for most of my life, has affected my health, self-esteem, ability to function optimally, and even my desire to drive up the coast from VA to see you and Mom. Though I do drive home, because I know you, Mom, and I need to see each other.

How much time could we possibly have left, Dad? Is this really how you want to leave me … anguished by the ponderous weight of your disapproval? I want to squish you back down to age fifty, so we have a better chance of resolution, more time, and more opportunities.

I know you must see the growth in me from living in Virginia these past ten years. Apparently, I had to move away to define

303

myself and grow into a clearer understanding of who I really am. In Virginia, I made time and put effort into grasping the gospel and enhancing my faith, which has allowed me to embrace *G-D's* view of me.

I have also been graced with a new population of people. These are not the people I grew up with, but rather new friends and colleagues who have introduced me to authentic me. It's uplifting and startling to experience people experiencing me. In Virginia, I am not only respected, but my presence, my views, and my ability to influence kids to see the beauty in themselves and reach for the best in themselves, is coveted.

It isn't that I *need* your approval in order to have a successful life, Dad. Learning G-D's view of me has changed who I know myself to be. But I can't think of anything I want more than for you to see the Leah Rebecca so many others see.

We have written each other letters for decades now, and I have made this plea to you before: that we try to resolve our issues or at least table them and see where discussion leads. But we never do table them. On the phone you might acknowledge you've received my letters, but no conversation develops after that.

I don't know that I will plead again, Dad. I feel like a wooden horse on a merry-go-round, endlessly going fruitlessly round and round. It's your move now, Daddy. We may resolve nothing, but we may resolve everything. To me, it's so worth the effort.

My whole essence, through to the center of me, loves you unabashedly. And so forever,

I am yours, Leah Rebecca.

*****

When I called home to speak to Mom a few days later, Dad answered the phone. He acknowledged he had received my letter and then handed the phone to Mom.

But things between us changed by tiny increments after Dad received the above letter. In June of 1996, I was gratefully able to write the following Birthday letter to him, because we were negotiating a truce.

*****

1996

Dad,

You are eighty-four today. This is positively momentous when I ponder the reality of what might have been your family's plight. If all of you had not braved the issues, sacrifices, fears, Bolsheviks, and walked from Russia to France to catch a ship going west, what additional atrocities would you have faced? I think about this more and more as I age and face your and Mom's mortality.

Although you and I have been geographically separated for many years, you are permanently sketched inside of me. When I see you, I see your desk with organized piles of self-instruction. What amazing things have been accomplished as you sit at the helm of your notes and magazines and editorial musings.

I see your arms folded while one hand holds your chin and you peer over the top of your glasses. This stance signals to me you are contemplative, listening, and formulating thoughts.

You know I love you with my whole heart, Dad, and isn't that what it's really all about? I would bet most fathers, as they assess their lives, would long to know they are deeply loved by their children. You can say that and really mean it. Regardless of the issues and tempests the four of us have weathered, we have come through it all able to say we're still pretty madly in love with each other.

Your years have been filled with a lifetime assortment of family, friends, and colleagues. These are the people whose lives you have touched and might certainly have altered. You have earned our love because you have been to us an advisor, friend, comfort, and support. You have cared about us, shared your bounty with us, and given us your time, wisdom, and attention. That you are dearly loved is a testimony to who you are and how you have lived.

And oh my G-D, Dad, just four years ago, in your plant, while handling textiles and encouraging employees, three assailants entered your private world and demanded your money. On your way to retrieve it, one of the men shot you twice at point-blank range with a twelve-gauge double-barreled sawed-off shotgun. Once in your chest and once in your leg. You sank to your knees and watched your organs fall to the floor.

An ambulance and Mom were called. I was in Virginia. Ruthie sped to the hospital, and Mom, in her negligee and silken robe, drove to the plant in confusion. Then she sped to the hospital. By then, you were in surgery. You survived, *miraculously*.

When you and I spoke the next day, you said, "Leah, when the surgeon came in this morning to check my wounds, I thanked him for saving my life." He said, *'Mr. Kline, I did not save your life. There is no earthly reason, not even one, that you should be alive today. We scooped thousands of pellets from your interior cavity; none of them penetrated major organs. Then we sewed your organs back into place. Surely, it was not medicine that saved your life.'"*

And then you said to me, in a voice that sounded to my heart like a celestial choir, "Leah, this doctor believes as you do. He thinks G-D saved my life."

I said, "Right, Dad. There's no other explanation, and you might want to think about that fact while you recuperate."

You said, "I will, Leah."

Daddy, could a family be more grateful? Could the community of people who love you and immediately surrounded you at the hospital be more grateful? I don't think so. You were saved for a purpose. The story will unravel in your heart, mind, and spirit, and your life will be forever changed. How could it be otherwise?

307

Allow me to close by making sure you know this: the conversation we had when I was home in January of this year was the most significant we've ever had. Because Dad, I have operated under the assumption since I was a little girl, that although I knew you loved me, I've been equally convinced you have not liked me. It wasn't that you just didn't like some of my choices or behaviors, but that you genuinely didn't like or respect me.

This has been a life-shaping belief. It also always seemed you were not interested in being a recipient of my love. As I have adapted to being single and celibate, I have adapted to what felt like your total disgust.

This might sound over the top to you, but that last conversation we had in January, altered my interior worldview and cleared my understanding of how you perceive me. You admitted you more than love me, more than like me, but that you're proud of many things about me and see parts of yourself in me … the drive, resolve, determination to beat the odds, the staying power, the set goals that are reached, the guts, and the passion. Holy kreplach, kasha, and matzah ball soup!

I awakened the next day feeling released from the bondage I've lived in for most of my life. I could barely believe what you said. It sounded like a script, or that a puppeteer put words in your mouth. But visits home have been so good since our talk, I know it really was you who formulated those words.

You pointed out that I don't seem happy in your home and that I'm moody. Well, yeah! I've been in a defensive posture in your company since I was a young girl. But it's all gone now, Dad. We are where we always could have been, but the milk spilled long ago and yesterdays are irretrievable. I stand grateful and awed by our talk; it has changed everything.

This is landmark stuff, Dad. Now we can love each other openly and maybe even laugh together or take a ride or go to a deli and split a pastrami on rye. Happy 84th, Dad.

You have my heart, Leah

June 14, 1996

Oh, Deb. I am ready to write the story of last month. The day was ripe with spring's May sun and silky clear air. Swirling, fragile wind currents played in my yard, and the scent of lilacs filtered in through the kitchen screen. Robins sang, sea gulls dove and soared. It seemed like a standard-issue budding and birthing spring day. But now, I know what happened that day will live in me forever.

On Monday, May 13, 1996, I started to plan the logistics of how I'd work my day. I had a gazillion things to do on the road in the great outdoors.

I wrote in my journal and did some Bible study. I put on the soundtrack from *Waiting to Exhale* and did some jive boogyin' around the spaces of my home. I talked to Mom. I talked to Ruthie. I showered and put on an outfit that made me feel subdued and foxy all at once.

My watch read 1:30 P.M. Barnes and Noble was on my list. I needed a blank artsy Birthday book for Mom, into which I will put recent photos of her favorite people. Although Barnes and Noble wasn't clocked in until way later in the day, I felt "led," as we say in spiritual word-speak, to change my plan and stop at the bookstore *right then*. One would be a fool to ignore a prompt from one's Spirit.

I took my time handling the gorgeous handmade paper books that filled a corner of the store. I chose a creamy white one with parchment pages. It felt like coffee break time to me, so I sauntered over to the café and scanned the room for a free table. My eyes lit on someone who looked more than vaguely familiar. I had an adrenalin rush and my mouth turned to cotton.

Nah, I thought, couldn't be. I moved a little closer to his table. Yeah, it's him. Oh my G-D, it's Robert! I couldn't speak. My voice cannon-shot from my body. I moved into close proximity to him to force him to look up. He did so, inadvertently, and then casually looked back down at the book he was reading. He then mimicked the classic double-take number and said, "It's you!"

My voice jumped back into my body, and I said, "Well, I guess that means it's definitely *you*."

He gestured for me to sit down. I last saw this man twenty years ago. We were young adults. Now we aren't. His physical beauty was still staggering to me, but he'd traded in his Botany 500 suits and his slick blond haircut for beastly ragamuffin attire and stringy sun-whitened hair past his shoulders.

"So, Dr. Robert England," I said as casually as I could master, "what is it exactly that you do these days that allows you to walk around looking like a homeless person?"

"Long story," he said.

"I've got time," I said.

I was perched on the edge of my seat because I figured any second now his wife, Elaine, would appear from behind one of the stacks. She'd sit down and he'd lie and say, "Honey, I'd like you to meet Leah Kline. She and I were colleagues at Penn."

"Are you visiting some friends here?" he asked. It was a logical question because he knew I used to drive to Virginia Beach often from my home outside of Philly.

"No," I said. "I've lived at the Beach for eleven years."

"You're not serious," he said.

"Perfectly serious," I said. "Why?"

"Where exactly do you live?" he asked.

"Near Mount Sidemore."

"How mind blowing," he said. "For eight out of your eleven years, we were damn-near neighbors. We lived about a mile and a half from each other."

Now *I* said, "You're not serious!"

"Okay. That's eight out of eleven. Where have you been for the past three? Tell me, Rob. Please."

"Elaine left me. I quit my job at the University. I shut down my consulting business, sold my properties and divested myself of my securities. I've been sailing the oceans of the world alone ever since."

Well, that explained his sun-bleached, derelict fashion statement.

I was still dealing with the "Elaine left me" sentence at the beginning of his last package of words, so I asked, "Why did Elaine leave you, Rob?" I internally braced myself for, "Because I had a series of affairs after you and she found out." Or, even more hurtful could have been, "I fell hopelessly in love after you. Elaine found out and left me."

Instead, he said, "Mind if I answer that one later? Don't feel like talking about it yet."

No biggie. I can drop a hot potato about as fast as anyone.

I tried to create his life in my mind and asked, "Why are you doing what you're doing, and what do you do out there on the wide blue sea?"

"I always dreamed of someday sailing the oceans for indefinite time," he said. "It's romantic and dangerous. Lonely too. And what I do out there is sail, read, and ponder the great mysteries of life."

Ponder the great mysteries of life? Words of ecstasy caressed the airwaves, and I smiled an invisible smile.

There was something about him that looked wounded. Lost. That thirty-six-year-old cocky professor of aerodynamics from the late 1970's didn't seem quite so cocky anymore.

When I finally computed he and Elaine were truly divorced, a shield inside me fell with a clamor to the hardwood floor. I let my eyes really take him in. I loved the piercing clarity of those pastel blue ponds of light; his eyes excited me. The toned strength of his body enticed me. I loved his long hair. He looked like a Nordic Viking weary and shell-shocked from battle.

Mostly, he looked healthy and fit. And then there was that face. Oh, how that face did draw me in again. Robert, as ever, was delicious.

Now ask me how thrilled I was about the following little exchange.

He said, "Really Lee-Lee … enough about me. Please tell me what you've been doing."

And I casually, nonchalantly, and with a humility which was not feigned, said, "Well, Rob, I've written a book and it's on one of those shelves over there. Want me to get you one?"

In one lightning-fast moment, I knew he knew the sick, scared, suicidal, twenty-eight-year-old woman of my past … had died.

"You're an author! You've written a book? Yes, I want a copy. Wait, tell me what it's about."

"It's about my relationship with G-D," I said.

"Your 'relationship' with God? So, what gives? Are you guys on a first name basis or something? Leah, you're joking. So come on, tell me! Are you a Jewish Buddhist, a Talmudic scholar?"

"Neither of the above," I said.

"So, what then? Come on. Come on."

"I'll get you a copy of the book, Rob. Hold on."

"Leah, before you go, listen. I was just kiddin'. Really, whatever it is your book is about, I can see that 'it' or something has touched you, changed you. Your face and body are similar, but there is something in your countenance that's completely transformed."

WOW, I thought I'd pass out.

The reasons why I grew to love this man so much during the sizzle and drama of our youth began to feel familiar. That insight. That perception. That lust for truth. That depth. That radar sensitivity.

"Be cool, Leah," I kept pleading with myself.

I went to the stacks to bring him a book. I couldn't find them where they usually reside, so I went to the front desk to have someone check it out. They were out of stock.

I reported back, "They're out of stock."

"Out of stock!" he said with a voice and expression that echoed amazement and delight.

"That's great. Out of stock." He shook his head in near disbelief.

I went to my car and retrieved a book. He looked at it with intensity and vigor. He flipped it over, and when he saw my picture on the back cover he said, "Now that's the real Leah. They caught you. I like it."

He looked at the table of contents and picked the piece called "Princess Di and the Toothless Drunk." He read it and winked. I turned to one I thought he'd like about migrant birds. He handled the book as though it were a treasured newborn.

I took it back from him to write an inscription. Although I'd personally autographed over seven hundred books, ironically, all I got to write in his was the date and his name before he had me distracted and talking about something else.

"So, where's your boat docked?" I asked.

"Charleston."

"Damn," I thought.

I said, "Then why are you in Virginia Beach, and more specifically, why are you in Barnes and Noble?"

"I flew in a couple weeks ago to take care of some legal matters. I'm staying on the boat of a friend who's out of town. My now blind and deaf golden Lab is with me. Remember Sandy? I'm in Barnes and Noble because my lawyer's office is across the street and I had some time to use before the appointment. In fact, I have to be there in five minutes. Will you wait for me?"

Will I wait for him? Is rain wet? Are flowers fragrant?

I told him I had changed my route and stopped at the bookstore several errands before I had planned. I wanted him to understand this reunion was not by accident or chance.

"Yeah, I'll wait for you, Rob. Take your time. I'm not in a hurry."

Then I went to the bathroom and said, "Oh my G-D," about three trillion times. I checked my makeup. I washed my hands. I went back to our table. I drank some decaf. I looked through the pile of books he'd been reading on sailing the seas alone. I waited.

He came back winded, and I asked him why.

"Because I was afraid you'd leave."

More barricades, barriers, and buttresses fell crashing to the floor. I felt the melt down begin.

We sat for a while more as he pulled the summary of my past twenty years from me. I never could, nor did I ever want to hide anything from Robert. First and foremost, in the late 1970s, he was my friend. His titanic intelligence always made it easy to share things with him. He always "got" it. He could extrapolate. He had a bird-dog's way of homing in on a target. Although it was his face that initially magnetized me, it was his mind that captured my heart.

"I've got to go to The Camera Shop," I said. "Want to come with me?"

He wanted to. I was at last calm and capable. My stomach had settled, and my heart rate was even.

At the camera shop I was ready to conduct some business with the store manager, and Robert got involved with the telephotos. I was talking to Mr. Green about buying film in bulk when I felt a tug on my dark paisley shirt.

As if all at once, Robert had become a little boy who said, "Mommy, I have to go to the bathroom and I really want a lollipop."

I said, "Mr. Green, my little boy seems to be in need of your facilities, and would you mind if he has one of these Tootsie Pops?"

"No problem, little guy," five-foot-seven-inch Mr. Green said to six-foot-one-inch Robert. My "son" postured a humiliatingly nerdy grin at Mr. Green and waddled off. I wanted to kiss him and kill him at the same time.

When my business with Mr. Green was completed, I drove Robert back to his rental car. I asked him if he wanted to follow me over to my apartment. "You'll just love it, Robbie. It's precious … sort of like an oversized dollhouse."

"Leah, you told me you've been celibate for ten years. I don't want you doing anything you'd regret. You must really trust me."

"No, I don't trust you, Robert. But I do trust myself."

His first response to the pretty little palace was, "My God … It looks like a designer did this place!"

"A designer did," I told him. "I went back to school in my mid-thirties and got another degree, this time in interior architecture and design."

He walked around like a little boy at *Toys 'R' Us*. Dazed. Amazed. Soaking up the details. "Are you the blue-ribbon prize winner for neat-freak or what? I remember your home being organized and tidy, but this is ridiculous. What happened to you?"

"I found out a lot about who I really am after the divorce. Our place reflected Max and me. This place is thoroughly Leah."

He looked carefully at each of the excessive photos I had all about. "Your Dad is so distinguished … and your Mom is simply elegant."

I realized at that moment how little we really knew of each other. We had an affair. Our time together was on the run. We hadn't taken the time to talk much about our lineage or ancestry.

Twenty years ago, he reeked of aristocrat. Ralph Lauren clothes that were faded and worn. Custom-made suits, if the moment called for it. He had the look and feel of a blue-blood, and that's the category I knew he hailed from. He knew I'm Jewish, but who knows what else he'd conjectured about me.

Once we got to my office, he sat in the rocker. "Wait. I've got to assimilate this before I see any more. All these books. Oh, Leah, I could sit here forever and read the books." He said it so plaintively I wanted to hug his little heart.

"Oh yes, Robert," I thought. "Stay forever. Read the books. Let me love you."

I sat on the floor in front of his chair. We were both facing the window and the weeping willows that grew into their majestic fullness. He slowly and methodically ran his hands through my hair … almost but not quite mindlessly, hypnotically. We moved into our own silent space. Time hovered, waiting for us to sigh or create or speak.

When the shadows in the room changed angle, I rose, took his hand and said, "The tour is about to recommence, Dr. England. Will you join me?"

When he looked at the bank of photographs on my bathroom wall, he said, "You're so connected, Leah. You know a million people, and obviously you care enough about them to have their images wallpapering your home."

"I know a lot of people, and care deeply about several, but honestly, Rob, most of my time is spent alone. I'm really not Miss Congeniality, nor do I blossom with a house full of people."

"Oh, Lee-Lee … I remember how you interacted with people. You have a genius for it. You thrive on it."

"I don't thrive on it," I explained. "I know I can and do interact effectively and that I have a talent with children. But G-D gave me gifts that require solitude for their expression, so He also gave me a nearly unquenchable lust for silence and time alone. Otherwise, the work wouldn't get done. I'd be more interested in playing with people than playing with words."

I don't know why, but he smiled a half smile and kissed the end of my nose.

We moved into my bedroom.

"This is an entirely different expression, Leah. The other rooms are warm, fanciful, and imaginative. This room makes me want to whisper. It looks like a bedroom for a doll-baby or a princess. It's so feminine. You're so feminine. My God, Leah, you are a princess. Princess Leah."

"It's been done, Rob. Princess Leia in *Star Wars*. Intergalactic heroine. But thanks. That's sweet."

"You embarrass so easily with compliments. I remember that about you now. Well, hang on. Here's more. What I see when I look at you now, twenty years past the heat of your youth, is that you truly are the real thing, Leah. You're a bona fide princess. Hell, you're a real live goddess. And I'm not talking about stereotypical

JAPs, as some women are so unappealingly labeled. You're a Cinderella princess, unassuming and unsung. And by goddess, I do not mean a sultry vixen. You're Aphrodite, little Leah. You're irresistible."

I thought to myself, "Am I in the middle of a movie script? Who's writing these lines?" It's all happening so fast. I want to pull each moment back into existence. I want him to say it all over again. I want him to take me in his arms … sort of like Errol Flynn would … and tell me he will never again leave me, ever, never, not possibly.

I want him to hold my face and look intently into my eyes and say it surely must be destiny that brought us back to each other. I want him to say he could imagine some unanticipated, extremely influencing events that could unfold and lead us into a joint life that is unique and resoundingly strong.

But inside I thought … "Wait a minute, Leah. Essentially all the guy said is he thinks you have a dimension of princess-shtick and a sensuality that's engaging. These observations do not a combined destiny make. Sooo … Take stock. Drop back. Be cool. Don't push."

The sky had muted into the inviting tones of dusk. I noticed he looked truly tired. "Rob?"

"Yeah?"

"Would you like to take a shower and wash your hair?" He didn't reek, but he was moving toward ripe. I knew how great my shower felt, and I knew he'd enjoy it. I wanted him happy. I wanted him cared for.

"Really? Yeah, I'd love to. Those stall showers at the marinas are sorry. Thanks, Leah. I appreciate it."

I laid out soft, generous towels. On top of these I placed a new toothbrush in its unopened box.

Within moments he appeared in the living room, where I was thinking about what to share with him next. He was holding up the toothbrush in its box. In a combination presentation of both his little boy at The Camera Shop three hours ago, and an emotional and tired man glad for a moment of something that felt sort of like home, he said, "I can hardly believe it. I'm going to have a toothbrush on land. Oh boy! Oh boy! Oh boy!"

I laughed at his vast appreciation for something so small and soon heard water from the bath. It physically felt like I was walking through a combination dream and fantasy. All day I thought, felt, and often said, "I can't believe you're in my car. I can't believe I'm seeing your face and hearing your voice. I can't believe you're in my home, drinking from my glass."

When he reappeared, although in the exact same crap-o duds, he looked like a new man. Brighter. More focused. Less intense.

"Want a glass of cabernet?" I asked.

"Sure. Sounds nice."

We moved in silence around the kitchen. I held the bottle steady while he hoisted the cork. I pulled out my two favorite glasses, thick and hand-blown, sea green and navy.

We walked onto the deck. I'd just started to plant geraniums, and the earthen soil smelled so rich. There were three families of ducks on the lake. Sea gulls swooped by in aimless formation. A kid in a canoe moved slowly past.

"Come out on the sea with me, Leah. You could write *our* story. I'd take care of you. Come with me."

"I can't do that, Baby. Not possible. I have a life. I have a purpose. I don't want to disenfranchise myself from the world. I'll offer you the same invitation. Come back to land, Robert. I'll take care of you."

"You're on a mission, Leah. I'm not part of your world."

"You could be. I know lots of people who you'd like, and they'd stimulate your hungry mind."

"Leah, let's make love. Please let me hold you. I need your naked warmth next to me."

"Stop, Rob. Please. I beg you. Stop. This isn't easy for me. Now hear this, my passion has *not* ebbed. I walk around on fire a lot. I want you naked next to me too. But I can't and I won't. My decision is intractable. Please, Rob, don't push."

"I don't understand how you could remain celibate for ten years. The Leah I remember couldn't have."

"I'm not that Leah anymore."

"Well, what is it you do exactly to avoid being asked out? You're sexy and classy. You exude raw sensuality. What's the deal, Leah? Do you wear a 'Don't mess with me' sandwich board or what?"

"Cute, Rob. Really cute. I don't know why men don't ask me out. I guess I'm not exposed to many single men. It's not like I'm having to beat off the masses with a heavy stick. Hell, I haven't even met a single man I want to have a cup of coffee with … much less hold hands."

My shampoo in his hair caught my attention as I moved around him to see the last of daylight fall onto the west end of the lake. I felt his strength and weight and height behind me.

He said, "May I kiss you once? I promise I won't push."

I didn't answer. I couldn't. I just moved slowly in a half circle so that our bodies were touching and our eyes were kissing.

He took all of my head into his enormous hands. He just looked into my eyes for a long time. "Those brown eyes. They pull me in so deep. Your body feels stronger. Everything about you feels stronger. I love who you've become. I knew she was in there screaming for release. You really are some kind of miracle,

Leah. No one who knew you in your twenties could deny you are radically changed. Isn't it amazing, Lee-Lee, when we knew each other, you were so nervous and uncertain; you had no idea who you really were? You were scared and you were lost. Now you are solid and grounded, and it's I who am lost."

"You're a generous man, Robert. Lots of people might see what you've seen, but I think few would be kind enough to share it. Thanks for seeing me clearly. It's validating. It's even vindicating. I love you very much."

"I love *you*, very much."

And we meshed and melted into each other through a long, languid, luxurious, unhurried, and passion-saturated kiss. He never took his eyes from mine.

I wanted to stay right there forever. I wanted us frozen in time. I wanted to feel the dimension, complexity, and rawness of his love for every second of eternity. There was ecstatic joy in this kiss and something so indefinably sad, I almost cried. I moved away from him slowly. It was time. I did not want us even close to that inexorable point of no return.

"Lee," he said as he held me, and we swayed.

"Yeah?"

"You asked me earlier why Elaine left me. I'm willing to answer that question now."

I released myself from him because I really didn't want us touching when he told me about the babe he might have fallen for after me.

His look turned shy, somewhat withdrawn. "After you and the abortion, I couldn't make love to Elaine anymore, and after several years she left me."

Now I'm *positive* I'm in the middle of a movie script. Sentimental melodrama at its most exhaustive. I said nothing. What was there to say really? Something like, "Oh, come on, Rob. Can't you think of something less theatrical than that?" or, "Sure, Robert, you're maxin' out. Don't lie to me." Instead, I kept focused on the light his eyes radiated.

"When I'm out at sea and feel like thinking about something warm, protective, fun, and lovely, it's you I think about. I just never really let go of the memory of you. We met each other too late, Leah. Both of us were married and promised to someone else. We had no choice but to abort our baby."

I felt flushed. The wine had made me slightly light. I wanted to walk up to that male beauty, believing every word he said was golden with truth … and hug him into peace and wholeness. I wanted him mine. I wanted us joined for all time.

"Oh, Robert. You touch chords in me that are staggering. Isn't it gorgeous that we can pick up so easily? As though twenty years of separation never even happened. Do you think this is a living, breathing example of kindred spirits rejoined by forces stronger than themselves?"

"I don't know, Leah. Right now, I don't feel as though I know much of anything."

I said, "Wait here, Baby, I've got something you need to read." I went to my office, reached for a file, and pulled from it a letter I had written to Robert in 1991, during post-abortion counseling, fourteen years after the death of our baby. It was an assignment given by the therapist … to write never-to-be-sent letters to the fathers of our aborted children.

I filled his glass with more crimson cabernet and explained about the counseling that helped me through a midnight-black period in my life when I confronted the pain of the loss of our baby.

From the chaise he read, then looked up at me. Two sea-salty tears sank down his face. "So we have a son in heaven?"

"That's how I see it, Rob. Our child is safe and lives in another dimension as well as forever in my heart."

I could see Robert's face remembering that time in our lives. Now he has new information. Now he is confronted with my inalterable truth that it was not a nebulous clot that emerged by force from my womb. It was our boy … and I felt deeply it was Robert's turn to deal with the choice we had made back then.

"My God, Leah. How can you be so sure? How can you know with such determined certainty the baby now exists somewhere else? Couldn't it be you just need to believe this, and your mind has conjured a way to deal with your loss?"

"Faith is an invisible and inexplicable phenomenon, Robbie," I explained. "That there is more to a person's life and spirit than the linear perception of earth time we embrace, seems more than just logical to me.

"It was not our child's fault nor choice to be aborted. See, Rob, I believe a baby has person-hood from the moment of conception. His DNA carries every genetic attribute he will ever have. Because I believe G-D to be just, I also believe at the moment of our baby's earth-death, G-D intervened and whisked our son speedily back to Himself. His spirit was not killed off, only his opportunity to experience life on earth.

"For me, Robert, concepts such as multiple other dimensions, eternity, and timelessness are wholly and entirely conceivable and believable. That our son can and does exist somewhere in the inestimable beyond is just reasonable to me. It's my truth, Robert, unequivocally."

"Okay. I hear ya. I'm willing to think about that. Leah?"

"Yeah, Rob?"

"Can we make another baby?"

"Can we make another baby?" I repeated to myself. That's the kind of question that can both break a heart and patch it up in one lightning moment. The question he posed had a particular tone of voice designed to cover a submerged hunger to create life. And it was joined with eyes that looked so young, hopeful, injured, and expectant. He seemed caught up in a fairy-tale vision that was coming through the most handsome and vulnerable face I'd ever seen.

Someone can deliver a line like that and leave an imprint on the recipient like a steer branded with fire. That's how I felt. Imprinted and laid bare by the innocence and freedom of a very vulnerable little-boy Robbie.

I climbed onto the chaise with him and we held each other. Again, there was no room or need for words. The sun was gone. The night was dark.

"I've got to go, Lee-Lee. The dog needs to be fed and walked. What are you doing tomorrow?"

"I'm busy until four."

"I'm busy until about then too. Write down your address and phone. I'll either call you at four or be here at four. How's that sound?"

"Like a symphony."

At the front door we hugged and swayed in silence. I knew he didn't want to let go. I knew he knew I didn't either. He clutched his copy of my book to his chest and started down the stairs.

I said, "I love you, Robert. I love you."

He came back to me, cupped my face in those hands toughened by ropes and sails, and said, "I know you do, Princess. I love you too."

From the street he blew me a kiss and disappeared into the lilac-scented spring night air.

I slid to the floor in near disbelief. I reviewed every second. I played with it. I memorized it. I couldn't move for a long time. Sleep wasn't even an option.

I walked through the spaces of my home and collected things for him. Some written by me, some by others. From my extensive collection of Bibles, I chose one for him. It had my name engraved in gold on the lower right-hand corner. In it I wrote:

May 13, 1996

Robert ...

In giving you my very own Bible, though I do have several more, I am giving you the very best of me. I do not know why our life paths have once again crossed, but I am certain I need not conjecture. The drama will un-ravel and I will not squeeze it in one way or push it out another. Yet I concede, you make my being sing.

May the WORDS IN HIS BOOK from the HEART OF HIS HEART, sweetly touch the heart of you.

EVER ...

LEAH REBECCA

May 14, 1996

It feels as though 4:00 P.M. will never come true. I bought him fruits, figs, French bread, and brie. Only two more hours until I breathe in his beauty and listen to the workings of his mind. I feel as though every electrified nerve ending in my body has risen to the surface of my skin.

We'll have four days together until he flies back to Charleston. Lives and destinies can change and form in four minutes. What will four days bring us?

Don't be late, Robert. Not even five minutes.

LORD G-D, You are astonishing! Have You really brought him back to me? I believe You have! Dare I believe You really have?

*****

(Letter to Robert)

May 17, 1996

Robert,

You were to arrive at 4:00 P.M. I was so excited. Every molecule of me was expectant and eager. Five o'clock. Six o'clock. Seven o'clock. Silly me. It wasn't until eight o'clock it dawned on me that you weren't late. Truth was, you weren't coming. I did all the girlie things one might expect. I cried. I paced. I swore. I prayed. I pondered. Eventually, I sobbed myself to sleep fully clothed, ungracefully spread across my down comforter.

It took forty-eight hours to grasp the fact that you have disappeared without a trace. You left me with no ability to contact you. How indicative of a superbly trained Viet Nam Green Beret. I will write because it is what writers do. I will stop when I've examined the pain and confusion of what I'm feeling.

May 17, 1996

How quickly everything built after I realized you and Elaine are divorced. All the love I ever felt for you was permitted to quantum leap. The barricades I fought against while loving you so many years ago disappeared like mist at dawn. There has been enough time and distance between us to allow us to see each other clearly. In the clear and honest light of day, I tell you, Robert England ... despite your disappearance, you are loved by this little lady.

Like a childish schoolgirl, I actually believe you'll be back, because what we shared for those four hours was equally intense for both of us. I know this. You know this. It stands as immutable truth.

Where are you, Robert? Did you split the Beach early? Are you too overwhelmed to even speak to me? Are you thinking about Jesus and wondering if He truly is humanity's Savior?

Are you trying to guess why our paths have again crossed? Do you see an eternal connection?

Have you let our boy pass through your thoughts, travel through your emotions, enter the space in your life he deserves to hold?

As for me, I've had to work through all the scenarios to realize I can deal with any outcome.

If I never again see your face or hear your voice, I'll still know I was granted precious time that marked me indelibly. I felt loved. I felt recognized. I felt I was permitted to inhale the fact I really had impacted your life. I thank G-D for those hours.

I have learned by reaping in searing pain that to fight the design of G-D's will is frustrating in its futility. If you listen for His voice and take His advice, Robert, I will have no choice but to do the same.

In so many ways we complement and blend. Didn't you too feel that sensation with torpedo strength? We're both unconventional, gutsy, solitary. We're both daredevils on the cutting edge. We're pioneers. We're trendsetters. I know I have met my match in you. I pray you've met yours in me. If you have, I hope that thought entices you and doesn't repel you.

Neither of us is an easygoing, soft-wired person. I can only assume if it be G-D's will our lives are joined, there is an eternal purpose far weightier than either of our selfish quirks and ease with aloneness. If we are to share our lives, He will give us the strength of character to see each of us victorious.

327

I love and adore your pink-and-purple toothbrush in my bathroom. Purple is my favorite color. I don't even know your favorite color. I don't know your birth date. I don't know if you have siblings. I know so much and yet absolutely nothing. But I love you and know that you love me.

Believe this too, Robert. I have not for many, many years wasted my love nor handed it out frivolously. The words I write are sincere and bleed with truth.

We made a baby. He lives in another dimension. He would be nineteen. He may have looked like you. You and I have already shared the most significant thing two people can share. We created life. How could you not be deeply embedded in my psyche, memory, and subconscious?

You are me. I am you. He is us. Run from me if you must, Robert England. I will likely be here for a while. Call … don't call … write … don't write. Do as your being compels.

I will pray you are better able to sleep. I'm so grateful you look healthy and fit. Your face gives a type of pleasure to my eyes that makes orchids and sunsets seem pale. Be safe.

Ever, Leah

May 20, 1996

Robert, know this … I am overly accustomed to the deep wounds that can be delivered only by someone whom we love. Although I was not prepared for your magic trick of "Poof, I'm gone," once the dust settled, I realized I wasn't surprised.

I don't really know you, Robert. We only related in the context of an illicit affair. The amazing thing is that I have a type of peace. This reaction to your disappearance is so antithetical to the reaction I would have had prior to a relationship with G-D, I know this peace *must* be G-D given. In handing the reins of my life over to

Him, He covers me with warm, luminous light, and His unimaginable grace and mercy. I'm just crazy nuts about G-D! I love His heart. I love His attention to detail. I love how magnificently He loves.

It's also possible, Robert, that our son needs us to jointly acknowledge what we did. We were both having affairs, which resulted in the death of our boy. There's nothing like reckoning with the TRUTH to be liberated from things you don't even realize you're bound by.

May 23, 1996

I need to tell you something, Robert. I feel altered because of seeing you. I feel different knowing there is a man on the planet who genuinely loves me. It makes an impact on my being that I don't feel inclined to squish into words ... I would risk distortion or diminishment.

May 26, 1996

I think to myself ... if you were not fabricating or exaggerating, your words implied you've thought about me over the past twenty years. Well, now you have something new to think about. Now, our past has a present. We've shared time. We've shared secrets. We evoked emotion in each other. You walked in and among my things. You held me. We fantasized. We dreamed.

May 28, 1996

Tonight I re-read the journals I wrote during our time together twenty years ago. The lasting feeling from reading those journals is how grateful I am that the Leah of my past ... died. I almost feel in writing about her that she was a "her" and not a "me." I remember her vividly because of the words that recount her, but I can no longer relate to her. Geez, what a sad, disordered, sick, groping, anxiety-ridden bundle of complexes that Leah truly was. I wonder where that Leah would be today if G-D had not intervened.

Another point about those journals, Robert, is this. Recollection is not always fact based. I remembered some of our relationship accurately, but much of what I remembered wasn't true.

It's as though our minds can only deal with so much, and then we mutate the truth in order to be able to live with it. But if one keeps meticulous journals, the truth cannot be twisted and the recorded past remains silent, only to be recaptured when one so wishes, and today I did so wish.

But I seem unable to write more just now. It makes the past too fresh. Too emotion drenched. So many lives were affected by the choices I made back then ... most powerfully, our son's.

June 2, 1996

Tonight, I re-read the letters I wrote to you twenty years ago and that you always handed back to me. I didn't like having an affair, Robert. But I had all the necessary ingredients for being able to carry one off, back then.

- I could deal with a titanic amount of stress if I wasn't ill.
- I was drawn to the danger.
- I could lie without much remorse back then.
- And I wanted more than anything in the whole world to be loved.

I had drunk the Kool Aid and bought the fairy tales, Rob. I was one of those 1950's girls who read *Snow White* and *Cinderella* until the books fell apart and had to be replaced.

I believed I too was a princess who would meet her prince. But there has been no prince, other than the Prince of Peace.

And I know for certain there is little sanity or satisfaction with the wrong prince. So I became the predictable: the face on billboards that silently shrieks, "Lookin' for Love in All the Wrong Places." I became reckless and promiscuous and desperate for love.

But the "man" thing and even the "people" thing never worked out too well. I was constantly leveled by the people I loved the most. So, here's my bottom-line lesson, Robert. I can only really trust G-D because everyone else is just a person trying to work out his or her own stuff.

This realization has fried all my fantasies, and that's a really good thing. Now I play by the codes laid out in G-D's book, the Bible. I don't always hit the target, but I do always reach for the mark of His highest calling. The Bible is my manual for how to live. It covers every contingency.

So, now I've got it. I cannot afford to love anyone more than I love Him. He must be my core and center. And finally, I cannot afford to follow my whims, but only His guidance. That's what I want for you, Robert. Why would I not want someone I love to reap the inestimable rewards of a committed walk with G-D?

You are on a journey, Robert. But you are not yet on a pilgrimage.

July 15, 1996

Something happened to me today. I realize what I'm doing in writing to you is playing mind games with my own mind. Surely, if you had chosen, you could have sent a postcard during these past two months. Just any old something, like: "Sorry, Lee-Lee. Can't deal with you or Jesus or American soil or commitment or anything

331

that seeing you or communicating with you might compel me to have to deal with. It was a swell four hours. Have a great life."

I will continue to pray you are safe and well, and most significantly, that the Bible has lured you into its fathomless depth, astonishing story, elegant literature, and mind-expanding truth.

I will internally release you to fly on eagles' wings, sail the seas, and be whomever it is you are meant to be.

G-D give me strength to honor this path. G-D help me to let go of something that never even was. Safe journey, Robert.

*****

I filed this letter in my "Letters Never to Be Sent" file, and there it shall remain.

*****

December 8, 1996

My dearest son, Gabriel,

You have been in my mind and heartbeat since 1990, when I was yanked out of denial and realized what I had done to you. But you have been in the forefront of my every day since your Dad and I met seven months ago in Barnes and Noble in Virginia Beach.

That encounter sent me into an orbit that doesn't even feel as though it's part of our stratosphere. You have become so real to me that some days I think I sense you around me. I think I hear a whisper that may have come from you, or a scent that might represent you. If it is not you, I'm grateful for whatever it is that allows me to sense you so near to me.

Who would you have become, my boy? The combination of Robert's and my genetics may have produced a dynamo. Might you have been part of a team that finds a cure for some incurable malady? Could you have been an astronaut? Your Dad might have been had he not chosen to teach aerodynamics to Ph.D. candidates.

Or would you have acquired my proclivities and instead written books or concertos or written and directed Broadway plays? Could you have been a Nobel Laureate in literature? Or might you have chosen to teach gifted musicians cello or piano?

It wouldn't have mattered what you chose to do as long as you were content, fulfilled, and grateful. If you had pushed wheelchairs around hospital corridors and made a difference in the daily lives of patients, I would have cheered if you exuded peace and a measure of joy.

One of the brightest men I ever knew said he could drive semi-trucks cross country and be fulfilled because of the amount of time it afforded him to "just think." From that moment on, I understood that what one does is irrelevant if there is fulfillment as defined by that person himself.

There is scant doubt we would have loved hangin' out together. Kids are my favorite people no matter their age, and I believe you and I would have truly enjoyed each other.

I'd have made mistakes as a parent, and the older you became, the more you would have forgiven me and seen the genesis behind the "mistakes." As a parent, you would likely have skirted my parental failings, but made your own failings with your children. Because that's the way of it. It's inevitable.

Because you were denied an earth-life, you avoided the pain that cannot be avoided on this sphere in this phase of history. It's the only consolation I can conjure. Your baby spirit ran right back to G-D, and you have not been burdened with life's travails.

But it is not a consolation that eradicates my daily knowing that you and Esther had destinies of your own to fulfill. And that the two of you would have satiated my life with all that I long for still, all these decades past the abortions. And if G-D created you, what made me so flippant as to believe I had every right to eradicate you?

Women say, "It's my body. No one should dictate to me what I do with it." I don't see it that way anymore, Gabriel. These bodies are shells that encase our spirit. G-D has loaned them to us for a specific amount of time. When He says, "Your time here is finished," it is finished. He removes our body, and our spirit continues its journey.

Sooner than later, Gabriel, you and I will craft G-D's heavenly work together, whatever that may be. Until then, I will do what G-D has prepared me to do. I will do it with largesse and the gift of knowing I may help post-abortive women and men and may dissuade a girl or woman from a choice she only thinks she wants. There truly are far better options, not only for children, but definitely for their Moms.

One of the strangest aspects of my life is that I miss you and we've never met. I miss you with inexpressible and unquenchable longing. You are my son, and that is the singular impetus behind the yearning.

Until soon, my Love-Boy,
Your, Mom

*****

1997

Deborah, in four months I'll be fifty. I've begun to think about how I want to celebrate the occasion. I don't want a party. I don't know enough people, who, from their hearts, care how old I am.

So, how about a trip to somewhere I've never been? But alone? Nah. It feels like I need to do some more praying and pondering. I'll let you know when I've figured it out.

Got it! The only two people walking the skin of this earth who would lay down their lives for me and love me with unyielding love are Mom and Dad. That's what it comes down to. That's the not-dressed-up truth. On August 2, 1947, they were the two people who were jubilant.

So, I want the three of us to go to New York and see a few shows, eat some great food, walk some fab-o districts, window shop, people watch, and sit at the bars of crowded restaurants and chat with other chatters from around the globe. Perfect!

I've already checked with Mom and Dad. They like it a lot. It's not over the top or littered with people who just don't care much if I'm turning fifty or one hundred and six.

And now for another segment of *As the Stomach Churns.* Dad's in the hospital. Some stomach flu-ey thing. Of course, all plans for New York are scrapped. I'm in his hospital room now, as are Mom and Ruthie.

(Later) Dr. Joel just said Dad will be fine in a couple of days. So, Dad had Dr. Joel convince Mom and me to go to New York without him. He said Dad would probably be home before we were back from New York, and Ruthie's in town and available. This is not a big medical megilla. But this is my Fiftieth Birthday, not the same as turning thirty-seven or forty-eight.

In Dad's hospital room today, Dr. Joel asked me why I love to write. His daughter's majoring in creative writing at Bennington College and he wanted some insight into her passion.

Here's what I wrote, which I gave to him.

*****

Writing

It heightens awareness. Transcends the moment. Teaches communication. Augments appreciation. Strengthens mental agility. Requires discipline. It's lonely and requires solitude. It's sometimes agonizing. It's expanding, and forces focus. It energizes interpretation. It is clarity producing. It's a need. A hunger. An expression. An art form. A calling. An educator. It demands observation and stimulates creation in other media. It's exhausting. Exciting. Challenging. Cathartic. Expository. Linguistic. Frustrating. Inciting. Enticing. It encourages individuality.

IT'S INEXHAUSTIBLE.

*****

Dr. Joel smiled, kissed my cheek, and said, "Thanks, Leah. This actually really helps."

July 31, 1997

New York! New York! It's a hell of a town. Lovin' every second.
So different from living here with Max in the early 1970s, with
little money and with me mentally ill.

The adrenalin rush kicks in as soon as we exit Lincoln Tunnel.
Windows down, the stinkin' air of the city assaults us. Then the
cacophony of horns and drivers screaming and bikers streaking.

Skyscrapers of hard-edged steel and walls of glass hold hands
via walkways with older architecture whose rich choices of detail
and time-honored crafts form facades of sculptural wizardry. Fab-
o! We're staying at a European hotel near the Theater District.

More later. I don't want to miss a thing.

August 3, 1997

Just got back to Pennsylvania and I'm still zooming. It couldn't
have been more fun or jam-packed. Mom and I are so fabulous
together. We quietly transform ourselves into pretzels to please
each other. I am happiest when I see her flourishing, giggling, and
reveling in our love.

We did everything I hoped we would. Saw three Broadway
shows. Ate in extravagant restaurants and popular dives. Pranced
up and down Madison Avenue and Fifth Avenue, SoHo and Tri-
beca. Mom bought a to-die-for-cream-yellow-baby-blanket-soft
leather shoulder bag. I shot film and wrote in my journal. We
had drinks at dusk every night at a New York eatery while we
chatted up people on bar stools from countries all over the globe.
And we flirted with Charles, the bartender … a cutie-patootie
from Holland. He introduced us to the regulars, and we acted like
sophisticated, fun-loving coeds ready for action. Harmless, but just
ever so, ever so …!

On our last night we listened to a harpist in a room off the lobby. Little pastry delights were served. She was everything one might expect from a harpist. Demure. Hair just so. A long pink satin gown and matching dyed flats.

I had to sneeze, and when one must, one simply must. How was I to know it would be four sneezes that were *not* demure? I blew into Dad's oversized monogrammed handkerchief. Mom giggled until both of us were almost out of control. People stared as though we were hecklers. We left.

Mom peed into her little silk panties before we got to our room, and I had icing all over my nose. She and I get punch-drunk-stupid over the same things.

Next day: Neither of us wanted to leave, but it was time, so I drove south for ninety miles, and here we are, in our living room, telling Dad our adventures.

Eventually Dad said, "Leah, Samuel Becker (*father of my first aborted baby*) called today to wish you a happy Fiftieth."

"Did you guys talk or was it just a one-sentence volley?" I asked.

"We talked for over an hour. Here's his number. He wants to take you out to dinner."

"Does he? And this is fine with you, Dad? You're not incensed?"

"That was over thirty years ago, Lee. I really wanted to know what he'd been up to and how he is. Invite him over for drinks before you eat dinner."

"Okay," I said.

Samuel and I had spoken many times over the past thirty years, but not for the preceding three or four. He came over. Mom, Dad, he, and I talked for another hour and then he took me out for a sumptuous Fiftieth-Birthday lobster dinner at a neighborhood hangout.

During dinner I had a protracted amount of time to talk about Esther. Samuel hadn't thought about the abortion of over thirty years ago, but he got the drift. I had more than thought about her. I was still mourning her. It was impossible not to tell him about how Jesus came into my life and heart, because it was Jesus who prompted me to deal with my abortions.

Samuel's reaction was calm. Although Jewish, he was not aghast about Jesus. He was just thrilled I was healed of those deadly depressions and didn't care if I thought it was Jesus or Bugs Bunny who healed me.

By dinner's end he was crying. For our lost child. For the pain I suffer. For his own disregard of the life we'd extinguished.

He devised a plan. He would drive down to Virginia Beach in a week or so, and he did. I had a small gathering at my apartment for some friends, prayer partners, and members from my Messianic Jewish synagogue. We planned a memorial service for Esther to take place the next day on a remote sand dune at the beach.

It was a poignant day. Everyone wore white and came prepared. Jews wore yarmulkes and tallit. Psalms were read. Self-written odes and poems were recited. My friend Mike made a Star of David from twigs and wove tiny Baby's Breath and Lilies of the Valley through the thin, delicate reeds. Samuel read the Mourner's Kaddish in Hebrew, and I joined him along with others who knew this Hebrew prayer spoken over the deceased for millennia. We all joined hands and recited the Lord's Prayer. Samuel prayed an eloquent benediction, and then we all walked along the ocean's edge for a half hour or so.

What touched me most was that Samuel legitimized our daughter. He told me, "Her name is no longer Esther. It is now Esther Becker." When he returned to his new hometown of Tucson, he had a plaque made with her name inscribed on it and hung it next to his parents' plaques on the memorial wall of his synagogue.

Samuel made a gesture that helped mend my heart. He was willing, even anxious to claim her as his own. That's class ... a man willing to hear the truth and do all he could to make everything concerning Esther less gruesome and macabre. Now our daughter has both a Mom and Dad, and she was put to rest with both honor and respect.

I'm so grateful for G-D's kindness, and for His ability to turn a nightmare into a dream.

*****

G-D opened wide the doors that allowed me to have closure with the fathers of my two children.

In 1996, Robert England reappeared in my life at Barnes and Noble in Virginia Beach and we spent hours talking about our son, Gabriel. Although Robert vanished the next day, there was most definitely closure.

In 1997, Samuel Becker reappeared in my life and our daughter Esther was memorialized in a sand-dune ceremony. And in her memory, a plaque honoring her now hangs on a synagogue memorial wall in Arizona. There was closure.

*****

(Letter from Mom)

August 2, 1997

To lovely Leah Rebecca, on her 50th Birthday,

Our pattern from the time you were a little girl has been to write letters, each to the other on our Birthdays and other meaningful occasions. The letters have been kept and treasured, and so they record the journey of our lives.

Re-reading some of those letters from you today, a truth was confirmed that I've always known. You are a writer: a poetic, provocative, powerful, and poignant writer who will be recognized as an author of merit.

Never stop believing your work is worthy. There is so much published trash today that demeans us. Your elegant prose with its spiritual intent challenges our minds and hearts. So, you must keep writing, Leah. You need to be heard. You have a message of enlightenment written in golden prose, taking the edge off soul-searching subjects, with your refreshingly off-beat humor.

Reading your beliefs is both palatable and positive. You'll see. Your Mom-friend is on target; you won't always be the best-kept secret on the East Coast.

When I look back on your earlier years, plagued by self-doubt and crippling depression, I marvel at your resilience. Many hellish storms paved your way to health.

And too, Leah, you made choices in your life which bring you to age fifty without a husband or children or other traditionally grounding forces in life. Yet, somehow, through the passion and pain, you have found your own way to emerge with grace and uncommon wit as a stable and productive woman, firm in purpose, absolutely adorable, and the essence of substance.

Our dynamite Tiny Mite has come of age.

When I was twice diagnosed with breast cancer, you launched into searching for the finest specialists and the best forms of treatment. It was your hand holding, your comfort, and your constant love that pushed me gently through the anguished awfulness of treatments. Never ever has your concern missed a beat when other crises in our family needed your loving attention.

341

When people beyond family or friendship require your gifts of heart and talent to help with their problems, again you never miss. Yes, Leah, you have always been a champion of those less privileged. Need I tell you, my daughter, you have a heart abundant with compassion?

Your sense of silliness makes you irresistibly delightful. My pride swells at the depth of your character, your flair, the multiplicity of your artistic expressions, and your resolute integrity.

But what I most treasure is the richness of our friendship. It is a mother-daughter bond strong enough to hold a ship at anchor, yet delicate in its tender respect for each other's flaws and limitations.

No mother could be prouder than I to be able to say, "Happy 50th Birthday, Leah Rebecca, my daughter, a razzle-dazzle ruby."

You live in my heart with boundless love, Mom

*****

(Letter from Dad)

August 2, 1997

I am alone in the house as you and Mom are in Manhattan. I know there is no one else either of you would want to be with on your 50th Birthday. Not feeling well, I would have slowed you down, and that would not have been what I wanted for either of you, my ladies, the two of you and Ruthie, the women in my life who give meaning and substance to my every day.

Fifty years have sped by since I first held you in a tiny blanket. Just writing that makes me feel old, nostalgic, and somewhat tired; I'm eighty-five.

I often wonder if I would have reached this age if my family had stayed in Russia. I would have had children, no doubt, but they would not have been you, and you have been a singular experience.

Leah Rebecca, my oldest daughter, from birth I have adored you. (Though I know you feel I have not.) Were we to have another child, I told Mom I just wanted another "Leah." Ruthie is not "Leah," but Ruthie captured my heart the minute I held her too.

In so wanting another "Leah," I did not know what I was bargaining for. Because what I got with you is a small bundle of dynamite. You're a huge enigma to me, Leah. I understood the toddler but have never understood her adult counterpart. You challenge me and many times I've "lost," and I am not a man accustomed to losing.

But my ardor, love, and admiration have always been there even when exasperated. I've given my deepest and best to you. I hope I have not failed you.

You need to know something I have only recently realized. When I overhear you talking with your friends about G-D, when I see our tables covered with Bibles and commentaries, when I listen as your modulated tone debates someone who does not share your beliefs, I must tell you, I have come to appreciate some things.

First, I now know you are not part of a fringe group or crazed cult you will ultimately tire of.

Second, I acknowledge your beliefs have been honed through over two decades of study. You have applied yourself in order to understand what you proclaim. When you speak, you share your knowledge with intelligence, substance, and even eloquence.

Third, neither Mom nor I can dispute you have not had an episode of severe depression for over seventeen years.

Fourth, and finally, to not state you are sound and sturdy on your 50th Birthday would be unkind and ungracious. I know you have longed for my approval. Now, you will have it in writing.

Leah Rebecca Kline, I am proud of you, and you have earned my respect.

Happy Birthday to you.

My Tiny Mite has become My Fair Lady.

With everlasting love, Dad

*****

EPILOGUE

In 1992, I had lived in Virginia for eight years. I had a network of friends with whom I played and worshiped, prayed, worked, and traveled. It wasn't a big network, but I never needed a big network.

A close friend from Philadelphia, Michelle, called me in the spring of 1992. Her voice trembled; she was shaken and needed counsel. I'm her mother's age, but we seem more like big sis and little sis to me; sometimes she's the big sis.

Michelle reported that her roommate, Sally, was pregnant and had an abortion scheduled in three days. I knew I had to fly home to Philly and help. Sally and I were casual acquaintances, so I really had to be nuanced in my approach. Food is always a good start, so on Saturday night, once in Philly, I asked Michelle and Sally if they'd like to go to the Barclay Hotel in Philly for their dazzling Sunday brunch the next day.

We had a grand time with sumptuous food and fun conversation. As soon as the last of the desserts were sampled and the final cup of java poured, I said, "Sally, I'd like to talk to you about something."

"Like what?" Sally inquired, almost indignantly.

"Like the fact that Michelle told me you're pregnant and have an abortion scheduled for Tuesday."

Sally's face fractured and bloomed into crimson rose. Her fury at her roommate was palpable as she seethed out loud, "I'm going

345

to kill you, Michelle!" This was hyperbole, and I wasn't really concerned.

My turn: "Sally, I don't know if you know this, but I've had two abortions. One when I was nineteen, your age, and one when I was twenty-nine."

"Yeah," Sally said, "and that's supposed to be of some importance to me? Well, hear this loud and clear. I don't care if you had twelve abortions. Mine is scheduled and I'm keeping the appointment."

I had not expected a different response.

"Sally, I've got a lot of years on you, and I know a thing or two. Please just listen for a minute. I've had an illegal and a legal abortion and I feel like an expert. I've completed a program on grief counseling for the aftermath effects of abortion."

Sally interjected, "I don't care a twit what you have to say. That was *your* life. This is mine, and you can't force me to have a kid I don't want."

"That's for sure, Sally," I said. "No one could have made me have a kid I didn't want either. *No one!* That's why I had two abortions. I didn't ask for or receive any advice. I too wouldn't have cared a lick what anyone's opinion was. But time changes things, inevitably. And now I wish someone who was post-abortive *had* talked to me.

"Talking to a man never could have impacted me. And talking to a woman who had never chosen abortion would have been equally meaningless. It would have had to be someone who was post-abortive. And guess what, Sally. I told my parents about the abortions more than two decades after the second one. They said I had chosen wisely, and they would have advised me to do exactly what I did. But here's the thing: they weren't post-abortive.

"I was in denial for over twenty-three years about what I'd done. I was a sophomore in college when I first conceived, and having a

346

baby was not on my radar. No way! In my fantasy world, I would have a baby when I was married, my career was in place, my husband's career was advancing, the nursery was painted, and there were onesies in the drawer. No other scenario even occurred to me. Abortion was all I ever considered."

"Then why are you preaching to me when you know exactly how I feel and what I'm going to do?" she asked. "Who do you think you are? This is *my* business. Take me back to the apartment now!"

The drive back to her place was silent, but my mind was steady hard at work.

Once I was safe at Mom and Dad's house, I reluctantly called Sally. "I've got an idea," I said. "Can we talk for a couple minutes?"

"Why?" Sally demanded.

"Because I have a suggestion. Would you consider postponing the abortion for one week? Not more. Not less. You can call the clinic tomorrow and change the appointment. All you'd lose is one week."

"Like I said, 'Why'?"

"Because you haven't given yourself a chance to think things through. Give yourself a minute. Your choice can be exactly the same, but you will have time to consider other viewpoints."

I didn't mention it, but, truly, I needed time too. I knew there would be several Crisis Pregnancy Centers in the area and I needed their counsel.

Miraculously, Sally agreed to the one-week postponement.

I found a center close to where Sally and Michelle live. For a couple of days, I spent hours at the center and embraced a strategy they've found helpful in some cases. They have video tapes, brochures, and questionnaires that will prompt Sally to probe her own psyche and determine what she really wants for her baby's life and for her own.

I was entering sacred ground now, and I wanted to do all I could to allow her decision to be based on knowledge and not pure emotion. A skyscraper-tall order.

I remember every minute of the days and weeks leading up to my two abortions. And I wasn't even in a decision-making mode. My decision had been branded into me from the moment I heard I was pregnant.

By Wednesday, I was ready to escort Sally to the center. She had bitten her nails to the quick, her hair was unkempt, and her face revealed a this-is-not-so-easy attitude, as opposed to her bravado-based stance at the hotel brunch.

Everyone at the center was low-key. No pressure. No being pushed from room to room or any hint of hard sell tactics. These were gentle and compassionate women who had their own stories to tell and who were committed to their path and their passion.

Sally disappeared into a room with one of the senior counselors. When she reappeared, I knew she was pushing back the swell of emotion that was rising within her.

In the car, she whimpered and told me to say nothing. I understood; silence was good. It allowed her to begin to sort through what she had seen and heard in that room.

In about twenty-four hours, she surfaced for air and was hesitantly prepared for the conversation that had to begin.

Sally said, "They really didn't have to go much further than the first video they showed me. Have you ever seen their video of an actual abortion?"

I nodded. Although I hadn't seen it until twenty-some years after both abortions.

Sally said, "The young girl is lying on a gurney covered with a flimsy blanket. She whimpers through the whole procedure. At one point, she can no longer stand the pain and cries, 'How much longer?' The doctor says, 'Just a couple more pieces to go.'"

I knew this wasn't fabricated melodrama. Women I've talked to over the decades have heard that same stabbing sentence about a body part. All of this, as they muffled screams during gripping contractions as the vacuum extracted their tiny baby from their throbbing womb.

Sally continued, "The young girl is now almost unglued, and the nurse attempts to shut her up so she doesn't scare off the other waiting mothers. They sure did start their propaganda in an excellent place, wouldn't you say? What more would a pregnant woman need to see or hear? That's it. No more. I couldn't even do that to a pregnant frog. Damn. Damn it all.

"What about the guy who got me pregnant? What about where I'll live and how I'll live? I don't know if I even want to keep this thing or give it away."

It all made perfect sense to me. Her utter despair, confusion, revulsion, fear, incredulity, the prospect of telling her parents and having to quit work.

Now a great-big unanticipated wrinkle developed for Sally. As if she weren't under enough pressure, when she called her parents, they demanded she have an abortion. Sally is African\ American and the baby's dad is Caucasian. Her parents were having none of it. They threatened to disown her. They were outraged and besotted with both fear for her and disgust with her.

Sally was a teenager. She wasn't used to defying the authority figures in her life. Not having any family support, just the support from me, Michelle, and the women at the Crisis Pregnancy Center, just wasn't cutting it. She was crestfallen. Her fear heightened, and her decision status was put into temporary jeopardy.

But Sally couldn't shake the visuals from the abortion video, and she moved ahead with her plans to cancel the abortion.

She did not know this yet, but having the team which would develop for her (*her personal preg-o team*), would be the biggest blessing of her coming year, possibly her life.

"You've made a brave decision," I told her. "G-D will honor you for it, Sally. You'll see. None of it even looks possible right this minute, but the minutes will pass until nine months have passed and there will be answers for you and your baby. What do you need?"

"What do I need?" she shrieked. "I need everything in the world. I don't even know how to answer that question. Give me a minute. My mind is mush, and how should I know what I need? Shut up for a second, will ya?"

No problem. I shut up. She'd just had her mind blown, and her former decision to abort had been washed down a sewer drain.

I decided to stay in Pennsylvania for the duration. Have computer will travel and there was nothing I couldn't do in Philly that I was doing in Virginia. Staying with Mom and Dad gave me stability.

It did take a few weeks for me to do all I had to do to help Sally as though she truly were a daughter. And it wasn't hard to enlist the help of three more women who I'd met at the local Messianic synagogue.

Now that her preg-o team was in place, we helped Sally decide what to tell her boss. Her boss, just for your info, was the proprietor of an adult bookstore in a not-too-swanky part of Philly. Sally did what she had to do to pay a portion of her rent, buy food, clothes, cigarettes, makeup, and all her other teenaged girl needs.

This bookstore guy also had a girlie bar where Sally bartended, waitressed, and if need be, danced on tabletops. From me, there was no judgment. My early twenties were sex, drugs, and rock n' roll too and I have never had much to say about other people's behavioral choices anyway.

We applied for Medicaid and all the social services she was entitled to. We each kicked in enough money to cover her portion of the rent. We bought groceries, took her for counseling at the Crisis Pregnancy Center, and began our nightly talks about what she thought she wanted to do regarding the baby. She didn't really know, although I knew she really did know.

She's a smart and practical young woman. She knew she had neither the will nor the resources to raise a child. But none of us would press any of our predisposed opinions onto her wavering thoughts and heartbreaking emotions. Her hormones were enough for her to deal with, and although she had our support, we knew this decision must be hers.

Open adoption was something we now investigated. There are many well-organized and well-conceived adoption agencies in the United States. Some are government funded. Some are private.

The self-made books, resumes, and letters of "Why you should choose us as your adoptive parents" started to pour in. Fascinating! These couples were so hungry for the tiny bundles that make a family a family. An amazing journey began, and my education was enhanced. These self-made packages arrived wrapped with pro-fessionalism, humor, anecdotes, and photos that would comprise the finest "Choose me! Choose me!" creations ever created. Sally was beginning to like the idea of people clamoring for her baby. In that this baby was going to be biracial, many of the applicants were biracial couples.

Stories unfolded, phone calls were exchanged, and several couples were chosen for final consideration. The couple Sally chose in California bailed when we learned that Sally's was a high-risk pregnancy.

A high-risk pregnancy! Can we add any more drama to this already melodramatic tale? Why sure we can, because now Sally must be treated as though she's about to lay a Faberge Egg. She must be restricted to bed and have her pillows plumped, her orange juice squeezed, and her prenatal care adjusted. We slid into fifth gear. Nobody had much of a life outside of caring for Sally.

Finally, Sally began serious talks with a biracial couple from Chicago. These people were lovely and caring; they sent money and maternity clothes. Eventually, once cleared by her doctor because of the high-risk pregnancy, Sally went to visit them. A love-in began and Sally was certain this was the couple.

Thank You, G-D! One of the biggest decisions was made, and things started to swing into perfect order.

A week before her scheduled delivery, Sally went to stay with this Chicago couple. We talked to her every night; she seemed calm and steady. We all felt this was the best decision for everyone, and spirits climbed in anticipation of the birth.

It's a girl! A big, healthy, round, gorgeous, curly-haired, brown-eyed girl! The couple was euphoric, and Sally, although having pangs of separation anxiety and all the concomitant hormonal issues, was truly pleased with her decision. She knew this adoptive couple would do as they said and send monthly photos and call when things settled down.

Perhaps never in Sally's life had she experienced the love and care this past year afforded her. She was changed, more rational, more tranquil. She was so pleased she had not aborted her daughter. I freely admit, although I was grateful to have been part of this life drama, a section of my heart was envious. Undeniably, I was deeply thankful that Sally would never know the loss, mourning, and torturous regret many post-abortive women know. I *was* sincerely happy for her; I just wished I had the same reason to be sincerely happy for me.

In that Sally had nine months of pampering and tons of time to reevaluate her own life, she now made decisions that included a move to a Western state and entrance to a college where she would major in marketing. She began a wholesome life she probably secretly believed could never be hers.

So here are the bottom-line truths: This was a win-win-win-win story. The baby girl won. The birth mother won. The adoptive parents won. And the four women who assisted and loved Sally through her pregnancy and decision-making process also won.

This became the story of how a crisis pregnancy can transform itself from a shrieking trauma into a gorgeous blessing.

I conclude, it is not picketing that will get the job done. It's not the protests and arguments. It is people standing up and giving all they have to these girls and women in crisis pregnancies.

It is hands-on help that will get the job done. It's putting our money where our rhetoric is. It's having teams of professionals who can guide women through the strategic steps that lead to victory for everyone. "Actions speak louder than words" has never experienced a more apt application.

Check this out: When the girl who was adopted turned ten years old, her parents were adopting another child. This little girl was now old enough to understand the whole adoption process, and she wanted to meet her own birth mother. That was arranged, and Sally and her birth daughter became forever friends.

When Sally moved to Kenya, her daughter visited her there and they now travel together regularly. Sally also proudly attended her daughter's high school graduation and applauded her decision to become a college accounting student.

This child has become a well-adjusted young woman with a gaggle of friends and a group of swooning boys hanging around her aching for a date. She oozes charm, stability, and joy.

Is this not one of the most poignant stories you have ever heard? I have photos of Sally and her daughter in my home. When I glance at them, I swell with pride, a sense of accomplishment, and a deep knowing that two lives were saved the day Sally decided not to abort.

Her daughter was given an opportunity to experience life on earth. Sally was afforded the time and encouragement to reimagine her own life into one of creative productivity and a guilt-free, shameless existence.

Was every second of our intense involvement worth the fabulous-ness of this story's outcome? Yes! Resoundingly, I proclaim, ABSOLUTELY YES!

I know that without G-D's unparalleled involvement in every nuance of this story, none of it might have happened the way it did. We were just four friends, four Bible-believing women, committed with unremitting resolve to our Lord and Savior, and ready to be of service to someone in need. The Holy Spirit encased us in His life-breath. He afforded Sally, her daughter, the women at the Crisis Pregnancy Center, and Sally's preg-o team, to be led to the agencies, people, and ultimately, the perfect adoptive couple for this priceless little girl.

This is a G-D-infused epic story, and we were willing clay vessels in our Lord's capable hands.

Blessed be our G-D, the Miracle Maker. And forever, thank you, LORD, for allowing me to hear Your voice in the music of my heart.

*****

Allow me to reference back to the letters I received from Mom and Dad on my Fiftieth Birthday. I received them twenty years ago. Then and now, they remain my favorites.

These passing decades have not been easy. I had to cope with my own two cancer diagnoses. Both of my parents transitioned to another dimension. I also lost, mostly through death, another nine people in my world who had been there since birth or for at least thirty years.

There's simply nothing comparable to that degree of loss. It sticks to you with the tenacity of Velcro. Clearly a relationship with G-D *did* bolster and encourage me to continue my own journey with courage and purpose. And slowly, ploddingly at first after each loss, but eventually, I would find a way back to my center and my raison d'être.

Last thoughts:

- There are choices that we make along our paths.
- There are forces that shape these choices.
- These choices often have distant-reaching consequences that cannot possibly be anticipated when the moment of choice arrives.

I share this last thought about choice because I know it to be true north; I know that every cause has an effect. And I know that sometimes our limited maturity or myopia deter us from thinking clearly or projecting into a future that is invisible and unknowable.

Conclusion: Choose wisely, with deliberation, with the input of others, and listen especially carefully for the voice of G-D which is very soft, and of maximum wisdom.

I also want you to know something I know: I am just another sojourner scaling the skin of planet earth … different from you only in the incidentals, the particulars. Within the simple or stunning, startling, or staggering stories of every one of us … there lives a story.

So, it is with a cornucopia overflowing with varied emotions that I offer you the interior of my life and my world.

May G-D radiate His light and joy upon you!
Toni Lisa Brown a\k\a Leah Rebecca Kline

Indulge me: one last short piece about a profound honor I experienced on January 22, 2013.

January 22, 2013

January twenty-second, 1973, was the day *Roe vs. Wade* was passed by the Supreme Court.

That was forty years ago. Every year since, a national organization hand-selects about thirty speakers to meet on the steps of the Supreme Court in Washington and give their testimonies about their abortion(s). There is always a gigantic crowd on the National Mall.

I was chosen to be a speaker in January, 2013, and I sprained my ankle three days before the D.C. event.

My friend, Robert James, asked if he could drive me to D.C. in a blizzard of snow-sleet-and-ice, and then wheelchair me from our hotel to the Supreme Court steps. Really? There are such people? It's not as though the man had nothing else to do. He is one of the most prestigious and respected attorneys in his field, known all over the United States. He is also, without doubt or question, a treasured man because of who he is. All heart. Dignity. Fun. Sophistication. An adventurer. A man of impressive diversity. That he is my friend has been a sheer delight.

The irony of Robert being there that day was not lost on me. His mother could have chosen to abort him but instead chose adoption. He has had a terrific life, and what he has given to people just because of the largesse of his heart has impacted and brightened countless lives. I was so thrilled he was with me that day.

On the Supreme Court steps, I didn't choose to talk about my abortions. Instead, I read the letter I had written to my daughter, Esther, in the late 1980s, decades after she was aborted (*June 21, 1989, is where that letter appears in this book*).

In spite of shocking cold, wind, snow, and ice, a half million people were on the Mall that day. The applause and thunderous roar that moved toward me in waves after I read my "Letter to Esther" were sounds and sights that drenched me in humility.

The next day, Robert and I left, sated from the festivities, the banquet, and the sheer volume of people who know there is a wiser and more humane choice for babies and their Moms.

So, let's not talk anymore. Let's open residential facilities for expectant mothers. Let's staff them with professionals who can help these girls and women with the months that lie ahead.

Let's make the change happen through actions that flourish from the sheer force of love.

LET'S DO IT! Stop the pickets, arguing, slurs and bullying that don't work anyway.

In every conceivable dark-life circumstance, love will forever be the answer. AMEN.

ACKNOWLEDGMENTS

Zee Sailer was my tenth-grade English teacher. We were the best of friends for many decades after I completed high school, until she passed away about two years ago. I miss her deeply. She was the first to tell me I had a flair for writing, and I wish I had known to take her seriously when applying to colleges. Zee read at last two drafts of this book and never stopped encouraging me. We had season tickets for at least two theaters in Philadelphia for a dozen years. We met for lunch often. We talked on the telly. She was my stalwart friend and mentor.

Pat Aurilio has been a consistent friend and cheerleader since 1984. She was the person who all but made me sit down and write my first book. She read everything I wrote and re-wrote, and she had things to say about all of it. She never gave up believing I would be published. To have someone in your corner for decades encouraging you not to quit, and reinforcing belief in your ability, is a gift of incomparable worth.

Marlene Bagnull. I attended Marlene's monthly critique writing group in Pennsylvania for about six or seven years. Marlene is a human force … an author, editor, speaker, publisher, and the director of annual writing conferences in Colorado and Philadelphia through her ministry, *Write His Answers*. She edited this book and her comments were invaluable, especially the ones that assured me my work has merit and my writing is sound. Sublime joy quietly erupts when writers have this kind of response from valued professionals. I love this woman. Just love her. I also admire and respect her and am a little awed by her too.

Marlene suggested that when I finished and perfected the book, I should have one more edit. When it was time, I called Marlene and she recommended Christy Distler. Christy's were the final formatting, punctuation, and minor grammatical changes. Our relationship was brief but effectual, and I am grateful to anyone who improves my work. Thank you so much, Christy.

Tiarra. Tiarra, you're a gifted editor. I am so grateful to be a recipient.

Carole Rosenfarb, thank you so much for your encouragement and knowledge.

Guy Matthews was involved at various stages for legal advice. And as the years passed and the work came closer to completion, his involvement grew too.

Although writing is a solitary venture, once a piece is complete, all the players must rally to bring the batter across home plate. I am dripping in fortune from the crew of people who cared about their contribution and believed in this project with their tireless effort, knowledge, and encouragement. G-D bless each of you for the work you do for so many, and especially for the work and friendship you have offered me. I will remember you always.

OTHER BOOKS BY TONI LISA BROWN

Awakenings: A Jewish Woman's Search for Truth

Stories * Observations * Quips * Lessons Learned.

Look for a series of children's books that are in progress, and an anthology of stories and essays.

tonilisabrown1919@gmail.com
www.toni-lisa.com

CPSIA information can be obtained
at www.ICGtesting.com
Printed in the USA
JSHW010206060722
27525JS00001B/1